PRAISE FOR GREG KEYES

THE BRIAR KING
"A wonderful tale . . . It crackles with suspense and excitement from start to finish." —Terry Brooks

"The characters in *The Briar King* absolutely brim with life . . . Keyes hooked me from the first page and I'll now be eagerly anticipating sitting down with each future volume of The Kingdoms of Thorn and Bone series."
—Charles de Lint

"A thrill ride to the end, with plenty of treachery, revelation, and even a few bombshell surprises."
—*Monroe News-Star* (LA)

THE AGE OF UNREASON
"Features the classic elements of science fiction: high-tech gadgetry, world-threatening superpower conflict, a quest to save the world, and a teen hero who's smarter than most of the adults . . . Powerful." —*USA Today*

"Seems likely to establish Keyes as one of the more significant and original new fantasy writers to appear in recent years."
—*Science Fiction Chronicle*

THE WATERBORN
"A satisfyingly robust, impressive debut that offers some genuine surprises."
—*Publishers Weekly*

THE REIGN OF THE DEPARTED

THE HIGH AND FARAWAY BOOK ONE

NIGHT SHADE BOOKS NEW YORK

Night Shade books may be purchased in bulk at special discounts for sales
promotion, corporate gifts, fund-raising, or educational purposes. Special
editions can also be created to specifications. For details, contact the Special Sales
Department, Night Shade Books, 307 West 36th Street, 11th Floor, New York, NY
10018 or info@skyhorsepublishing.com.

Night Shade Books® is a registered trademark of Skyhorse Publishing, Inc. ®,
a Delaware corporation.

Visit our website at www.nightshadebooks.com.

10 9 8 7 6 5 4 3 2 1

Library of Congress Cataloging-in-Publication Data

Names: Keyes, J. Gregory, 1963- author.
Title: The reign of the departed / by Greg Keyes.
Description: New York : Night Shade Books, [2018] | Series: The high and
faraway ; Book one
Identifiers: LCCN 2017031334 | ISBN 9781597809375 (pbk. : alk. paper)
Subjects: | GSAFD: Fantasy fiction.
Classification: LCC PS3561.E79 R45 2018 | DDC 813/.54--dc23
LC record available at https://lccn.loc.gov/2017031334

Cover illustration by Micah Epstein
Cover design by Claudia Noble

Printed in the United States of America

7/30/18

To Kenneth Hoffman Carleton

PROLOGUE

Aster shrieked as a huge wave struck the silver ship and hurled its prow toward the bleak sky, but her voice was lost in the howling wind and steady drum of thunder. Her feet slipped from under her, and only her grip on the handrail saved her from being flung over the side. The wave roared under them, and then her stomach went all strange for a moment and her body seemed to weigh nothing at all.

Then they slammed back into the sea, and the rain-slicked deck was beneath her again.

She saw him now, standing on the bow of the carrack, his red hair streaming like fire in the wind. He spoke words louder than the thunder. Dark things beat at him from out of the storm; sometimes they seemed to have faces.

He had fought them before—in the glass city, in a forest of singing trees, on another sea, on another boat. And he had battled other things more terrible still. She didn't remember all of the nine years of her life, but as far back as her memory went, he had been fighting something.

But now he seemed to be losing.

She struggled toward him, gripping the rail, trying to recall a Recondite Utterance, but all she could remember was a Whimsy for opening flowers.

He stumbled to one knee and a hundred smoky fingers seized at him. From the clouds, gigantic wings appeared, supporting the coiling, sinuous body of a serpent that dwarfed their little ship. The monster gaped a mouth large enough to swallow a man whole.

"Daddy!" Aster screamed, running toward him.

The next wave struck, and the ship spun half around, and once again the few pounds her body possessed were taken from her.

But this time she wasn't holding on to anything.

She saw her father's face; it seemed far away. The silver ship, too, fell away—and then the sea swallowed her. Water pressed at her lips and nostrils, trying to fill her up. She flailed her arms and legs, but she didn't know which way the surface was.

Something gripped at her ankle and pulled. She turned, and in the murky light she saw the ill-shaped form of the thing and knew it wasn't her father. She fought, but it towed her with awful strength. She needed air. Her panic was a cloud of bees in her.

Suddenly she knew the surface because it blazed red-gold, like fire seen through beveled glass. The creature clutching her was a black shadow against it, and for a moment, all seemed still and quiet.

Then the monster dragged her out of the water. It had something like a face, and it was grinning. Aster's greedy lungs sucked in air that stank of sulfur and soot.

Her captor stopped grinning when it saw her father, a yard away, still on the prow of the silver ship, no longer kneeling but standing tall as a tree. His eyes blazed with familiar fury.

Her father spoke a word, and the thing split in half and each half into another. She fell again, but not far; her father seized her leg where her captor had been gripping it. As it turned into a mist of ash, he pulled her up.

The storm was swiftly receding in all directions. They were in the center of a widening circle with blue sky above. Little yellow flames danced here and there on the waves and the ship, and on the broken and blackened body of the winged snake that was slowly sinking into the sea.

Her father cradled her in his arms.

"Streya, Streya," he murmured. He smelled of lightning and whisky.

"I told you to keep below."

"I wanted to help, Daddy," she said.

"I know," he said. "But I cannot lose you, do you understand? If I lose you nothing I have done will be worth it. So when I tell you to keep below, keep below."

"Yes Daddy." She smiled a little. "You beat them. I was afraid you were going to lose."

"I had hoped to win without the use of such an Utterance," he said. "I had hoped to escape their attention, to put them off the trail. This—this will be noticed."

"I'm sorry Daddy."

"It's not your fault, Streya," he said. "Come below. I need a drink."

He was shaking a little; she could feel it. Whenever he did something really big, he shook.

They went below, and she fetched him his bottle. He drank straight from it.

"It's no matter," he said. "The curse is following close behind us. All we need to do is outrun it. I know a place where you will be safe."

"But you'll be with me, Daddy, right?" she said. "You'll be there too."

"Of course I will, Streya," he said.

He looked very tired now, and sad. She knew that could last for days.

"I wish I knew more," she said. "A Whimsy to lift your spirits. A Recondite Utterance to slay your enemies."

He took another long drink.

"Where we go, Streya, I pray you have no need of such knowledge. And as for my spirits, I will not be satisfied until you are safe."

She nodded.

"Do you miss it Daddy?" she said, after a moment. "Do you miss her?"

He looked away from her.

"Yes," he said. "And yes." He took another drink.

"Do you remember that place?" he asked her.

"I think so," she said. "There was a garden, and peach trees, and my room was blue, with stars on the ceiling."

"Yes, that's right," he said. "And do you remember her?"

She shook her head. "I try," she said. "I only remember her voice, singing."

"She had a beautiful voice," he said. "She was beautiful, just as you are."

Aster nodded. He had told her that many times.

"Can we ever go back?" she asked.

He was silent for a long time.

"No," he said. "No, Streya, we can never go back."

She felt the emptiness in him when he said that. And it showed in his eyes.

"It's just you and me then," she said.

"Just you and me," he echoed.

"That's all I need, Daddy. That's all *we* need."

He tried to smile, then nodded, and the little silver ship sailed on.

PART ONE

WAKING

ONE
MOSTLY DEAD

The way he remembered it, Errol hadn't set out to kill himself. That had sort of evolved after he found his father's things, things his mother had hidden away in the attic. One of them was a bottle of scotch, which he started in on immediately. When he was a little drunk he found the painkillers. Even then, he only meant to take one or two, to feel better and forget everything for a little while. But after a few of the pills, forgetting *forever* sounded pretty good, and he took the rest of them. He thought he would fall asleep and just fade away, become a hole the universe would quickly fill.

That's not how it went. His body fought death and he got sick, very sick, and then he became scared and finally utterly terrified. He tried to dial nine-one-one—only by then, it was too late. The numbers were blurred and unfocused, his body was wracked with spasms, and he couldn't get his fingers to cooperate. The numbers faded entirely, and all he could see was the glow of the phone, and soon that darkened, too.

So he didn't exactly remember dying. But he did remember coming back.

The first thing he knew he was lying in his great-grand-mother's feather bed with the comforter pulled over his head. He knew that from the faint smell of cedar, the call of the rooster outside, the chirping of birds as morning came to the woods and pasture that surrounded her house. She would be in the kitchen already, making biscuits, and soon he would get up, eat the biscuits with butter and lots of jam and spend the day exploring the forested hills that went off what seemed like forever in all directions.

He had spent a couple of summers here with Granny, passing his days in solitude and in her comforting, undemanding presence. Those days were the only times of pure contentment he had ever known in his seventeen years.

He heard her calling him to breakfast, but he stayed in bed. He would pretend to be asleep until she came to wake him with a light, dry kiss on his cheek.

She called again, but this time something didn't sound right about her voice. It had a strange edge to it.

The next time she spoke he was sure it wasn't her.

He tugged the covers tighter over his head, remembering the scotch and the pills and that Granny had been dead for years. Something grabbed the covers and yanked them back, calling his name again, and this time it didn't even sound human and he screamed because there was nothing else to do.

He had been screaming for a while before he realized he hadn't yet drawn a single breath—and that he still didn't need one. He also became aware that he was sitting up. His panic seemed to have washed every emotion out of him, and he felt oddly calm. The darkness was gradually lightening as well, and he began to make out that he was in a room he didn't know, with dark blue walls and lots of antique furniture. And books, books everywhere.

"What's your name?" a familiar voice asked.

"Errol," he said, without thinking. "Errol Greyson." The voice was behind him. He tried to turn, but the high back of the chair blocked his vision, and he couldn't stand up—he seemed to be strapped into the thing. But he knew who it was, by her unmistakable and singular accent.

"Aster?"

"Yes," she said. "That's me. So you know who I am. That's good. Now, try not to freak out."

"I'm pretty freaked out, Aster," he said, as she stepped into view.

"I've put a calming charm on you," she said.

Aster Kostyena had fine, flyaway hair which aspired to be red, but wasn't quite. Her head was large and sort of onion-shaped. She had big, green eyes and long thin limbs and she had always reminded him a little of the Christmas elves in stop-motion TV specials.

She had first appeared at Sowashee Elementary in fourth grade; rumor had it that her father had been a mafia boss in Russia and was hiding out in America because things had gone badly for him over there. Errol had had sort of a crush on her back then, because of her accent and because she was so different from anyone he knew. Of course he had never told anyone that, especially not her. They had been friends for a while, but by seventh grade they hardly talked to each other anymore. Even now he had the stray thought about her—at least before his thing with Lisa. But his friends all thought she was strange and didn't think she was all that pretty, so there was no way he would have ever asked her out. She would have told him no anyway, most likely, just another rejection to add to his résumé.

"Calming charm," he repeated.

"Yeah," she said. "Kind of like magical valium."

Which just sounded crazy. Like the whole situation.

"And you've tied me to a chair," he said, glancing down.

Looking down was a mistake, but now he believed her about the calming charm. Otherwise he would be screaming again instead of merely being very, very alarmed.

Up until then he had been piecing together a scenario where Aster had somehow come into his house and found him passed out. For whatever reason, she had kidnapped him, tied him up . . .

But no.

What looked like his arms, legs and chest—what *felt* like them—were not. What he saw instead were limbs of carved wood, held together by bolts and wire. The hands were perhaps strangest, both delicate and strong-looking; some fingers were black, some white, as if they had been made from piano keys. The torso was built of slats, put together like a barrel with steel bands.

He flexed his fingers. The digits moved.

And he *was* tied up, with several coils of heavy rope.

"This isn't real," he said. "I'm dreaming."

"You can believe that if it helps," Aster said.

He felt a little panic pierce through the unnatural calm. "Am I—am I dead?" He looked up at her. "Is this Hell? Are you really Aster?"

She knelt down so their faces were level. She was wearing a denim jumper over black pants, an outfit she'd worn at least once a week since tenth grade.

She looked him directly in the eyes.

"This is not Hell, Errol—this is my house. You pass it every day on your way to school. And you aren't dead. You are only *mostly* dead."

That was enough—suddenly he couldn't take it anymore. Errol started jerking, trying to wriggle out of the ropes.

"Get me out of this," he demanded.

"Don't do that," Aster said, but he wasn't listening to her anymore. Whatever this was—hell, a bad dream, a drugged-out hallucination—he was done with it.

The ropes were strong but, he realized, so was he. The chair began to splinter, and that loosened his bonds, and then the chair slammed to the floor. He got one arm out, and then the other.

"Stop it, Errol," Aster said.

He didn't, of course.

"*Svapdi*," Aster shouted, and everything went black.

Thank God, was his last thought.

T he next thing Errol knew, he was flat on his back. The broken chair was all around him, and Aster stood a few feet away, looking a little vexed.

And he was still a giant puppet. Apparently.

"That was a perfectly good chair," Aster said. "I have to say . . ."

She stopped, closed her eyes, and drew a long breath.

"Look," she said, "I'm sorry I tied you up. But I couldn't be sure I was going to get—*you*. I don't summon up spirits every day, you know. Or ever before, really. If I had made a mistake, there's no telling what might have showed up—a *dhves* or a *leme* or worse. Now I know it's you, so I won't tie you up again. But what you need to know—what you need to understand before we go any further—is that I can stop you with a word, anytime, like I did just now. I can send you right back where you came from."

"Back where?" Errol yelped, still on his back. "Where did I come from? What's happening to me?"

"You can get up," Aster said. "I have something to show you. It might help."

Errol did get up, albeit clumsily. The wooden body was a little bigger than his real one, and it didn't move exactly like a human body. That sent a chill through him because it made everything seem somehow more real. Details. In dreams things just sort of *were*. And they weren't usually this consistent.

Aster took something off of the table and handed it to him. It was a copy of the Sowashee Sentinel. It was folded, and an article was circled in red ink. There was picture of him, his last school picture. The caption of the article read, "Local Boy in Coma."

He read the article numbly. It described how his mother had found him, how by the time EMT's arrived he had stopped breathing, how they had managed to revive him. How the brain damage had been too extensive. That it was unlikely he would ever awaken, and even if he did, he would probably never be normal. It mentioned that students at Sowashee High were being offered counseling to help them cope, and to hopefully head off any more such suicide attempts.

Like anyone at school was going to have trouble "coping" without him. And he noticed it didn't say anything about him being suspended.

He went back and read the whole thing again. An awful sickness started in his belly, panic and terror and grief and everything else jumbling around together.

"Oh my God," he sobbed, and understood he was crying. He wiped at his face and found only wood — no tears, of course. But it *felt* like crying, and it wracked him from head to toe. Aster didn't say anything, she just let him go. Her expression was unreadable at first, but after a while it became a bit impatient.

"Okay," she finally said. "Suck it up. It's not that bad."

"Not that bad? I'm brain-damaged! This — whatever it is — is probably all just what happens when your last few brain cells die. You're probably not even real. Jeez, like in that stupid movie—"

"Believe what you want," Aster said. "Rationalize it any way that works for you. But I'm going to need you to do some things, and so I can't have you moping on about this forever."

"Moping on about . . . Forever? It's been like five minutes! Are you insane?"

"Yeah, I don't know," Aster replied. "I don't have much to judge by, frankly. But just—listen. Yes, your body is in a coma, and yes you have brain damage. But *you*—the you who makes you who you are—your soul, if you wish—that's right here, right in front of me. I summoned you here."

"You did this?"

"I've said it twice now. Why else would you be here?"

"Who the hell knows?" Errol said. Then it sunk in. "For God's sake, *why*?"

"Don't be ungrateful," Aster said. "Would you rather be trapped in a brain-dead body until someone decides to pull the plug? Or would you like to have another shot at life?"

"In this?" he asked, shaking his hands to indicate his puppet-body. He didn't want to touch it. "In this—what the hell is this, anyway?"

"Call it what you want," she said. "I prefer *automaton*. Sound's scientific, although it soooo isn't. Until a few minutes ago it was a bunch of lifeless junk. Now it's you, at least for the time being."

"Time being?"

"It might be possible to heal you," she said. "To bring your real body back to life. If you want. Or I can let you truly die, if you prefer—"

"Why would I prefer that?" he snapped.

"Well, you did try to off yourself," she pointed out.

"It was an accident," he said. "I didn't want to die, I just . . . I mean I didn't—" he paused and closed his eyes and was surprised how big and thick his lids were. He wondered what they were made of. He hoped to God his head didn't look like that of a ventriloquist's dummy.

"Just—what are you saying? About healing me?"

"Errol," she said, "if you're good, maybe one day you can be a real boy."

For a moment he didn't have any response to that.

"Oh my God, is that a joke?" he finally sputtered. "You think this is funny?"

"Just trying to lighten things up," she sighed.

"Lighten—" he tried to get hold of himself. If he lost it, she would just send him back to nothing—or worse, to whatever that was pretending to be his grandmother.

"Just for the sake of argument," he said, "let's say I believe all of this. You're some kind of witch and you made—" he waved again at his body " —this, and took my soul out of the hospital. Why? In four years you've barely even spoken to me."

"Nor you to me," she said.

"Okay, whatever. Why?"

"Ah, now we get down to it," she said. "I need someone like you, someone caught between, not living and not dead."

"Why?"

He wasn't sure if she was even planning on answering that, but if she was, she didn't get the chance. The whole house shuddered—not shook, but shuddered. The walls seemed to ripple like water struck by a stone.

The lights all went out, and it was as dark as the inside of the water tower at night.

"*Zhedye*," Aster said. "Not now."

She grabbed his hand. It felt tiny in his palm, and distant, as if it was muffled in layers of cloth. But he shouldn't have been able to feel *anything*.

"Come on," she said, pulling him along. He heard a door open, and then they seemed to be in a hall. For a moment it was quiet, but then the house reverberated with a dull booming.

"The front door!" Aster gasped. "Quick."

She led him through a couple of turns, and just as they took the second one the house rattled and Errol heard a massive splintering sound. Moonlight flooded in through what had once been a door but which now lay flat in the foyer. A hulking shadow stood on it; all that he could make out were two faint green orbs, and although they didn't have pupils, he knew they were eyes. He somehow had a sense of smell—although like his touch it seemed muted. Nevertheless, something stank to high heaven, like a dead animal in a blender with burnt cake.

"Oh, *zhedye*," Aster said, and for the first time she sounded scared. "How did he do that?"

"How did who do what?" Errol wondered. Then the thing rushed them.

Errol threw up his hands to protect himself, just as the shadow hit him like a battering ram. It hurt, but at least he didn't have any wind to knock out. He heard Aster yell something, but he couldn't understand it.

All of a sudden, the fear blew out of him like a storm had come through, and for the first time since before he'd found the box of his father's things, he felt like himself.

Which was to say as pissed as hell.

He balled up his fists and hit his attacker as hard as he could. And boy, did that ever feel good. He felt the crunch, like the time he'd broken Colin Fielder's nose, but more and better. This little body was *strong*. Then he was just slamming the monster, over and over again until all of a sudden it—well, exploded. Now the smell was staggering. He heard Aster vomit.

"The door . . ." she managed, between heaves.

Another monster was already at the door. With a bellow, Errol charged it before it could come after him, striking it low and pushing it up and out. It was lighter than the first, and he forced it back through the opening. In the glow of a three-quarter moon, he saw horns and a long snout with bone showing through. It was four-legged, and ribs stuck through dry, tight skin.

"Jesus, it's a cow!" he gasped, heaving it back.

The first two were just a warm up, because here came the herd—about twenty of them now breaking into a trot, at least those with four legs. Several limped on three, and one was dragging itself with only forelimbs. The whole back half of it was gone. And pushing through all of these was the biggest bull he had ever seen, probably six feet tall at the shoulder. It didn't seem to be in a hurry.

Zombie cows. It might have been funny, if it were in a movie he was watching. But in fact it was mind-meltingly horrible. It would have been better if they had been some sort of three-eyed monsters.

One of these things he could handle. But a whole herd . . .

"The door!" Aster repeated. "Pick it up!"

"It's broken," Errol said, unnecessarily.

"Just hold it closed," she said.

He did, bracing for the impact of the lead bull. Aster started muttering in a language he didn't know, and then he saw her hand outlined in blue flame. She touched the door, and he felt it sort of harden in his grip. He stepped back and it stuck in the frame as if held by magnets.

"That will hold for a while," Aster said.

"A while?" he said. "What the hell is going on? I just exploded a zombie cow."

"Animals bloat up with gas when they start to decompose," she offered.

"That is so not the point."

"Stay here," she said. "We don't have all night. I've got to stop him."

"Stop who?"

"If the door gives, don't let them in," she said.

Then she left.

The door shook as one of the things outside banged into it. They were making a noise now, a low-pitched buzzing that sounded something like a swarm of bees and nothing at all like cows.

TWO

THE ELF-WHISPERER

S crew this," Errol muttered, but then the door cracked in the middle. He dithered for a second. If those things got in . . .

Then what? He didn't know. He didn't know anything except that none of this was possible. He felt panic returning and he hated it. He loathed fear—it was the most useless emotion imaginable.

He looked around for something to fight with, but nothing in the hall looked like a better weapon than his ebony-and-ivory fists.

The door cracked further, and moonlight spilled through. He shoved his palms against it and braced his legs.

Thoom, thoom, thoom.

"Aster!" he hollered. "Whatever you're doing, hurry up!"

A horn came through the crack, nearly catching him in the face, and the door leaned in on him. He doubled his effort, and suddenly the horn was gone. The pressure let up.

Finally, he thought.

Then the door erupted in a thousand pieces, hurling him to the floor and back fifteen feet.

The bull stamped in the opening. Its huge eye sockets glowed with flickering blue fire as it lowered its head, aiming its huge, curved horns at Errol.

"Come on, then," Errol snarled, standing up. He was tired of thinking, of trying to figure things out. Fighting he understood.

It hit him like a freight train; braced as he was, he didn't feel like he slowed the bull down at all. The horns missed him, but the head lifted him high and slammed him into the ceiling. He felt something in his body crack. Then he crashed down onto the monster's back. He grabbed at it and wished he hadn't, because his fingers tore through the stiff hide and into the putrid flesh beneath. He tried to get a grip on the backbone, but then it tossed him like a bad rodeo clown, and he smacked into a wall. He tried to get up, but one of his legs wouldn't work. He watched as it backed up and took aim at him again.

Somewhere something chimed, like a crystal bell, and the bull stopped. It stood for a moment, and then began to back up. It backed out of the hall onto the lawn and began to walk leisurely away. The rest of the dead cows followed it.

Errol was checking out his leg when Aster returned. One of the wires had snapped, and his thigh had a crack in it.

"Look," he told Aster.

"I can fix that," she said. "I'll be right back."

Once she had changed out the wire, he could walk, but she wanted to repair the thigh, so she led him toward the back of the house.

The workshop was a big room with a skylight, but without the sun it was dim, lit only by a few fluorescent lamps. The walls were covered in odd contraptions; some looked like clocks and others like elaborate shadow boxes. One in particular caught his eye, perhaps because it was the largest and because he could see the parts moving behind the glass. In it a golden sun seemed to dance with a silver moon, while a glittering star moved alone, until the Moon moved to dance with it. When this happened, the metal disk of the sun spun to reveal a dark back. Then the moon also turned, to expose a reverse still silvery, but covered in dark blotches, like the real moon.

Then the whole thing reset and began again. Below the action, the gears driving it were all visible.

There were also all sorts of puppets, mechanical hands, and two life-sized manikins, built of what looked like found objects and worked wood.

And there were loads of tools—a big circular saw, lots of hand tools, a lathe and plenty of things he didn't recognize at all. The room smelled of sawdust and oil.

"This where you made me?" he asked.

"Yes," she replied.

"That calming spell still on me?"

"No," she replied, putting a c-clamp on the cracked leg and tightening it down. He felt the pressure.

"See how calm I am?" he said.

"You seem very calm. It's a little worrisome. Reminds me of how you were just before you beat up Roger Bickle. You aren't planning on beating me up, are you Errol?"

"That depends," he lied.

She held up a bottle. "Wood glue," she said.

"You're going to *glue* me back together?"

"Dowel," she went on, showing him a thin wooden cylinder.

"So I'm really in a coma."

"Yes."

"And you really are a witch?"

"I'm okay with that word," she said. She held up something gun-shaped.

"Electric drill," she said.

"Oh, no you don't!" Errol yelped, drawing back.

"Yeah, that'll hurt," Aster mused, chewing her lip.

She smiled. "*Svapdi*," she said.

"Hey—" he began. But then everything went dark again.

A ster finished her work on the automaton and regarded it for a long moment. She thought about calling Errol back, but he was scared and angry and full of questions, and she didn't want the distraction. Not now, when she needed to think about what had happened.

She should be feeling triumphant right now; not only had she successfully summoned Errol's soul, her automaton also worked admirably well. And yet she somehow felt things hadn't gone as they should. She supposed she had expected more gratitude from him, some thanks for at least giving him another chance. Instead it felt as if she hadn't accomplished anything at all.

But she hadn't done it to save him, had she? She had done it because she needed him. So she shouldn't be bothered that he wasn't all brimming with appreciation.

Anyway, all of that paled next to the appearance of the dead bull and his herd. She hadn't even thought it was possible for a summoning to appear outside of the house. What if it was already too late? She had Errol, but not the others.

She spent the next four hours cleaning up exploded cow, replacing the front door with one of the hall doors, and building stronger wards around the house to deter any future invasions, necro-bovine or otherwise. When she was done she glanced at the clock and saw she only had three hours before school.

She went to her room, set the clock to let her sleep for two hours, and closed her eyes.

A ster went over the whole thing again in second period. Mr. Watkins was droning on about ancient Greek poetry, which ordinarily she might pay attention to. He was the most interesting of her teachers, and he always seemed excited about his lectures, despite his audience. She pretended to take notes, but actually she was sketching and scribbling. Something about the lines emerging onto paper helped structure her thoughts, and today she really needed to come up with some answers. After years of nothing happening at all, suddenly it was all too quick.

"The Elf-Whisperer is in rare form today," someone hissed. She wasn't sure who; a girl, but that didn't narrow things down. But then another girl giggled, and she knew it was Jenna Morgan. Which meant the crack had come from Sara Carver.

When Aster scribbled, sometimes her lips moved. She couldn't help it. That had earned her several inventive nick-names— "The Girl Who Talks to Her Pencil" (in fourth grade) "Lip Reader" (fifth grade) "Psycho Scribbler" (sixth) and, of course, "Elf-Whisperer." That one had stuck, right through to her senior year.

She felt her face warm, but she kept her head down and pre-tended she hadn't heard. It shouldn't bother her at all, but it had been Errol who actually coined the "Elf-Whisperer" epithet. She had a tendency to depict dragons and hippogriffs and—well, elves. When they were younger, Errol had often asked her to draw pictures to go with the stories he wrote. They had even done a little comic book together. But now Errol didn't write stories, and "Elf-Whisperer" still had a little sting in it.

"Maybe she's drawing herself a boyfriend," Sara whispered. "It's the only way she'll ever get one."

Aster turned so she could just see Sara. Then she winked and blew her a kiss.

"Oh, gross," Sara said, a bit too loudly. "You can only dream."

"Ms. Carver?" Mr. Watkins said. "Is there something you would like to share?"

"Not with *her*, Mr. Watkins," Sara said.

That got a pretty good laugh.

"That will be enough, Ms. Carver," Mr. Watkins said.

Mr. Watkins called her over after the bell rang and asked to see her notebook. He thumbed through a few pages.

"It amazes me that you never take any notes, and yet you ace all of my tests."

She didn't know what to say to that, so she kept quiet.

"There's some interesting stuff here," he said. "Do you read a lot of mythology?"

"I guess I do."

"I don't recognize some of these guys," he said. "Are they from Slavic myth?"

"They're mostly made up," she replied.

He sighed. "Well, the drawing is really quite accomplished. You're a talented young woman, Aster. I wish I could convince you to enter some of your work in the art fair this year."

She felt a little glow of warmth at that, and knew a smile had crept onto her lips. Mr. Watkins was pretty young, for a teacher, and he was nice-looking in a soft sort of way. And he was smart about the right things.

"Well, I really just draw in my notebook," she said. "I don't know anything about framing, or matting, or any of that."

"If that's the only problem, I don't mind helping you with it."

"Right," she said. "I just don't think it's my thing."

"It might help," he said. "It might make people see you in a different light."

"What do you mean?"

He scratched his head. "It's hard to be different in high school. It's hard to accept who you are when others don't. I'm saying you need to take control of your talent. Make it a positive."

Now something in his tone made her uneasy, but she couldn't put her finger on what.

"I just scribble, Mr. Watkins," she said. "I don't think of myself as an artist."

"Well how do you think of yourself?" he asked, softly.

She didn't want to tell him the answer to that, so she just shrugged.

"Look," he said, "high school isn't the real world. Some day—probably in college—you're going to meet people who see how much you really have going for you. The real you."

He smiled and stared into her eyes with his big brown ones.

Oh, my God, Aster realized.

"Thanks, that's good to hear," she said. She glanced at the door.

"Okay," he said.

"Okay," she said, and started to go.

"There's something else," he said. "Ms. Fincher wanted to see you before lunch."

"Okay," she said. "Thanks."

"Think about what I said," he told her. "And I'm here anytime you want to talk."

I'll bet you are, she thought, but she just smiled and nodded.

"Desvadanya," he said.

"Sir?"

He looked flustered. "Did I say it wrong? I thought you were Russian."

"Oh," she said. "No, not Russian. Lithuanian."

"Really?"

The warning bell rang. "I have to go," she said, and scurried off.

Great, she thought. Another damn thing to deal with. How dumb does he think I am?

And now she would have to learn some Lithuanian, for when he tried to "relate" to her in *that* language.

Ms. Fincher stood up behind her desk and indicated a chair with an almost karate-chop motion. She wore a red dress—that, along with her small frame and darting eyes made Aster think of a cardinal—the bird, not the clergyman. She was pretty. Her father had flirted with Ms. Fincher once, when he thought Aster wasn't listening.

"Have a seat, Aster," she said.

She sat.

Ms. Fincher smoothed her skirt and settled back into her swiveling chair. She adjusted her red-rimmed glasses with her index finger.

"Aster, is everything okay at home?"

"Yes, Ma'am," she replied.

"Your father—I've been trying to get in touch with him. He hasn't returned my calls or letters."

"He travels a lot," she said.

"I understand that. But I really must speak with him."

"What about, Ms. Fincher?" she asked.

"About a number of things," the counselor replied. "Things I've tried to talk to you about."

"You mean college," Aster said.

"Yes," she said. "Among other things. If I can't talk sense into you, maybe I can convince him."

"It's my decision," Aster said, "not his."

Ms. Fincher pursed her lips.

"Is there some reason he might not want you to continue your education? Some cultural reason, perhaps?"

"No Ma'am," she said.

Ms. Fincher looked doubtful.

"Does your father ever take you shopping?" she asked. "Do you ever buy new clothes? What you wear is all but threadbare."

"Sure, Dad—well, I'm not really a clothes kind of girl. I just wear things until they fall apart, and then I get new ones."

"Most girls your age take some interest in their appearance."

"Most girls my age don't think of much else," she replied.

Ms. Fincher smiled. "A new outfit or two won't hurt you. If it's a money problem—"

"It's not," she said.

Ms. Fincher was silent for a moment.

"When your father is traveling, who takes care of you?"

"I'm seventeen, Ma'am," she said.

"How often is he gone?" she pressed. "How many days a week would you say you're alone?"

"One, maybe sometimes two."

"Only one or two?" Ms. Fincher sounded dubious.

"Some weeks he doesn't travel at all," Aster said.

Ms. Fincher patted her desk. "Is there anything you would like to tell me, Aster? You're safe here."

Aster didn't feel safe. She didn't feel safe at all.

"There's nothing, Ms. Fincher."

"Well," Ms. Fincher said, with evident frustration. "Tell your father to call me. Soon. If not, we'll be forced to look into your home life a little more closely."

Aster nodded and left. Her heart felt like a rock in her chest.

Getting her father to make that call was going to be interesting, and not in the fun way. And even if that went okay, it wasn't going to help for long.

But maybe just long enough.

THREE

ACTUALLY DEAD

Errol smelled wet leaves and soil, but he couldn't see anything at all. Still, he knew he was in a forest. It was night and it had just rained. He reached out and took a step, felt the rough, damp bark of a tree. An owl hooted off in the distance, and now he remembered this: the night he'd been lost in the huge stretch of hills between Herbert and Bethel. He'd been scared at first, terrified, but as the night wore on, he had lost most of his fear and learned to love the woods in moonlight almost as much as he did in the day.

But now he wasn't so sure. The owl called again, and it sounded wrong, like his grandmother's voice back before Aster woke him.

He caught a bit of movement from the corner of his eye, something white, but when he turned to face it, all he saw was a slight haze. He rotated his head further and as the light moved back toward the edge of his vision, it sharpened a little. It seemed to move closer, not straight toward him, but sort of circling in.

And then it—or rather she—came into view. At least he thought it was woman, because she wore a long white dress, and her snowy tresses fell the full length of her back. Her face was hidden by her hair, and all he could see was her chin. But as he continued to stare, she lifted and turned her head, and he abruptly knew he did not want to see her face, *could* not see her face. He spun and ran, smacking into a tree, feeling his flesh tear on the bark, and he heard her soft laugh.

A nd he was looking at Aster again.

"You there?" she asked.

"Jesus," he replied. "Oh, man."

"What's wrong?"

"I was just someplace," he said. "Someplace bad. What are you doing to me, Aster?"

"I fixed you," she said. "See?" She pointed to his wooden leg. He could see where she had drilled holes and pushed in dowels to hold it together.

He suddenly realized Aster had changed clothes — she now wore jeans and a brown t-shirt, untucked. And her hair was in a ponytail.

"How long?" he murmured.

"Well, the glue had to dry," she said. "Plus, you haven't been the best company."

"How long?"

"Three days," she said. Her brow crinkled. "What do you mean, 'someplace'?"

He wanted to be mad, but all of that was leaching out of him now. What he knew was that he could *not* go back in those woods, could never look in that woman's eyes.

"Aster," he said, "I don't understand what's happening. But please don't do that again. Don't send me back there."

"What happened?" she persisted.

"Just please don't do it again. Whatever it is you want me to do, just tell me, and I'll do it, and — whatever. But keep me here."

She regarded him seriously before responding. "I won't send you back unless I have to," she said.

She didn't explain what she meant by "have to." He knew what she meant.

"Anyhow," she said, "I woke you up because we're ready for phase two."

"What's phase two?" he asked.

"I'll explain on the way," she said. "Let's get you dressed, first."

E rrol regarded himself in the mirror. In jeans, boots, sweater and work gloves, he looked sort of normal, if a bit wide. But the face . . .

He wasn't sure how to take the face. The dummies in the workshop had had blanks with mere holes for eyes and mouth. But some work had gone into what he was looking at now. The light, fine-grained wood had been painstakingly carved into a semblance of his real features — his tapered chin, thin nose, high eyebrows and full lips — all there. The cheekbones were in the right place, and the expression was a little sullen, which he had to admit was probably right, most of the time. The eyes were glass balls, like big marbles, and didn't look real at all. Maybe they *were* marbles. All in all, he thought it was creepier than a totally blank face would have been. At the same time, it was somehow comforting, although he couldn't figure out why.

He had an image of Aster, at her desk at school. She almost never looked up from it, was always doodling and drawing no matter what was going on around her. She filled notebooks with pictures of knights, elves, dragons, and weirder, made-up creatures along with strange symbols and letters that he was also pretty sure she made up. She got teased a lot for that, and he wondered guiltily if she was aware he had coined the nickname "Elf-Whisperer," and hoped desperately that she did not.

"And this should do it," Aster said, sticking a baseball cap on his head.

"I look like a scarecrow," he muttered.

"Oh, but you're more like the Tin Man," she replied.

More with the jokes, he thought, but he held back saying it aloud.

"So now what?" he asked.

"Now we go for a little drive," she replied.

He recognized the battered old Honda; Aster had begun showing up at school with it a few months before. It started up after a few complaints, and she backed it out of the driveway and headed west on 293.

"Keep low when we meet other cars," she said, unnecessarily.

"Where's your dad, anyway?" Errol wondered.

"Business trip," she replied.

He thought about all of the weird stuff in her house.

"Does he know you're into all this?" he asked. "Does he know about me?"

She shrugged. "Yes and no." She turned right onto Powers Road.

"What does that mean?" He asked.

"Means I don't want to talk about it," she said. "Eventually, but not now."

Errol digested that. He had only seen Aster's father half a dozen times, always outside of the house. Even when they had been sort of friends, Aster never invited him over; she either came to his house—or more often, they wandered in the hills and pastures of Mr. Bound's land.

Jesus, he thought to himself. What if he's dead? What if he's lying on some bed in that house, just a skeleton? What if she . . .

They passed a logging road, and Errol remembered parking there with Lisa, kissing her salty neck and fumbling beneath her shirt. The memory was so strong that for a moment it blotted out everything else, like being rolled under by an ocean wave.

"Where are we going?" he asked, to try and distract himself.

"Attahacha Creek," she said. "Below the falls. How far, I'm not sure."

"Why?"

"Okay," she said. But then went quiet for a moment.

"Okay," she started again, "but when this starts sounding crazy, I want you to remember what I've done, right?"

"You mean me," he said. "This." He touched his wooden face.

"Exactly."

"Okay," he said.

She nodded. "Well, Errol, I'm on sort of a quest. And for that quest, I need companions, three of them, and I have to get them in order. You were first; the mostly-dead. I need you to find *her*."

"Find who?" he said.

"The completely dead," she replied. "Veronica Hale."

"I don't know who that is," he said.

She turned left onto a dirt road that wound up into the hills. Toward the falls.

"A girl," Aster said, "a year or so younger than us. She disappeared somewhere around the falls. They found one of her shoes four miles downstream. But they never found her."

"I don't remember hearing about that," he said.

"That's because it happened thirty years ago," she said.

"Oh."

They turned on a logging road and reached the falls a few minutes later.

The best thing about Attahacha falls was that they weren't that great; the waterfall only dropped about six or seven feet, not like Bourne's falls or Silas Creek, which were more impressive and always crowded in the summers. Pretty much only local teenagers went to Attahacha, to skinny dip, drink, smoke, and make out. You could hear a car coming for a mile, giving you plenty of time to reform your behavior or hide before the sheriff or some random parent showed up.

Which meant that although they looked deserted as Aster pulled her car up, they might well not be.

"What day is it?" he asked, suddenly.

"Monday, October 4," she said, climbing out of the vehicle.

"You're missing school? You never miss school."

She shrugged. "Come on." She closed the door and began walking along the bank, downstream. After a reluctant pause, he followed her.

"This quest of yours," he said, kicking an old soda can from his path. There was litter everywhere, as usual. "What's it about?"

She smiled thinly. "Water," she said. She reached into the bag she had across her shoulders and pulled out what looked like a little perfume bottle. It had a few drops of clear liquid in it.

"I don't get it," he said.

"The water of life," she said. "You hear about it all the time in legends."

"Do you mean like the fountain of youth?"

"That's something else," she said. "The water of life restores life to those who have lost it."

"You mean it brings people back from the dead?"

"Sort of."

"Can it bring me back?" he said. "In my real body?"

"No," she said. "You aren't dead. What you need is the water of health, which is an altogether different thing. And that's what I need, as well."

"Why? Are you sick?"

Aster's thin brows pinched together, which he knew meant she wouldn't answer that.

"The point is," she said, "our quest is to find the water of health, and for that we need this." She held up the vial.

"You're going to bring a dead girl back to life?"

"Not just a dead girl," she said. "A special kind of dead girl. And I can't find her by myself. That's what I need you for. I won't be able to see her. You should. When you do, take hold of her until I can sprinkle her with this."

Errol peered down nervously at the water.

"You know all of this how?" he asked.

"Well, Errol, I consulted a sort of oracle," she said. "It's supposed to be very reliable."

"What exactly am I looking for?" he asked.

"I don't know. But I'll bet you know it when you see it."

Errol really didn't like the sound of that. When he was younger, he'd had nightmares about skeletons coming after him, and he hated movies with zombies. If this girl had been in the creek for so many years, she was probably going to be pretty disgusting. *Take hold of her?*

Aster reached for his hand, and he flinched away.

"Don't get any ideas," she said. "I *have* to hold your hand."

"Oh," he said. When she reached again, he let her fingers lace between his.

It felt really strange, walking with her like that. Her hand seemed like an intruder in his. It sort of made his heart ache, because he ought to be holding Lisa's hand. He didn't understand how her feelings could change so quickly. How could you love somebody and then suddenly not? How was Brandon Alewine better than him?

But that was a stupid question. Everybody liked Brand. He was smart and funny, a great football player—and his family had a house on Baybell Lake. And a motorboat. Now he had Lisa.

And Errol was holding hands with the Elf-Whisperer.

He was so intent on all that, that at first he didn't notice anything strange. It got darker, but initially he thought that was just clouds overhead. But then he tripped on a root, a big one. He'd been down this path a hundred times and never seen that root.

Or the tree it was attached to, for that matter, a huge oak that he was sure he would have noticed before. There wasn't any more litter, either—no cans, bottles, or cigarette butts. Just ferns higher than his waist and a forest way more open than he remembered, without the understory of saplings, bushes, and brambles that had sprung up after the logging that had gone down a few years back.

"What the hell," he murmured. "This isn't here."

"It's here," Aster said. "This is why they never found her. Because she got stuck *here*."

"Where?" he demanded.

"In-between," she said. "Haven't you ever had a dream about a house you knew, but in the dream it had extra rooms you had never noticed before? Rooms that couldn't really exist, because there was no place for them to be?"

He realized as she said it that he'd had that dream regularly about his grandpa Burn's house, back when he was maybe five. He had looked for those rooms for several years after that, and then gradually forgot the whole thing. Until now.

"You know how some dining tables are made so you can pull them apart and put in an extra piece, so more people can sit at them?"

"Leaves," he said. "They're called leaves."

"This is like that," she said.

He stared at her. She was serious.

"That makes no fricking sense at all," Errol said.

"And yet here we are."

"But—"

He was never sure after what he'd been about to say, because his brain at the moment went through a sort of temporary erasure. They had just come around a bend, where the creek got really wide, almost like a small pond. And standing in it just up to her knees was a naked girl.

Embarrassed, he tried to look away, but then he noticed her expression, how she tilted her head.

It's okay, I don't mind if you look, she seemed to be saying.

"Errol?" Aster asked. She sounded very far away, a voice from another room. "Errol, what's wrong?"

The girl ignored Aster. She had skin the color of milk and her eyes were black. Her wet amber hair was plastered on her shoulders. He thought he had never seen anyone so beautiful.

"Errol, stay with me," Aster snapped. "Don't let go of my hand. Where is she?"

When the girl suddenly giggled, beckoned for Errol to follow and took off splashing down the creek, he wasn't surprised. He jerked his hand out of Aster's and hauled after her, laughing. She was mischievous, this girl, and bold, and he wanted to know her better.

Aster might have shouted after him, but he couldn't be bothered with that. The girl sprinted downstream, lithely vaulted onto a half-submerged stump and from there sprang up onto the opposite bank. It was amazing jump, and for an instant he could only stand there, admiring. But then she crooked her finger and sped off through the ferny underbrush.

He lost sight of her, but then she giggled again, and he followed the cheerful sounds.

He was vaguely aware that the forest was growing denser and darker, but the girl's flesh seemed almost to glow, making her easy to follow. She vanished into a canebrake, and he continued after, the canes rattling musically against his head and arms.

He hurtled out of the thicket and found her waiting for him at the edge of a pool. Heavy, leaf-laden branches blotted out the sky, and the air smelled like a storm coming.

"Hey honey," the girl said, the first words she had spoken. "Come here."

So he did, completely as if in a dream. It almost seemed like he heard music as she took his hand in hers. Now she seemed almost shy; she put her head down. But when she lifted it back up, he knew he was going to kiss her.

It was a small kiss at first, just their lips touching. Her eyes were open, and he could see it all, straight through to her soul. She was playful and bold and yes, mischievous—but never cruel or fickle. What he saw in her eyes was honest and real.

And she saw him, how he would love her, protect her. She gave a little sigh and pressed close as the kiss deepened. Her skin was both hot and cold, like a hot fudge sundae, like being in a warm lake but feeling a cold current come along beneath.

He felt happier and more peaceful than—well, ever.

He had a moment of dizziness, and he saw her hair was fanned out around her face, so she looked like a flower. It confused him at first, the lack of gravity, but then he understood that they were underwater. He wanted to laugh. That was her, always playful, pulling him in like that.

In the dim aquatic light, he saw her grin, and then she wrapped her arms around him and pressed the side of her face against his chest. He squeezed back, wondering how deep the pool was.

Then he felt his feet touch bottom, but it wasn't the mud he expected. Something snapped beneath his wooden feet.

He started to look down, but she caught his chin and brought him back to her lips. As they tipped over backwards he wondered distantly how he was able to kiss with lips of wood. It sort of didn't make sense.

They fell slowly, to settle horizontally on the floor of the pool.

He rolled so she was beneath him and there it was, her perfect face.

And a foot to the side, a much less perfect one, a bare skull, in fact, and now that he was looking around he saw that they were making out in a real bone yard. He saw at least four skulls and hundreds of other bones.

That snapped him out of it. Sort of. If he was flesh and blood, he would be dead by now, drowned. But he knew she wouldn't do that, didn't he?

Yeah, right. Like he had any judgment about women.

He broke away from her and began to swim toward the surface, half of him still willing to lie on the bottom forever, as long as she was with him. But he knew now it was a trick. Hell, it was always a trick, wasn't it?

He was halfway up onto the bank when she caught his foot. He turned and saw her emerging, looking more hurt than he thought anyone could, and all of a sudden he just wanted to hold her and tell her everything would be fine. With a sigh of surrender, he turned back toward her.

He was half-dead anyway, right? What did he have to lose?

When Aster reached the pool, she saw only ripples. She waited, trying to peer through the murky water, every part of her wound tight as a wire. She hadn't expected Errol to run off, although she should have. Even under normal circumstances he was a sucker for a pretty face, and most of his thinking was done way below his brain. But he only had to hold off for a few seconds, and he hadn't even done that.

If she failed here . . .

But suddenly Errol erupted back out of the water and grappled with the bank. He only did that for a second, though, before he whipped around toward something she couldn't see. Then he let go the land once more.

Aster flicked the water of life behind him, knowing that it was all she had, all she would ever have if this went wrong.

For a moment nothing happened, and she was sure she had missed, and everything she'd striven for was in ruins. But then the algae-covered bones of Veronica Hale's skeleton appeared, clinging to Errol like the shell of a cicada to a tree. Water and mist swirled up from the pool, enveloping the bones, forming on them, until she was all there. Her skin was so white it was nearly translucent and her long fair hair fell more than halfway down her back. Her features were human, but her expression wasn't, and the horror of it drove Aster back a few steps.

The mad eyes focused on her, and with a terrible little shriek the *nov* bounded at her, fingers outstretched like claws. But then her feet went wobbly and her features took on an air of terrible confusion. She opened her mouth and water poured out, and then she began coughing up more. Finally, panting, her eyes unfocused, Veronica looked up.

"What?" she said, and sat down on the mossy bank. She tucked her knees under her chin and began to rock.

"What, what, what?" she whispered.

"It's going to be fine," Aster said. "You're going to be fine. Look, I've brought you some clothes."

The girl kept rocking.

"Veronica," she said. "I've brought you some clothes."

The girl's motion slowed and stopped.

"That's my name," she said.

"I know," Aster said. "Why don't we get you dressed? I wasn't sure what size you were."

She pulled out some old khakis and a big t-shirt. Veronica, shivering, nevertheless stared at them for a long moment.

"I don't remember . . ." she mumbled.

"I'll help," Aster told her.

"What have you done to me?" Veronica moaned, as she pulled the shirt over her head.

"Restored you, at least partly."

"I don't understand," she said.

"I'll explain," Aster said. "But let's get to a safe place first, okay?"

"It's too late for that," the girl said. "He's almost here. He won't like this. He'll catch us."

"He who? What?" Errol interrupted.

Always with the questions, Errol. As if he couldn't think without talking.

"Just lead us out of here, Errol, now," she said. "Everyone hold hands."

A strong wet wind whipped the tree branches into a frenzied dance and a raindrop struck her shoulder. Thunder rumbled above.

She grabbed Errol's hand and placed Veronica's in his other.

"Don't let go this time, okay?" she said.

Errol looked like he was still in something of a daze. He kept staring at Veronica.

"Errol, she can't get out of here without your help," Aster said. "Neither can I. *Get* it together."

He nodded and then began walking, retracing their steps. The rain came, falling in sheets that tore through the canopy and stung her shoulders. Back behind them she heard something louder, something wetter and more massive than any storm.

She's mine. It went through her head like the keen of a buzz saw.

She reached in her pocket and pulled out a small paper packet of *gheizhe* and scattered it in the rain behind them, hoping it might throw him off for a few seconds, anyway. It was a small hope, as she wasn't even sure what was coming. She had only expected to find Veronica.

They sloshed across the creek to the path. When she had chased Errol across it, it had only been a foot deep or so. Now it came up to her waist. The stream pulled at her viciously, personally. She fell, and her scream was cut off by water flooding into her mouth, but Errol didn't let go; he gripped her fingers so tightly they hurt. He dragged her through the stream until they were on the bank, stumbling back the way they had come.

Witch! You do not dare!

He was too close. They weren't going to make it. She looked left at the river and saw the dark form building in it. Her feet were getting heavy.

She reached into her pocket again, and brought out something she had hoped to save for later. It didn't look like much, just a little silver sphere, but it had been her mother's.

She tossed it toward the thing.

"*Belas,*" she murmured, and suddenly it was as if the sun had come for a visit. A terrible, decidedly inhuman shriek cut though the downpour and then they were out of it, tripping through beer cans and candy wrappers.

Witch, the voice was very faint now. *Thief. I smell the Northeast Wind on you. I mark you now.*

It hung in her mind, as Errol began babbling questions again and Veronica made baby noises.

That was unexpected, she reckoned, and bad, but not as bad as being caught by whatever-it-was.

And now she had two of her companions. Just one to go.

FOUR

DADDY

V eronica.

She gripped the name, tried to open it like a book and see all that it contained. She remembered new, white tennis shoes, and the woman who gave them to her. She remembered looking down at them and the waterfall beneath . . .

Right here. She stared at the falls, so close, and yet for eternity so unattainable. How many times had she tried to swim that way? And how long since she quit trying?

"I've been here," she said, aloud. Not for the others, but for herself.

The skinny girl with the brown hair answered anyway. "Attahacha falls," she said.

"Yes. I—Veronica—was here before."

The girl had done something to her, freed her from *him* and those dark waters. It was almost as if she had placed a shining crystal inside of her mind, lighting up all of the places that had been dark for so long. At first the shock of the change, of stepping back into *Veronica* had been frightening. Now, here, in this half-remembered light, all of her fear drained away.

"Veronica," the girl went on. "Do you think you can tell me what that was that came after us?"

The girl seemed serious, although the question was a pretty silly one.

"*Him*," she replied. "The Creek Man."

"Oh," the girl said. "A *vadras*. Bad news."

"I don't know that word."

"There's no reason you should," the girl replied.

But Veronica thought she should. She wanted words again. She wanted to fill her head with them.

"What's your name?" she asked the girl.

"Aster," she replied. "Aster Kostyena. And this is Errol Greyson."

"I remember you, Errol," Veronica said. "I kissed you."

"Yeah," Errol replied.

"You're made out of wood. I didn't notice that before."

"That's kind of funny," he said. But he didn't sound like he thought it was funny at all.

"I guess that's why you're still alive," she said.

"So you were *trying* to kill me," he said.

"I wasn't *trying* to do anything," Veronica explained. "I was just doing what I do. I don't think about it."

"How many men have you killed?" he said, in a fairly noisy way. Anger? Was that what that was?

"I think we can agree they basically killed themselves," she replied.

"No!" Errol said, more loudly than before. "I don't agree with that at all. Aster, this is nuts. Do you know how many bodies were down there?"

"I'm sure Veronica will be a good girl from now on," Aster replied.

"I *am* a good girl," Veronica said. "My father always said so." She smiled, then, at the sudden image of his face.

"I remember my father!" she said.

"You will remember more and more, as time goes by," Aster said. "You'll remember about being human."

"But I'm still not human, am I?"

"No, you aren't," Aster replied. "But you're closer than you were."

Veronica felt like laughing again when she saw the car. It was funny-looking — not like the cars she remembered — but she knew what it was. Her head was filling up with words again.

T hings could have been worse; the yellow Toyota could have been waiting for them when they arrived, instead of pulling into the long driveway just as Aster was getting the house door open.

"Get in, Errol," Aster said. "Take her and hide her someplace."

"That's Ms. Fincher," Errol said.

"I know who it is," she snapped. "Get going."

She watched the car arrive, stop, and Ms. Fincher step out. And not just her, but Mr. Watkins, too. She fought off panic and tried to smile.

Behind them, she noticed a murder of crows settling in the field across the highway.

"Hello, Ms. Fincher, Mr. Watkins," she said.

"Hello, Aster," Mr. Watkins said. "We missed you at school today."

"Yes, I'm sorry," she said. "I had a doctor's appointment. I was going to bring a note tomorrow."

"You're soaking wet," Ms. Fincher said. "Exactly what sort of doctor's visit was it?"

"It rained," she said.

Ms. Fincher looked up at the clear sky and cocked her head. "It rained."

"Yes, Ma'am."

"What about your friends?" Mr. Watkins asked. "Did they have appointments as well?"

"Those are my cousins," she said, noticing as she said it more crows arriving in the field. "They're just staying for a few days."

"Visiting from out of the country?" he said. "How exciting."

"Yes, I suppose," she said.

Ms. Fincher smiled. "Here's the thing, Aster. We would like to speak to your father. Now."

"He's not here right now, Ma'am."

"We're here to help," Mr. Watkins said, soothingly.

Ms. Fincher's smile faded. "Listen to me, Aster. If we leave, we're coming back. And when we come back, we'll have the sheriff with us. Do you understand?"

"I don't see why the sheriff would be interested, Ma'am," she said, trying to stay calm. "I'm not a kid. This is my first absence this year. I had a doctor's appointment. I'll bring the note tomorrow."

"Why not just show it to me now?" Ms. Fincher asked.

Mr. Watkins looked apologetic. "There's no need—look, just let us talk to your father, Aster."

Aster blinked. Ms. Fincher was glaring at her and Mr. Watkins was looking earnest, but they were suddenly the least of her worries. A black mass rose up from the field, a whirling tornado of cawing, shrieking birds, thousands—hundreds of thousands—of them.

"Oh, not *now*," she groaned.

Ms. Fincher heard the noise and turned.

"Sweet Lord!" she squealed.

In that instant, Aster had two plain choices; duck inside and slam the door, leaving Ms. Fincher and Mr. Watkins to bear the brunt of this latest conjuration — or pull them in, as well. If she did the first, she at least wouldn't have to deal with them anymore. But then the police would come anyway, wouldn't they? There would be questions.

So she grabbed the two of them by the hands and hauled them in, just as the avian storm struck the house, a shuddering blow.

"What in heaven's name?" Ms. Fincher let out. She backed away from the door. Mr. Watkins' mouth was working but sound wasn't coming out.

Aster kept hold of their arms and led them to the first room down the hall.

"Just have a seat here," she said. "We should be safe inside."

"Safe from what?" the woman gasped.

"I'll get you something to drink," Aster said. "How about some orange juice?"

"Safe from *what*?" she shrieked again, as Aster ran down the hall.

"Wait," Mr. Watkins called. "Aster—"

She reached the door to her father's room and paused for a moment, then with a sigh unlocked it and pushed it open.

Errol led Veronica back through the winding maze of the house, but they hadn't gone far when a shock struck the building, and all of the power went out.

"Great," he muttered. "Again."

"What is it?" Veronica asked.

"Cows, maybe? I don't know."

But he started back toward the front door. Halfway to the foyer, he saw Aster dart across the hall, and followed her instead, figuring she would know what was up.

He caught up with her just in time to see her open the door.

The room looked like a tornado had been through it, and it appeared that the tornado had made a stop at the liquor store first. Whisky and vodka bottles littered the floor or stood empty on tables, chairs, and bookshelves. He could see all of this because of two oil lamps sputtering at either end of the room.

In the midst of all of that stood a tall man with red hair and green eyes. He had on pajama bottoms but no top, and Errol could see he was tattooed with what appeared to be stylized animals, stars, and moons.

The fellow's head jerked toward the open door, and his eyes widened when he saw the three of them.

He shouted something Errol didn't understand, but he felt a sort of crackle, like electricity.

"What's he saying?"

"Here," Aster said, touching him at the base of his head. "*Veidi.*"

". . . destroy you and your hellish golem, as well!" the man finished. It was weird—he could hear that the words weren't English, but they made sense now.

"Don't come into the room unless I tell you," Aster said, stepping through. "He can hurt you there."

"Come no closer, apparition!" the man shouted, hoarsely, brandishing a brown whisky bottle. Errol now noticed something else about him; he was staggering drunk. He also finally recognized him.

"Calm down," Aster said. "You know me."

His brows furrowed. "Nevese?" He muttered. "But no, you are very like, but too young—"

"I am your daughter, Aster," she said.

He stopped pacing and stared at her.

"You lie," he said. "Aster is but nine years of age."

"The wall, Dad," she said. "Look at your wall."

Errol followed the line of her finger, just as the red-haired man did.

He would have noticed the wall first, if it hadn't been for the crazy man. It had seven large pictures on it, all of Aster. The first had been taken probably about the time she had started at his school. She looked about nine. In the next she was about a year older, a year older in the next, and so on. Underneath the pictures were numbers, painted in big bold strokes; 4621, 4622, 4623, 4624, 4625, 4626, 4627 and 4628. And above all of this, painted in even larger characters, was written, "Kostye Dvesene: You can't remember anything since 4621."

Lots more was written there, too, whole paragraphs, mostly too small to read from where Errol stood.

The man dropped the brown bottle he was carrying.

"By all that is and can never be," he murmured. "What has happened? Time, the years . . . This is all written in my own hand. I don't remember . . ." He looked back at Aster. "How long? How long before I forget again?"

"If I stay here with you," she said, "hours maybe. But if I leave for a quarter of an hour, you won't know me when I get back."

"How many times have we had this conversation?"

"Hundreds," she said.

"Oh, my daughter, how did this happen to me?"

"I don't know," Aster said.

"A curse," he muttered. "A curse, but from whom? Who found us?"

"We don't know that either," she said. "But Dad, listen—I need you to release the spirits that you summoned to attack the house. The birds."

He took a rather large drink from the bottle. "Yes, I did that," he said. "I'm trapped in this room—this and the next, anyway.

Did you know that? I woke, and found myself imprisoned here. I summoned help—"

"Well, if you don't send them away they will kill me," Aster said.

Aster's father's look became suspicious, and he took another drink.

"How can I be sure?" he asked. "This could all be some elaborate enchantment. Who trapped me here? Who is powerful enough to have done that?"

"You did it yourself, Father, because you feared what would happen if you got out."

"Myself?"

"It's on the wall!" she snapped. "Read it!"

Aster's father looked from her to the wall, and then something inside of him seemed to collapse. He waved his hand and muttered something. The house stopped shuddering.

"Thank you, Father," Aster sighed.

"Do I make such summonings often?" he asked.

"You've called many things to this room," she said. "Spirits you hoped could cure you, the imp that brings your liquor—"

"And things intended to kill you," he finished.

"Because you don't know who I am," she said. "Because you find yourself trapped."

His eyes moistened. "Aster, I'm so sorry. For everything, all of it . . ."

"Yes," she said, softly. "You've said that before." She shrugged. "None of the earlier spirits ever escaped this room," she said. "And in time they returned to their proper places. But twice now you summoned something from outside of the room, outside of the house itself. You've never done that before. How did you do it?"

"I—I don't remember."

She nodded. "It's getting worse. You're getting stronger somehow. It may be too late."

"Too late for what?" he asked.

Her face hardened. "I've got to go, Dad. I've got things to do."

"No," he said. "No, Streya, I don't want to forget you again."

"It's okay, Dad," she said. "You'll remember me. You'll just remember me as being nine."

"But you're not," he said. "You're a woman." His gaze finally shot past her and fastened on Errol. "What is that?"

"A—he's a helper."

"A helper?" A look of fear came over his face, as he noticed Veronica. "Two of the three? The half-dead and the *nov*? Streya, what are you planning?"

"I'll do what I must, Father," she replied.

"Don't." Again he looked at Errol and thrust his index finger toward him. "You there. Don't let her go through with this. She has no idea—"

"I have no choice," Aster said. "I waited years for the first companion. Now I have the second."

"You aren't ready!" her father shouted.

"I'll have to be," Aster said. "And in a few minutes you'll forget we had this conversation, and you won't be worried. I'm going. I'll be back. And I love you."

He looked for a moment like he was going to continue the argument, but then he sighed. "You should hate me," he said.

"I do hate you a little," Aster said. "But the love is more."

"Mr. Kostyena!"

It was Ms. Fincher, pushing her way into the room. Mr. Watkins was just behind her. She took everything in, the smell, the dozens of alcohol bottles.

"This is honestly worse than anything I imagined," she said.

"Wow," Mr. Watkins said. He gave Errol a startled glance, but his gaze quickly returned to Aster's father.

"Streya?"

"Father, this is Ms. Fincher—the school counselor—and my teacher Mr. Watkins."

"We've met before," Ms. Fincher said. "Under better circumstances, I must say."

"Have we?" he muttered. "What are you here for?"

"Listen," Mr. Watkins said, pushing forward. "We're worried about Aster's welfare, that's all."

Her father's brow lowered, and he somehow grew steadier. He set the bottle down.

"Are you?" he muttered. "Or have you come to take her from me?" He took a step forward. "Whole kingdoms have I fought and cursed to keep my Streya safe, to keep us together. Righteous and terrible wrong have I worked. I have given up all but her—and she, I promise you, I shall never give up."

"Mr. Kostyena, you need help," Ms. Fincher said. "Anyone can see that. We're not here to hurt anyone, but Aster can't live like this—and neither can you."

Aster's father nodded, and then snapped his finger. Ms. Fincher and Mr. Watkins went all wavery and then turned into black clouds of smoke. The smoke coiled and twirled into the empty whisky bottle. Then Aster's dad shoved a cork in it.

"Well, that's one solution," Aster murmured. "You can restore them, I presume."

"Of course," he said.

"Fine. I guess for the time being . . ." She chewed at her lip.

"Are you nuts?" Errol said. "What did he just do to them?"

"They're fine," Aster said.

"If you say so," Errol said. "But you can't just kidnap two teachers. Surely they told someone they were coming by here."

"Yes," Aster said. "I need a Charm to hide her car."

"The big purple book in the library," her father said. "Under 'diverse obscurements'."

"Thanks, Dad," Aster said. "Errol, Veronica, let's go."

"I won't tell you anything else you need to know!" he shouted after her. "I won't help you do this thing!"

"Okay," she said.

W ell, that was pretty intense," Errol said when Aster came back in from hiding the car.

They sat in the kitchen, a neat little room with windows above the sink. The table was enameled on top, a sort of burnt orange color. Aster had poured herself some water from a stoneware pitcher and made a peanut butter sandwich.

"I guess it was," Aster said.

"How long has your dad been like that?" he asked.

"Since we got here," Aster said. "But he used to be better. He could remember for longer. As long as I stayed with him, almost. So we could go to parent-teacher conferences, shopping, that sort of thing. But now—sometimes he forgets in seconds. And it's getting worse."

"Have you thought about maybe seeing a doctor?" Errol said.

She shook her head. "Not at all. It isn't a medical problem. It's a curse."

"Are you sure? Because I'm not expert, but it looks like your dad drinks—uh,—kind of a lot. That can affect memory, can't it?"

"I don't suppose it helps," Aster replied. "But that's not his problem."

"Then what is?"

"Do I eat?" Veronica asked, suddenly.

Aster tilted her head. "Veronica," she said, "I'm not sure. Technically you're still dead—"

"Whoa," Errol interrupted. "I thought you said the water of life would bring her back to life."

"It's brought her one step back," Aster said. "She has life — she has her soul — but not health."

"Like me," he said.

"Sort of. Like you, she also needs the water of health."

Errol got it then. "So does your dad."

Aster wagged a finger at Errol. "You're very clever, Errol."

The way she said it didn't make him feel remotely clever, but he pushed on.

"So this quest we're on — it's about healing your dad."

"We're on a quest?" Veronica asked. She had pulled the knife out of the peanut butter and was sniffing at it.

"I used to like this," she said. She licked at it experimentally, and made a face.

"I don't think I eat," she said.

"Probably not," Aster agreed.

"What about Mr. Watkins and Ms. Fincher?" Errol said.

Aster spread her hands. "If I let them go now, we're done. Dad goes to a hospital, you stay in a coma, and Veronica — well, I'm not sure what happens to Veronica."

"I'm not breathing," Veronica noticed.

"That will get you noticed, sooner or later," Aster said.

"I usually get noticed sooner, don't I Errol?" Veronica leaned over and put her hand on his shoulder.

"Okay, Veronica, you're freaking me out," Errol said. "Really bad."

"You're a big talking puppet," Veronica said. "How do you think *I* feel? And you were all *over* me . . ."

"That wasn't my fault," he said. "That was magic or something. Like a spell."

"That much is true," Aster said. "Few men — or boys — can resist a *nov*."

"Is that what I am?" Veronica asked.

"Where I'm from that's what we call you, yes. The ghost of a girl who died a virgin—a *nov*."

"Well," Veronica said. "I *told* ya'll I was a good girl."

Errol found himself staring at her again and looked away. Veronica was different—different from what she had been back in the in-between-place. She even looked different. Now that her hair was dry it was a golden blonde, but it was much more than that. Now he could see her nose was a little crooked and her eyes were a bit too far apart. She wasn't the most perfectly beautiful woman he had ever seen anymore. And she was starting to act and talk more and more like a semi-normal person. But when he looked at her, he still remembered how he felt, how he had loved her, wanted her, more than anyone or anything. He felt he had been robbed of something, just like when Lisa dumped him. He also felt sort of dirty about the whole thing.

And of course, he had seen her naked *and* she had tried to murder him.

All in all, he hadn't thought he could be any more confused, and yet here he was.

"So," Veronica said. "We're on a quest. What next?"

"Now," Aster replied, "we need a giant."

"You mean like a circus giant?" Errol asked.

"No," Aster replied. "I mean like a bona-fide giant."

Errol digested that for a moment.

"We're not going to find one of those around here, are we?"

FIVE

THE CREEK MAN
AND THE SHERIFF

Dusk paused her horse Drake at the stream. He stamped once and then bent to drink. From the corner of her eye, she saw the water begin to collect, to bulge up.

"Do not *dare*," she said. Her tone was more confident than she; she had never done battle with a vadras, not this near the Pale, where her power was diminished. The vadras fed on death and decay, and there was plenty of that in the dark world beyond the Kingdoms, or so she had heard. It was said to be a world *made* of death.

The vadras wondered, too. He didn't move toward her, but he was still gathering himself.

"Who are you, who invades my demesne?" the vadras asked.

"I am one who goes where she will," Dusk replied. "I am a seeker."

"Indeed. In my experience that word often means thief."

Dusk bent forward in her saddle. Her heart-shaped face looked back up at her from the water, framed beneath her conical helm. Her breastplate glimmed softly in the uneasy light.

"I am not lightly accused, grandson of the ancient deeps. I'll tell you plainly why I've come to this wretched place."

She reached into the haversack slung on her saddle and produced a small, golden orb.

"Do you know what this is?" she asked.

"I know it," he said.

"They are few, and they call to one another. Mine was called, and I followed. And here I am."

"You have come for the orb?" the vadras said. "Then you *are* a thief. It burnt me, did me harm. It is mine, now."

"I have little interest in the orb," Dusk said. "After all, I have my own, do I not? But I have a great deal of interest in who hurt you with it."

The water boiled in agitation, and she put her hand to the hilt of her sword.

"Come now," she snapped.

"A witch," the vadras rumbled. "A witch and a man of wood. Thieves. They came and took my daughter."

"Your daughter?" Dusk said. "A *nov*?"

"My very own," he said.

"Tell me about this witch."

"She came from beyond the Pale, but she had the stink of the Northeast Wind on her. Like you."

"Take care whom you insult," Dusk said, softly. "The wind blows everywhere."

"Rarely here," the vadras said.

"Let me see it," she said. "The orb the witch brought."

"For what reason?"

"I may be able to tell a thing or two from it. Then I will go on my way."

"I think instead I will have yours," he said.

The pool exploded and rose up, a dark beast of mud, filth, and human corpses. Drake reared up and kicked at the monster as it rushed from the water. It slapped the horse and sent him rolling. Dusk leapt free, drawing her blade. She danced forward, dodging the ill-formed hands that groped for her, and then leapt high, plunging Polestar deep into the mass the vadras had formed. An ordinary blade would have had little effect, but hers was no ordinary blade, any more than she was an ordinary traveler.

"*Gelde*," she shouted, as she withdrew the weapon.

The effect was immediate; the muddy fist swinging for her slowed instantly to a stop, literally frozen. She watched as ice walked itself across the pool and upstream, and the air became bitter chill.

Lady, please. I did not know who you were.

"Now you do," she, holding up her little globe. An answering glint came from within the frozen hulk. She carved at it for a time until it came free, ignoring the moans of the vadras.

Drake seemed to be mostly okay; blood flowed from one great, soft nostril, but that would heal soon enough. She stroked his neck and kissed him near his eye. Rather than mounting him, she walked him upstream, until she came to the Pale, beyond which she could not pass. But she could see dimly through it. She could mark it in her own geography. Now she knew where they were hiding.

"The sorcerer couldn't have come through here," she told Drake. "Not if I can't. We'll have to backtrack out of these faded, broken places. But now that I know where his path leads to, it will make it that much easier for us to find the right way through."

She patted the horse. "Are you ready to bear me again?"

Drake whinnied, and she mounted up. The vadras was still whimpering for forgiveness when she rode past, but she looked at the blood on Drake's muzzle and decided to kill the thing.

When she was done, she put the Pale to her back and rode away. And for the first time in years, she felt some hope that her mission might be fulfilled.

T he sheriff approached the stream, watching his hounds sniff about in agitation. He reined his mount to a stop.

"Vadras," he said. "It's the sheriff."

He got no answer.

The sheriff swung down and examined the tracks in the mud.

He found the vadras dead. He didn't care much about that, or the about the one that had killed him, for that matter. But the trail that led into and out of the marches was a different matter. Unnatural things were walking beyond the Pale, and that was very much his business. And something was familiar here, something a nagging in the back of his mind told him was important. Something to do with his exile.

Maybe something that would end it and give him his name back.

He patted the white dog on the head, then mounted back up.

"Let's go hunting, boys," he said.

SIX

THE VIRGIN GHOST

S o, why?" Veronica asked, as Aster fiddled with three large backpacks in the corner of the kitchen. They already seemed to be mostly packed, but she was adding tins of food, crackers, and an assortment of fruit.

"I thought that was understood," she replied. "I have to cure my father. If I don't—well, you saw what he did to Ms. Fincher and Mr. Watkins. There's no telling what he might do if he ever manages to leave the house."

"No," Veronica said. "I mean why are you here? You and your father? He said something about kingdoms . . ."

Aster paused. "We really need to get going," she said.

"Going where?" Veronica pressed.

Aster zipped up one of the backpacks and started on another.

"The fact is, Veronica, I don't really know why we're here. I think we're lost. Dad was running from someone, or something. We were on the run for a long time. And then we came here, and he said we were safe. But he's never told me who we were running from, or why. I think it has something to do with my mother. I think she was killed, or . . . I don't know. I've gone through his things, but there's nothing about her. Only I did find out how to go back."

"Back to whatever he was running from?" Errol said.

"It's the only way," she said. "Unless you know someplace in *this* world where I can find the water of health."

"Is it the same place I was?" Veronica asked.

"Dad calls them the Kingdoms," she replied. "They're all connected but sometimes it isn't easy to get from one to another. Some parts of the Kingdoms are nearly impossible to reach. We could go back in where I found you, but the vadras would be waiting for us, and for all I know that place is a thousand miles from where we want to go. So we won't go that way, not when I have an easier route."

"So when do we start this quest?" Veronica asked.

"Right away," Aster replied. "As soon as I'm done packing."

"Aces!" she said. "Can I go to the bathroom first?"

"Sure," Aster said. "Down the hall to the left."

"Thanks."

E rrol tried not to watch Veronica go, without success.

"Oh, dear," Aster said.

"It's not like that," he said. "You know about this stuff. You said it yourself. Geez, why didn't you warn me?"

Aster shrugged. "Maybe I should have, but I don't think it would have done any good."

"Well, I don't trust her," Errol said. "How sure are you about this whole 'three companions' thing?"

"I'm sure," she said. "I needed you to find her, I need her to enter the Kingdoms—yeah, I need all three of you."

"But if you only needed me to find her, then why do you still need me?"

"Because I do, Errol, okay?"

"Listen," he said, "no need to get testy. I told you I'm with you. Just—she makes me uneasy, is all."

"I've never heard it called *that* before," Aster said.

"Ha, ha." He watched her pack for a moment.

"How can we leave him alone? Your dad?"

"I don't want to," she said. "But I've got no choice. He has a bathroom, and he can summon food and drink . . ."

"Mostly drink, from what I can see."

"Yes," she said. "The main worry is if someone else comes, like the police. But I have no solution. There isn't anyone I trust to watch him. We'll just have to hurry, that's all."

"It's like leaving a ticking A-bomb. Except you don't know when the timer is going to go off."

"He's my father, Errol. I—wait."

He followed her to her workshop, where she rummaged for a bit before finding something that looked like a necklace made of amber pearls. Then she went back to her father's rooms.

"You can listen," she said, "but stay out of sight."

She opened the door.

"Streya?" her father murmured. He sounded even drunker than before, close to passing out. He spoke very slowly and deliberately. "I was just looking at your pictures. Reading this— is it true?"

"It's true," she said. "Listen. You understand why you're trapped in this room?'

"I did it myself," he said.

"Right. But now you've begun to summon things from out-side the house. I've nearly been hurt twice."

"I don't remember," he said.

"It happens when you don't read the wall. When you panic."

"Yes, I see that," he said.

"I can't always be here," she said. "I've got to go to school."

"I know," he said. "You've grown so big. You look like your mother . . ."

"There's no time for that," she said. "Just listen. You sorceled a woman and a man into that bottle there," she said. "You need to extract one of them, or I'm going to be in big trouble."

"The man or the woman?"

"The woman," Aster said.

After a pause, Errol heard a sort of burping sound.

"Thanks Dad," she said. "I'll be back."

"Oh!" he heard Ms. Fincher say. "I don't—what are you doing?"

"Come with me, Ms. Fincher," Aster said.

Ms. Fincher appeared in the hallway. She was wearing the necklace.

They went back in the kitchen.

"Ms. Fincher," Aster said.

"Aster?" Ms. Fincher replied.

"First off, don't ever take that necklace off, or ask anyone else to take it off for you, okay? And don't get close enough to my father for him to take it off you."

"Okay, Aster," she said.

"Second, I need you to tell anyone who knows you visited my house that everything is fine here, that there's nothing for anyone to worry about."

"But that's not true."

"Right. You'll have to lie. Use your imagination."

"Okay," Ms. Fincher said.

"Also, you know my father forgets. When he forgets, bad things happen. So I need you to stay here and remind him every twenty minutes or so about what's going on."

"But what about my job?" she said.

"Get a leave of absence. Tell them somebody died or whatever you think is most plausible. And under no circumstances are you to take any orders from my father, or anyone else but me."

Ms. Fincher nodded.

"That's all," Aster said. "Best get on those things now."

"Very well, Aster," Ms. Fincher said. "Can you tell me where a phone is?"

"Down the hall," Aster replied. "Past the clock."

They watched her go.

"What did you do to her?" Errol asked.

"The necklace, a trinket of my father's," she said. "I'd almost forgotten it."

"How could you forget something like that?" he asked. "You could get Sara Carver to wear it and make her do *anything*."

Aster smiled slightly. "I can't say I haven't thought about it. In detail. But using this stuff—especially outside of the house—is dangerous."

"Dangerous how?"

"Dad says it can attract attention," she said. "The wrong kind."

"Then maybe you shouldn't—"

"You were the one who said I needed to do something," she reminded him. "Now I have a little piece of mind."

Then she frowned. "Where's Veronica?"

"She went to the bathroom, remember?"

"That was a while ago," Aster said, her voice rising in alarm. "And anyway, if she doesn't eat—"

"—then why does she need a bathroom?" Errol finished.

She wasn't in the bathroom or indeed in the house at all. Veronica, the virgin ghost, was loose.

Veronica ran as fast as she could—not because she was afraid the witch and Pinnochi-Errol might catch her, but because she loved the feel of it, the bare soles of her feet on the asphalt, the wind in her hair. It was a little upsetting that her lungs weren't heaving for breath and she felt no pulse of blood in her body, but hey—you got what you got.

She laughed, trying to imagine the looks on their faces when they figured out she was gone. Holy cow, did they think she was nuts? Why in the world would she want to be mixed up in any sort of business with Aster and her crazy father and some Kingdom who-knew-where? If she went with them she would as like end up in another swamp with another creek man—if not the same—and that she wasn't up for.

She noticed she wasn't getting tired, which seemed like a bonus of her condition. What did being alive have on this, really?

She laughed with delight when she spotted a red bicycle in the front yard of a trailer, and a few minutes later she was cruising in style, remembering how she could ride without hands. She wasn't at all concerned by the woman shouting after her, demanding she bring her son's bike back.

She started trying to figure out where she was. The ride from Attahacha Falls hadn't been that long, so she wasn't that far from home, but nothing looked familiar, so she just followed the road until she came to a crossroads, and she sat there for a moment. She thought she knew where she was, then, and turned left. If she came across Tucker's store in the next half-a-mile, she would know she was on the right track.

She hadn't peddled a hundred yards, though, before she started having some doubts. There was a big brick house where one shouldn't be, and it didn't look new, and a little farther on a right turn that ought not to be. But then she saw the familiar sign with the dinosaur on it and Tucker's store, exactly where it should be.

But then she got closer. The sign was there, yes, but all cracked, and a chunk with the dinosaur's tail missing. The concrete around the pumps was all broken, with weeds pushing up through the fissures. The windows were all either shattered or boarded up.

She rested on the bike, balanced on one foot, remembering. There had been a jar of pickled pig's feet on the counter, and every time they went in, her dad had offered to buy her one, and she always made a face. On hot days, she would go inside and put her nose down into the open coolers and suck in the cold hair until her hair felt frosted. They had fifty kinds of penny candy. They had a cup on the counter from which they sold single cigarettes. She had taken one when she was thirteen while Mr. Tucker was busy with another customer. It had been her first.

How long had she been dead?

A little less upbeat, she continued on down the road. When she came to the junction with 25, she got another surprise. She didn't remember anything being on that spot except pine trees; now a big, bright, mostly orange and yellow building stood there. She sat wondering at it for a moment.

It was about twice the size of Tucker's store, and it had eight gas pumps instead of two. Two cars were at the pumps, but she didn't see any attendants. It looked like the people were just pumping the gas themselves. It was all very bright.

Inside she found no open coolers—they all stood upright, like refrigerators with glass doors. She saw lots of drinks—especially beer—but she didn't see any grape Nehi. Even the stuff she recognized looked weird.

Of course, she didn't have any money anyway. And she didn't eat or drink.

"Kid!" someone shouted—a fat lady behind the counter.

"Ma'am?" she said.

"You can't come in here barefoot."

"I can't?" They hadn't cared at Tucker's.

"No, you can't. Now get on out."

Veronica returned to her bike and peddled on. She knew where she was going, but more and more she worried about what she would find there.

T he little blue house she remembered wasn't there, but plenty of others had taken its place. They were all big, and they all looked kind of the same. They all had really nice lawns.

She couldn't even tell exactly where her house had been, so she knocked on the door that seemed about right. When no one came, she rang the bell, but that didn't get her an answer, either, so she moved on to the next one. There was no one home in that house, either, but about that time she caught a familiar smell, a sense of something. Humming, she rode down the row of houses until she found the right one, and knocked on the door.

He was kind of lanky and had a little beard. He was wearing a swimsuit and his hair was wet. She wasn't sure how old he was.

"Yeah?" he said.

"I was wondering if you could help me," she said. "I'm looking for a Mr. and Mrs. Hale."

"I don't know anyone by that name," he said. "Do they live around here?"

"They used to," she said.

He laughed. "No one used to live here," he said. "They built all of this last year. Some of the houses still aren't finished."

"I'm sure this is where they lived."

He was taking her in, now, and liking what he saw. She smiled.

"Do you — uh — want to use our phone?"

"I wouldn't know who to call."

He looked down at her bare feet. "These people you're looking for, the Hales — are they relatives?"

"My mama and papa," she said.

"You don't know where your parents are? What — did you run away or something?"

"Yeah," she nodded. "Something."

"Well — look, come in. We'll check in the phone book, okay? You can't just wander around . . ." he didn't finish, but just waved her in.

"Well, that's really nice of you," she said.

Inside the house was big, too, with high ceilings and a fancy kitchen. In the back were glass doors, and past that she could see a patio and a big swimming pool.

"You must be rich," she said.

"My dad does okay," he said.

"What about you? Do you go to school around here?"

"Yeah, at the community college."

"Oh, college man," she said.

"Yeah," he said, rummaging through kitchen drawers. "Where is that phone book?"

"I hope you didn't invite me in under false pretenses, sir," she said.

"I — no," he said. "Just looking for the phonebook." But he paused.

"Hey — how long has it been since you've eaten?"

"It's been a while," she said.

"I can make you a sandwich. You want something to drink?"

"That would be lovely," she said.

"How about a beer?"

"That sounds great," she replied.

He opened two beers. She forced herself to swallow a little.

"I'm not sure where that phone book is," he said. "Mom always puts it in the weirdest places."

"I'm in no hurry," Veronica said. "I was just noticing what a lovely pool you have out back. I'm afraid I must have interrupted your swim."

"That's okay."

"I love to swim myself."

"Yeah?"

She could see it now, the thing she had smelled. He had been careful not to ask her age, hadn't he?

"I don't think we have a suit that would fit you," he said.

"I can make do," she told him.

T hey had only gotten a hundred yards down the road when a lady waved them down.

"Look limp," Aster said. Errol tried to oblige.

Aster rolled her window down.

"Hi Ms. Wesley," she said.

"Hello, Aster," Ms. Wesley said. "I—what in the world is that?"

"That? Oh, science fair project. What can I do for you?"

"Huh," Ms. Wesley said. "Well, listen, a blonde girl just came by here and stole Billy's bike. You know, the red one?"

"Yes Ma'am."

"I called the police, but I don't have a car. She can't have gone that far. If you see her . . ."

"I'll do what I can, Ms. Wesley," Aster said.

A ster wheeled up to the quick-stop and dashed in. She came out under a minute later. Errol stayed ducked down in the seat.

"She was here," she said. "A girl on a red bike."

"So we're on the right track," Errol said. "Good guess."

"Not so much a guess," Aster said. "She's going home. Or thinks she is. Her parents moved to Atlanta twenty years ago, and there's a new subdivision where she used to live."

"You know a lot about her," he said.

"I've been researching her for years," Aster replied. "I had four candidates for a full-dead, but she was the most likely."

She sped along and turned onto new pavement and into the subdivision.

"Oh, yeah," he said. "I remember them building these."

"We can't miss her here," Aster said. "If we miss her here, there's no telling where she'll go next."

"Calm down," he said. "There's the bike, over there."

She pulled up in front of the house and knocked. There was no answer. She tried the door, but it was locked. Errol watched her run around the side and pull herself up to look over the cedar privacy fence.

She dropped down.

"Oh, crap—Errol, get over here, fast!"

No one seemed to be around, but he still felt exposed loping across the lawn. Aster had climbed the fence by the time he got there, and he found—to his delight—that he could easily vault over it.

At first he didn't see what the fuss was about, but then he realized two people were at the bottom of the swimming pool.

He dove in.

Veronica wasn't happy when he pulled her off of the man, but she relented after a few hard tugs. He grabbed the fellow and brought him up to the surface.

"Crap," Aster said again. "Is he dead?"

"He's not breathing. Do you know CPR?"

"No," she said. "Do you?"

Errol dropped down and pumped at the man's chest. Water spewed from his mouth. He bent to blow in air, and realized he couldn't.

"You're gonna have to do this," he told Aster.

"Oh, right. Walk me through it."

Errol kept one eye firmly fastened on Veronica, who slid into a lawn chair and watched them with obvious amusement.

"Veronica," Errol said, "get dressed."

"Fine," Veronica said, and reached for her clothes.

The man suddenly sucked in a breath on his own.

"Oh, foo," Veronica said.

"Let's get the hell out of here," Errol said.

"Yes, let's," Aster replied.

They left the man, gasping and still unconscious.

W hat the hell was all that about?" Errol demanded, once they had Veronica dressed again and in the car.

"I was looking for my folks," she said. "They used to live around here."

"Yes, but how do you go from that to drowning some guy in his swimming pool?"

"I got bored, and I guess a little frustrated."

"That doesn't explain *anything*."

"It's a habit," Veronica said. "Don't you have habits?"

"I chew my nails!" he said. "That's a habit. I don't kill people."

"Admitted," Veronica said, "it may very well be a *bad* habit. But that guy had terrible things on his mind."

"You can read minds?"

"When I'm kissing, yes. So, like when *you* were kissing me it was all 'I *looove* this girl, I can see into her soul, I want to *marry* her—'"

"Because of a spell!" Errol objected.

"Maybe," she said. "But my point is, you were all sweet. That guy—that's not the sort of things he was thinking. What he was thinking was really nasty, and maybe had me dead at the end, and there wasn't anything about love in it."

"Really?"

"Really."

"But wait a minute," Errol said. "Let's say he was a bad guy. You were going to kill me, even though I wasn't planning to hurt you."

"Sure."

"So what does it matter what he was thinking?"

"Because if I killed you, I might feel a little sad about it. But not that guy."

"Veronica," Aster interrupted, in a cold, flat voice. "Listen to me. You can't run away again. You have to help me."

"I surely don't see why."

"Every time you go out, there's a chance you'll slip back into an in-between place, and you'll be just like you were before, only this time no one will come for you, because no one will know where you are. And even if you avoid that—for a while— eventually you're going to be caught by the police, either for this attempted murder or whatever you do next. Once they fig- ure out your heart isn't beating and yet you continue with the flirting, I shudder to think what will happen to you. Probably you'll be dissected, or something. Stay with me—help me—and if we succeed, you get your life back. A real life, the one you didn't get to have. You can eat chocolate, get married, have kids, whatever you want. I'll help you find your parents, if that's what you want. But no more running away. You do what I say."

Veronica was quiet for a moment.

"But if I go with you," she said, "into that place. I might get caught there, too?"

"You won't because you'll have *us*," Aster said. "Errol and me."

"Hey, speak for yourself," Errol muttered.

"You'll have both of us," Aster said, shooting Errol a stern look. "We'll have your back. But you have to have ours."

Veronica looked out the window.

"Everything is so different," she murmured. Errol realized suddenly that she had tears on her cheeks.

"Don't cry," he blurted. "It's like Aster said. We'll watch out for you."

"It's okay," Veronica said, patting his arm. "I didn't know I could cry. Now I do." She straightened up. "Let's go find a giant."

"Hang on," Errol said.

"What now?" Aster sighed.

Something had been building in Errol, something bright in the pit of where-his-stomach-ought-to-be, but only now did the light reach his head.

He paused, remembering the terrible woman in the forest. The fear that Aster might send him back there knotted in him.

"If we're really about to wander off into Fairyland or whatever I . . . I want to see me. My body. In the coma."

"Are you kidding me?" Aster snapped. "Are you flat-out jackass kidding me? Because *no*."

"You're in a coma?" Veronica asked.

"So I'm told."

"And it is a fact," Aster insisted.

"But don't you see?" Veronica said. "I needed my answers— Errol needs his."

"What answers?" Aster asked. "There's a subdivision where your house used to be? I could have told you that."

"It's not the same as knowing," Veronica said. "All that talk about having each other's backs — let's see it then. I want to see you have Errol's back."

"Look," Aster said. "You just nearly killed a guy. My father turned Ms. Fincher and Mr. Watkins into poofs of smoke, and he's getting more out-of-control as we speak. Now you want to go down to the hospital? What next, go downtown and start shooting out the blue lights on police cars?"

"You made Ms. Fincher's car invisible," Errol said. "Can't you do the same for me?"

"No," Aster replied. "That spell only works on immobile objects. Once in motion, the illusion breaks."

"Oh, surely that's no problem for someone as talented as yourself," Veronica said, sweetly.

"In time I might be able to figure out how to do it," Aster said. "But that's time I don't have."

"Well," Veronica said, folding her arms, "I've changed my mind. I'm not helping you find any giant until you help Errol."

Aster stamped on the brake, and the car came to abrupt halt. Veronica yelped and bumped into the back of Errol's seat.

Aster sat there for a moment, glaring, it seemed, at the car horn.

"Okay," she finally said, softly. "Errol, reach up behind your right ear. You'll find a little stud."

He reached back.

"Got it," he said.

"Push it in, then toward the back of your head."

He did as she said and then was suddenly dizzy. His body felt weird, far away. He moved his arm, and felt it move, and yet he could see that it *hadn't* moved.

"Push forward," Aster said.

Again, he felt his hands come up, but his vision said they weren't moving. He felt a flat, invisible surface, and pushed. It clicked and opened, and he had a brief instant of terrifying blindness.

"Wow," Veronica said. "How weird."

He was looking Veronica level in the face, but she was huge. So was the car. Everything had grown about fifty times bigger except for him.

But at second glance he got it.

He was standing inside the head of his puppet body; the face had opened when he pushed it out. He was now in another body, much smaller—obviously, since it fit into the head of the big one.

And this little body seemed to be carved almost entirely of something white, like bone.

"You weren't going to mention this?" he asked, after a few long moments of dumb silence.

"When it became necessary," Aster replied. "Which I suppose is now."

Her hand appeared, enormous. Reaching for him.

"Hey!" he shouted.

"Calm down," she said, "I'm just putting you in my backpack."

SEVEN

BED OR COFFIN

T hat's not me," Errol said, when Aster finally let him peek from the backpack.

"Just who do you think it is, then?" Aster whispered back.

Errol would have frowned if he had had eyebrows.

Even in a mirror, Errol had never thought his face looked quite right — not like it looked in his head, anyway, when he pictured it. The pallid features nestled on the white hospital pillow seemed to have even less in common with him. But now, studying it in mute horror, he recognized the scar over his left eye, and the small birthmark below his right ear. The mouth was covered by a respirator.

"Huh," he said, because he didn't want to say anything else, or let the strange and terrible sadness welling up in him show itself to the others. "Well, okay."

He looked around the otherwise empty room. When imagining this visit, he'd pictured his mother, sitting by the bedside, tears in her eyes, asking him to come back to her. And maybe some of his friends, too, Darren or Tommy at least. And Lisa, full of remorse for breaking up with him. But not only was no one here, there wasn't much sign that anyone ever had been. No cot, no blankets or pillows on the chairs, no paperbacks.

"You're kind of cute, Errol," Veronica said. "Not a movie star or anything, but not too bad."

She cocked her head.

"You look just like you're sleeping."

Errol remembered that's what someone had said about Granny, too, when she was in her coffin at the church. He hadn't thought she looked like she was sleeping at all.

"Except, you know, for that thing on your face."

"Visitors," someone said. He caught a quick glimpse of Dr. Sanders with his long jaw and balding head before Aster shoved him quickly back down in her backpack.

"Ah, Aster. Back again."

"Uh—yes. We checked in at the desk."

"I know. I was on the floor and thought I would come over and say hello. I don't think I've met you, Miss."

"I'm Veronica," she said.

"You look awfully familiar," he said. "What's the last name?"

"McCartney," Veronica lied. "Like the Beatle."

"Do I know your folks?"

"I don't think so, sir," she replied. "How is dear Errol?"

"Well, there's no change, I'm afraid," he said.

"Is there any hope for him?"

"There's always hope," Dr. Sanders said. "For all of our technology and advances in medicine, we still can't really say what makes a person who they are. And the brain—well, it's more resilient than most people think. I had a patient with a bullet hole all the way through his head, and in the end he was pretty much the same after the incident as he was before."

"So he was retarded before?" Veronica asked.

Dr. Sanders lifted a greying eyebrow.

"Now, young lady, that's not a nice thing to say," he said.

"I'm sorry, doctor," she said. "I didn't know that."

Errol felt like screaming. Why did Veronica keep calling attention to herself?

The Doctor cleared his throat, the way he did right before telling you that you had to have a shot.

"I'm glad to see you girls here," he said. "He needs visitors. Aster, I heard you talking to him last time you were here. I encourage that, too. Keeping him connected here is the most important thing; until he wakes up, there's nothing else we can do."

"What if he never wakes up?" Veronica asked.

"Well . . ." Dr. Sanders trailed off. "Let's just pray he does, okay? Talk to him, girls. Encourage him to come back to us. And encourage his other friends to come around."

"Bye Doctor," Veronica said, as the sound of footsteps began and receded.

"You've been here before?" Errol snapped, pushing his head out of the bag.

"Yes," Aster said.

"What for? How many times?"

"A few," she said. "I needed to—you, know, do some things here."

"What things?"

"Well, I had to have a little of your blood, for one thing," she said, stiffly, "and part of the spell had to be recited here."

"Are you—are you—" but he stopped himself. What if she *was*? What if she was keeping him in a coma?

"Am I what?"

"Are you in love with him, I think he means to say," Veronica smirked. "Spells, schmells. You were in here *talking* to him."

"This is very stupid," Aster said. "Are we done here, Errol?"

"No! I mean — if you were here before — did you ever see my mom?"

Aster chewed her lip for a moment.

"Once," she finally said.

"Out of how many times?"

"Six, I guess."

"Did she — did she say anything?"

"Not really," Aster said. "She was — a little drunk. And with some guy. Tall, blond guy. He didn't really want to hang around, I think."

"Roger."

"I think so."

Errol closed his eyes. Goddammit mom, really? First Dad and now me?

"Okay," he said, after a moment. "I'm done here."

His body's room was on the third floor; they took the elevator down, which opened down the hall from the emergency room. Errol was peeking from Aster's backpack, and saw a familiar face. He was awake and sitting in a wheelchair, but Errol had no trouble recognizing him as the guy Veronica had tried to drown.

"Hey!" the guy shouted.

Beyond the fellow in the wheelchair, way back in the waiting room, someone looked up. A man, older, with salt-and-pepper hair cut short and a deeply tanned face. Incredibly, Errol could see that his eyes were ice-blue, and even more impossibly that those eyes were focused on *him*.

"Hustle," Errol said.

In response, Aster picked up her stride. The guy yelled again, but by then they were going through the revolving door, into the hot evening air. The blue-eyed man was on his feet, walking swiftly.

"Really," Errol said. "Someone is following us."

Aster broke into a trot.

Errol, still looking back, watched the revolving door start to turn again, and the man emerge.

"Hurry," he said.

Aster and Veronica went to a flat-out run. They reached the car and piled in, but the man was almost upon them. Aster started the engine and threw it into gear just as he arrived.

"You don't belong here!" the man shouted. "None of you belong here!"

The tires screeched as they peeled away.

"There will be a reckoning!" The man's voice followed them. "I'll find you!"

"Says you, lunatic," Aster muttered.

But her voice quivered, and her tone was anything but certain.

PART TWO

OUT FROM THE GHOST COUNTRY

ONE

DELIA

A ster pushed down her panic and tried to get her thoughts in order. Errol, as usual, wasn't helping.

"What was that all about?" he ranted. "That guy knows something. He *saw* me."

"I don't know, Errol," Aster said. "I'm trying to work it out."

"Well, work it out fast. I think he's following us. A truck pulled out of the hospital lot right after we did. You've turned twice and it's still behind us."

Aster glanced in her rear view mirror and saw a battered white pickup.

"*Zhedye*. Great," Aster swore, stepping on the gas.

This was it. No more time to plan. No more time to be careful. No way to even go back to the house, to make sure she had everything.

For the first time in a long time, she actually felt lighter. Freer.

"I've seen him before," Veronica said, softly. "The man."

"Where?"

"I don't remember. But I'm afraid of him."

"Yeah, well he's damn spooky," Errol said. "I'll give you that."

The truck was a good ways back, but gaining ground. Aster sped around the next curve and then turned hard right onto Sugarloaf Road with its narrow twists and turns through pine forest.

"Go, mama," Veronica whooped. "Race that dragster."

"I would say you're going to get us killed," Errol said, "but since you're the only one that applies too . . . hey!" He yelped as she fishtailed onto a dirt road not even a lane wide.

"Errol," she snapped. "Get back into your head."

"I'm not the one losing it," he shot back.

"No, dufus, I mean literally. Into the big body. You're going to need it soon."

"Where are we going?" Veronica asked, with a bit of strain in her voice. "This doesn't feel right."

"Hold my hand," Aster said.

"Well, I'm not a little girl," she said.

"Hold my hand, *now*," Aster commanded.

Veronica complied, and Aster felt a palpable jolt.

"Now, hold on to Errol."

The dirt road became a muddy, rutted red-clay trail, but she kept the car going as fast as she could, fearing becoming mired.

"We're in-between again," Veronica gasped.

"Hang on, Veronica," Aster said. "We aren't staying here. We're pushing through."

They were going downhill, now, and the car began to pick up speed, sliding crazily from rut to rut and scraping hard against the ground. She felt a terrible jolt and heard a metallic clang, and the engine doubled the noise it was putting out as she left her muffler behind. She could feel it now, like a wind, pushing against her; everything became a blur, as if they were hurtling through a tunnel of green and blue and red.

Then midnight slapped her in the face.

I s she dead?" Veronica asked.

"She's breathing," Errol told her. Despite her seatbelt, Aster's head had hit the windshield when the car crumpled against the tree. She had a nasty cut and a bump the size of a baseball and was leaning forward on the steering wheel. "Check and see if she's got any first-aid stuff in the glove box."

"Whatever you say, Mister Boss," Veronica replied, sighing.

"C'mon, she's bleeding."

Veronica popped open the glove box and gave it a diffident inspection.

"Nothing there," she said.

"The backpacks, then."

"Shouldn't we get her out of the car, first?"

"I don't think you're supposed to move people after an accident."

"Right. But don't cars explode, sometimes?"

"Yeah," he said. "Okay. Let me out your side, so I can go around."

She complied in her usual unhurried fashion, but when she pushed on the door, it fell out onto the ground. Figuring it was broken from the crash, Errol stepped out after Veronica did.

It was then that he noticed that the car no longer seemed to have any paint on it, and was in fact covered in rust. He brushed at the roof, and a cloud of red dust travelled after his hand.

Aster's door actually fell apart when he tried to open it. As he carefully cradled her and pulled her from the vehicle, the axels collapsed and what had moments before been an automobile became a rough hump of corrosion.

Errol laid Aster out on some moss and then pushed into the reddish pile, extracting the backpacks.

"Now why would it do that?" Veronica asked, as Errol began to search through the packs.

"I'm nearly at the point of not asking questions like that," Errol told her. "None of this makes any sense. I keep coming back to this being some sort of nightmare I'm having."

"So you think you're dreaming me?"

He caught the way she said it, but he plowed on as if he hadn't. "Why not?" he said. "Whatever. It doesn't matter. I'm just going with the flow, from now on."

"And Aster is the flow."

"Apparently."

"And what if we didn't?" Veronica said. "Why should we let her tell us what to do? We can leave her. Now would be good."

He paused for a moment. What about that? Could Aster send him out of this body if he was too far away to hear her? Was it the sound of the word she said that did it, or was it something more substantial?

He realized it didn't matter.

"I won't abandon her," he snapped. "I'm not like them."

"Them?"

"I mean I'm not like *that*."

He didn't find any medical supplies in the first pack. He started searching the second.

"Like it or not," he rationalized, "she's the only one who knows what's going on."

"I don't think she knows as much as you think," Veronica said. "She didn't know who that guy chasing us was."

"Maybe not," he said.

"But you're going with the flow."

"Yes. Yes I am."

"That doesn't seem like you," Veronica said.

"You don't know me," he said. "Nobody knows me."

"Poor lil' ol you," she sighed.

His hand hit a flat metal box, and he fished it out. It had a red cross on it.

Veronica stood. "Well there you go," she said. "Me, I'm going to have a look around while you play doctor with Miss Witch."

"Don't go anywhere," he snapped.

"Huh. Does someone think he's the boss of me? Because I can assure any such a person —"

But she stopped in mid-sentence.

"Did you hear that?" she whispered.

"No," he began, but then he did. It sounded kind of like a trumpet, but more raw in tenor. And close behind it came the baying of hounds, two of them.

"I don't think we ought to wait around here, anymore," Veronica said. She pulled nervously at her blond locks and darted her gaze all around them.

"You know what that is?" he asked.

"It's him," she said. "The man from the hospital."

"How do you know?" he asked.

"I can't remember. But I know." She looked more agitated by the second.

Errol looked back at Aster.

"Let me bandage her head. Then we'll go."

Delia felt a crackle in her hair and clothing, as if lightning had parted around her. The bloodshot eyes examined her, up and down, and she stood still for the scrutiny. Again.

"Who are you?" he demanded.

"My name is Delia Fincher, Mr. Kostyena. I've brought you something to eat." She proffered the tray and the peanut butter sandwiches that lay on it, neatly sliced.

He frowned. "My name isn't Kostyena," he snapped. "Kostyena means 'daughter of Kostye.' I am Kostye. Kostyena is my daughter's name."

"Well," Delia said, "in that case you've lied to the school system, and judging by your mail, the power company and at least one bank."

He appeared confused, and looked as if he was trying to hide it.

"Again, who are you? Your name is meaningless to me."

"I'm the counselor at Sowashee High, where your daughter attends school."

"My daughter is nine. She isn't in high school."

"Read your wall," she said.

She waited while he took it all in and then sat heavily in an armchair. He reached for a bottle of gin.

"You really should eat something," she told him. "I've only been here a short while, but in that time your diet has been entirely liquid."

His unsteady gaze came back to her. He looked at the gin and back at the sandwiches. He took a drink of the gin.

"Yes," he said. "Why are you here? Have you come to take my daughter from me?"

"I wish that I could," Delia told him. "You're in no condition to look after her. Surely you must know that."

"I know only that no one will take her from me." He tilted his head.

"You should think of what's best for her."

He pointed at her throat. "That necklace," he murmured. "Where did you get it?"

She took a step back. "Aster put it on me. Apparently while I'm wearing it, I have to do everything she tells me to do."

"And what did she tell you to do?"

"I was to assure the school that all was well here. She also told me to take a leave of absence from my job, which I have done. And I'm also to look after you. I don't want to do any of these things, mind you—"

"Yes, I understand the effect of the necklace," he said. Then his eyes widened.

"Where is she?" he roared.

"I've no idea. She left yesterday and hasn't returned."

"Was she alone?"

"No. There was a sort of walking puppet with her, and a young lady I do not know." It sounded ridiculous as she said it, but she had never been shy to face reality. This man and his daughter could perform what she could only characterize as magic. She could only theorize where their abilities came from—mental powers, mutant abilities, Satan—but given her situation it would be insane to deny the obvious facts. She was quite certain that she herself was not insane.

"A walking puppet?" For a moment he looked dazed, and then he began shouting in a language she didn't know. He picked up the gin bottle and hurled it against the wall, where it shattered, intensifying the already strong smell of alcohol in the room. Delia stepped back and reached to shut the door. In a bit he would forget whatever was upsetting him, and next time he asked where Aster was, she would tell him she was at school.

A long wail tore from his throat, followed by a sob, and tears began streaming down his face. Her hand was on the doorknob, but she didn't move.

"She will not survive," he told her. "Do you understand?"

"No, I don't," Delia said. "I understand very little about any of this."

"We came from a place," he said. "Another place, where she is under threat of terrible danger. I think she's gone back there."

"You mean Russia?"

"No," he sighed. "Not Russia. We aren't Russian. We only told you that—" he stopped, staring at her.

"I *do* know you," he said. "Your hair was different. You didn't wear glasses. You wore a grey suit. And a wedding ring."

She rubbed the place where her band used to be.

"Yes," she said. "You noticed. You said my husband was a lucky man."

"Yes," he agreed. "Where is it now, the ring?"

"My husband didn't share your opinion," she said. She tried to smile. "But of course, he knew me better. I knew at the time you were trying to flatter me. You were trying too hard in general, and I figured something was wrong. You seemed desperate. The rumor was you were hiding out from the mob."

He laughed bitterly. "If only it was so simple," he said. He looked around him.

"I'm trapped here," he said. "I cannot leave these rooms."

"I know."

"Then you must go after her," he said. "You must bring her back to me."

"Aster instructed me not to take any orders from you," she told him. "And so I shan't."

"Then someone must."

"I can't tell anyone about this," she replied. "Aster saw to that."

He sighed and seemed to crumple back into the chair.

"Tell me about her," he said. "About my Aster."

"Well. She's bright, very bright, but she's always seems distracted. I've tried to talk to her about colleges, but she's never seemed interested, although with her grades she could have her pick. She keeps to herself. Lately, her teachers—" she stopped.

"What is it?" he asked.

"Heavens," she said. "I just remembered."

"What?"

"Poor David. One of Aster's teachers. He came here with me. They're going to wonder where he is—"

"What happened to him?" He asked.

"You sort of—put him in a bottle."

"Ah," he replied. "Well then."

"But you have to let him out."

"Does anyone know he came here with you?"

"Well, no, but when he doesn't show up the police will be involved. They might find it suspicious that he and Aster vanished at the same time—and at the same time I took a sudden leave of absence."

He nodded thoughtfully.

"Do you know where the bottle is?" he asked.

"Yes."

"Bring it, then. And be quick, before I forget."

Delia nodded and trotted back to the kitchen where the whisky bottle still stood on the table. When she returned, she found Kostye staring at the pictures of Aster.

"Here," she said.

At first she thought he had forgotten her again, but then he nodded and took the bottle. She half expected him to rub it, but instead he said a few low words. There was a quick rush of smoke, and David appeared.

"What?" David demanded, his eyes full of panic. "What's happening?"

Kostye pressed two fingers against the teacher's forehead, and she heard a sort of hissing sound. David squealed. Blood dribbled down his brow.

"I lay this curse on you," Kostye intoned. "You will have no pleasure from food or drink or any other thing until you find my daughter Aster Kostyena and return her to me, safe and whole. My blood gives you passport and direction."

David staggered back, and Delia saw the blood was indeed coming from Kostye's fingers. The red blotch on David's forehead seemed to glow like fire, but then it faded.

"Oh my God," David gasped.

"Hush," Kostye said. "Now listen as I tell you where to go, for she will have taken the path out that we took in."

"Wait," Delia said. "You can't—"

But he waved his hand, and the door slammed in her face.

One good thing about being a wooden man, Errol reflected, was that he didn't get tired. He had all the backpacks on and Aster in his arms and had been trotting for half an hour and he wasn't feeling a thing. Veronica also seemed tireless.

He didn't have any idea where he was going; the woods seemed endless. In a way, he didn't mind. This was the forest that trees must dream of. He'd grown up with two sorts of woods; pine plantations—which were dull because nothing else lived in them, and the trees were all the same size and distance apart—and the hilly forests which had been heavily logged. That left only a few really big trees, so they were thick with scrub and briars and saplings scrapping to be larger.

This place might have never known a chainsaw or an ax. Oaks reached up mighty, twisting arms, and hickories bigger than he had ever seen stood like gray columns to support the sky. Grapevines bigger than his thigh coiled up their trunks and wove between branches to cast a dense net of shade. The spaces between the trees were broad, and the floor was green moss and feathery ferns.

He noticed a distant stand of cypress, thought it probably meant water and plunged that way as the dogs grew louder. He was right; beavers had dammed a meandering stream. He sloshed through it, ran about thirty feet, and then came back and waded into the stream. A snake—a little copperhead—wriggled away from his footfall, and darters on the bottom of the creek broke in all directions.

"Trying to lose the dogs," Veronica murmured. He wasn't sure if it was a question.

"It's worth a try," he said.

"Maybe we should split up," she offered.

He remembered the conversation from before. "You really want to do that? What if they follow you instead of me? I probably don't have much of a scent. Being wood, and all."

They sloshed on for another twenty yards before she answered.

"No," she said. "I suppose not. Guess we're stuck together."

Despite his efforts, the hounds grew steadily louder. He quit the stream and struck off overland. He wished Aster would wake up. As scenic as the woods were, it would be nice to know which way they ought to be going. Plus, he was starting to get worried. What if she was hurt worse than she looked? What if she wasn't going to wake up?

"Do you have any idea where we are?" he asked Veronica.

"We're still in-between," she said. "Aster was trying to push us through to someplace else, but she hit the tree first."

"Well, maybe—I was able to see you in-between when she couldn't. Maybe you can see the way to the Kingdoms."

"I get glimpses of something," she said. "Like something through the trees. But it never holds steady."

"Well, that's more than I'm getting," he said. "You lead. Hold my arm and guide me."

"Okay."

She didn't make any jokes or flirty comments. She was scared, he thought—a lot more scared than he was.

So they ran across the open floor of the forest. The horn blew again, and the dogs howled in unison with it.

"This way," Veronica said. "I think I see a path."

Errol didn't see anything, but he followed her tug. Glancing back, he noticed something white flash in the trees.

At first he thought it was the woman from his nightmare, and terror shocked through him. But then it appeared again, and he saw it came on all fours.

A dog, white as a snake's belly, and behind it another black as coal, and something else, something bigger.

Veronica wasn't running straight, anymore, but was winding as if through some maze he couldn't see. That was slowing them down, too much.

The lead dog was only forty feet or so behind him; he was about to put Aster down so he could fight when suddenly something broke from the trees in front of them.

It was another rider, this one on a dark red horse and wearing armor, like a medieval knight. He had fallen for the oldest hunting trick of all—he'd let himself be driven right into an ambush.

But the rider cut around them.

"Keep going," the knight yelled. "I'll get them off your trail."

Errol watched the horse gallop by, open-mouthed.

Veronica tugged on his arm again.

"Come on!" she shouted. "See?"

To his surprise, he did see it, a trail on the forest floor. They started running again, and the forest began closing in around them, growing denser with saplings and blackberry briars, so that soon only the trail was near, and then even that became so overgrown that they had to fight their way through the weeds.

Finally, they burst into an open pasture, beneath a wide blue sky. He smelled the familiar scent of cow dung. They were next to a persimmon tree, and yellow jackets were buzzing around the rotting fruit. He might have been anyplace around Granny's house, and a sudden feeling of belonging swept through him, of home.

"I'm tired of running," he said, and turned around again, facing the forest. He settled Aster gently on the ground and then stepped a few yards in front of her.

"I don't think we have to run anymore," Veronica said.

"Either way," he replied.

The moment stretched until Errol started feeling a little silly.

"I don't think you're going to get your fight," Veronica said.

TWO

DOCTOR SHECKY

Y ou're not fixed on *her* now, are you Errol?" Veronica asked.
It had been a while since they had emerged from the
forest, but Errol was still waiting. She had resisted the urge to
light out on her own several times. By some miracle they had
escaped — but for how long?

"What?" Errol said.

"Miss knight-on-a-horse," she said. "You aren't that fickle,
are you?"

"That wasn't a woman," he said, looking genuinely confused. "Was it?"

Veronica laughed. "Boy, you need glasses," she said.
"Totally female. And part of you knows it, even if your brain is
slow catching up. But you've already got one hurt girl to tend
to, unless you want to switch 'em out."

He finally relaxed his guard and faced her.

"Right," he said. "We'd better get Aster some help."

But he still seemed reluctant.

Veronica was starting to realize that Errol had a problem. He
was *loyal*. He was loyal to Aster, for no reason she could fathom.
And now he suddenly was willing to risk both of their — well,

not lives, but existences—for a stranger just because she had done them a good turn. He acted like he didn't care about anyone, but he cared like it was a disease.

An odd, unwelcome thought followed that. Had she ever been like that? It almost seemed like she remembered feeling that way, and why it made sense. But she couldn't really get the feeling to hold still to examine—nor did she really want it to.

"This way," she said, walking off toward the low hills in the distance. She liked hills.

She didn't look back, but after a moment she heard the crunch of his wooden feet on the grass.

"Do you have any idea where we are?" Errol asked, when he pulled even with her.

"I guess we're in the Kingdoms," she replied. "I think I glimpsed them before, back when I was in my in-between, but the Creek Man wouldn't ever let me come here."

"It feels different here," Errol said.

Veronica knew what he meant. "Yes," she said. "It feels like we belong here. Us freaks."

"Kind of," he agreed.

"Aster hasn't told you anything else?"

"There hasn't really been time," he replied. "Things have been happening kind of fast."

"Maybe she doesn't want you to know anything," Veronica said. "Gives her more control over you. Only now—what if she dies? What then?"

"She's not going to die," he said.

He didn't snap or say it mean, but something about the *way* he said it really dug into her.

"So your mom hasn't been coming to see you at the hospital," she said.

She wished he had a real face, so she could see the hurt on it.

"I guess not," he replied.

"Hanging out with some guy instead. What about your dad? Is he not fond of you either?"

"He's dead," Errol said. And she could hear it, then, the hollow ache in him. "Died of cancer."

"Oh, dear Errol," she said, "I'm so sorry." She remembered words like that, and knew when to say them, but wasn't sure what they meant.

"Don't bother," Errol said. "Why don't you just shut up and quit asking me questions."

"Just pulling wings off a dragonfly, honey," she said.

"What's that supposed to mean?" he muttered.

It was funny that he didn't get it.

"Just passing time," she said. "I figured a little conversation might be pleasant."

"That's what you get for figuring," he said.

Half an hour later, Errol noticed a huge buzzard circling overhead. At first he reckoned it had found a dead animal of some kind, but after a while he realized that it was actually following them. When Veronica figured it out, she giggled.

"He obviously hasn't had a good look at Aster," she said. "There isn't enough meat on her to feed a little bird, much less one his size."

"Buzzards like dead things," Errol replied, still feeling pissed off from their earlier conversation. "Maybe it's you he's after."

"Well, that would show better taste," she replied.

But about ten minutes later, the buzzard flew off and didn't come back.

He wondered where the cows were. He saw plenty of signs of them, but he started to realize that most of that could be days old, if it hadn't rained. They must have been moved to another pasture.

He thought it odd that they hadn't seen any trace of a building so far; cows meant people, and people meant houses, barns, fences.

And they were running out of pasture. He was beginning to think they should go back the other way, skirting the edge of the clearing, when he saw smoke drifting up through the trees. He steered them that way.

They found the house just inside the edge of the forest. Errol wasn't sure what he had expected, but what he saw was a small cabin built of slightly overlapping planks with a tin roof. The unpainted wood had weathered to a gray color. Beyond a screen door, a hall divided the house in two—he could see daylight through another door on the other end.

On the porch, an old man sat, whittling. He looked up as they arrived. He was clean shaven and almost bald. Dark eyes peered at Errol over a dramatically hooked nose.

"Well, you're an unlikely bunch," he said. He ran his gaze up and down Errol. "I guess you're never too old to see something new."

"You don't seem all *that* surprised," Veronica noticed.

"Well," he said. "I *have* seen plenty." He gestured at Aster.

"Something wrong with your friend?"

"She hit her head," Errol said. "She won't wake up. We're looking for a doctor."

"Well," he said, mildly, "I'm something of a doctor. Best in these parts, anyway. Maybe I can take a look at her."

He stood and dusted the wood shavings from his denim overalls and stuck out his hand.

"Dr. William Shecky, at your disposal."

Errol shook the offered hand.

Dr. Shecky opened the screen door and gestured inside.

Errol hesitated, obviously enough that the man nodded.

"Wait there," he said, and went into the house, leaving the screen door to squeak closed behind him.

"Convenient," Veronica whispered.

"Yeah," Errol said. "That's what I was thinking."

A moment later the man returned, carrying a black leather satchel. He opened it up and showed Errol the interior, which was occupied by a stethoscope and various other medical-looking tools.

"Well . . ." he said.

"I don't blame you, son," the man said. "But sometimes luck does find you."

It sure seemed that way, Errol reflected. First the woman on the horse, now a doctor when they needed one. But what did he know about the Kingdoms? Magic was obviously involved. Maybe this was just how things happened here.

"Okay," he said.

"Bring her on in," Dr. Shecky said.

He led them down the hall to the second door on the right. He opened it up, revealing a smallish room with an old-fashioned looking iron stove, a big table, and a cupboard.

"Lay her on the table," he said.

Errol did as the man asked. Aster looked ashen and drawn, and he hoped they weren't too late.

Dr. Shecky picked up a kettle. "There's a well out back," he said. "I'd be obliged if one of you took this and filled it up."

"Veronica," Errol said, unwilling to leave Aster with a stranger. "Would you mind?"

"Tricky question," Veronica said.

"Please."

She took the kettle and sauntered out the door.

"Nothing I can do for *her*," Dr. Shecky said, nodding after Veronica. "That one is beyond my skills." He peered more closely at Errol. "Same for you, I'm afraid."

He listened at Aster's chest with his stethoscope and then checked her pulse at her wrists and temples. He inspected the blow to her head.

"Fetch me that box over the stove, will you?" he said. "The yellow one." He began laying out instruments on the table — a scalpel, something that looked like tongs, some vials of powder.

Errol did as he was told. The box was full of small white crystals. It looked like salt. Smelling salts, maybe?

"What's wrong with her?" Errol asked.

"Head's busted," the doctor said. "Pressure building up in there, you know. Fetch me that jug, will you?"

He pointed, and Errol saw a big ceramic jug, the kind moonshine came in, at least according to the movies.

Sure enough, when Dr. Shecky opened it, he caught the unmistakable whiff of hard liquor.

"Anesthetic," the Doctor said, taking a drink of it. "I would offer you some, but there hardly seems a point."

"You're not going to cut her, are you?"

"Not much," Dr. Shecky replied.

About that time he heard a bloodcurdling scream from outside, and knew instantly it was Veronica. Before a single conscious thought entered his head he had already bolted out into the hall and toward the sound.

"Don't do anything until I get back!" he hollered.

Veronica was still screaming. She knelt at a well with low stone walls and was braced against it with her hands.

"It's got me!" she screeched, when she saw Errol.

That's when he noticed the pallid hand clasped around her wrist. He couldn't see what was on the other end of the hand, because it was in the well.

"Oh, crap," he said. He started forward another step, but then he had a horrible, sick feeling. Whatever was pulling at Veronica, she seemed to be fighting it successfully — at least for the moment.

"I'll be right back," he yelped, and ran back into the house.

When he got to the to the kitchen door it was closed, and when he tried to open it, he found it barred from the other side. Through the heavy oak he could hear Dr. Shecky humming happily, and a sound like knives being whetted on a stone.

And then he heard Aster scream.

V eronica saw Errol turn and run back into the house and knew she was on her own. She braced her knee against the stone and pulled, fighting the blackness that waited eagerly at the corner of her eyes and behind her head.

The bone-white hand clamped on her wrist held on like a steel band, but it wasn't pulling that hard. It couldn't draw her into the well. That wasn't the real problem — the real problem was the voice.

Come along, it whispered. *You belong down here, with your kind.*

Each word was a glob of oil dripped into her ears; each black drop invaded the brightness Aster had put in her, coated a memory. She was turning back into what she was when Aster and Errol found her.

And why shouldn't she? Aster's promises were worthless, and Errol had turned his back on her. His sickening loyalty evidently did not extend to Veronica Hale. If she went into the well, he would eventually come to see what had become of her, and then she would have him as she should have back in her old home. To rest in the water, to caress her bones once more . . .

But that would mean losing the light again. And forgetting. Again she recalled her tennis shoes, new and white, standing on the rocks above the falls. She tried to hold it as if her mind had a fist, but it was slipping from her.

"Not again!" she cried, and clawed at the grasping hand, panting, feeling her mind dim.

And then suddenly she fell back, landing on her bottom and flopping onto her back. The hand still had hold of her wrist, but it wasn't attached to an arm, anymore. She slapped at it, and it suddenly released her and scuttled back toward the well, leaving a trail of blackish blood across her shirt and pants leg.

A face appeared above her, framed in a silvery helmet. The rider from the woods.

"Are you injured?" the woman asked.

"No," Veronica said.

"Rest," the woman said. "Stay back from the well. I think your friends are in trouble."

A ster woke screaming, with a livid pain in her chest. She was lying down, and her arms were pulled over her head and tied to something. Her legs were likewise bound. A strange man stooped over her with a knife.

"Hush now, child," he said. "Just let Dr. Shecky operate."

She realized with horror that he had cut her shirt open and a bright pool of blood was collecting in the hollow just below her breastbone.

"Stop!" she said. "Don't!"

He just smiled and bent to her, bringing the scalpel down. She heard Errol yelling someplace, and a heavy pounding. She wanted to look around, but her eyes wouldn't leave the scalpel. It couldn't be happening.

And then she felt something else, alongside the fear. She felt the shimmer, the *elumiris*.

I'm here! She realized.

She suddenly felt very still and far away, and she remembered one of the first of the Recondite Utterances she had learned from her father, the Word of the Whirlwind.

She spoke it.

She sucked in a deep breath; her ears popped. The man with the scalpel blinked.

"Oh!" he said.

Then she exhaled.

The wind lifted him bodily from the floor and slammed him into the wall, but not just him; everything in the room not nailed down was whirling furiously about; she winced, expecting to be struck at any moment, but then she realized she was in the eye, and thus safe.

And when the wind died, nothing looked as it had before.

The house shuddered for a long moment, and Errol heard a roar like a tornado; then everything sort of blinked a few times, and when it stopped blinking, he saw that the door wasn't there anymore; what he had been hurling himself into was a tree four feet in diameter. The house wasn't there, either; instead he stood in a thicket of vines and briars. Through them, he saw Aster tied to a fallen tree-trunk, and something coming down on her. Not a man, but creature with gleaming talons and a long, wicked beak. He had an impression of black feathers and smelt a terrible sweet stench of rot.

"Aster!" He threw himself against the vines and began tearing at them. He had ripped a hole big enough for his head and upper body when he saw something come through from the other side.

Someone, rather. It was the knight from the forest, slicing through the brambles with her sword. And yes, he saw now she was female, and pretty—and she had a star tattooed on her forehead.

The thing over Aster was black confusion, at first nothing his eye would take hold of, but then suddenly a huge buzzard flapped heavy wings and leapt to the open sky above. The woman thrust after it with her weapon. The bird screamed as she sliced into his leg, but it flew on.

The woman looked up. "You would have been better off waiting for me," she said.

"I didn't know—" he was distracted by Aster, who was struggling furiously with the vines binding her hands and feet.

"What the hell is going on?" she demanded, darting her gaze from one to the other.

"Let me help with that," the woman said. She drew a dagger. Aster strained away.

"For the vines, not for you," she said.

"Who are you?" Aster asked.

"My name is Dusk," the woman replied.

Then Aster vomited, and not just a little.

THREE
OBSESSION

David hadn't believed, at first. Aster's father was clearly as mad as a hatter, and he'd somehow gotten to Delia as well. She kept babbling about magical spells and other nonsense. Possibly drugs were involved; certainly something had caused him to pass out, because he had a big gap in his memory.

So when he left, the first thing he tried to do was go to the police, even though the thought of doing so made him a little sad. Still, he had to consider Aster's welfare. Who knew what went on in that house?

He only made it half a mile down the road before that diminutive sadness became depression so crushing he almost ran his car into a tree just to make it stop. Moaning, he turned around and headed toward Sugarloaf Road, and almost immediately felt better. He had the overwhelming sense that he was doing the right thing.

Before long it was difficult to believe he had actually felt as bad as he had, and so once again he turned around, only to return to the deepest despair he had ever known. He didn't try to escape again, but drove until he reached Sugarloaf Road and saw the narrow logging ruts.

He had always been skeptical of hypnosis, at least the sort done with a shiny watch and soft words. But Kostyena had been in the Russian mob, and maybe the KGB before that, so who knew what he had training in and access to? Secret brainwashing drugs, possibly. It was like something out of a ridiculous pulp spy novel, but it was the only explanation that actually made sense.

When the road got steep he got out of the car and stared down into the pine forest. Now that he understood what was wrong with him, his mind had found something else to worry about.

What was he going to find down in those woods? Aster's corpse? A gang of Russian thugs holding her hostage? If the latter, what was he supposed to do? He didn't have a gun or even a knife. Aster's father had just said to find her and return her. He hadn't said a thing about what had happened to her.

Waiting was only making matters worse, so he started down the road. He thought about Aster and her drawings and her strange accent, the way her lips moved when she was concentrating, as if everything she did was some sort of incantation. He had been a lot like her in school; lost in books, not very popular, a person a lot of people didn't notice at all.

But he noticed Aster. He had watched the thing inside her, the glow she kept hidden, first surrounded by the body of a girl, and now by that of a young woman. He had seen that glow before, in others—only to watch it fade, flicker and go out when they became adults.

He felt he had so much to teach Aster, so much to show her. Sometimes he thought that later, after she graduated, when it was more appropriate . . . after all, he was only a few years older than she . . .

He tried to shake that out of his head, but he found that the only thoughts that made him feel even remotely happy were thoughts of Aster. So although he knew he should resist them, instead he let them come and play themselves out in scenes. If he didn't like the way the scenes ended, he would go back and rewrite them. None of it, after all, was real.

And so the pines gave way to spreading oaks and a deeper forest than he had ever seen, and the logging road became a trail.

And off in the distance he heard hounds.

"Probably fox-hunting," he muttered under his breath.

The kind of fox hunting people did around Sowashee wasn't the equestrian sport in which the hunters wore stylish red outfits. It usually consisted of a bunch of rednecks in pick-up trucks releasing first a farm-raised fox and then their hounds. They would then stand around, drinking beer, listening to the sound of their dogs baying as they chased the poor animal.

David didn't see how that qualified as sport.

He continued on, his thoughts alternating between Aster and the increasingly strident yowling of the dogs, until he realized that they were pretty close to him. He swung around, wondering if he should climb a tree. Then he saw them, huge beasts, one sable and the other albino.

And they weren't chasing a fox; they were coming right for him.

With a yelp he turned to flee, and in a dazed panic saw a low hanging branch. He grabbed and pulled himself up the tree, just as the dogs reached him. He yanked his foot up barely in time; the volume and pitch of their howling was terrifying, and he realized he was screaming in abject terror.

It wasn't long before the huntsman came along.

This wasn't an English fellow in Jodhpurs, either. He was hard-looking man with cerulean eyes. He had on worn jeans, a khaki shirt, snakeskin boots and a cowboy hat to complete the image.

Actually the twin six guns and the Winchester rifle completed the image; the saber muddled it a little. He sat his massive piebald horse, staring at David in a clinical sort of way.

"Are these your dogs, sir?" David asked.

"Yes," he said. "They've run you up that tree because they know you don't belong here."

"I don't mean to trespass," he said. "I never saw a sign."

"You didn't get here on your own," the man said. "You had help."

"I don't know what you mean," David objected. "I just came here to . . ." He broke off. Maybe this was one of the men who had Aster. Surely he was.

"Go on," the man said.

David didn't say anything.

The man sighed. "I've had a long day," he said. "I've chased abominations and trespassers I should've caught. I've been interfered with by them that has no business interfering. Now you tell me what you know."

"I don't know anything," David said. "I was just hiking."

The man sighed and drew his pistol. Without pause he lifted it and fired.

David screamed at the sound, unable to believe what was happening to him. He felt a sharp sting on his cheek.

"Oh, God!" he said.

"You're not killed," the man said. "Yet."

David realized the bullet had struck the tree a few inches from his face, and that it was flying bark that had stung him. He felt blood dribbling down his chin.

"He sent me," he said, his ears ringing from the gunshot so his words sounded muffled. "He sent me to get Aster. Hypnotized me. Maybe drugged me. Please don't shoot me. I just—she's just a girl. I don't know what you want with her —"

"This Aster," he interrupted. "She have companions with her? A fellow made of wood, a blond girl?"

"A fellow made of wood?" David said.

Was everyone crazy?

But then he remembered, back at Aster's house. There had been a sort of puppet or automaton made of wood and wire standing in the doorway. He'd pushed past it and been startled when it moved but then other things had taken his attention. And he remembered the girl, too, golden-tressed and pretty but with something weird about her eyes.

"Yes," he said.

"And then who sent you after them?"

"I shouldn't tell you."

The man raised his gun.

"I can't tell you!" David shouted. "He hypnotized me. I know it sounds crazy, but that's what happened."

But the man cocked his hand and spit before sheathing his gun.

"So you've been made to find her?" the man said. "Not of your will?"

"If I try to do anything else—"

But even the thought was so devastating that his whole body went weak, his hold loosened on the tree and he smacked into the leaf-littered floor of the forest.

He closed his eyes, already feeling the dogs ripping him apart with their teeth, but when nothing happened he opened his eyes.

"Get up," the man said.

David did so.

"I'm trying to find the girl too," the man said. "But my dogs have lost her scent. So here's what we'll do. I'll deputize you and you'll come along with me. And we'll find her."

"I don't know—" David began.

"Or I can shoot you and let the animals gnaw your bones."

"Yeah," David said. "Right. The first option."

"Fine. You're a deputy of the Marches. Now you just keep on where you're going, and I'll follow."

"Who are you, sir?" David asked.

"Why, I'm the sheriff," he replied.

FOUR

CHILD'S PLAY

E rrol carried Aster out of the thicket, where they were joined by Veronica, who gave Aster a curious glance. She had drawn the remains of her shirt tight, and the front of it was now soaked with blood.

"Is she dying?" Veronica asked.

"It doesn't look that bad," Dusk replied. "A spring just down here, I think. Come along."

"How long was I unconscious?" Aster asked Errol.

"A few hours," he said. He gave her a brief sketch of what had been happening, including their meeting with Dusk.

By that time, they had reached the spring. Dusk unfastened her helmet and set it on the ground. Long locks of auburn hair tumbled out, and Aster suddenly realized that Dusk—despite her bearing—was probably not much older than she. But she was a great deal prettier. Just above her brows a small, six pointed star gleamed faintly golden in the sunlight.

"The wooden fellow," Dusk asked. "Is he an enchanted person or a living thing?"

"He is a person," Aster replied.

"Is he your husband?"

"My . . .?" she started. "No."

Veronica laughed.

"Then he should stand at a discreet distance," Dusk said.

"I can hear you, you know," Errol muttered. "I'll turn around."

When he had done so, Dusk pulled her shirt open. Her concerns over modesty were a little excessive, given that Dr. Shecky hadn't cut through her bra; since he had apparently intended to gut her first, there hadn't been any need too. Still, she felt exposed, and weak, and not a little terrified and was grateful to have someone thinking of her feelings.

Dusk cleaned the cut with a wet rag, but dark blood welled back up.

"You're from here?" Aster asked, to take her mind off of the blood. She already knew the answer; the star on Dusk's forehead said it all. But she was hoping to learn more.

"From this place?"

"From the Kingdoms."

"Yes," she replied. "Although I was born very far from this demesne." She whistled a short little tune, continuing to dab at the wound. Aster heard magic in the melody and began to feel alarmed.

"Don't worry," Dusk soothed.

She felt something tickle her ribs, and saw a large black ant was crawling up her side. She gasped and reached to slap it, but Dusk gently stopped her hand.

"No," she said. "Bide."

She caught the ant and brought it to Aster's wound. With her other hand, she squeezed the cut closed. That hurt, a lot.

Then she pushed the insect right up to the incision. It bit her with its fierce-looking pincers. Dusk gave a deft little twist, separating the ant's body from its head. The head remained clamped on her cut, like a suture.

More ants were on her belly, now, and in a matter of moments, Dusk had the gash closed as tightly as if she had used stitches.

"There," Dusk said. "That will do for a while, until we find better help."

"Thank you," Aster replied.

"I have no garment to lend you, I'm afraid."

Aster had seen the backpacks hanging from Errol's shoulder.

"Errol should have one," she said.

"The wooden man?"

"Yes," she said.

"I'll look," Errol called, and started going through the pack. Dusk walked over and took the shirt he came out with.

Once Aster was dressed again, Dusk swung back up on her horse.

"We should go," she said. "The Sheriff will pick up your trail soon enough, and he has authority to follow you here."

"The Sheriff?" Aster said. "The man with the dogs? Why is he after us?"

"His task is to keep the borders between the Reign of the Departed and the Kingdoms," she said. "You must have violated his authority." Her gaze wandered significantly over Errol and Veronica.

Aster nodded. Now some of her father's warnings made more sense. More, she remembered something now, when she was little, when she and her father were running.

The howling of hounds.

"How do we stop him?" Errol asked.

Dusk shrugged. "He would be difficult to kill. But he has other duties—if the chase becomes too drawn out, he might recrudesce to his station."

"Why do you keep saying *we*?" Veronica asked.

"I intend to go along with you, if there is no objection," Dusk replied.

"But why?" Veronica said. "You don't know us."

"I know you are in jeopardy. I am in position to be of assistance. This is all I need to know."

But Veronica wasn't ready to back down, just yet.

"It's just awfully convenient," Veronica said. "The way we met you in the in-between, right when we needed you. That you saved us in the nick of time back in the thicket."

Dusk's brow puckered. "The first was fortuitous, I suppose, although I was following the sound of the horn and the dogs, interested to see what had aroused the sheriff. But as to the second, I merely followed your footsteps. Errol's are not easy to hide." Her frown deepened slightly. "I'm surprised you feel I must explain myself."

"You don't," Errol said. "Veronica is just being — Veronica."

Aster actually thought Veronica had a pretty good point, but thus far Dusk had been nothing but helpful.

"Maybe," Veronica said. "But it still doesn't explain why you decided to help us. Did you have to fight the horseman?"

"No," she replied. "It wasn't necessary — I merely led his hounds on a fruitless chase. Drake here can outrun almost anything." She patted her horse's neck.

"As to why I'm helping you — I suppose I'm intrigued. You seem an interesting lot. You came from the Reign of the Departed, and I've never known any such before."

"I don't think that's where we're from," Errol said.

"It's what they call our world, Errol," Aster told him.

"Departed?" he said. "As in dead?"

"It would take some time to explain," Aster said.

"So I'm right, in any event," Dusk said. "To come into the Kingdoms from that place requires no small magic. You must have a reason, and a compelling one, to attempt it. I have an instinct that in helping you, I might further my own cause."

"What cause is that?" Aster asked.

"I'm on a quest, of sorts, but I've reached an impasse. I don't know where to go from here. I think I was meant to meet you, go where you go, and in doing so find the inspiration I need." She shrugged.

Aster reflected that Dusk still hadn't really told them what her cause was, but she wasn't prepared to press any further, because she didn't want Dusk asking her similar questions about her own undertaking.

And that star on her forehead, what it might signify. She needed to know more about this girl, although there was danger in that.

"We are grateful for your help," Aster said.

"Thank you," Dusk replied. "I advise we not tarry here. The Sheriff is surely back on your path now."

"Right," Aster said. But when she tried to stand, she found she couldn't. Her legs felt like rubber bands.

"You may ride Drake," Dusk said, preparing to dismount.

"I'll carry her," Errol said. "We can go faster."

"Very well," Dusk said. "Then all we need is a direction to go in."

Aster hesitated for a moment. She didn't have the first clue where to begin her search for the giant. She had supposed that it would somehow just be at hand when she arrived. As loath as she was to tell anyone what she was up to, Dusk was the only person present who might have any idea where she should search.

"I need to find a giant," she said.

"A giant?" Dusk repeated. "A true giant?"

"Yes," Aster told her.

"That could be difficult," Dusk replied. "Most giants live in the most distant kingdoms, in the old high places. Finding such a place—*going* such a place—they are separate things, and both very difficult. It could take years."

Aster felt a sort of plummet in her belly.

"Years?" she said, weakly.

But Dusk was still thinking. "Perhaps a lost giant." she said. "They are few, but they exist. What do you need a giant for?"

"I only know I must find one," Aster said. "Just as I found these two." She gestured at Errol and Veronica.

"So you consulted an oracle? You have some reason to expect there is a giant to be found?"

Aster nodded.

"Well, then there must be one," Dusk replied. She turned her mount toward the mountains.

"There is a good place to start," she said. "Giants like mountains."

"I like mountains," Veronica piped in.

"Are ya'll kidding?" Errol exploded. "Are we just going to set off in some random direction?"

"It's not random," Dusk said. "Giants like mountains."

"Hang on," Errol said to Aster. "You knew where to look for Veronica, and you knew you needed me to find her."

"That's true," Aster replied.

"If you knew that, why don't you know where this supposed giant is?"

"I did a lot of research to figure out where Veronica was," Aster explained. "I went to the library and read old newspapers and records. I talked to old people who remembered her. And I still might have been wrong. I got lucky. But researching the Kingdoms from our world—that's more difficult."

"You don't have any clues at all?"

Aster sighed, and flicked her gaze over at Dusk, then back.

"Just that an orchard is involved, or some sort of walled garden," she said.

"Giants like orchards," Dusk said.

"Well," Veronica said, pointing northwest. "The mountains are that way."

They struck across the pasture and then into the woods. Dusk led, and she kept the pace brisk, but she took every opportunity to mislead the sheriff and his dogs, stopping at times to erase tracks and sprinkle something from a bottle she kept in her saddlebags, walking up and down streams. She even collected some of her horse's droppings and laid a false trail or two. Errol thought he heard the hounds once or twice, but they didn't seem to be getting closer.

He didn't like the way Aster looked. Her normally pale face was bone white, and she kept drifting off.

Dusk noticed, too.

"It may well be the creature was septic," she said, during a pause. "It would not be unusual."

"I don't have any magic for that," Aster murmured.

"Aren't there any towns?" Errol asked. "Anyplace with real doctors?"

"There was a village," Aster murmured. "I remember we went around it."

Dusk looked at her with an odd glint in her eye.

"You've been here before, then?"

"When I was little," Aster said.

Night had crept close upon them when Dusk's horse whickered nervously. Dusk swore something which—though Errol could not understand the words—sounded unladylike.

Something crouched in the shadows at the side of the road. Errol felt an involuntary shiver.

In shape, it was more catlike than anything else; it might have been the biggest cougar he had ever seen. But it was hairless, covered instead with slick scales and patterned like a rattlesnake. When it twitched its long, catlike tail from side to side he heard it rattle.

Aside from its tail, only its eyes moved at first, looking from one member of their little group to the other. Then it bunched up tighter, and aimed itself at Dusk and her horse.

Dusk hadn't been waiting idly. She had unlimbered the long, wicked-looking spear she carried on her mount. But Errol had big doubts she could stop the thing. Everything about it was wrong, and his senses told him that it was the most dangerous thing he had ever seen.

"Aster?" he whispered.

"Can't think," she said. "Put me down. Help Dusk."

He started to do that, when Veronica made a disgusted little noise and started over toward the thing like it was a housecat.

It growled — a horribly unnatural sound — and shifted back, the muscles under its sleek scales bunching strangely so that instead of a cat it appeared almost manlike, as if the bones under its skin could shift at will.

"Stop that, you," Veronica said, and before Errol could yelp a warning, she had touched it on the muzzle. For a moment the growl stretched, but then Veronica knelt and scratched it under the jaw, and soon it was nuzzling her like a big kitten. Except that the looks it was sending over Veronica's shoulder suggested that although *Veronica* might be all right, it still considered the rest of them to be either food or a scratching post.

"Go on, silly," Veronica said, after a moment. "Before someone gets hurt."

Incredibly, the monster reluctantly did just that, its tail rattle fading as it drew further from them.

"Wow," Errol said. "What the hell was that?"

Veronica shrugged. "I don't know what to call it. There was one that used to visit the Creek Man, and we would play. Sometimes we would — you know — eat together."

Errol did his best not to picture that.

"I hope it doesn't have any relatives around," Aster said.

Dusk was still having trouble controlling her horse.

"Something is wrong," she said.

"Is it coming back?" Errol asked.

"No," Veronica said. "I think it's probably them."

But by then he saw them too.

They were surrounded.

T he first thing Errol noticed was that they had guns. For some reason, he hadn't really expected that, but there they were. They were rifles and shotguns for the most part, and really old-fashioned looking. About half of the boys — none of them looked much over seventeen — had bow-and-arrows instead. They were motley in dress — some wore overalls, others vests and pants — with or without shirts — and some were stripped down to the waist. Their faces were as variable; some were as dark as anyone he had ever seen, and others as fair as Aster, with pretty much every shade between. Their eyes were black, green, brown and blue. Most had brown or black hair, but a couple of them were dirty blond.

"Miss," one of them said, talking to Dusk. He was a muscular fellow with short brown hair.

"Miss, I advise you to put off that gizzard-sticker. And you," he went on, nodded at Errol, "whatever you are, just walk on back."

Errol realized he'd balled his fists and set himself as if for a fight. He glanced over at Dusk, who, after a moment's hesitation, returned her spear to its place beside her saddle. Errol unclenched and tried to look harmless.

"What *do* you reckon he is, Jobe?" another of the boys asked.

"Deviltry," another of them shot in. "I say we pitch 'im up and set 'im afire."

There was a little murmur of agreement at that.

"Why don't you come over here and talk like that?" Errol said. "Without all your buddies in front of you."

"Easy, Errol," Aster said.

The boy who had suggested burning him was now blushing.

"Ain't no sense in going to fists with deviltry," he muttered.

"You ain't much for going to fists with nobody, Jake," Jobe chided him. "Hush up and let me deal with this."

He looked back at them, and then walked toward Dusk.

"What's this?" Jobe asked, pointing at the star on her forehead. "That looks pretty high-and-far-off."

"My homeland is distant from here," she said. "Very distant."

"Uh-huh," he said, sizing her up. Then he turned his attention to Errol.

"What are you, then?"

"He's enchanted," Aster broke in. "He's just a normal person, but a witch made him like that."

"I know he can talk," the boy said. "Let him tell me himself."

"Yeah," Errol said. "Like she said."

Jobe frowned and then shrugged. "Your tracks come out from the edge, off toward the Ghost Country. Are you ghosts?"

Errol realized that at least two of them were, sort of.

"We're just travelers, passing through," Dusk said. "We were in the Marches for a short time, that's all. We intend no harm to you or yours."

"No, of course you don't," Jobe said. "Nobody ever does. And yet harm seems to happen, just the same."

"We're just leaving," Errol said.

"No," Jobe said. "You ain't. At least not right away. We've got questions for you, and it's best we not ask them here, not with night coming. You can walk or we can carry you. And by carry, I don't mean gentle."

"She's hurt," Errol said, pointing at Aster. "Any one of you tries to drag her or whatever, and we'll see how many of you I can take."

"Well, I reckon you'll walk, then," Jobe said. "And lucky for you, we've got some as can doctor."

"As long as the doctor's name isn't Shecky," Errol muttered.

"Shecky?" Jobe said, and the others murmured. "So it *was* you who cut him."

"He was trying to eat Aster," Errol snapped.

A ripple of laughter passed through the boys.

"I reckon he might have been," Jobe said. "Now let's go on—we don't want to be out after sundown."

Only a few turns of the trail brought them to a rambling wooden building that looked as if it had been added onto a lot. It had a big covered porch that went most of the way around it. It had also seen better days; even in the fading light there was a sort of run-down look to it.

Chickens pecked at the bare dirt yard, and a couple of harmless-looking old hounds were stretched out near the porch.

They were led up the rickety steps and through the front door. Aster examined the details of the house, remembering Shecky's illusion, and said a True Whimsy under her breath, but nothing changed in appearance. Weakness came and went over her like waves, but each time the troughs seemed deeper. She closed her eyes for a moment, and when she opened them again, she realized that she had lost time. She was in a largish room, golden with candlelight. She was lying on a small bed.

Besides her companions and the boys who had coerced them into coming here, she saw about fourteen more people. Most were girls; the oldest looked about sixteen, and she was pregnant. The youngest was probably around seven.

Something is wrong, she thought. No adults.

What were they talking about? She tried to focus. Then it all seemed to be over, and a couple of the girls came over to her while everyone else left. One had thick, frizzy hair caught up in a bun and eyes that tended to cross a little. The other was the pregnant girl, whose eyes were a startling green color.

They gave her something hot and bitter to drink, then they undressed her and cleaned around the wound, which she felt pulsing like a living thing. She bit back a scream when they touched it.

"It's alright," the green-eyed girl murmured. "Just you rest."

After a while she did sleep, but it wasn't restful. She dreamt of a forest of giant spiders, a city made of glass, stone-lined canals, a tall ship in a storm. And she knew it was all real, all things she had really seen, and always he was with her. Her father, carrying her in his arms as Errol had, and she was hurt, worse than this. Her father speaking words that no man should know, parting darkness and flame or casting it forth as suited his purpose. And he told his purpose often, so often it had become a part of Aster's flesh and bones.

"I will keep you safe, Streya. I will find a place where they cannot touch us."

It all unrolled behind her closed lids in colors more vivid than reality, memories from before she could talk, spoken in the language of dreams.

When she woke, she was talking.

"Daddy, daddy . . ." She was whispering, again and again.

A rooster was crowing, someplace. She opened her eyes, half-expecting that she would be in her own house, that everything had been a dream—but she was in the same room as the night before. The candles were out, and daylight filtered in through a little window.

She touched her chest. Some sort of bandage was wrapped all the way around her torso, and they had replaced her shirt over it. The pulsing ache of the night before was gone, although it still hurt. But her head felt clear. She tried to sit up, and found she was able to without feeling dizzy.

"Well," she murmured. "At least I woke up. That's a good sign."

She heard some girls chattering somewhere and followed the sound. The house seemed empty.

Four girls, all on the younger side, sat in cane-bottom chairs on the porch. They were shelling butter beans, and they stopped their talk when Aster appeared.

"You sure you ought to be walking?" one of the girls asked. "Mattie said to keep you in bed all day."

"I'm feeling fine," Aster said. "Where are my friends?"

"Are you hungry?" another of the girls spoke up. This one was missing two teeth, but she looked about seven, so that made sense.

"No, thank you," she said. "I just want to see my friends."

"You'll see them when they get back," someone else said. She turned, and realized a boy was on the other end of the porch. He looked about thirteen and he was cradling a shotgun under one arm.

"Get back? Back from where?" she asked. "Where is everyone?"

"Most are in the fields or hunting," one of the girls said. "They left us back to look after you."

"Are my friends in the fields?" Aster asked, trying to keep her temper — and her fear — in check.

"Heck, no," the boy said. "I thought you knew. You was there last night when the deal was struck."

"I had a fever," Aster said. "I don't remember much of what was said."

"Well, we made us a bargain, us and your friends."

"What sort of bargain?"

"Jake, I don't think you're supposed to be talking about this," one of the girls said.

"Aw, hush, Nellie. You're just a girl. You don't know nothing."

"I know Jobe can wear you out when he gets home," she shot back.

That seemed to give Jake a little pause.

"I think Jake knows what he's doing," Aster said. "He's practically a man. After all, they left him with a gun, didn't they?"

"That's right," Jake said, and stuck his tongue out at Nellie.

"You were talking about a deal," Aster prodded.

"Yeah," Jake said. "We nurse you, take good care of you. Their end of the bargain is they kill the Snatchwitch."

"Snatchwitch," Aster repeated.

"On account of she snatches us," Jake said.

"Kushikanchak, they used to call her," Nellie said. "Back when."

"You ain't old enough to remember that, Nellie," Jake said.

"How come I know it, then?" She said.

"Probably made it up."

Nellie looked defiant. "You ask Jobe, or any of the olders," she said.

Jobe? An "older"? Aster remembered that she hadn't yet seen any adults.

"Don't you have any parents?" she asked. "Where are the grownups?"

"Sure we have parents," Jake said. "Of course we do. That's half the trouble, ain't it?"

"Jake," the other girl said. "Best you hush up, now, and remember what Jobe told you."

Jake's brow lowered almost comically. "Well, I ain't told her nothing, and you're a liar if you say I did," he said.

"How long have they been gone? My friends?" Aster asked.

"Left a little before daybreak," Jake said.

"Can you show me the way?"

"Oh, no Ma'am. You're to stay here."

"What if I don't?"

He hefted the gun. "Jobe said I couldn't kill you, but I can sure shoot your foot off."

FIVE

THE SNATCHWITCH

"That's her place down there," Jobe whispered.

"Down there" was a muddy red-clay clearing in front of a gaping hole in the side of a hill. The wind was blowing from that way, and it brought with it the sweet scent of putrefaction. In the crooks of tree branches around the clearing, human skulls gazed about with empty eyes. Near the cave mouth stood a log about a yard in diameter and six feet high. It was hollow, or partly so; he could see a hole going down through the top.

"Not exactly a gingerbread house," Veronica said.

"Reminds me more of where I found you," Errol said. "Dusk, you know anything about this?"

She shrugged. "I have some experience with witches and ogres and such, but I know little of this demesne."

"Have you tried shooting her?" he asked Jobe.

"She snatches us up and eats us," Jobe said. "What do you think? Bullets don't hurt her." He eased back. "Anyway, there she is. Good luck, and maybe we'll see you back at the house."

"You're not staying to help?"

"I think you're missing the point of our deal," Jobe said. And like that, he slipped off.

"We're missing something, all right," Errol muttered. "I just don't know what."

There was a stir down at the cave, and presently she emerged.

She was tall, very tall, and spindly as a spider except for her head, which seemed about twice the size it ought to be. She seemed to be grinning, a grin which literally stretched from ear-to-ear. Her tattered dress was made of skins—what sort didn't bear thinking on—and her long grey hair was caught up in a ponytail.

She went up to the log, bent her elbow, and stuck it into the hole. *Thump!* The sound echoed off into the forest.

She lifted her elbow out and brought it back down again. *Thump!*

"What do you suppose she's doing?" Veronica asked.

"Damned if I know," Errol replied.

"She's pounding something," Dusk said. "As with a mortar and pestle. Her elbow is the pestle."

"Pounding what?" Errol asked.

"Bones," whispered Veronica. "It smells like bones."

"That's sick," Errol said.

Veronica shrugged and smiled.

"The question is, how do we kill her?"

"The question is," Veronica said, "why should we kill her? She's done nothing to us."

"She eats children," Errol said. "Look at the skulls."

"She hasn't tried to eat us," Veronica said, "and probably won't if we leave her alone."

"Jobe and his bunch have Aster," Errol said. "If we don't do it—"

"Well, you know where I stand on *that* subject," Veronica said. "But if you insist she's worth killing for, why don't we kill Jobe and the rest?"

"That was well put," Dusk said. "I mislike being used as an assassin." She looked down at the clearing. "Still, she is a wicked creature, by the looks of things."

"Jobe and his boys have guns," Errol said. "And there are too many of them."

While they were talking, the Snatchwitch stopped her pounding long enough to pick up some bones from the carcasses in the yard and toss them in the log-mortar.

She was set to pound again, when a sudden yell came from inside the cave. It sounded like a girl, hollering for help. The witch turned and went back through the dark opening.

"Okay, that does it," Errol said.

"Agreed," Dusk said. "The question is one of strategy. Drake and I can come around from over there, where the slope is most shallow. If you can bring her into the open, Errol, I can try my spear on her. It has never failed me."

"Sounds like a plan," Errol said. "Veronica—"

But Veronica was gone.

The smell of death was strong in the clearing, and Errol had a sudden, vivid memory of his father, that last day. His dad had been a big, strong man. He would whirl Errol around by the arms like he didn't weigh anything. He could kick a football as high as the moon. But in the end, his muscle had all been eaten away, and he looked so thin and fragile Errol could hardly believe it was really him. He had watched him waste away, had seen him the day before, but there was something extra missing that last day. Only in his eyes could Errol still see his father.

The memory didn't make him sad. It made him angry, so angry that when he shouted and the monster came back out of her cave, he wasn't scared of her. He thought of Aster, as he had last seen her, stretched out on a strange bed, eyes closed, breathing so shallowly it was hardly noticeable.

"Well," the witch murmured, almost as if to herself, "not much to like about you, is there? No bone, no liver, no lights. You might be fun to take apart, though."

"You've got somebody in your cave," Errol said. "I can hear her."

She stepped forward. The way her limbs moved seemed all wrong.

"They sent you, didn't they?" she said. "The little rascals."

At that moment, Dusk and her mount broke into the clearing. He could see the fierce, determined grin on her face behind the shining spear point, and he felt a sudden savage lift.

What a woman! He thought.

And then the Snatchwitch snatched him.

He hadn't imagined how fast she was, or how strong. Claws gripped into his wooden body; she yanked him off of his feet and held him up as a shield. For a moment he thought Dusk would hold her course, but at the last instant she broke to the right. The witch hurled Errol and he crashed into Dusk and her horse with enough force to knock them over. He rolled and came back to his feet, seemingly intact, and just in time to see Dusk hurling her spear at the witch.

The Snatchwitch opened her mouth, and kept opening it. It was like her lower jaw was a zipper, unzipping her whole long body into one huge maw. The spear went in—and vanished.

Then she closed her mouth.

Dusk drew her sword and leapt forward. The lean, bright blade sliced right through the witch's neck, and her head toppled from her shoulders and rolled along the ground. Her body swayed, still upright. She didn't bleed.

"Wow," Errol said. "Beautiful." He didn't just mean the wicked attack, but also the fierce expression on Dusk's face. She regarded her weapon, saw it was clean, and sheathed it.

"Jump back up," said the Witch's head.

And that's what it did. It sort of did a little bounce and then flew back up onto her neck. Dusk yanked her sword out again, but the witch slapped the blade from her hand and then grabbed her.

Errol howled and leapt forward, punching the Snatchwitch's belly. His fist did more than connect; it actually went through her skin, which felt sort of like rubber. When he tried to yank it out again, it wouldn't come. He kicked at her with his leg, and that stuck, too.

Dusk was as caught as he was. Drake had regained his feet and was stalking toward the monster.

"No, Drake!" Dusk shouted. "You bide in the woods. Don't let her get you, too."

The horse paused, and then—with seeming reluctance— turned and galloped back up into the trees.

With a sigh, the witch started back toward her cave, effort- lessly dragging them along. Near the opening, however, she paused, took a grip on Errol, and yanked him out of her. She held him suspended for a moment, at face level, but too far away for him to hit her in the eye.

Then she set him down on his feet and continued on, Dusk still attached to her and writhing furiously.

He fought back the urge to hit the witch again, knowing he would just stick, and instead looked around for Dusk's sword. He saw it a few yards away and started to get it.

Or at least he intended to start. His feet wouldn't move, and he had a funny, tickling sensation all over his body.

Leaves and tendrils began sprouting from every inch of him, with the speed of a time-lapse movie. He felt his toes digging through earth, deeper, deeper, yearning toward the center of the planet.

Aster clenched and unclenched her hands, thinking about all of the things she might do to Jake. Several choice possibilities rose to the top of her mind, but the problem was that none of them would likely get him to tell her where Errol and the rest were, and if she made a mistake it might get her shot. So instead she tried to calm down and think things through. She sat down on the edge of the porch.

"I'd like some water, please," she said.

"Nellie, run get her a drink," Jake said.

"I don't see why—"

"Because I'm in charge," he said.

Nellie went and got the water. She didn't look happy about it.

The water came in an old, chipped clay cup. It was cool and delicious, with no chemical taste. She listened to the girls chatter, hoping to learn something useful, but it was all about boys and dresses. Jake didn't say anything; he took out a knife and started to whittle.

After a while, Aster felt the call of nature and told the girls so.

"The outhouse is out back," Nellie told her. "By the woods."

"I'm scared to go back there by myself," she said. She knew Jake would have followed her anyway, to keep her from running off, but maybe this way she could score some more points with him. He wasn't that smart, and without the girls around he might let something slip.

"I'll keep guard," Jake said. "Come along."

He led her around the house to where she could see the out-house, a little shack a hundred feet behind the main building.

"I bet you're pretty good with that gun," she said.

"I reckon I'm a better shot than most."

"Did your father teach you to shoot?"

"We don't do much shooting on Sunday," Jake said. "Mostly I learned from Jobe."

"You only see your father on Sunday?"

He looked wary. "I ain't supposed to talk about that."

"Who says?" Aster asked. "You just said you're in charge."

"Well, I am. And I don't expect I'm going to talk about that, you hear? Now there's the outhouse."

She remembered outhouses, now. She had used them when she was little. This one, at least, was more than a hole in the floor. It was a little shack with a door, and inside was a bench, about the height of a toilet, with a hole in it, corncobs for toilet paper and a bucket of sand for covering up after. She closed the door and latched it and stood in the darkness for a moment, still wondering what she ought to do. Why would the adults only be around on Sundays? Where were they the rest of the week?

She proceeded to use the facilities, such as they were. It didn't seem dark, as her eyes grew accustomed to the ample light leaking in through cracks between the boards. Up in one corner she noticed a small wasp nest, but the insects didn't appear disturbed by her presence.

From the verge of her vision, she glimpsed a movement, a change in the light. It took a few seconds before she realized Jake had his face pressed at a knothole in the wood.

She tried not to react, tried to pretend she didn't know he was there. She felt revolted, weak, and exposed. She wished she could shrink to the size of a bug.

None of this was going as she had planned. She had entered the Kingdoms unconscious, and had been either insensible or weak since. The companions she had conjured to help her had run off with someone she didn't know at all to fight some monster Jobe and his tough guys were afraid to take on. They might never return, and if they did they would probably consider her too weak to lead them. Now this indignity.

Enough. She was Aster Kostyena. She had power.

She turned her gaze straight at the knothole.

"What is wrong with you?" she snapped. "You little pervert."

Jake bumped into the board; obviously he hadn't known she knew he was watching her. She saw, through the cracks, him backing away. But then he came back.

"I want you to take it all off," he said, "so I can see you naked."

Well, that's a first, she thought, unexpectedly amused. Certainly no one had ever asked that of her before. The idea that he wanted her to do a strip tease, in an outhouse, and show off her twiggy legs and mosquito bite breasts was so ridiculous she actually barked out a rough laugh.

"Don't you laugh at me!" he growled. "I'm in charge. I've got the gun."

She heard something dangerous in the margin of his voice.

"Let me finish this in peace," she said.

"And then?"

She didn't say anything, but he backed off, and she finished up her business. Then she reached up for the wasp nest.

"*Me kelbede,*" she said, softly. "*Me Gelede.*"

The insects, disturbed, flew a few orbits around her hand before settling on her fingers. She winced at the first sting, but held still until they were all done. Then they returned to their work.

When she opened the door, he was two yards away, gun raised.

"Now do what I said."

"Why in there? Why not out here? Or in the house?"

His eyes widened; his command had obviously been an unplanned impulse, a reaction to her catching him in the act of peeping. A way to save face. He hadn't thought through all of the possibilities yet. Looking into the dark outhouse from the bright outside, he could probably barely see her.

"Alright," he said, gesturing with the gun.

As they walked back toward the house, she remembered reading that rape wasn't so much about sex or attraction as it was about violence and control. Jake probably hadn't started out planning to rape her, but he might well be coming around to it now. There were no adults around, no older kids, and the girls wouldn't be able to stop him even if it occurred to them.

"Jake?" she said, as they reached the door. He had dropped the barrel of the gun toward the ground so he could undo the latch.

"Yeah?"

"You've got something on your face." As she said it, she brought her hand up, not too fast, and brushed at his eyes. He was so surprised and her gesture so non-threatening, that his only reaction was to blink, so her fingers lightly touched his lids.

"*Eza gela*," she whispered.

Jake screamed as her fingers stung him. He dropped the gun and slapped his hands to his face. Then he fell to his knees. Aster suddenly realized he was after the gun. He almost got it before she seized it and backed away.

"Now," she said. "*I'm* in charge. And you are going to tell me where my friends went."

"What did you do to me?" he howled.

Aster heard someone gasp and turned to see Nellie and the other girls staring around the corner of the house before they darted off.

"Hurry," she snapped "Tell me, or I swear I'll shoot your foot off."

"Don't do it," he pleaded. "They went to the cave down by Ashy Creek. North, on the trail."

"You're coming with me," she said. "You'll lead the way."

"I can't *see*," he bawled.

"You can give directions," she said.

"Leave him be," a quiet voice from behind her said. She turned, bringing the gun around, but he caught it with his hand.

He had dark skin and golden-brown eyes. His hair was curly and as black as obsidian.

He had a pistol in his other hand.

"Ease up," he said. "I'll take you to your friends."

SIX

SATURDAY NIGHT

Errol reached for the latch on his head and found it, just before his arms stiffened and refused to obey him. Again he experienced the dizzying shift of perspective as his consciousness fled the large body for the small one.

He pushed at the face and it moved, but only a fraction. He put all of his strength into it, but that wasn't very much. It opened just enough for him to get one arm out. Moments later, greenery covered the face, and he couldn't see anything.

He slumped back against the inside of the wooden skull, glumly examining his polished white limbs. He figured that since they were bone or maybe ivory the spell that was turning his wooden body into a tree hadn't affected this one. That was good, but it could also be very bad if he never figured a way out. It wouldn't take long to go crazy in such a small cell.

Hours passed, and although he tried everything he could think of to pry the face the rest of the way open, he was forced to admit that it wasn't possible. To make matters worse, what little light coming through the foliage surrounding him started to fade. He remembered Dusk, fierce and beautiful, and tried not to imagine her dead, meat for the Snatchwitch.

He worried about what would happen to Aster, when he never returned.

"The story of my life," he muttered to himself. No matter what he did, not matter what he tried, he didn't make a difference. Not to his father, not to his friends. He might as well never have lived at all.

He wondered what he would do now, if he had a bottle of whisky and some pain pills.

He started when something creaked and his dark little room shuddered. Had the witch come back for him?

Everything shook again, and suddenly wind stroked his face, and the face swung open. An enormous, moonlit visage suddenly filled his view. He balled his fists, thinking if he could put out one of her eyes, he might have a chance.

"My, Errol," Veronica said. "You're just so awfully cute like this."

The relief actually made him a little dizzy.

"You came back," he said.

"You could say that," she replied.

"Thank you," she said.

"The witch has Dusk—" he began.

"Oh, *her*," Veronica pouted. "She's still alive, or at least she was when I last saw her."

"You've seen her?"

"Sure. While you two were bravely getting creamed, I slipped into the witch's cave. She never knew I was there." She paused and looked thoughtful. "I think she can't see me."

"That doesn't make any sense," Errol said.

"Well, she looked right at me a couple of times. I was holding still, but she should have seen me." She held out her hand. "Come on."

"Where are we going?" he asked.

"Back in the cave," she replied. "The witch is asleep. I want to show you something."

T hey're already after us," Billy said. That was his name, the boy with the copper eyes. He didn't talk a lot, and when he did say something it was with a slow deliberation, as if every word had to be considered several times before speaking it.

"Why?" Aster asked. They were making their way along a narrow hillside trail through the woods. Her breath felt like fire in her chest, and her head pounded. She was weaker than she had believed, and she was slowing Billy down, she could tell.

"They want to stop us," he said.

"Stop us from what?"

"No talking, now," he said. "It's getting dark. Things will hear."

"But—"

"If you want to see your friends again, listen to me."

She nodded, having used what little wind she had left, noticing as she did so that Billy's feet made no noise on the forest floor — nor, to her even greater surprise, did hers.

She still didn't hear any signs of pursuit, but a few minutes later, Billy took her by the arm. His grip was sure, but it wasn't hard. He guided her through a maze of grapevines and into the hollow of a huge tree. Then he pressed a finger to his lips.

She never heard them, but after a bit she saw movement back up along the trail, and after that she sorted out Jobe and some of his boys, most on horseback, moving along at a trot. It seemed like a long time after they passed, before Billy gently prodded her to come out from cover and continue, this time in a different direction.

The sky was silver. Night was near. Off in the distance, something made a sound like nothing she had ever heard, or wanted to hear again.

E rrol rode on Veronica's shoulder. Now he figured he knew what a pirate's parrot felt like, except that a parrot had claws and didn't have to cling to the pirate's hair in order to not fall off. Veronica didn't seem to mind, however.

The cave smelled worse than the clearing, and he was glad he couldn't see clearly why. The moonlight spilling in showed mostly a few large shadows, and one seemed to be the witch. He caught at Veronica's ear when he saw something moving.

"It's Dusk," she whispered. "She's still stuck to the witch."

"Oh," he said. Then he remembered. "We heard someone in here, a girl—"

"Yeah," Veronica sighed. "It's sort of too late for her. Probably the reason Dusk is still alive."

"Oh." A hard chill passed through him. Someone had been alive yesterday, and they weren't now, and he might have saved her.

But he hadn't, of course.

The sting of it soured in his belly, and he felt nauseated. But he couldn't do anything about that either.

"Come look here," Veronica said.

He numbly watched as she squated down by what he could vaguely make out as a grotesquely clawed foot. Was that really what Veronica wanted to show him?

"Is this really what you want to show me?" he whispered.

"There," she said. "Look." She pointed toward the heel.

He did see it, then. The witch's skin glowed a faint reddish color, but only in a patch a few inches across. The patch was shaped like an eye. It was kind of disgusting and he wanted to look away, but he kept staring, and it seemed to him something was moving, deep down below the translucent skin.

"Okay," Errol said. "That's nasty."

"I think it's her weak spot," Veronica said. "I've looked all over her and I think this is it."

"What makes you think she has a weak spot?" Errol asked.

"Well, if she doesn't, we can't kill her," Veronica said. "If she does, this is probably it. Really, Errol, can't you follow the simplest logic?"

Errol guessed he couldn't, but he didn't say so.

"If you stab her and it doesn't work, it's going to wake her up," Errol pointed out.

"That's why you're going to do it," Veronica said. "You can scurry off and hide."

"I thought she couldn't see you."

"If I try and kill her, she might become more attentive, but that's not really the problem. The problem is, I think it has to be something magic. I tried to pick up Dusk's sword, and it hurt me. On account of my nature, I think."

"Well I can't pick it up," Errol said. "Not like this."

"No, but you could use this," she said, rising again and walking a few steps to where something glittered.

"It's the spearhead," Veronica said. "She yacked it up a while ago. I think it must have been hurting her stomach."

"It's in a pile of vomit," he muttered.

"It might have been worse," she said. "She might have passed it through. Anyway, I can't touch the spearhead either."

"Fine," he sighed. She put him down and he waded into the stuff. It smelled something like dog food and something like rotten shrimp, but he got the spear head. It was almost as long as he was, but it was light, and he managed to lift it.

And, typically, that was just when the witch chose to wake up.

She yowled like a beast and bounced to her full height as if she'd been sleeping on springs. He heard Dusk yelp. He stood his ground, gripping the blade, defiant, ready to do what fighting he could.

But the witch's purposeful stride took her away from Errol, not toward him.

And then he heard Dusk hollering.

"Aster, run!"

And then Errol was running, stumbling and slipping in God-knew-what, as the witch grew more and more distant. It would take him forever to reach her . . .

But then Veronica scooped him up. He heard her gasp as the cold metal of the blade brushed her hand, and he held it up and away from her.

Outside was confusion. He heard Aster yelp, and someone else, a male voice. He didn't see either of them.

He thought they would make it; but at the last instant whatever had protected Veronica failed, for the Snatchwitch suddenly turned and swatted her away. Errol went spinning through the air—still holding the spearhead—before slapping into something sticky. When he got his bearings he saw the witch above him, her eyes glowing red embers. She snatched, but he darted, and there it was, her ankle, and the flushed eye-spot, and with an inarticulate yell he flung himself at it, stabbing down, a gnat attacking an elephant.

The blade sank in, and then clawed fingers closed around him, lifting him up, bringing his tiny body toward her gaping maw.

Then she dropped him and toppled without a sound.

Once again he smacked into the earth, and once again things were different when he got up. Dusk was free, and she had her sword raised. The witch was still alive, feebly clawing at Dusk. She drew back the weapon to cut.

Then thunder boomed, or so Errol thought, until he realized it was a shotgun. He followed the sound and saw Aster holding the weapon.

"Stop!" she shouted. "You can't kill her."

"And why not?" Dusk asked, tersely.

"Because," a male voice said. Errol saw him step forward. He couldn't tell much about him in the moonlight except that his eyes were a sort of amber color.

"Because she is my mother."

The shotgun was louder than Aster had imagined, and her shoulder ached from the kick. Dusk hesitated, her gaze flicking to Billy, then back down to the felled witch.

"Your mother?" Errol said. He was in his bone-corpus, so his voice was tiny. Aster wondered what had happened to the automaton. If the Snatchwitch had torn it up, that was going to be a bother.

"Yes," Billy said.

Aster noticed Dusk was now looking at something behind her, and quickly turned.

"Just loosen your hold on that shooter," Jobe said, as he and his boys entered the clearing.

Aster thought about that for a second, but instead she pointed it straight at Jobe's head.

"You're way outnumbered," Jobe said.

"That may be," she said. "But if you come another step closer, you won't care anything about that."

She tried to hold the weapon steady, wondering if she could really do it.

The boys next to Jobe inched away a bit.

On the ground, the Snatchwitch moaned.

"She'll get back up," Jobe said. "And when she does she'll murder us all."

"You know better than this," Billy said. "That's why you tried to have the strangers do it. Then what were you going to do? Hang them?"

The witch stirred again.

"Kill her Rand," he told one of the boys. "Kill the witch."

Billy shifted his pistol to a gangly, freckled boy.

"You said we wouldn't have to do it, Jobe," Rand said.

"Well, it looks like we have to now," Jobe replied. "It's our best chance. Sunday will be here soon, and after that she'll be fit again."

"And tell the folks what you've done," Billy said.

"I'm about past caring what any of them think," Jobe said.

He suddenly drew his pistol and aimed it at Aster, throwing himself down as he did so. Aster was so startled she pulled the trigger. She stumbled back and almost fell. She thought she heard more shots, but couldn't be sure for the ringing in her ears.

Jobe was rolling on the ground, hugging his knee to his chest. Billy followed him with his pistol. But now all the other boys had drawn, and most were pointing at Billy.

"Just do it, God's sake," Jobe howled.

"We'll have to shoot Billy first," Rand said.

"Well do that, goddamit," Jobe said.

"You oughtn't," Billy said.

"And why is that?" one of the boys sneered.

Billy just pointed with his index finger to the second group of boys who had just arrived. The new arrivals numbered a few more than Jobe's bunch, and they were clearly on Billy's side of things.

"Anyway, it's just about Sunday," Billy said.

"What's that got to do with anything?" she heard Errol ask.

"All right," Jobe said. He'd gotten to his feet with help. He didn't seem all that injured. He looked around defiantly.

"We're walking out of here boys," he said, and began hobbling backwards.

"The deacons are going to have something to say about this," Billy said.

"I reckon they will," Jobe said, "but I ain't going to hear it now."

"They'll just hide out until Sunday's over," one of the new arrivals hollered.

"Let 'em go," Billy said. "We don't want no one getting shot."

And so Jobe and his boys slunk off into the woods as noiselessly as they had come.

Suddenly the witch cried out in agony, a sound that began like that of some animal but ended in a very human sort of whimper. And when Aster looked, the witch wasn't there anymore; only an old woman covered in skins far too big for her.

SEVEN

SUNDAY

E rrol's triumph at bringing down the Snatchwitch faded into one of helplessness and confusion as events unfolded that were literally too large for him to affect. So when the witch screamed, he did the one thing he knew he could do, and lifted the blade, intent on stabbing her foot again if that was what was needed.

But he found himself eye-to-eye with an old lady who looked nothing like the witch. She was lying on her side, blinking a little, as if she had just wakened from a dream.

"Hello there," she said.

The boy named Billy quickly knelt by her.

"Mother, are you okay?" he asked.

"My foot is awful sore," she said, "but I'll live."

Billy helped her to her feet, and now Errol was just at her ankle again. But Veronica hadn't forgotten him, and a moment later he was back on her shoulder.

The old lady gave them a peculiar look.

"Here you are," she said. "I reckon I expected you a little earlier, but here you are."

"What does that mean?" Errol asked. "You knew we were coming?"

She grinned. "Well, when you have part of something," she said, "you reckon the rest will be along directly. Needs tend to find one another."

"Are you really her?" Errol asked. "The Snatchwitch?"

"Six days a week," she said. "Today is my day off. Now, young man, where did we put your bigger self?"

T he body Aster had built for him didn't feel the same exactly, and it wasn't the shoots and leaves that persisted in places even after the old lady somehow withered off the parts that immobilized it. It felt somehow more alive, and he suspected it was, in a way—the wood he was made of was now green and full of sap.

They marched through the remains of the night.

The woman's name was Hattie Williams, and she promised to explain once she was fully herself, whatever that meant.

Just after dawn they reached the town of Caneshuck. There wasn't a lot to it; two dozen houses, a church, and what looked like a general store.

And for the first time since leaving the hospital, Errol saw more than one adult at the same time. Most were streaming into town from outside, most in rags, but some were well dressed. Shockingly, one of them was Dr. Shecky; four children of various ages were embracing him. It appeared to be a reunion.

Similar meetings were happening all around the square, though some children notably hung back. All of them shifted their gazes when Errol and his companions came into view. Their expressions varied from embarrassed to unfriendly.

Hattie and Billy hustled them into one of the houses.

"This business isn't for outsiders," she said.

Inside, the house was neat and spare. Billy led them to a long table with two benches and brought water, biscuits, butter, and jam while Hattie excused herself. Errol watched as Aster and Dusk ate like starving wolves.

"Are you okay?" he asked Aster. "They were supposed to fix you up."

"You shouldn't have left me, Errol," she said. "You should have waited before running off on your little adventure."

The injustice of the remark stung Errol, and he bit back a response. Veronica, however, did not remain silent.

"You're being a real you-know-what," she said. "They didn't give Errol that choice. It was either kill the Snatchwitch or they were going to let you stay sick. Jobe said they might even help you on, a little, if we didn't go."

Aster frowned, and looked ready to continue the argument, but then Billy put a hand on her shoulder.

"They had to get it done before Sunday," he said. "They wouldn't have waited."

Aster pursed her lips and nodded.

"Okay," she said.

"Okay?" Veronica said. "How about 'thanks you guys, for risking your lives against a horrible monster'?"

"I'm not always such a horrible monster," Hattie said, coming back into the room. She had plaited her hair and donned a dress of brown homespun.

"Sorry," Errol said. "We didn't mean—"

"Oh, don't you apologize for me, Errol Greyson," Veronica said.

"It's fine," Hattie said. "I know this must all seem very confusing."

She glanced sidelong at Dusk. "Perhaps not as much so for you, my dear."

Dusk nodded. "No, I see now."

"You're under some sort of curse, is that it?" Aster asked.

"Yes," Hattie replied. "But it isn't just me."

"I saw Dr. Shecky," he said.

"They met Uncle Roger, too," Billy added.

"Uncle Roger?" Errol asked.

"That snake-cat-thing on the trail," Aster said. Then, to Hattie. "How many of you are cursed?"

"All but the youngest," she said. "Any man or woman of age to conceive a child fell under the curse. Six days of the week we are changed. Most are just animals, but those of us with the most shimmer, we become monsters. On God's day we come to ourselves."

Errol could see Aster trying to hide something in her expression.

"When did this happen?" she asked.

"Eight years ago," Hattie replied.

"Eight," Aster repeated. "Why? Who cursed you?"

"We've no idea," Hattie said.

Aster ticked her index finger on the table. She had the fierce, focused look Errol knew so well.

"Why did Jobe want us to kill you?" she asked.

"Jobe is nearly grown," Billy said, in his soft voice. "He's sick of the elders showing up one day a week and telling him what to do. A lot of them are like that."

"Sometimes I think he's right," Hattie said. "The danger we pose—"

"No, Mother," Billy said. "We've all learned to be careful, to go quietly, to ward the houses and yards."

"Life would be easier without us," Hattie said. "Jobe sees that."

"But why did he want us to do it?" Errol asked.

"Wanted to make it look like strangers did it," Billy said. "But then once everyone got the idea that one elder could be killed, it might convince them to go after the others, the most dangerous ones first."

"But eventually all of them," Veronica said. "Sure. And easiest on Sunday, I would think."

"I can't believe they would murder their own parents," Aster said.

"Some wouldn't," Billy replied. "Right now more than half wouldn't. But it used to be that no one considered it."

Errol heard the door bang open and a moment later Shecky limped into the room. He heard Aster gasp.

The man stood there for a moment, his eyes sorrowful behind his crooked nose.

"Miss," Shecky finally said. "I owe you my deepest apologies. I'm terribly sorry for the hurting I gave you."

Aster's face had drained of blood but was otherwise utterly without expression.

"Everything has been explained to me," she said.

"That may be," Shecky replied. "But there is them that drink and do a thing, and claim the whisky done it. And maybe it did; maybe without the whisky he'd be a fine man. But I think it's something in him the whisky brings out, and so he's accountable. That's how I feel about these things."

"We can remember what we do," Hattie said. "Not always. And this kind of curse, it finds something in you. Maybe something little, and it twists it all up."

"I tried to take my hand to myself once," Shecky said. "I couldn't, and I'm ashamed."

"It's the curse, Will," Hattie said softly. And the way she said it made Errol think she knew that from experience.

"Anyhow," Shecky said, producing a squat glass jar. "This here is a liniment. It's good for most scrapes and suchlike, and will draw out poison. I'd be obliged if you took it."

Aster regarded the proffered gift for a moment, then reached for it.

"Thank you," she said.

"Is there anything we can do?" Errol asked. "Any way to break the curse?"

"You are already on a quest, Errol," Aster reminded him.

"I'm not jumping ship, Aster," Errol said. "But if we could do something for them, something that wouldn't get in the way of what you want—why shouldn't we?"

He remembered what Hattie had said about needs finding one another.

"You already seek the holy water," Hattie said. "It might be that could benefit our situation."

Aster started. "Who told you that?"

"I see things, child. I know things. You need one more companion, a rare sort of companion indeed."

"Yes," Aster said.

"It's my sister you must speak to," Hattie went on. "She knows more of these matters than I."

"Can you tell us the way?"

"Billy will guide you," she said.

"Mama, no," Billy protested.

"Hush child. They need someone who knows the land and its dangers. And after yesterday, I would rather you were far from here. Jobe and his won't take kindly to what you've done."

She took Billy in her arms. "You've been a good son to me, as true as any born of my blood. So mind me now; go with them. They might be able to find the cure for our curse."

Billy lowered his head and nodded.

"Good," Hattie said. "Now, I fear there is little time. You must leave while it is still Sunday. Shecky here will see you armed, mounted, and supplied."

She smiled. "Take them, Billy. I can't stand a long farewell. God bless you all."

D avid was tired of walking, and his feet hurt. He still had on the dress shoes he'd worn to work that morning, and he could feel the blisters painfully squishing around in them.

"Keep your pace," the Sheriff said.

Easy for you to say, David thought. You're on the horse.

But he did walk faster.

"Where are we, anyway?" he asked. Aside from a couple of collapsed wooden buildings that probably dated from a hundred years before, he hadn't seen any sign of human beings, unless one considered the pastures themselves, which often had terraces. He kept expecting that they would cross a highway. Northern Okatibee County was pretty rural, but he had been walking all day without encountering even a barbed wire fence.

Or seeing an airplane go by overheard, or hearing a car in the distance.

Maybe they had somehow slipped by Highway 33 and they were clear over in Hardy County, he thought.

It was near sundown when the hounds sent up a noise, and the sheriff took them down a little path.

"This doesn't feel right," David said.

"They came through here," the Sheriff replied.

"Okay."

The trail brought them an old shotgun house that had a few rooms added on to it. Watching them arrive were a bunch of children, mostly girls. None of them were Aster. The girls wore long dresses and the boys wore overalls, and he wondered if they had wandered into some sort of snake-handling fundamentalist cult hidden away in the woods.

The few boys were all pretty young. One—about thirteen— had eyes swollen nearly shut; it looked like bees had stung him in the face. He placed himself in front of the porch, as if to say he was in charge.

"Hey there, mister," he said.

The Sheriff didn't beat around the bush.

"I'm looking for two young women," he said. "And a thing built of wood that walks as a man. They were here."

"Yeah, they was," the boy said. "That sick one give me this," he said indicating his face.

"Jake," one of the girls said. "Them's grown men."

"I know it," Jake said.

"But they came in past the wardings. So they ain't . . ."

"Where have they gone?" The Sheriff demanded.

"They went to Ashy creek," the boy said, "to kill the Snatchwitch. Well, three of them did. That hellhexer stayed here, on account of the deal, but she done this to me and lit out after 'em. And now Jobe's gone after her." He shrugged. "That's been a while. I hope they had to shoot her skinny self."

The horseman seemed to consider for a bit. Then he indicated David.

"I'm the Sheriff of the Marches," he said. "This is my deputy. I need a horse for him, or a mule."

"Jobe took all the horses," Jake said.

The sheriff looked at David, and he felt a searing contempt in his gaze that made his legs go weak.

"Well, I don't guess you can walk at night," he said. "We'll stay over here and set out in the morning."

"Mister," Jake said. "It's polite to ask if you want to stay someplace."

The horseman stared at Jake for a moment. Then he got down, drew a pistol, and before the boy could do much more than cower, clubbed him on the side of the head with it.

"Please," the Sheriff said, "might we stay here for the night?"

Jake was holding his ear, elbows on the ground and back arched up. Blood leaked from between his fingers. He was crying.

"Yes, sir," he managed to whimper. "I reckon you can."

D avid sat on the porch, listening to the crickets and tree frogs, drinking cold water from a ceramic cup and soaking his feet in a small basin. A clump of girls sat further down the porch. Most of them were in long cotton shifts, now — presumably what they slept in. He was clearly the object of their attentions, because they kept giggling and pointing toward him.

"Can I help you girls with something?" he asked.

"We was just wondering how old you are," one of them said, a pretty, moon-faced girl with frizzy dark hair and emerald green eyes. It was hard to guess in the moonlight but by the way her shift fell straight he thought she was probably eleven or so.

"I'm twenty-five," he said.

"And it not even Sunday," she said. "I've never heard of such."

"Well, he ain't from around here, Nellie," another said.

"He must not be."

"What school do you girls go to?" he asked.

"School?" Nellie said. "I don't reckon we have a school no more. It got burnt a few years ago. We have our lessons in the Church, what ones we get."

"And what Church is that?" He asked.

"The one in town," Nellie said.

"No, I meant — what denomination are you?"

"I don't know what that means," Nellie said, "but it sounds sort of dirty."

The girls all giggled.

"I mean Baptist, or Methodist, Presbyterian, or whatever."

"Well, I been Baptized," she said. "I never heard of those other things."

The girls abruptly clustered together, whispering in a rush.

"No you don't do it, Sarah!" Nellie suddenly shouted.

"Hey mister!" another girl said. "Nellie's wondering if you're looking to find a wife."

The world did a sort of half-turn, and David felt his cheeks burn.

"I think maybe I'm a little too old for you," he said.

Nellie stopped slapping at her friend and looked suddenly deadly serious.

"I'll have you know I'll be thirteen come July, same age as mama was when she got hitched. My daddy was right near forty at that time. Just because you're the only growed man around don't get big ideas. I got prospects."

"I didn't—" he began, but then thought better to change the subject. "Where are your parents?"

"Well, they ain't around are they?" Nellie said. "Except on Sunday."

"Why only on Sunday?"

"Cause the rest of the week they're man-eating monsters," Nellie said.

"Tie-snakes and water panthers, snatchwitches and life-eaters," Sarah said.

"Now you're having fun with me," David said.

"Mister, you walk out in them woods, you'll see what kind of fun we're having with you."

The oldest-looking girl stood up, and David saw she was pregnant.

"Come on, girls, it's past bedtime. Let's let Mr. David here have some peace from your jabberholes."

D avid woke with something warm snuggled against him, and found it to be Nellie. At first he wasn't sure what to do. Everyone slept all together in one room, in pallets on the floor, but he'd found a whole other room with beds which were apparently reserved for the missing older kids or parents. He'd taken one of those, a down mattress that had seen better days but was a lot softer than the floor. At some point, Nellie had apparently followed him in.

He lay still for a moment, feeling her shallow breathing, and then tried to disengage himself.

She wasn't asleep, though, and gripped him tighter.

"I ain't want no husband," she whispered sleepily. "I just want to pretend you're my pa. And I don't want Jimmy to come along messing with me like he does. Please, mister."

He hesitated, then with a sigh he lay back down. She tucked her head on his chest, and in a few minutes her breathing evened out. He wondered what kind of 'messing' Jimmy did. What kind of Lord of the Flies situation had he stumbled into? These kids needed help. This needed reported.

After he found Aster.

Suddenly the warmth of Nellie's body against his felt like pain, like loss. It should be Aster next to him. He should be with her like this. Protecting her, hearing her regular breathing. That it wasn't she gnawed at him. Only when he began to pretend it *was* her was he able to sleep.

A stir of voices and footfalls woke him next. He pushed Nellie over—a little rougher than he meant to, because he knew what it might look like—and jumped up to see what it was, only to find found himself face-to-face with a hard-looking boy in his late teens.

"Well, now," the boy drawled. "Who are you, come here to help himself to our women?"

"No, it's not like that," David said. "I was just—she . . ." He stumbled back, noticing as he did that the boy's leg had a make-shift bandage on it.

"And in my bed," the young man went on. "A fine thing. I oughta blow your brains out."

"Oh, hush Jobe," Nellie said. "He didn't touch me."

"Well, who would, Nellie?" Jobe snapped. "Get out of here. You know better than to come in here."

He turned to David. "Now, you."

"He's with me." The Sheriff's voice rumbled. Where he had been this whole time, David didn't know; he hadn't been sleeping in any of the rooms set aside for that. But David was suddenly happy to have him back.

"And who the hell are you?" Jobe demanded.

"I'm the Sheriff," he replied. "The young woman, Aster, and her companions. Where are they?"

"What have they done?"

"That's not your concern," the Sheriff said. "Where are they?"

Some of the hardness went out of Jobe's eyes, replaced by uncertainty.

"I reckon they're in town," he said. "Or will be soon."

"Well, then," the Sheriff said. "I'll need you to take me there and help me apprehend them."

"Sheriff, you say?" Jobe said. "I ain't never seen you."

"Sheriff of the Marches," he said.

Another of the boys gave a low whistle. "I've heard of him. He's got the authority, he does. They'll have to give them over, in town."

"That suits me just fine," Jobe said. "But you have to guarantee my safety."

"You've committed no crime I care about," the Sheriff said. "You're my deputy now, and as such inviolate."

"Well, then," Jobe said. "Let's saddle back up, boys."

PART THREE

OUT FROM THE MARCH

ONE

THE WATER GETS DEEP

Aster was watching Shecky bring the horses when she saw a young boy run up to him; they were far enough away she couldn't hear what the boy said, but it seemed to light a fire under Shecky, who all but dragged the mounts along.

"Best hurry," he said, when he got near. "They say the March Sheriff is coming for you. If he finds you here we'll have no choice but to hand you over."

He clapped Billy on the shoulder. "Jobe and his bunch are riding with him."

"We'd best go, then," Billy said.

Dusk had already loaded some provisions onto Drake. Billy hurriedly strapped more on his, then put a rifle into a sheath fastened to his saddle.

Veronica hopped onto her mount, a small red mare—without effort. She looked comfortable. Even Errol sat the big, barrel-chested animal he'd been brought with what appeared to be confidence.

She stood, gazing at the horse proffered her, a spotted grey mare she'd been informed was named Lily.

Billy noticed.

"Have you ever ridden?" he asked.

She remembered hoof beats, and a storm at night, her arms gripped tight around her father's waist.

"I've been on a horse," Aster replied. "But I don't know how to ride."

He came over and took her hand. It was unexpected, and confusing, but then he placed it on the muzzle of the horse. She felt the velvety soft hair, the warm suspiration from Lily's nostrils.

"Lily will be easy on you," he said. "She'll follow, so you won't have to do much."

He led her around to the side.

"Always mount from the left," he said. "Put your foot here, in the stirrup, now throw your other leg over."

In the saddle, she took a deep breath.

I can do this, she thought. She had always wanted to ride. Here was her chance.

"Remember," Billy said. "Holding the saddle horn or the reins won't keep you on. You have to hold on with your legs and keep your weight between them."

"Got it," she said, not certain that she really had, but feeling the Sheriff drawing nearer in her mind.

"Let's go," Errol said.

They started at a walk, which was easy enough, but when they got beyond the town and onto the road, Billy brought his horse to a slow trot. As promised, Lily followed. It was a bit bouncy, but not so bad.

"Okay, Miss," Billy said, coming alongside her. "We're going to a fast trot, and that can be hard on your backside. So you want use your legs in the stirrups to sort of take up the bounce. Watch me."

He sped up, and she saw what he meant; his horse was rising and falling, and his legs were pumping against the motion.

"We call it posting," Dusk said. "It's not hard, and it will save you a lot of pain."

As the other horses pulled ahead, Lily took their example and broke to a fast trot. At first it hurt, but then Aster found the rhythm—tah-tun, tah-tun, tah-tun—and again she remembered clinging to her father's back, that same double beat lifting her up and down.

"A horse can't run for long, Streya," he'd said. "But a good one can trot forever. Remember that."

I *can* do this, she knew, and grinned.

Then she remembered the Sheriff and looked back, but the road was clear except for their dust.

They soon found themselves rising and falling through low hills, and the road took itself along a wooded ridge top. There they stopped at an overlook from which they could see the open fields, and more distant yet, the smoke rising from the chimneys in town.

"There they are," Billy said.

At first all she saw was a dust cloud, but then she made them out; a bunch of riders. Two were further out in front than the others, and flanked by a pair of dogs.

They weren't on the main road, but were cutting across the fields.

"They're going the wrong way," Errol said.

"No," Billy replied. "They aim to cut us off before we get to the river. They know where we're headed."

"How?" she wondered. "We've passed at least three turn-offs."

"They know where we're going," Billy repeated.

"Well," Aster said, "let's go someplace else, then."

He seemed to think about that for a long time.

"If we're going to Aunt Jezebel's, we have to cross the river," he said. "And there's no other place shallow enough to ford in a hundred miles."

"I don't get it," Errol said. "If the way they're going is quicker, why didn't we go that way?"

Billy shrugged. "I thought they would follow us, and I could lose them in the hills."

"This river," Dusk said. "How wide is it?"

"The Sinti? A good stone's throw."

"Is there any place it is particularly narrow?"

"Up north a few miles, I reckon, it pinches up a little."

"I have some arts," Dusk said. "Let's try it there."

Oddly, instead of Billy, Aster realized everyone was looking at her.

"We've no chance at the crossing?" she said.

"I would say no, Miss," Billy replied.

She looked at Dusk. "You can do this?"

"If the river is narrow enough, I daresay yes."

"Then north we go," Aster decided.

They soon took a branching trail, and then Aster learned what it was like to run, for Billy took them to a canter. Surprisingly, it was vastly smoother than a trot, and after the first slight panic at the rush of the forest on either side it quickly became intoxicating. Lily responded to her hands at the reins, but she knew that control was only partial, that the horse might suddenly choose to do almost anything, and a deep thrill somehow wound all through that.

They didn't run for long, but went down to a walk for a bit, then back to a trot, to let the horses get back their wind. Then they were running again.

Night fell, but Billy pushed them on under the light of the moon, which was waning but still nearly full. Nightbirds called, and the shapes of the trees grew grotesque. Their pace slowed to a walk.

"When do the adults change back?" she asked Billy.

"They clear out of town around nine," he answered. "They change at midnight."

"So we won't run into any monsters tonight."

"No, we might," Billy replied. "There are other towns, and lots of people just scattered about on homesteads."

"Wait—you mean it's not just your town? The curse affects everyone in the Kingdom?"

"Yes," Billy said. "The curse is everywhere."

She worried at his words for the next half an hour, until they slowed to a walk. The trail was narrow, so the group strung out some, and Aster suddenly realized Errol was riding alongside her. The carved features of his face didn't register anything, but she sensed he wanted to talk.

"What is it, Errol?" she asked.

"Eight years," he said. His tone was low; even she could barely hear it. The next closest rider was Veronica, twenty feet ahead.

"What about it?" she asked.

"Their curse started eight years ago," he said. "That's about the time you showed up at Sowashee Elementary."

"I'm aware of that, Errol," she replied.

"Hey, look," he started, and she felt the sudden bitter sense she was making a mistake, that she shouldn't have spoken to him like that. The problem was that she was angry at Errol, but she wasn't sure why.

"I'm sorry," she said. "I shouldn't have treated you that way back at Hattie's. And it was smart of you to figure of the eight-year thing."

"I'm not dumb," he said.

"No," she replied, "But you've been acting dumb for so long now, I forget, sometimes, how smart you can be."

"Is that supposed to be a compliment?" Errol said.

She shrugged. "Anyway, yes, father and I left here eight years ago. And eight years ago my father's memory began to go bad."

"Do you think there is a connection?" he asked.

"Yes," she said. "I don't believe in coincidence. Not at that scale."

"I don't either," he said. "Did you notice how Hattie talked to Dusk? Like she might know something about this?"

"Yes."

"Maybe you should ask her about it."

"I don't know about that," she said. "We still don't know a lot about her."

"I know she's saved our asses more than once. I think we can trust her."

"Look," she said, "I know that Dusk is . . . Impressive. She's strong, and she's brave, and she's hot. But try not to . . ." She sighed.

"What?" he demanded.

"When it comes to women you . . . make mistakes."

"Are you still going on about when I ran off after Veronica?" he said. "Because you know I couldn't help that."

"No," she said. "I'm talking about Lisa."

He was silent for a moment.

"That's mean," he said.

"You were her puppy dog, Errol. She played with you long enough to make Brandon notice her, and then she dumped you."

"That's not true," he said.

"And this is what I'm talking about," Aster said. "When girls are involved, you can't separate fact from fiction. So watch what you say around Dusk. If I decide to talk to her about this, I will."

"Yes, Ma'am," Errol said, sarcastically.

"I'm not trying to hurt your feelings, Errol," she said.

"Well, God help me when you try to, then," he muttered, and rode up ahead, toward Veronica.

V eronica smelled the river long before they reached it; the clean rush of the channel, the corruption in the eddies and pools along its banks, the musk of the water snakes hunting frogs on sandbars. She felt a longing for the depths, for at least one swim down to the slippery sediment, to run her fingers through the empty shells of crawfish and the broken skeletons of catfish and water birds, to fill her dead lungs with living water.

She remembered the hand from the well.

Part of her wanted what Aster promised. Each day her remembrance of her few living years sharpened, and a sense of possibility was developing in her. Every day she felt changed, not always for the best. She had come so close to leaving when Errol and Dusk went down to their futile confrontation with the Snatchwitch. She still wasn't sure why she hadn't.

But at least she was on a horse again. She was certain she'd had a horse, way back then. And she liked to run.

They wound down to the sandy littoral; the moon was behind the trees, so Dusk asked her to lead, because Veronica had the best eyesight at night.

And she felt Him, in the deeps. Big. He hadn't noticed them yet, and she hoped he wouldn't.

"We—" she began. She had meant to say, "We should go quietly."

But she was cut off by Dusk, who thrust the point of her awful sword into the water. Veronica gasped, almost as if the blade had pricked her own skin.

"*Gelde*," Dusk said.

Cold struck Veronica, and she was once again reminded of thrusting her head into the open coolers at Tucker's store. She watched as frost spread across the water and felt ice in her own veins.

And she felt Him and his abrupt fury.

And then, before she could say anything, a gunshot exploded downstream.

"They're here," Billy said, as another detonation rang through the night air.

Veronica saw them, then, by the flash from the gun. They were south, on a ridge overlooking the stream.

"Quickly," Dusk said. She led Drake out onto the ice. The others followed.

"No, wait," Veronica said.

But then the ice shattered, as *He* smashed up through it.

His massive, spade-shape head reared toward the stars, drawing a serpentine body behind. But the form he wore was no snake. His skin was slick and without scales, and he had two forelegs so tiny they made those of a Tyrannosaurus rex seem big by comparison.

For a moment, Veronica stood unmoving, staring as Errol and the rest struggled in the water. She felt something like an angry insect hiss past her head, and then the bark of another gunshot.

The monster darted its open mouth toward one of the horses. The poor beast shrieked, breaking Veronica's stupor. She stepped into the water, feeling the sweet, metallic taste of the horse's blood on her tongue and felt rather than knew what to do.

When the ice broke, Errol had a single glimpse of their attacker, but it was as clear as a flash. He had seen one before, although it had been much smaller. His grandfather had called it a conger eel, but he had later learned it was really an *amphiuma*, a kind of amphibian. He remembered that they had teeth like razors.

As he sank, he swam furiously toward the thing. If he could get hold of it, he might be able to pull it under and give the others a chance. But he couldn't see anything in the pitchy darkness, and once again he felt the weight of failure settle on him.

Aster had a Recondite Utterance forming on her lips, but the shock of the cold choked her, and then her mouth filled with water. She realized with horror that her hand was tangled painfully in Lily's reins, and the terrified horse was dragging her along. They were in the middle of the river, and the current was strong. She and the horse were spinning in a kind of ghastly waltz. A horse screamed, and it was one of the worst things that Aster had ever heard.

Then she went under. She closed her eyes, furiously trying to focus on something. She could feel the untamed magic all around her, but couldn't bend it to her will. The water was crazy with noises, but she couldn't tell what they were.

Then a sort of light flickered in her mind, the same light that illuminates dreams. She was still in the water, but she was comfortable, at ease even. Powerful. She felt herself growing, reaching up and downstream. She saw herself in the water, and Errol, sinking toward the bottom, Dusk thrashing toward the monster, Billy trying to aim his pistol and swim at the same time.

And as all that slipped away toward darkness, Aster knew this wasn't her dream—it was Veronica's.

And Veronica was changing, becoming, like a moth splitting out of its chrysalis.

Then the vision left her, and strong bands tightened around Aster. A sort of ticklish cloud lifted her back toward the surface. She was separated from Lily, and a moment later her feet touched the muddy bottom as whatever-it-was dragged her toward shore.

As she found her own footing and they released her, she realized what had saved her from the river.

Cottonmouths. Copperheads. Water snakes. Eels.

It was too late to scream. She could only sit and stare as her companions were brought ashore in the same way. She didn't see the monster anymore, but then its head broke the surface, far down the river, toward where the gunshots had come from. At the base of its head, she thought she saw a person clinging.

TWO
IF I WERE ALIVE

They had lost two horses and half the provisions—and, it seemed—Veronica.

"We should at least move back from the river," Billy said. "They can't cross, but they can still shoot us."

"I'll stay down here," Errol said, feeling stubborn. "It's not like a bullet will hurt me that much."

"Don't start feeling invincible," Aster warned him. "If a bullet goes through your skull and smashes the homunculus, you'll be back in your hospital bed."

"Well, that's good to know," Errol replied. He wanted to say something sharper, to demand why she hadn't told him that sooner, but her words were quiet, and a bit faltering. It sounded like she was genuinely concerned about him. Then she completed it.

"Sorry," she said. "I should have told you that a long time ago."

"It's okay," he said. "How did you do that trick with snakes? That was . . . I mean it worked, but—"

"That wasn't me," she said. "That was Veronica. And she took that whatever-it-was downstream toward the Sheriff."

She sighed. "Errol—I don't know that she's coming back. Something changed in her. The magic was so strong I felt it. For a moment I felt like I *was* her."

"What was that like?" he asked.

"Disturbing."

"Can she be killed, too?"

"I'm not sure," Aster said. "I doubt it, since she's already dead, but she could be torn into pieces too small to stick back together. But that isn't what I meant. When I . . . felt her . . . I think—she felt—she might not *want* to come back."

"Yeah," Errol said. "I can see that."

"Oh ye of little faith," a voice said from behind them. Errol turned to see Veronica emerging from the water. Her eyes seemed faintly luminescent, and he felt a thrill of the same desire he'd had when he first met her, mixed with not a little fear.

"We got a few of them," she said. "But the Sheriff has some pretty good juju. Fire and brimstone and all. Anyway, they won't be crossing here."

"You saved us," Errol said. "How did you do that?"

"Honey," she said, "I have no idea. It doesn't pay to think about these things too much. I felt like I could take Big Slinky on, and I did. I felt like—" Her brow puckered and she looked briefly confused. Then her eyes widened as if she had seen something wonderful.

"I felt like I had a reason to," she said.

D aylight found them a few miles from the river, in a prairie brilliant with wild flowers. Billy still hadn't had any sleep, but Aster was dozing in Errol's arms. Her horse Lily was one of the survivors, but Veronica now rode her. Billy and Dusk still had their own mounts.

"That was pretty neat, the way you froze the water," Errol opined to Dusk. She hadn't spoken much, and he didn't think it was just from being tired.

She laughed, bitterly. "It was nearly the end of us," she said.

"You couldn't have known the amphiuma king was hanging out right there," he said.

"If I had waited to hear what Veronica had to say, I would have known," she said. "My mother always said I was too certain of my abilities, too quick to act."

"There's nothing wrong with being confident," Errol said.

"Well," Dusk said, stroking the mane of her horse. "May I ask you a question, Errol?"

"You can ask," he replied.

"How did you become what you are?"

He glanced down at Aster. Her eyes were darting about beneath her lids, and her lips were moving slightly, so he knew she was dreaming.

"Back home," he said, "my body is hurt. It can't wake up—I'm in what we call a coma. Aster took my soul and put it into this."

"So that you might help her in her quest," Dusk said.

"Yes," Errol said. "But it also gives me a chance. Without the water of health, I—my real body—will probably never wake up."

"So that is what you seek."

Oh, man! Errol thought. He knew Aster had wanted to keep that a secret. This was only going to confirm to her that women made him stupid.

Of course he *knew* that, but he didn't like to hear it from her.

"I had already guessed," Dusk said. "Hattie mentioned the sacred water. She could only have meant the water of life, of health, or of death. Given that she wants to end a curse, the water of health seemed most likely."

"Oh," Errol said. "Right. Wait—there's a water of death?"

"Naturally," she said. She frowned slightly.

"You knew Aster before you fell into this false sleep," she said. It wasn't a question, but he nodded anyway.

"How were you injured?" she asked.

"It was an accident," he said. She looked like she was going to press on that, so he took her earlier cue and changed the subject.

"You called my world the 'Reign of the Departed'," he said. "Why? What does that mean?"

A brief cloud of annoyance passed over her face, but she got the hint. She looked thoughtful for about a minute before saying anything.

"When people pass out of the Kingdoms, your world is where they end up," she told him.

"You mean when they die?"

"Yes. No. I mean, not everyone who dies goes there. It has to do with what my people call *elumiris*. It's the magic that shimmers in living things, that gives them their natures. Those born in the farthest, most ancient kingdoms have the most elumiris and shine the brightest. Here—in the kingdoms nearest the Pale—the light is dimmer. Imagine a man in the highest, most faraway kingdom. When he dies, his soul is born to another body, but often in the process, elumiris is lost. His soul grows dimmer, and he is thus born into a lesser kingdom. And the next time he dies, his shimmer might wane further. If the day comes that his soul has little or no elumiris, he is not reborn in the kingdoms at all, but into your world. He has departed."

"Why would he lose this stuff?" he asked, dubiously. "This elumiris?"

"That's a difficult question," she replied. "Many answers have been given, and none is believed by all to be the correct one. But one can gain elumiris as well as lose it. Even beyond the Pale, in your world, some have spark enough to pass back through unaided, at least into the Marches. If the Sheriff doesn't stop them."

"So it's sort of like reincarnation," Errol mused. "But what if someone dies in my world? Someone without the shimmer?"

Dusk was silent for a moment.

"Some say that it is the end of them," she said, quietly— almost apologetically. "That their souls cease to exist. That your world is the last chance, the final stop before oblivion."

Dad, he thought. He remembered the terrifying woman in the forest, the one whose gaze he knew he could not meet. Was that how it ended? Was her face the last thing he would see? That his father had seen?

She noticed his silence.

"Some have other notions," she said. "Only those who have died such a death know the truth."

"Or they don't know anything at all," Errol replied.

His family had never been particularly church-going, but in the depths of his heart he had always imagined that something, some other existence lay beyond death. If he believed what Dusk said, it did. For some people.

Just not his father, or him, or the other several billion people who had somehow lost their magic. That hardly seemed fair.

But then he already knew the world wasn't fair.

On the second day after crossing the river they came across a herd of buffalo. They were larger than Aster had imagined, but Errol—who had seen them once in Oklahoma—assured her they weren't of unusual size. Billy took them carefully around the beasts, also avoiding the huge cats that prowled the edges of the herd, waiting for a weak member to stray a little too far from the rest. She steadily became more impressed by his competence in such matters. He remained mostly quiet, and he usually had a far-off look in his eyes. Over the next few days she took to riding more and more with him, because he offered and because she felt like an intruder when Errol started talking to Dusk or Veronica, which he did frequently. Clearly the adventure they had had while she was being peeped on in an outhouse had drawn them tighter to one another, if not to her. Having them chat while Errol carried her like a baby was intolerable.

If she was completely honest, she liked the physical closeness of riding double with Billy. At first she had felt weird about it, but when he brought Tom to a run, she had no choice but to put her arms around his torso. He didn't seem to mind, and he also didn't seem to take it as an invitation to anything else.

Although now and then she thought it might be nice if he did. Of course, such thoughts also made her feel frivolous and a little guilty. She needed to stay focused on the task before her.

She asked him about Hattie's comment suggesting she wasn't his real mother, and he answered that she wasn't, but that she was the only mother he had ever known. He'd been told he just wandered into town one day, but he didn't remember that, or much of anything before Hattie adopted him.

They crossed another prairie, where sunflowers hummed strange, low harmonies. From a distance, they saw a war between cranes and tiny men with long, rigid tails. Once, Billy urged them all undercover just before a hawk the size of a private airplane flew over.

On the fifth day, on a trail through low scrub forest, they met a pair of riders on the trail. They had black hair, sun-darkened skin and high cheekbones. They wore turbans of brightly patterned cloth and long coats that looked sort of like the military jackets from the American Revolution—lots of buttons.

Crescent-shaped silver gorgets adorned their throats, and their ears were jangly with rings and bangles. One held a long rifle casually in one hand. The other had a bow across his lap.

Dusk trotted Drake up alongside Billy.

Aster caught a slight motion from the corner of her eye, a flash of silver off to their left.

"Billy—" she whispered.

"Yes," he replied. "I know."

They drew up near the two in the trail. This time she wasn't surprised that neither seemed much over sixteen.

Suddenly the one with the bow in his lap pulled a pistol from his jacket and pointed it at Billy's forehead. Aster felt a jolt, and her vision went white at the edges.

"Can you still dodge a bullet, Billy Nomother?" the boy asked.

She felt Billy sigh. "I never could dodge a bullet, Chula," he said. "You're just a terrible shot."

Chula leaned forward in his saddle, bring the muzzle closer to Billy. Aster began an Utterance, but before she could voice it, the other boy laughed and put his weapon away.

"It makes a better story that you can dodge bullets," Chula said. He looked at the rest of them.

"You've got a funny bunch here."

"Yeah," Billy said. "Ma sent them to see Aunt Jezebel."

"And you to guide them," Chula said. "How are things back there?"

"Can I tell you as we ride?" Billy asked.

"You got trouble following you?"

"Maybe. Could be days back, could be less."

"All right, then," Chula said. He turned to the fellow with the gun. "Snapper, you take over here. Scout and see if his worries are near. But come on back before sundown."

"Okay, Chula."

They rode another hour with Chula chattering on about relations and Billy answering in his usual laconic fashion, until they began passing through corn fields. A little later they reached a village. Some of the houses looked like log cabins, but more appeared to be made of mud or plaster, and had steep roofs of wooden shingles. Each house had a little garden, although Aster didn't recognize the plants in them. Chickens wandered about free, and lots of dogs.

Chula gestured at one house that towered above the others.

"You can stay in the townhouse 'til Sunday," Chula said. Then he nodded at Aster. "Except her," he said. "You know where she needs to go."

"Yeah," Billy said. "I guess I didn't. But okay."

"Where I need to go?" Aster asked. "What are you talking about?"

The house Billy took her to was a hundred yards from any other building. It was next to a little stream and mostly hidden by trees from the rest of the village.

"Why here?" she asked. "Why not with the rest of you?"

"It's a special house," he told her. "Sort of holy."

She noticed he had stopped about six yards from it and seemed unwilling to go any closer.

"Go on in," he said. "Introduce yourself. It will be fine."

Puzzled, she walked toward the building. Like most of the cabins, it didn't have a door as such, but rather an entrance that went in a few feet and then turned hard to the right before leading her into the single room within. Four girls from about thirteen to her age looked up with surprise as she entered. It was smoky from a little fire in a pit in the center of the dirt floor. The girls had been playing what looked like some sort of game using sticks and markers and lines scratched on the dirt.

"I'm, uh, I'm Aster," she said. "They said I was supposed to come here. Chula said."

"She said her name!" the youngest girl gasped.

"Hush," the eldest said. "Be polite." She gestured at Aster. "Come in, Miss."

"I didn't mean to give offense."

"You didn't," the girl said. "It's just—we don't give names lightly."

"Chula said his," Aster pointed out.

"It's his nickname," one of the other girls said.

"I see." Aster said. An uncomfortable silence followed.

"So," the elder girl said. "You've come from far away, I take it."

"Very far," Aster agreed.

"On important business, I guess."

Aster nodded. "Do you have nicknames?" she asked.

"Oh, sure," the elder girl said. "They call me Sensible." She then named the others in what appeared to be descending age order; Mockingbird, Yelps, and Wiggler.

"It's my first time," Wiggler confided.

"First time for what?" Aster asked.

"To have the Moon's Portion and stay in his house."

"I don't know what that means," Aster said.

Wiggler stared at her, and then began to giggle.

"She is from very far away," Sensible said. "I'm sure they have another name for it."

"It's the time when you bleed," Wiggler laughed.

Aster felt her face blaze red. How had Chula known?

She wasn't sure if she was more angry or more humiliated. Or confused.

"Oh," she said. "You have to stay apart from the rest?"

"Of course," Sensible replied. "Otherwise, it would be terrible. The boys would get sick, they couldn't hunt or fight—where are you from you don't know this?"

"But that's ridiculous!" Aster exploded. "It's demeaning. It's sexist. Menstruation is a natural thing."

"Like snakebite," Mockingbird said.

"Or a flood," Yelps added.

"Or lightning," Wiggler said.

They were laughing at her, she realized, albeit politely. As if this was something everyone knew.

"But, I mean — do the boys ever get shut up alone like this?"

"They don't get the Moon's Portion," Wiggler said, gently. "Don't you know that?"

"Besides, they go off alone all the time," Sensible said. "To hunt and fight."

"It's not the same," Aster insisted. "That's doing something."

"Listen," Sensible said. "Most of every month we are always *doing* something. Breaking fields, hoeing them, tending them, shucking corn—"

" —pounding corn," Mockingbird took up, "shelling beans, cutting cane, making baskets, cooking, sweeping."

"Or carrying heavy pots of water. We're always doing something," Yelps said.

"But not here," Wiggler said.

"No, indeed," Sensible said. "We're not *allowed* to work when we're here."

"Except to feed ourselves," Mockingbird said.

"And take long soaks in the creek," Wiggler put in.

"That's not work, my dear," Sensible told her.

"Well it's my favorite," Wiggler said.

"What do you do, then?" Aster asked.

"We eat, we play games, and we talk," Mockingbird said. "It's wonderful that you're here. I'm sure you have the best stories."

Oh, God. Aster thought. This is going to be awful.

At least she only had a day or two to go. But then it occurred to her; what if what the girls said was true? In the Kingdoms it might very well not be a superstition, but an actual fact that a menstruating women could do damage to a man.

What then, of Billy? Had she hurt him by riding with him these last few days?

It seemed ridiculous.

When Errol went out of the townhouse, he heard Billy vomiting again. He'd asked before if he could help, but it had only seemed to embarrass him, so rather than repeat the mistake, he went around the other way. Above, the night sky blazed, glorious to behold. Even in rural Okatibee County it was never like this; the light of Sowashee bled into the sky, and most houses, no matter how isolated, had lights outside. Here the only illumination was that falling from the heavens.

It had been a long time since he had looked up at the stars. The last time had been when he and Bobby and Jay had gotten hold of a bottle of Thunderbird and drank it out in Bound's pasture, lying on their backs. He had started naming the constellations, and Jay had made fun of him. That was when he was still learning to keep his mouth shut about such things. When he had been little, it had been with his dad, before he got sick. Once they had watched the sky wheel by for half a night, naming each constellation and planet as they rose.

And once with Aster.

The sudden remembrance startled him. She had known the stars, too, but she'd had different names for the constellations — Ursa Major or the Big Dipper was Thunder's Cart, and the Milky Way was the Path of Birds. They had been eleven or twelve.

Why had he forgotten that?

He lay on his back, half-fearing that in the Kingdoms, even the stars wouldn't be the same. But soon he began to pick them out, like old familiar friends.

Something rustled nearby, and he sat up, ready to fight, but the dark silhouette against the Milky Way was Veronica.

"Do you want to be alone?" she asked.

He did, but he didn't want to say so. Typically, she interpreted his silence the way she wanted to, and lay down next to him. Her arm touched his, and he twitched in startlement. It almost felt real, her touch, rather than the muffled half-sensation his puppet body made do with. He relaxed and felt the smoothness of her skin; it was the same temperature as the night air, which was to say hot.

"Can't sleep?" she asked.

"Something like that," he said.

She was quiet for a moment.

"Look, Errol," she said. "I know we got off on the wrong foot, with me trying to kill you and all . . ."

"You've saved me twice," he said.

"What?"

"You came back for me at the Snatchwitch's cave. You saved us all from the whatever-the-Hell-it-was in the river. I guess I can get over that one little thing."

"Can you?" she asked.

"Yeah."

"Huh," she murmured.

She started to lift up, but then relaxed back onto the ground. He was increasingly aware of the place where their arms touched, try as he might to ignore it.

"You like the stars?" she asked.

"I guess," he said.

"That's as good as a lie, Errol Greyson," she said. "You talk straight with me."

"I like them," he admitted.

"Tell me about them."

"You know — there they are," he said, pointing.

"Errol," she said quietly, "I don't know how many years I went without seeing a star, and I never knew anything about them before. But here they are in God's own glory, and I want you to tell me about them."

Errol might have sighed if he'd had lungs. Instead he pointed to the brightest light currently in the sky.

"That's Venus," he said. "The Evening Star."

"I thought Venus was the Morning Star," Veronica said.

"I thought you didn't know anything about stars."

"Well, I remember hearing that," she said.

"Well, she's both," he said. "She's really a planet, not a star, and she's between Earth and the Sun — so she's always near sunrise or sunset. We see her as the morning star for about 263 days, and then she disappears for a while and shows back up with the sunset for another 263 days."

"And where is she in between?" she asked.

"Out of sight," he replied.

"And that?" she asked him, pointing. "Is that the little dipper?"

"No," he said. "That's the seven sisters."

"Looks like a dipper to me," she said.

"No, that's little dipper, see?" He pointed at another, larger formation.

"Well, that looks like a plough," she opined.

They lay like that for a while, and he was just getting used to it when he felt the touch of her hand on his.

"Errol," she said. Her voice was still and small.

"Yeah?"

"I don't know what happened to me," she said. "I don't know how I died. I remember being at the falls. I remember I had new shoes. That's all I remember."

"Maybe that's for the best," he said, squeezing her hand.

She squeezed back.

"Maybe," she whispered. She sat up a little. He couldn't see her face, only the outline of it against the sky.

"Close your eyes," she whispered.

"Listen . . ."

"Hush. Close them."

He did. She still had his hand.

"Think about your body. Your real body, the one in the hospital."

"I'm afraid to sleep," he blurted. "I'm afraid that if I sleep I won't wake up. I have bad dreams."

"I know, Errol," she said. "Do what I said. Think of your body, lying here in the grass, just like this."

And so he did. He imagined himself, back in Bound's pasture.

"Imagine breathing," she whispered, "and your heart beating."

And as she said it, he did; he felt the pulse of life through him, the swell and collapse of his chest, the faint itch from the grass through his shirt, sweat beading on his skin.

And then he felt her lips touch his, warm and wonderful. And he felt his, as if they were made of flesh, and the luxury of it was almost more than he could bear. This wasn't like before, when he met her—there was no crazy lust, no loss of control; just a kiss so sweet it threatened to break his heart.

After a small eternity Veronica pulled gently away and lay by him again, and although the illusion quickly began to dissolve, a melancholy happiness lingered.

"If I were alive, Errol," Veronica said, her voice scarcely louder than the crickets, "that is exactly how I should like to kiss you."

THREE

BAD BOYS

What's the matter with you?" Jobe demanded. "You hurt?"
David didn't look at the young man.

"No," he said. "No, I don't think so."

He wasn't hurt, he knew. He had checked himself well for injuries, especially on the head, because a gaping skull wound would best explain the happenings of the last few hours. But, sadly, his scalp wasn't lacerated in the slightest. That meant that either everything he had lately seen was real — or he was clinically insane.

He had to consider the possibility that he was still suffering from the drugs Aster's father had slipped him. But that explanation made less and less sense as time went on. The monster he had just seen did not exist in his world, and neither did warm rivers freeze spontaneously. An old man in cowboy boots could not bring fire from dry leaves without a match — no, not just a fire, but a whirlwind of soot and flame — and he could not fire lightning from an old forty-five.

That meant he wasn't in his world, but in some sort of absurd fantasy land.

And he could not bring himself to believe he would hallucinate such a thing. Not when he spent eight hours a day trying to divert his students from such worthless drivel, to convince them to discover literature instead. He challenged them to read Homer, Virgil, the nameless author of Beowulf, Shakespeare, Chaucer, Dante, Swift, Blake, Cervantes, Milton, Voltaire, Melville, Joyce, Huxley, Faulkner, Vonnegut—authors who spoke to universal human conditions, whose works could increase the soul; not escapist pabulum by half-literate hacks about elves, fairies, dark lords, and dragons whose only notion was to entertain at the lowest level that writing could achieve.

Yes, he might hallucinate the boys—they could be straight out of Twain, or Faulkner. But the rest of it—the *magic*, for God's sake—no.

So that left him with it being real, which just made him feel dirty. It could only be worse if he was dropped into one of the teen romances the seventh-grade girls read.

Worse, but safer.

Fortunately, the Sheriff didn't give him much more time to think about it. Whatever magic he had, crossing deep moving water on horse was apparently not in it, so he pressed them south at a furious pace, until by noon of the next day they reached a ferry.

He paid the ferryman with a withering glance and a hand clapped to his pistols. It took them nearly an hour to get all the boys and their horses across. Then they started out again, alternating from painful trot to terrifying gallop. Still, David felt better now that they were actually moving toward Aster again. Even though he knew going south was the only way to catch up to her, it made him twitchy.

He knew the Sheriff was using him as a living compass, and he finally had to admit that that was magic, too. How could he know where she was? Her father's curse. Hypnosis couldn't give him what he now had to accept as supernatural powers. Or one magical power, at least.

He had tried talking to some of the boys, but they seemed singularly uninterested in anything he had to say, which was really okay with him. Teenage girls could be cruel, but they were usually subtle, which he could appreciate. Boys were cruel right on the surface, and usually physically so. He could tell they didn't think much of him, and he couldn't think of anything that might change that.

So he was surprised when Jobe rode up beside him the next day.

"So you're a schoolteacher," he said.

"Yes," David replied. "That I am."

"I used to like it when we had school. Before."

"Are all of the adults really—ah, cursed?"

"Every one," he said. "'Cept you and the Sheriff. Now the Sheriff is a special case. But that don't explain you."

"No, it *doesn't*," David corrected. "But I'm not from here."

"From another Kingdom, then?"

"From another world, I think," he said. "A different place."

"From the Ghost Country, you mean."

"Well, I'm not a ghost," David said.

"But you come from the same place as that girl, Aster."

"Yes, I *came* from there," David said.

"How come?"

"To bring her back to her father," he said. "Her father sent me."

"Is she your girl, then?"

He almost said yes, and for a moment he didn't know why. But examining it a little better, he knew.

"Where I'm from," he said, "it's not appropriate for a man my age to be involved with a girl her age."

"She's what, sixteen, seventeen?"

"About that, yes."

"I don't get it, then."

"Well, it's just the case," he said.

"But you're a man," Jobe said. "That ain't gonna stop you, is it?"

David laughed uncomfortably, but didn't actually answer.

"Yeah," Jobe said, "you sweet on her. You got that look in your eye. But you know as well as I do that there never was a woman that Hell didn't make. I keep back from 'em myself. Oh, I take what the Bible says, and all—I'm a man—but I don't get the feeling for them. That's just trouble, getting attached, ain't it?"

David was trying to think of something to say, but then Jobe slapped him on the arm.

"You whipped, son," he said. "And that means you doomed."

Laughing, he rode off ahead.

After that, the boys called him Whipped.

The next day they came to a village. It was about the same size as the last. They rode in about midday. A few chickens scattered in the streets as they arrived, but of human beings, David didn't see a sign.

The sheriff gave a loud blow on his horn, and then followed it with his own raised voice.

"I am Sheriff of the Marches. If any here harbors what is mine, I aim to collect."

After nearly a minute of silence a voice hollered from one of the unpaned windows.

"We ain't got nothing of yours, Sheriff."

"Come out and swear it to me."

After another pregnant pause a door cracked open, and thin girl with black curly hair and a complexion almost as dark stepped out.

"My name is Hannah Culpepper," she said. "And I testify there ain't no one here that you're looking for."

David already knew that. Aster wasn't here, hadn't been here. He told the Sheriff so.

The man put his blue-eyed gaze on David. For a moment he felt fear for his life, but then the Sheriff shrugged and kept riding through town. David felt a sense of relief without knowing why.

But the Sheriff's horse had only walked a few yards before Jobe spoke up.

"Sheriff, Sir," he said. "We're low on provisions. Lost the most of them back at the river, and I reckon we've got a ways to go."

The Sheriff nodded.

"Well," he said, "find what you can."

He started on again, and David's horse started after. David tugged at the reins, but the animal — as usual — ignored him.

"You heard him, girl," Jobe yelled at Hannah. "Load us up some provisions, quick."

David felt a sudden sink in his belly. Back in the town near where the boys lived, he'd thought there was going to be a fight. But there had been other adults, and Jobe and his rowdies were related to most of them.

Here, though . . .

"The Sheriff ain't got no right nor call to requisition of'en us," she announced.

"Don't he?" Jobe said.

"I know the law. You do too. We have to give up a fugitive. That's where it ends. Our crops been bad, and we got nothing to spare."

"Yeah?" Jobe said. He dismounted and walked up the girl.

"Listen, girl, you do what I say, and you do it quick."

For answer, Hannah lifted her chin in defiance.

Jobe punched her square. David heard the sound of her jaw snapping. He saw teeth spit out a moment later as the girl went to her knees.

A gunshot rang out, and wood splintered on the boards of the house, about a foot from Jobe.

Turning, David saw a billow of smoke from another window. Jobe drew out his pistol.

"They tried to murder me, boys," he said. "Let 'em have Hell."

"No!" David screamed, and tried to turn his horse, but the Sheriff put a hard hand upon his reins.

"Keep riding," he said. "I won't have you killed by a stray bullet."

"You can't let them do this!" He said.

"This is none of my concern," said the Sheriff.

David looked back, despairing as the figures became more remote and consequently more unreal. It looked like everyone was shooting now, and gray smoke billowed from several buildings.

As it turned out, David got to watch the whole town burn, because the Sheriff settled in on the next ridge to wait for his militia. They turned up hours later, their horses groaning with loot.

And girls. They had tied them all on one long string of rope. Some couldn't keep pace and were essentially dragged.

"We didn't lose a man," Jobe bragged, when they reached the hilltop. He winked at David. "I know the Sheriff wouldn't let you fight, but there's plenty to go around."

"You need to let those girls go," David said. "You can't do this."

"He's right," the Sheriff said. "They'll slow us down too much. Anything that's not food, drink, or ammunition stays here."

"Sure," Jobe said. "But we can keep them 'til morning, right?"

To that, the Sheriff merely shrugged and walked away.

"Jobe," David said. "Think about your own sisters. Your cousins."

"That's the brilliant thing, Whipped," Jobe said. "Ain't no one here I'm any kin to. Now, are you in or not?"

There was something different about Jobe, an odd cast to his skin, a metallic glint in his eye, a musky scent that David didn't recognize. And he knew there was no talking the boy out of this.

David surveyed the captives.

"Sure," he said, finally. "I'll take that one."

"Hannah?" Jobe said. "I was kind of looking forward to having her myself. But she's half rurnt, with that busted face. Go on, you get her. Do you want some whisky?"

It was tempting. Really tempting after what he had seen today.

"No," he said, "I had better not."

He took Hannah far from the rest, on a quiet hillside overlooking a lake. The sun was melting against the horizon. She studied him with eyes full of suffering and fear, but through all of that he could see the light in her. It wasn't as bright as Aster's, but it was lovely nonetheless.

"Have a seat," he said. "Let me have a look at that mouth."

"You don't have no call to hurt me," she said.

"I'm not going to hurt you," he said.

"No call at all."

He brought up a damp rag. "I'm just going to clean you up a little."

"Are you gonna kill me?" she asked. "I just want to know."

"No, Hannah," he said. "I'm not like them."

"You ain't?" she said. "What's that, then?"

She pointed at him, to show what she meant, but he already knew.

"That's . . . I don't know," he said. "It's adrenaline, I guess. It's not what you think. It's not my fault."

"You just like them," she said. "You just don't know it yet."

He put his head down, unable to meet the fierceness and the terror mingled in her eyes.

"I'm not," he said, feeling miserable.

"You ain't crossed the line yet," she said. "And I pray you don't cross it with me."

"I won't," he said. "I won't."

H ung over as they were, the Sheriff managed to get the boys up at sunrise. David watched the girls straggle back toward town, wondering what they were going back to. Had all of the boys in the town been killed? Would they starve when winter came?

It wasn't the Sheriff's business. Maybe it shouldn't be his, either. After all, there wasn't anything he could do to help them. That being the case, anything he felt about them was wasted emotion.

Get Aster and get back to the real world. That's all he should care about. It was all he should focus on.

But the Sheriff was a problem, in that regard. Because he had a feeling that once the Sheriff had Aster, he wasn't going to let David take her back to her father. So he needed a plan.

It got easier, after that, to have the single, practical problem to occupy him. That way he didn't have to think about Hannah, her bruised face and missing teeth, her misery and her defiance.

T hey didn't encounter any other towns of the size Jobe burnt, and the Sheriff kept them from ranging to look for more, but if they happened to come across a farmstead on their way — which happened more than David would have wished — it suffered the same fate. Now that they were released from what few inhibitions they had left, they had become truly monstrous, and he was certain now their bodies were changing as well. Most had taken to going shirtless, and the muscles along their arms and backs pulled in unnatural ways. Most had odd, discolored patches in their skin. The horses seemed more nervous around them.

Only the Sheriff could check them, but David foresaw that eventually Jobe might decide the fortune of his gang needn't be tied to the taciturn rider.

A couple of days later, they started down into a valley beyond which rose a line of hills.

They were greeted by gunfire.

First came the hissing of the bullets, like angry hornets tearing through the trees, and then the stuttered booms. A boy named Jeb screamed; his horse went wild and threw him to lie groaning on the earth.

"Dismount," the Sheriff shouted. "Take cover."

David was already scrambling down.

"They're at a good distance," the Sheriff told Jobe.

"Can't you proof against bullets, or some such?" Jobe asked. He didn't look or sound particularly scared.

The Sheriff didn't answer, but gave a low whistle. His dogs took off at a run in the direction of the gunshots.

"Bring the boys up behind that bank," the Sheriff told Jobe, gesturing at a creek about a hundred feet ahead of them. "Pass these out." He handed Jobe a box of cartridges.

David crawled over to Jeb, who was pretty much being ignored. Jeb looked up at him. He seemed in pain, but mostly confused.

The bullet had caught him in the collarbone. David guessed it was probably broken. He had steeled himself against the sight of the blood, but found that it didn't particularly bother him. What he wasn't sure about was what to do.

He cut strips of cloth from Jeb's shirt, got some water from the canteen and dabbed at it. Predictably, Jeb screamed, but

David kept at it. He was surprised to see the bullet, nested in pink, finely shattered bone.

"It's not so bad," he told Jeb.

But then he realized the boy wasn't breathing anymore, and his eyes were like glass.

"No," David said. "Jeb, you can't be dead. It's not that bad. It's hardly even bleeding anymore."

But Jeb kept that empty, accusing gaze on him, and the little light that was in him leaked away.

David only looked up at the crack of more gunfire, this time very near. Gasping, he scooted behind a tree, but then he realized it was the Sheriff and Jobe's boys firing. Even though it was daylight, the muzzle flashes hurt his eye, and the sound was high and sharp for rifles. A sort of dark cloud surrounded the boys, fretted with green strobes of light. As it grew thicker their bodies seemed to shift and change.

In the direction they were shooting, the sky was darkening with unnatural speed.

They were a hundred feet away, and none of them were paying him any attention at all. Still, he hesitated. If the Sheriff caught him . . .

But the familiar pain began. He had to get Aster. He had to take her back to her father.

So he ran, not toward the Sheriff, but off to his right. He ran as he had never run before.

Behind him, the gunfire continued.

FOUR
TO WAR

E rrol was sitting in the side of the square feeling everything was a little too calm, when he was proven right. Shouts went up around the village, and a minute later, strange riders came in. Errol swung up on his feet immediately, because these fellows looked more like Jobe's gang than Chula and his. But Chula greeted them calmly enough. After a few minutes of talking, things were less calm. Runners went off and more boys came back, armed.

Errol caught Chula and asked him what was going on.

"A gang is coming this way," he said. "They've been burning towns and homesteads."

"A man with two hounds, one black and one white?" Errol said. Chula nodded.

"That's the sheriff," Errol said. "He's after us. We should leave—then he'll leave you alone."

"You would deprive us of a chance to fight?" Chula said. "To show our bravery?"

He seemed as serious as cancer.

"If that's the case," Dusk's soft voice came from behind, "you must allow us the honor of fighting with you."

"If you wish," Chula said.

"How long will it take for them to get here?" Errol asked.

"The sun will be halfway from noon to sundown." .

"That's not long," Errol said.

"It's long enough," Chula grinned.

But Errol wondered if he really knew what he was in for.

T he boys painted black and red jags around their eyes — it
   looked like they were weeping lightning. They brandished
guns and bows, tomahawks and clubs. Errol's hands were too
clumsy to work either a bow or gun, so he chose a club, a single
solid piece of wood with a heavy ball carved at the business
end.

He was swinging it experimentally when Veronica came up.

"What are you going to do with that?" she asked.

"Fight, I guess. The Sheriff has caught up with us."

"Has he," she said. She studied the boys. "He's tough, Errol.
And he's mean."

"Well, he's our problem," Errol said. "It's us he wants."

She nodded. "I suppose I could tag along."

"Why don't you stay here?" he asked.

"I didn't ask permission, Errol," Veronica said. "Did you try
to talk Dusk out of going?"

He hadn't, and he didn't want to say so, but Veronica just
sighed and patted his arm.

"Oh, Errol," she said.

C hula took them up a winding trail to a ridge with a good
   view of the country. A dense marsh lay at the foot of the
hill, and a band of forest, but beyond that the land opened out
into prairie and little copses of trees.

"There," Chula said.

Errol saw them, tiny with distance.

Chula and six other boys came up to the front with long rifles and waited. Errol watched the riders enter the edge of the forest.

Chula and his shooters raised their guns to their shoulders and took careful aim. Errol wondered what they were aiming at—he couldn't see more than the occasional movements through the trees.

But they started to shoot.

After that, things got messy quick.

The air felt suddenly heavy, the sunlight dimmed. There were no storm clouds; it was more like dark glass had been passed between them and the light—and it kept getting darker until the solar disk was paler than the moon.

A cloud of what looked like black confetti blew up from the woods below, moving impossibly fast. Chula and the others threw themselves down flat, but Errol stood riveted by the sight.

Something slapped him in the face and in the arm and belly. He winced as cries of pain went up around him, but he didn't feel anything. He looked down, but something was covering his eyes.

He reached up and pulled off a scorpion nearly as big as his hand.

"God!" he yelped, crushing the deadly thing and batting off the others that had fastened to him. He saw Veronica calmly picking scorpions off of herself and smashing them underfoot. Dusk's armor had spared her; but half a dozen of Chula's boys were on the ground, racked with agony.

Those that could stood and shot again. This time they were answered with tarantulas the size of softballs.

Untroubled by their stings and bites, Errol set himself to crushing the vermin, but they seemed to be multiplying, somehow. He thumped spiders off of the nearest warrior, then stomped them on the ground. He was lifting his foot to smash another when a snake suddenly darted from behind him. Reflexively he yelped and hopped back, but then he saw the snake strike a scorpion and quickly gulp it down. A bullfrog the size of a kitten leapt on another, and suddenly the ridge was swarming with reptiles and amphibians all going after the bugs. He noticed Veronica standing alone, her eyes faintly glowing like phosphorescent algae and a weird smile on her face.

He gave her an uncertain thumbs up, and she returned the gesture.

A glance back down the hill showed him figures coming up the slope, fast. It was Jobe and his boys, but moving more quickly than seemed possible. It was not just that, but something about the *way* they ran that seemed all wrong.

Chula's remaining riflemen fired again. One of Jobe's boys pitched back and flipped several times as he went down the hill. Then he hopped back up and continued in the same, loping gait. Errol saw the Sheriff emerge from the woods and break into a canter.

Chula saw it too.

"Back," he cried.

The boys fell into a disorderly retreat, some dragging those who had fallen. Errol picked up two of the boys and started down the hill, trying not to stumble.

He followed Chula into the swamp on a winding little path. Thick columns of cypress thrust up from the surrounding water, and not far away, Errol heard something big stirring.

"Just hold off a few minutes, grandpa," he heard Chula mutter.

Then they were through, climbing to higher ground and a fallow field beyond. At the field's far edge, Chula stopped running, and had his warriors form up in a rough line.

Of the eighteen they had started with, only ten were still standing, and that counted Errol, Veronica, and Dusk. Most of the others moaned with pain, and a few had stopped moving altogether.

Errol remembered Shecky's ointment. He withdrew it and gave it to Veronica.

"See if this helps," he said. Then he turned to face the swamp.

He heard screams from the darkness, and a ragged crackle, like lightning. Something reared up above the trees, a creature that gave him an impression of both snake and crawfish before it plunged back from sight.

"That's grandpa," Chula said. "Let's hope he stays in there."

Errol was going to ask exactly what Grandpa was when Jobe and about six of his boys came out of the swamp.

As they drew closer, he saw their skin was all grey, and their teeth were sharp, like those of cats.

Dusk had hafted her spearhead onto a new pole; now she set it and charged. She struck Jobe straight on, and Errol figured that was the end of him, but instead Jobe just wrapped himself around the spear and pushed it into the ground. Dusk let go in time and reached for her sword, but another of the boys made an impossible running jump and tackled her off of Drake's back.

Errol bellowed and charged after her. He pulled the boy off of her and punched him in the face, as hard as he could, and then again. He dropped him as three more swarmed on him, and he was just realizing how *dense* they were, as if their whole bodies were made of bone. The recipient of his haymakers was actually coming back up on his feet.

Dusk rose and put her back against his, and together they fought whatever-it-was the boys had become.

One of them lost an arm to Dusk's shining blade, and they backed off. For a moment he thought they were going to quit, but then he heard a sharp report. Dusk made a funny sound and then sagged against his back. Errol punched the guy in front of him and swung around to see Jobe holding a smoking pistol. Dusk staggered forward, trying to lift her sword, and Jobe fired again. Then one of Chula's boys arrived, whaling away at him with a tomahawk.

Dusk had fallen on her face. Errol stood to defend her, knowing suddenly that they were going to lose this fight.

Then he heard Veronica singing.

Trees splintered, and 'grandpa' came out of the swamp, moving horrifyingly fast.

"Run," Veronica said. "I can't control him for long."

She handed him the ointment, and glanced down at Dusk.

"Go ahead," Veronica said. "I'll be along."

So he cradled Dusk in his arms and ran.

Her armor hadn't protected her from the bullets; one had gone through her chest and another a little above where her belly button would be.

He ran over a hill, followed closely by Chula and his warriors.

Fearing it was too late, he began undoing the fastenings of Dusk's armor, trying not to look at her drawn, bloodless face.

He got the breastplate off. She had a quilted shirt underneath, now wet and sticky with blood. He peeled it up, found the lower bullet hole and smeared some of the ointment into it. Then he shucked it up further until he found the second wound and treated it, too.

That was all he could do. He got back up, ready to fight again. Chula was at the top of the ridge, also looking back, but there was nothing to see except Veronica, walking slowly — and it seemed to him unsteadily — across the field.

A ster stepped outside when she heard the gunfire. Sensible
went with her, but cautioned the younger girls back in.

"That's Chula and his Reds," she said. "I wonder who
they're shooting at."

Whoever it was answered a few minutes later. Shadow
fell across the village, and in the distance Aster saw figures in
motion on the town square. She started that way, but Sensible
caught her arm.

"You can't help," she said.

"I can," she said. "I have some sorcery."

"That you may," Sensible said, "but the boys will wither if
you come near them. Stay here and protect us."

More shots rang out, and stranger sounds, like fabric
ripping.

"It's the Sheriff," Aster said. "I'm sure of it. He's here for
us."

"Of course it is," Sensible said. "And Chula is ready for
him."

They had begged Aster for stories, and not knowing that
many she had told them of her journeys in the kingdoms thus
far. She had done a fair amount of editing, but Sensible knew
about the Sheriff.

Sensible was probably right. Veronica had come to see her
the day before, and mentioned that Billy had taken ill. In fact,
Aster was pretty sure that was the only reason Veronica had
come, because she didn't have a lot else to say.

The gunfire went on for a while, nearly continuous at first
but then it dropped off until it was like the last few kernels of
popcorn in the popper, and then silence.

Aster went back into the hut. Yelps had gone back to the
village, but another girl, Summer, had joined them just after.

"Shall I plait up your hair?" Summer asked.

She wanted to say no, but the girl was so sincere and proud of her hair-plaiting ability, Aster just nodded and sat in front of her.

"I've never seen such fine, pretty hair," the girl said.

For a hot moment Aster thought Summer was making fun of her, but then the tone registered, and she could read nothing disingenuous in it, so she tried to relax.

"I wish someone would come from the village with news," Mockingbird said, making vocal Aster's own thoughts.

It wasn't long before the wish was granted. A girl nick-named Heedless showed up.

"Chula and his Reds tricked them in through the swamp," she said. "Snake Crawfish and the Horned Frog chased them back across Muddy Creek. Now it's Sunday, so they can't cross back, not until tomorrow, and I'll bet Jezebel will have a word about that."

"Were any killed?" Sensible asked.

Heedless nodded solemnly. "The chief's third son, the son of Walking Wolf, Mortar Red's youngest. Stone Breaker's son might not live out the night, but he might."

"And my friends?"

"Fought well," the girl said. "The one with the armor, Dusk—she was shot. She might not live. Jezebel is with her. The other two are okay."

"Billy?" she asked.

"He couldn't fight," Heedless replied, a touch of reproof in her voice.

J ezebel looked a lot like Hattie, but older. When she stepped out of the townhouse—which was now serving as a sort of hospital—her eyes fastened on Errol.

"She will live," she said.

"I wasn't sure the ointment would work," Errol said.

She smiled. "I've seen that ointment before," she said. "You've made the acquaintance of my cousin Shecky."

"Yes, Ma'am," Errol said.

"You can tell me about that later," she said. "I'm sure it's a good story, seeing as how the Sheriff was involved. Anyway, the ointment alone couldn't have saved her — it's not that powerful. But that and her high-and-far-off blood kept her alive until I could bring my modest skills to bear."

"Thank you," Errol said.

"I've others to tend to," Jezebel said. "Let her rest; give her until morning before you visit."

He watched her go back into the townhouse, uncertain what to do until he noticed Veronica, sitting in the shadows, legs crossed and head down.

He walked over.

"Well, you saved us again," he said.

"Yeah," she said. "Go, me." Her voice sounded strained.

"Are you okay?" he asked.

"Sure," she replied. "I just need to catch my breath."

He noticed she was holding her hand across her belly.

"What's that?" he asked.

For answer she took her pointer finger and poked at her dress. The finger went into her stomach all the way to the third knuckle.

"How do you like that?" she said.

"Jesus. Does it hurt?"

"Not in the least. But I have a hole in me, Errol. That's not right."

"Will it heal?"

"I don't know," she said. "I've never been shot before."

"Look," he said. "We're going to help Aster finish this thing, and we'll get that water or whatever, and we'll be fixed up. Good as new. Better."

"Is Dusk okay?" she asked.

"She'll live."

"She's awesome," Veronica said.

"You're awesome," he replied.

"Huh," she said. "Well, of course I am. Except for being dead. And this hole." She looked up at him. Her eyes seemed to swallow the moonlight.

"Admit it," she said, pointing at her wound. "You think it's nasty."

"Close your eyes," he said.

"Why?"

"Humor me," he said.

"Fine."

"Now imagine your heart beating, and air coming in and out of your lungs."

"Errol . . ." she began, but he stopped her with a kiss.

"If I had flesh and bone," he said when it was over, "that is exactly how I would like to kiss you."

Veronica leaned her head against his shoulder.

"That's really sweet, Errol," she said.

Then, after a moment's pause, she chuckled.

"What?" he said.

"You realize that 'freaks' doesn't even begin to describe us, don't you?"

FIVE

HIDDEN

Aster was clear of the "Moon's Portion" by morning, but she wasn't allowed to go anyplace until she had bathed in the stream. She did that as soon as it was light enough to see. The water was surprisingly cold, but she found herself enjoying it. She washed her clothes, too, as best she could, and hung them on branches to dry. Then she dressed in the clean clothes the girls had given her; a knee-length dress of soft deerskin and knee-high moccasins of the same material. She sat for a few minutes, and was watching a crawfish emerge from hiding in the creek bottom when she heard a soft footfall and looked up.

She had seen a lot of things most people wouldn't believe since crashing her car in the Marches; but she had been prepared for them, had been preparing her whole life, reading her father's books, questioning him when he would talk. Obviously she had gaps in her knowledge; she hadn't known about the menstruation thing, for instance.

Now, for the first time, she saw something that was to her not only unbelievable, but inconceivable.

"Mr. Watkins?" she said, rising and backing up.

"Yes, Aster, it's me."

She knew creatures existed that could take any form they wanted, who could read your desire and appear as its incarnation. But why would such a creature appear as Mr. Watkins? She hadn't given him a thought since her father had distilled him.

"You father sent me for you," he said.

"Okay," she said, more to herself than to him. "*That* actually makes sense."

She took in the whole image, then. When she had last seen Mr. Watkins he had been in his usual uniform; a stylish black suit and tie, white shirt, and snakeskin shoes.

The jacket and tie were gone, but he still had on the pants and white shirt, the latter of which was hardly white anymore but soiled with mud, ash, and what appeared to be dried blood. His normally neat hair was a mess, and a dark shadow of young beard had crept across his face. He also had a wild sort of look in his eye that she didn't care for.

It suddenly occurred to her that he had appeared conveniently soon after she had dressed.

"Yes," he said. "If any of this makes sense. He sent me for you, and now I've found you, so let's go while we can."

She took another step back.

"Mr. Watkins, I'm sorry if my father inconvenienced you by sending you to fetch me, but I'm not in need of fetching. I came here to do something, and I'm going to do it."

He sighed and took another step forward.

"If you only knew what I've been through," he said.

"I'm sorry," she replied. "But it was not my choice."

"Aster, there is a bad man near here, and he has with him some very bad young men. I won't tell you the things I've seen them do, because they are unspeakable."

"You mean the Sheriff."

"You don't know him," Mr. Watkins said. "He won't stop until he gets you, and then I really fear for what will happen to you. Please, let me help you."

"You've been with the Sheriff?"

"I was his prisoner," Mr. Watkins said. "I got away from him during the fighting."

"He can't reach me here," she said.

"He'll wait. And when you leave he'll catch you. Let me take you where you'll be safe."

He sounded sincere almost to the point of being unhinged.

"I must decline your offer, sir," she said. She backed away, but he sloshed into the stream.

"Wait," he said. "Just wait. At least tell me why. What's so important about this place you would risk your life?"

She suddenly felt sorry for him. She doubted that her father had talked Mr. Watkins into coming here; almost certainly he had compelled him with a spell of some sort. He deserved, at least, to know what was going on.

"My father," she said. "He's sick. There's something wrong with his memory."

"I gathered that much," Mr. Watkins said.

"There is something here that can heal him. I have to find it."

"Find what?" he asked.

"A special sort of water," she said.

"So you're on a quest for some sort of magical cure?" he said. "Aster, listen to yourself. Listen to me. What your father has is a damaged hippocampus. It's a well-known medical condition. It's not magical, and there's no miracle cure for it."

"You asked," Aster said. "I told you. Goodbye."

"Don't go," he pleaded.

"I have to," she said.

"I meant what I said at school," he said. "About you being special. How someone would eventually figure it out, and how lucky they would be."

She saw where this was heading now, and she really didn't like it.

"Stop this, Mr. Watkins," she said.

"Why would I say those things, do you think?"

She realized she was angry, now.

"Because I'm weird," she said. "Because I don't have any friends, and I'm not pretty. So that makes me easy. You think if you tell me I'm *sooo* special and *sooo* beautiful that no one can even see it but you, I'll gratefully fall into the sack with you."

His mouth fell open.

"That's what you think of me?" he said.

"Pretty much," she replied.

"But that's not true. Aster, I have feelings for you. I know I shouldn't—I don't want to—but I have them. You have a light in you —"

"This is nuts," Aster said. "And I'm not listening to another word of this."

"You have to!" he said. "I love you!"

He said it with such utter conviction, with such desperate desire. It wasn't flattering, or amusing, or annoying.

It was terrifying.

"You heard me," he said. "I can't think of anything but you. Without you I'll lose my mind. I'll wither away. I'll die, Aster!"

"Okay," she said. "I'm officially gone."

That's when he came at her with an expression on his face as unreadable as it was chilling. She didn't have time to be original; she used the same Utterance as she had against Shecky. When the wind died down he was lying, groaning, on the other side of the stream. She ran, looking back often, until he was out of sight.

When Errol peaked in on Dusk the next morning, he found her sitting up on the edge of the bed. She was dressed in the same buckskins most of the women in the village wore, and her hair was down, hanging in dense curls. He had seen her without her armor before, but she had always kept on the padded gambeson. Without it she seemed younger, somehow, softer.

"Errol," she said. "You saved my life."

"I did what you would have done," he said.

"Well, thank you," she said. "I'm in your debt. Again."

"Don't worry about it."

She nodded. "You fought well," she said.

"*We* fought well," he replied. "I think our teamwork has improved."

"Since we got stuck to the Snatchwitch?" she said. "I should hope so."

She looked past him. "And you, Veronica. I heard you turned the tide of the battle."

Veronica slipped in behind him. He felt her hand rest a little possessively on his shoulder.

"Just doing my usual creepy thing," she said. "Do I get to be included in the team?"

"Of course," Dusk replied. "The three of us are unstoppable."

Approaching the townhouse, Aster heard her companions congratulating themselves, and waited to enter until they were done.

Aster didn't ask if she was on their little 'team.' She didn't have to. Yet again she had been left out of their adventures.

"I'm glad to see you're all okay," she said, trying to keep the false little smile frozen on her face.

"Nice braid," Veronica said. "How was the sleepover?" She leaned against Errol.

Aster started to retort, but knew it would only make things worse, so instead she decided to get on with things, if she still could.

"Just aces," she said. "Except Mr. Watkins just tried to kidnap me."

"Mr. Watkins?" Errol said.

"Yeah. Apparently Dad had a lucid moment and sent him after me. He's been riding with the Sheriff."

"Well, where is he now?" Errol asked.

"I don't know," Aster replied.

"But you just saw him," he said. "Don't you think we ought to keep an eye on him?"

"Something is wrong with him," Aster said. "His cheese has slipped off of his cracker, if you know what I mean."

"I can say with certainty I have no idea what you mean," Dusk said.

"She means he's a few clowns shy of a circus," Veronica explained.

"That doesn't clear things up," Dusk said.

"She means he's crazy," Errol said. He turned back to Aster. "Crazy how?"

"He was . . ." she twitched her nose to the side and suddenly couldn't make eye contact.

"He tried to attack me," she said. "He was saying crazy things."

"Like?" Veronica asked.

She sighed, really not wanting to say. But they needed to know.

"Like, he loves me and can't think of anything but me," she said in a rush.

"Yes," Veronica said. "That's positively certifiable. This is that teacher, right?"

Errol was nodding, and at first Aster thought he was agreeing with Veronica.

"I don't know," he said. "There were rumors about him. And he kind of watched you a lot, Aster."

Aster felt her face warm. "What do you mean, 'watched me'?"

"I don't know. He would always look at you when you came in the door. And one time he asked me about you, if I knew what your story was."

"Yeah, that I believe," Aster said. "But that doesn't mean anything. Trust me, he's lost it. We are *not* inviting him along. And speaking of that, there are only so many hours in a Sunday. We should talk to Jezebel."

"Billy is already at her place," Errol said. "We were just waiting on you."

J ezebel's place turned out to be a treehouse perched thirty feet above the ground between two twin oaks on the outskirts of town. It had an odd, wandering floor plan dictated more by the limbs that supported it than by any sense of architecture. Jezebel had changed into a calico dress decorated with hundreds of tiny silver bells. Errol wondered if she was a snatchwitch during the week, like her sister, or if she took the form of some other sort of monster — perhaps something with wings, given the nest-like nature of her house.

Billy was seated next to her.

"Come in," she said. "Make yourselves comfortable. Billy has been explaining your quest to me — and some of your difficulties."

"I'm sorry the Sheriff followed us here," Aster said. "I didn't mean to bring trouble."

"Oh, it's the Sheriff," she said. "I don't blame you for him. And the boys that died did so bravely, which is all anyone can ask."

Errol thought one could ask for a lot more than that, but he didn't say so.

"I don't even understand what he wants," Aster said. "Not really."

"Well," Jezebel said. "You worked magic beyond the Pale, and that got his attention. He's supposed to prevent that sort of thing. And he's supposed to keep beings like your friends here from that world as well."

"Yes," Aster said. "But we aren't in our world. We're here."

"Ah, but in his mind you've broken the law, and must be punished."

"That's sort of psychotic," Errol said.

"Well, he's bitter," Jezebel said. "He once was someone in the Kingdoms, a powerful man. Becoming Sheriff was a punishment. He's exiled from the Kingdoms, except when his duty allows him here. He believes that if he keeps the law and enforces it well, he will be allowed to return." She patted Aster's hand.

"He won't come in my village. We have a different bargain in these parts, different laws, which is why he tried to enter the village by force. But if you leave this place, you will have to deal with him, I fear. You are welcome to remain here. Eventually the Sheriff will find other offenses to occupy him."

"I can't stay," Aster said. "I have to go on."

"Hang on," Errol said. "Do we even have a place to go? Do you know where we can find this giant?"

Jezebel nodded. "Yes. But I advise against the journey."

"I won't quit," Aster said. "And I won't wait."

Jezebel shrugged. "Beyond these hills lies the Hollow Sea. Cross that and you'll reach the Mountains of the Wind. In a valley on the slopes of those peaks you will find the orchard, and the giant. It isn't an easy journey, even without the hounds of the March on your trail."

"I didn't think it would be easy," Aster said.

"You will have my help," Dusk said. "If you still want it."

"I'll go," Billy added.

"Looks like you have all the helpers you need," Veronica said. She was standing close enough to Errol he could feel her presence. She was starting to seem more possessive, always close to him, leaning against him and such. He liked it, sort of, but he worried what the others might think was going on. Not that very much could be happening, obviously, and it was stupid to think Dusk would have any interest in him.

But there it was. As impossible as it was, he wanted Dusk to like him, and if she thought something was going on between him and Veronica . . .

He lifted his mechanical hand and looked at it.

Stupid, he thought.

He realized that Aster was talking to Veronica.

"I promised you I would do what I could to return you to life and health if you helped me," she said. "That still stands, even if you want to stay here." She glanced at Errol. "That goes for you, too."

"Okay," Errol said. "But I'm going. Whoever said anything about not going?"

Aster shrugged. "Okay then. Thank you."

Jezebel sighed. "You had best start packing now," she said. "Chula and some of the boys will escort you as far as they can and then lay some false trails. Now the rest of you get along. I need to talk to Aster alone."

O nce the others were gone, Jezebel sat her in a chair across from her. She stared at her so hard that Aster felt like an insect, pinned to a board by the woman's gaze. But then the old woman flashed a weary little smile.

"Hattie sent you to me with the hope that you could end our curse," she said. "But I don't know if I see that. At least not yet. But hope lives and hides in strange places, and I see no reason not to help you with your immediate troubles."

"Thank you," Aster said.

"I say 'immediate' because even if you succeed, you will only be opening a larger box of worries, dear."

"Well, I'll bear that in mind."

Jezebel shrugged. "I want to show you something," she said. She lifted the lid of a cedar box and brought out a hand mirror. She held it up so Aster could see her reflection.

"Did you know about this?" she asked.

A little shock when through her. On her forehead was a small golden star.

"No," she whispered.

"I didn't think so," the old lady replied.

"Dusk has a star like this," she said. "What does it mean?"

"To begin with," she said. "It means that you, like she, are a child of an Elder Kingdom, one of most high and far-off places."

"Are we relatives?"

"Can't you see the resemblance in your faces?" Jezebel asked.

"No," Aster said. "She's so beautiful, and I . . ." she shook her head.

"That is what prevents you seeing the resemblance," Jezebel said. "The way you think of yourself. Look harder, child."

Aster studied her face, realizing as she did so that it had been a long time since she had looked in a mirror. Why should she? She didn't wear make-up or do anything fancy with her hair. Any other use of a mirror was pure vanity, which she had no time for. And she knew what she looked like.

But now she saw what the old woman meant. She had the same high, broad cheekbones as Dusk, the same heart-shaped face, pointed chin, and large, almond-shaped eyes.

The face in the mirror had only a little resemblance to the one she held in her mind.

"This mirror," she said. "It shows hidden things?"

"The only thing about your face that is hidden is the star," Jezebel said.

"I guess Dad did that," she said. "But it must have been way back, or I would remember."

"I could make it visible," Jezebel said. "But if your father went to such great lengths—and he must have—to hide it, maybe it's best it remains unseen."

"Probably," Aster agreed.

"Good. Then go find your friends."

"I'm not sure they're all my friends," Aster said, and instantly regretted it. It was true, but why had she told Jezebel? She had just been told not to show weakness, and here she was whining about people not liking her.

"You'll sort that out too," the old lady said.

SIX
A RAINBOW AND A HOLLOW SEA

D avid felt it when Aster left town. He tried to follow her, of course, but the compass in his head betrayed him and brought him hard up against hills that proved unclimbable. Not that he didn't try; torn fingernails and briar scratches on most of his exposed skin testified to that. When the direct approach failed, he tried to find a way around or at least a break in the steep ridge that would let him to the other side.

It was daylight before he found such a place, and he felt Aster receding. But the going was easier beyond the hills, and the sickness in his heart relented. He was on her trail again.

He knew now that he had blown his chance, back at the stream. He shouldn't have tried talking to her. He should have grabbed her while she was bathing, gagged her, and tied her up with something. If he got another chance like that, he wasn't going to make the same mistake.

He'd only been across the hills for half an hour or so before he heard the hounds.

"Jesus, no," he muttered, and broke into a run. But even as he did so he knew it was hopeless. The dogs caught up with him an hour later, pinned him to the ground with their paws, and stayed on him until the Sheriff arrived.

Jobe's bunch was a little smaller, but all of the meanest ones seemed to have survived, which made sense. They also looked considerably less human than before, although they sounded the same when they talked.

He thought that the Sheriff would probably beat him, but not to death, since he still needed his unerring sense of Aster's direction.

But the Sheriff just signed for him to walk.

David took his cue and started in the right direction.

"You've got the smell of the north wind on you," the Sheriff said. "You talk to her?"

"Yes," David said. "For all the good it did."

"Did she say anything? About where she was going?"

David wasn't sure he ought to say anything, but he still felt the beating hanging over him, just waiting to happen. And he had been through enough.

"Her father is sick," he said. "She thinks there's some sort of water that can heal him."

"Ah," the Sheriff said. His gaze seemed to travel off toward the mountains. Then he switched his horse and rode ahead.

They all had horses again, so she no longer needed to ride double. Aster had mixed feelings about that, and wondered if Billy would even let her touch him, after what had happened. He had hardly spoken two words to her since leaving Jezebel's.

Without really wanting to, she found herself riding behind and watching the others. Veronica, Errol, and Dusk rode close, laughing and talking, but it seemed to her that Errol was paying more attention to Dusk than Veronica, despite Veronica's hovering about him that morning.

She regarded Dusk with fresh eyes. Her father was the only person she knew from her family, so she'd had no sense of family resemblance until now. She wondered where Dusk was from and what their actual connection was. But mostly she wondered what was really going on. What were the odds that she would meet a cousin so soon after entering The Kingdoms? A cousin who was also far from home, in the region of the Marches where Aster and her father had once fled to Errol's world? In a world bereft of magic, the probability was impossibly low. But in a realm where magical forces like destiny, fate, and weird were as much a part of the natural order as wind and rain, the impossible could become likely. And yet even here, coincidence was rare. Fate was the product of past actions, of curses and prophecy, of wishes and dreams. Some force beyond them both might have brought her and Dusk together.

But the cleaner explanation was that Dusk had been looking for her. But if that was the case, why? And why hadn't she said anything? She was so much a part of their group now that it was easy to forget that they had met her only just over a week ago, and that her stated reason for joining them was—to Aster at least—vague and unconvincing.

D avid saw the land grow dry and strange, over the next few days. The trees shrank to bushes and became few, while the grass grew taller. The land rose up like a staircase built for giants, now so ancient and weathered that it was only rarely any trouble to ascend it. About twice a day they came to a crumbling escarpment and found some slope to mount.

He experienced all of this in a nightmare of pain. Only three of the horses had survived the last fight, and one was the Sheriff's. The other two were used for scouting ahead, which meant David and the rest of the boys were on foot. It made them slower than Aster's group, who all had horses, so the Sheriff pushed them hard, and David's feet became a mass of blisters. His whole body ached.

It slowed them even more when the boys had to hunt for food, but game was scarce, and David's belly was flat and empty.

Jobe enjoyed tormenting him.

"You ain't much, are you?" the boy taunted him one day. "Running off from the fight like that."

"I went to find her," he said. "Aster."

"Yeah. And she bloodied your nose something good, didn't she. No, you ain't much."

"What do you know?" David said. "You're as ignorant as they come."

"Well, that may be," Jobe replied. "But I don't see as how anything you've learnt from your books has done you much good."

"It's kept me human," he said. "It's kept me from becoming an animal, like you."

"What do you mean?" Jobe asked.

It seemed an odd question to David. Jobe's eyes were a peculiar lead color, and his skin had become mottled with short, bristling fur. His ears had sharpened, too, and he had claws instead of nails. His body had a human shape when he sat, but on his feet his gait had become strange and quick. The other boys were broadly the same, with variations in fur and eye color.

Of course he hadn't been talking about Jobe's appearance anyway, but it was strange Jobe didn't even consider taking his comment that way.

"I mean the way you act," he said. "How you are when we come to a village."

A mean grin twitched on Jobe's face. "Oh, that. That's nothing to do with your learning. That's just you being scared. That's you being a whiney little girl."

"I'm not *scared* to hurt people," David said. "I don't *want* to. It's not right. It's not what good people do."

"You tell me, Whipped, what Goddamn good people you're talking about? Our parents, that kill us for sport six days a week and expect us all 'yes sir and ma'am' on Sunday? Is that who you mean? You mean *you*?"

"I try," David said. "I try to make a difference."

"And how do you do that?" Jobe asked.

"I pass on what I know," David said. "I teach young men and women how to reason. I lead them to what the greatest thinkers in history have said and written—philosophy, poetry, literature. And from that they can come to lead thoughtful lives, become better people. There's more to life than just surviving, Jobe. As a great man once said, 'the unexamined life is not worth living.'"

"What does that mean?"

"It means you should always be trying to know yourself, to understand your actions," David said.

"Hell, I understand myself," Jobe said. "I want something, I take it if I can and deal with it if I can't. I watch my boys and they watch me. It ain't too hard."

David shook his head.

"You know what you want," he said. "A dog knows that. It's not the same as knowing who you are."

Jobe stared at him for a long moment.

"And you reckon you know who you are?" he asked.

"I know I try," David said.

"Well," Jobe said. He scratched himself behind the ear.

"That fellow," he said. "That said that. He alive still?"

"No," David said.

"How did he die?"

"People didn't like some of his ideas," David told him. "They said he was corrupting the youth and sentenced him to drink poison."

Jobe grinned nastily.

"Well, he might have thought his life was worth living," he said. "You know, on account of the examining and all—but I reckon those that disagreed got their way."

"That's not the point," David said, wearily.

"Your problem, preacher," Jobe said, "is you think you have a point. But you go on, examine yourself."

David started to say something, but then something hit him from behind. He gagged on the pain and fell roughly to the ground. Someone kicked him in the ribs, and when he managed to open his eyes he saw them, maybe ten of them, standing over him, growling low in the back of their throats. For a second he thought it might be over, but then they came at him again. He screamed, which they thought was funny, and he suddenly knew he was going to die. The sheer terror of it was like nothing he had ever experienced; worse than the scalding water he'd once spilled on his bare leg.

But he heard the Sheriff's horn, and a deep-throated shout, and the pummeling stopped. He couldn't open his eyes, and his ears were filled with the painful, shallow breaths thrashing in and out of his lungs.

"We need him," the Sheriff said.

nothing was broken, but everything hurt. He couldn't keep any sort of pace, so the Sheriff put him on his horse, where he rode bent over the saddle with his head on the beast's neck, oblivious to and uncaring about the land his mount's feet trod. The next day was a little better. The Sheriff gave him whisky, and he drank it in little sips throughout the day.

Near sundown they came to a neat little village of sod houses. He and the Sheriff climbed a hill and watched the boys ride down on it. David wanted to feel something about it, but to his despair found he couldn't. He felt as hollow as the empty shell of a cicada, split open and abandoned. His one shameful thought was that at least he would have something to eat.

The screaming and shooting started, and David slumped off and found a rock to sit against, and finished the whisky.

Aster. His eyes watered up. He knew that her father had done something to him, but it didn't matter. He had imagined their meeting many times. Never had his fantasies involved the cold, dismissive rejection she had treated him to. She should have been grateful for his attention. Some girls practically begged him for it. Who was she to think she was better than he?

A painful nudge in the ribs made him realize he'd dropped off to sleep. The boys were standing around him, and for a minute he thought they were going to start beating him again, and the fear rose up in his belly. Then they shoved a girl at him.

She was young, pretty, terror writ clearly on her face.

"Go to it," Jobe said.

"No," David said.

"Ain't you a man?" Jobe demanded. "Go to it."

They were all looking at him, the way third graders looked at a classmate who had crapped in his pants. The disgust and disdain was palpable. Even the girl felt it; he saw relief creep across her features.

"Leave me alone with her," David said.

But they didn't move.

He looked back at the girl and saw the flicker of hope and gratitude in her eyes, the light inside of her, shining through him now, through the prism hidden within him. It had been present all along, but now it *turned*, so that the light passed through it and shattered into rainbow. Everything in him and everything beyond was suddenly impossibly vivid. The colors blazed on the girl's face, but deeper than that, to the shimmer in her. It was the most beautiful thing he had ever seen, and he wanted it. Had to have it.

It belonged to him, after all.

The disguise of her features fell away and he knew her for who she really was.

"Aster," he breathed.

"No," Aster said, but he knew she didn't understand.

"I'm not going to hurt you," he said. "This won't hurt."

She started screaming then, but he knew that before he was through she would stop, that she would understand what he was doing for her. That it was all for the best, and that then Jobe would leave the both of them alone.

"I love you, Aster," he whispered.

Well. That's a Hollow Sea," Errol commented.

"It's all right there in the name," Veronica agreed.

And yet Errol thought the name misleading. He had expected a big dry depression, with fish skeletons and such. This wasn't that.

For days the land had become higher and more arid, until finally it was a desert of red rock, sand, and scrubby evergreens. Now it suddenly plunged away in a nearly sheer cliff. It was less like a sea and more like the Grand Canyon, except the other side wasn't visible. Any more than the bottom was; looking down he could only see layers of progressively darker haze. It went off to the east as far as he could see, and west was the same except that mountains verged the rim.

"Do we know how far across this is?" Errol asked.

"Depends," Billy said.

"On what?"

"It just depends," he replied.

Billy didn't make sense a lot of the time.

Aster dismounted and walked along the edge. After a moment, Errol followed her.

"I hope you have some kind of flying spell up your sleeve, Aster."

He turned to look at her, and she had an odd glint in her eyes.

"I know this place," she whispered. "I've been here. With Dad."

"Do you remember how you got across?"

"Yes," she said, still softly. "I remember." She looked east and west.

"But I don't know which way."

Aster opened her mouth again, paused and shook her head. "It's nearly dark," she said. "We should find a place to camp. I'll figure it out."

T hey made camp in the ruins of a tower perched by the abyss, with a good view back the way they had come. As Billy started a fire, Errol asked him how far behind he thought the Sheriff was.

"Depends," he said. "Depends on how many horses they have, for one thing. And how much Chula and his boys managed to mislead them."

"Not much at all, I think," Aster said. "It's me."

"He wants us, too," Errol said.

"No," she replied. "So stupid. I should have known it as soon as I saw Mr. Watkins. That's how he keeps finding us."

"I don't get it," Errol said.

"Dad must have done more than just send Mr. Watkins after me. Think about it—once he was out of the house he would have gone straight to the police or whatever. So Dad cursed him to follow me obsessively. He probably gets sick or something if he tries to do anything else. That's why he seemed so crazy back at the village, I guess. But Dad must have also spelled him to sense where I am, or at least know what direction I'm in."

"So if we aren't with you, he can't find Errol and me," Veronica said.

Aster nodded. "That's right," she said.

"Too bad you didn't figure this out back at the village," Veronica said. "If you didn't, that is."

"I didn't," Aster snapped. Then she sighed. "But I should have."

Veronica was looking at Errol and he knew what she was thinking. So did Aster.

"It's okay," she said. "Like I told you back at the village . . ."

He had never heard Aster sound hopeless before. It was actually a shock.

"No," Errol said.

Veronica folded her arms.

"Now wait a minute," she said.

Everyone turned toward her.

"Aster needed you to find me," Veronica said. "She needed me to get here. She needs the giant for something-or-other. But what do we need *her* for?"

Errol sighed. "We can't—"

"Who is 'we'?" she snapped. "You let me finish."

"Fine," he said.

"What I mean," Veronica said, "is that *we* could finish this quest. Let her go back and hide out in the village. We'll go find the giant and the water and all that and then come back for her."

Errol blinked. "That's really smart," he said.

"I know that, Errol," Veronica said.

"She'll never make it back to the village," Billy pointed out.

"Oh, I bet she could," Veronica replied. "If she put her mind to it, and some of her witchy ways."

"I might," Aster granted. "But it won't work. I have to be there."

"Do you know that for sure?" Veronica asked.

Aster was silent for a moment.

"I don't know it for a fact," she admitted. "But I feel it. And no one is going on unless I figure out how to cross the Hollow Sea."

Veronica looked a little sour, but she nodded.

Billy and Aster scrounged firewood while Errol, Dusk, and Veronica explored the ruins. Errol tried to imagine what sort of people had lived here, on what seemed like the edge of the world. Whoever they might have been, they hadn't left many clues about themselves, or someone else had taken them all, because the tower itself aside, Errol saw no trace of human occupation.

As the sun set, Errol climbed to the top of the stone structure. He almost asked Veronica if she wanted to join him, but she seemed lost in her own little world, and anyway he wasn't sure he wanted to encourage her too much. He wasn't sure *what* he wanted.

Venus blazed in the west, and soon the other stars appeared. The silvery light of a crescent moon fell into the empty sea, and it seemed to him faint ripples, and quick, slender shadows stirred upon the abyss.

He looked at Venus and drew a deep breath.

A *breath*. It tickled in his ribcage like a bird trying to get out. He knew it was an illusion, that he couldn't really have taken a breath, so he felt his face to confirm that it was still wooden. It was, but it somehow felt more pliant, like hard rubber rather than wood.

And in his chest, he now realized, beat the faint ghost of a heart.

Something was happening to him. He was changing. But into what? A "real boy" as Aster had joked, or some kind of monster?

Or maybe he was just losing it.

"This is an uncommon place," Dusk murmured, as she climbed up beside him. He was a little surprised; he had heard the footsteps but assumed it was Veronica.

"This whole place is uncommon to me," he replied. "The kingdoms, I mean."

"Is your world so different?"

"Yes," he said. "Very different."

"And yet you wear an enchanted form," she remarked.

"That's a pretty recent thing," he said. "Up until a couple of weeks ago I was just a regular boy—flesh and blood, you know."

"So you said. But you never said what happened to you."

Errol could see Aster, down by the fire. Billy was beside her, and Veronica sat at the edge of the darkness.

He looked out at the dimming horizon. "I sort of got poisoned. It messed up my brain, I guess."

Her eyes widened, and an expression of what appeared to be shock passed over her features. Then something in her gaze sharpened a little.

"Who poisoned you, Errol?" she demanded. "Do you know?"

"Yeah," he said, reluctantly. "I kind of did it myself."

"You were trying to kill yourself?" She seemed incredulous.

"Maybe," he allowed. "I've been telling myself it was an accident, but maybe I was."

"Why?" she asked.

"Because I didn't like my life very much," he said.

"And now?"

"I haven't really had time to think about it," he said. "Thinking is what usually gets me in trouble, actually."

She was quiet for a moment. "I have a small question, Errol," she said.

"Okay," he replied.

"You put the healing salve on my wounds."

"Yes," he replied.

"One of my wounds was here," she said, touching her chest. He nodded.

"How shall I ask this?" she said.

"I didn't look," he told her.

"No?"

"I just sort of pushed it up under your shirt. I didn't see anything."

She smiled. "Well," she said. "Thank you for thinking of my modesty. I did not believe you were one to take advantage."

He knew that if he was flesh and blood he would be blushing. He had told her the truth, but nevertheless felt a bit like a liar. Because his thoughts about her weren't necessarily all that pure. That he hadn't taken advantage of the fact that she was bloody and dying to sneak a peek didn't really seem all that virtuous. You didn't get extra points for doing what you were supposed to.

And yet, he found that he would take them.

"So," Dusk began, after a little pause, "Aster plans to cure you and Veronica when she finds the water of health."

"Yeah," Errol said, happy to be back on the earlier topic. "And her father."

"Is he also asleep?" she asked.

"No," Errol said. "There's something wrong with his memory. He forgets things really fast. He thinks Aster is still a little girl, and she has to explain to him who she is every time they meet."

"An odd affliction," she said.

"She thinks it's a curse. But other people in my world get that kind of brain damage. I've read about it." He suddenly realized that he had gone on about Aster's personal life more than he should have.

"Look," he said. "Aster is pretty private about these things. Don't tell her I told you that, okay?"

"I shan't," Dusk replied.

A ster stood on the edge of nothing, and was afraid. Not so much of the drop below her; she could step back from that. Rather, she was afraid of what she had to do.

She had learned the spell long ago, but she had also read the cautions, which were many. She knew it could be done; she had seen her father do it. But he had nearly been lost, and he was far more powerful and practiced than she.

She heard a soft sound. In the dim light she at first couldn't see what it was, but then she made out Billy's profile. He was staring out over the gulf. She didn't think he had seen her, and she almost backed into the cover of a nearby bush. But she felt a sudden determination and instead made her way over to where he stood. Even when she was near, he at first did not seem to notice her; in the moonlight his eyes appeared huge, and for a moment she thought she saw the stars reflected in them. But then he blinked, slowly, and nodded at her.

"Nice view," she said.

"It feels like home," Billy replied.

"Back at Hattie's house?"

"No—home."

"Where is that?" she said. "I thought you didn't know where you're from."

"I don't," he said. "But this feels like it."

"Oh," she replied, still not sure she understood.

"You should rest," he said.

"Yeah," Aster said. And then it just blurted out of her.

"I'm sorry I made you sick. I didn't know."

"It's okay," Billy said. "I know you didn't."

"Then why haven't you been talking to me?" she asked.

He looked genuinely surprised. "I didn't have anything to say. If you want to talk, that's okay."

"Well, I guess I thought you were mad at me," she said, feeling really stupid, now.

"Why would I be mad at you?" he asked. "I like you."

"You do?"

"Sure."

She opened her mouth, but nothing came out. *Like me how?* Was what she wanted to say, but her tongue just wouldn't form those words.

"Okay," she said instead. "Good."

"What are you about to do?" Billy asked.

"What makes you think I'm about to do something?" she said.

"It's like your trying to set yourself for a big jump," he said. "You're scared."

Her first impulse was to deny it, but she realized Billy wasn't guessing, or he wouldn't have said anything at all. He knew.

"Yes," she said. "I am."

"Can I help?" he asked.

"Just be here with me," she said.

"I can do that," he replied.

She nodded, and reached into her rucksack and found the little case. Gingerly she removed its contents, a small dark feather.

"This is my father's," she said. "I took it from his things."

Billy didn't say anything. She stood there, holding the feather, trying to clear the fear from her heart.

"He said it once was nearly the end of him, Billy. I'm afraid."

"Whatever it is," Billy said, "you can do it."

The words felt like a cool breeze on a hot day.

"Okay," she said. Then she leaned over and kissed him on the cheek. It felt like the craziest thing she had ever done.

"In case I don't come back," she said. And before he could reply—if he even intended to—she touched her forehead with the feather and said the words.

"*Eza azmi karvas.*"

Pain stung every inch of her skin and a scream rose in her throat, but it never got out, because before it could a cold wind blew out from her heart and she exploded. She felt the bits of her, racing away from the center of a sphere expanding at the speed of sound. The edge of her passed over the camp through Veronica, Errol and Dusk; she felt their startlement at the sudden rush of chilly air. The farther she stretched out, the thinner she got, the more she felt herself fade. For a moment she almost let it happen without a fight, allowed herself dissipate, become nothing, forget her quest and her troubles and everything else.

No, she told herself. No.

She pulled back toward her center, but it felt as if she had waited too long. She no longer had the strength.

But then she felt Billy, in the middle, an anchor and an axis. He was singing something she didn't understand, but she grabbed onto it, onto him. She felt a strange well of strength and peace, and pulled.

She stopped expanding, and for a moment the world seemed still, as if time itself was taking pause.

Then she began to shrink, and then collapse at frightening speed, as if she was falling from hundreds of feet from every direction.

And when she slapped back together, she did scream.

But not with a human voice—rather, with the croak of a raven.

Dizzily, she lifted her wings, and without another thought dropped out into the open sky below. Her feathers caught the wind, each one a little wing in itself, turning, stretching, dancing her along the wind.

Mustn't forget, she told herself.

And she flew off east, along the rim, wondering what she had been afraid of. Flying was wonderful.

She flew until the moon had coursed half through the sky, and did not see what she needed to see, and so reluctantly turned back west, studying the rim a second time. Raven eyes were not so much better at night than human ones, but what she was looking for should be hard to miss, even under a crescent moon.

She passed a young man near the rim and her heart quickened with fear before she realized it was Billy. She was hungry, and tired of flying, and she ought not to be flying at night anyway. She wanted to settle on a limb and rest.

She was still Aster enough to know what was happening, but for how long?

West she soared, as the sickle of the moon stabbed into the horizon. Legs and arms seemed more a dream now than reality, a strange dream she'd had. Mountains rose along the sea, and a forest, which seemed familiar. But it made the hunt less certain.

Then she saw something pretty glittering below.

And she knew it.

She turned in an instant and flew back, but everything was sliding away, down her wings and off them so the wind could take it all. In her last moments she knew she could only keep one image, one thought to keep her going, one name, and so she

held hard to it. In the end it was more an annoyance than anything, a distraction. Why she should find the human sleeping
on the edge of the cliff and settle upon it was not only senseless,
but dangerous. Yet she was tired, and it was the only way the
buzzing in her mind would let her rest.

She fell asleep, and when she woke she was gripped tightly
in his hands, and knew she had made a fatal mistake.

SEVEN

SKY AND EARTH

idnight came, and Errol was surprised at how tired he felt, how sleepy. Dusk had asked him to wake her so she could take a watch, but he had planned on just letting her sleep. He was changing his mind; if he nodded off, he put everyone at risk. Veronica was dozing with her head on his chest, curled up like a cat in his lap, and he didn't want to wake her, either, so he gently lifted her and carried her down the stairs. She stirred, though, and her dark eyes blinked open.

"Wherever are you taking me, Errol?" she murmured. "Not going to throw me off the cliff, I hope."

"Probably not," he said. "I'm just relocating. It's Dusk's watch."

"I can do it," Veronica. "I've had a nice nap."

"Dusk asked me to wake her," he said.

"You don't trust me to keep watch, do you Errol?" Veronica accused.

"Of course I do," he lied. "I just want you to sing me to sleep."

"Well, that's awfully sweet," she said, in an uncertain tone.

He set her down on her bedroll.

"I notice Aster and Billy are nowhere to be found," Veronica said.

"Aster said she had something to do."

"Yeah," Veronica replied. "I bet it involves saliva."

Errol stared at her. It was hard to tell when she was kidding, sometimes.

"You think so?"

"Don't you pay attention to *anything*, Errol?" she said.

"I guess they've been kind of chummy," he said. "But Aster, I don't think she—"

Veronica snorted. "Are you kidding? Everybody is human. Okay—you're not, and I'm not, but Aster is. She had a thing for *you*, for goodness sake. Probably still does. Didn't you know that?"

"No," he said. "I know you used to joke about that, but—"

"I joked about it because it was so obvious," she said. "It was funny."

"I don't think that's true," he said.

She sat up and hugged her knees. "You're cute sometimes, you know that?"

He shook his head. "I've got to wake Dusk."

Dusk always slept on her back, or at least anytime he had ever seen her. She looked serene, and her lips were slightly parted, as if waiting for a kiss.

It was maybe because he was focused on that that he didn't see the snake at first. It was coiled on her belly, staring at her throat, its tongue flickering in and out. The diamond patterns on its back and the rattle trailing from its coils identified its species.

"Jesus," he murmured, and froze. The snake didn't seem to have noticed him. He tried to think it through.

Rattlesnakes hunted small animals, and they struck at big ones—like people—when they thought they were in danger.

But they didn't go *after* people. Tiny though snake brains were, they recognized something as big as Dusk was too much to eat.

So what was it doing? It was chilly, almost cold. Maybe it just thought it had found a warm spot.

But there was another, much uglier possibility, wasn't there?

The rattle started going. That only happened when a snake thought it was in danger.

Dusk's eyes opened, and she gasped.

Errol darted forward. Dusk still hadn't moved, so it was him the snake went for, uncoiling with amazing speed and burying its fangs in his arm. He felt the bright, sharp tips of them and yelped. He stumbled back, and the snake went with him, its fangs stuck in him.

It took a few seconds for rationality to assert itself. He was made of wood. The venom couldn't hurt him.

With his other hand, he gripped the snake behind the head and pulled it loose.

Veronica was up and staring at him.

"What's going on?" she said.

"You tell me!" he snapped, holding the squirming reptile up. She blinked.

"What?" she demanded.

"It would have killed me," Dusk said. She was standing touching her neck as if searching for a wound. She too looked at Veronica.

"Errol Greyson," Veronica said, "I know you're not implying that I had anything to do with that thing."

She was trying to sound angry, but Errol heard the hurt, too. But with Veronica, you could never be sure, could you?

"Why would you think that?" she demanded.

Without even thinking about it, he glanced over at Dusk and found she was looking at him.

"Oh." Veronica said. "I see."

She turned on her heel and strode off into the night.

"Veronica!" he shouted. "Just hang on—"

"It's a rattlesnake, you jackass!" Her voice came out of the darkness. "We're in a desert!"

He watched her go, wanting to follow. Yet something held him back.

"Would she do that?" Dusk asked. "If she thought there was something between us?"

"I don't know," he said. "But there isn't, so—"

"Is that so?" she softly interrupted. "We share some feeling, do we not?"

He heard the words, but they seemed impossible. Ridiculous at the very least. He groped for something to say.

"You're still holding the snake," Dusk reminded him.

"Yeah," he said. "I'd better take it off someplace."

"You aren't going to kill it?"

"Whatever is going on here," he said, "it's not the snake's fault."

He walked a few hundred yards from the camp and let the snake go. It slithered off without much commotion. When he returned to camp, Dusk was gone, having taken up her position on the tower. Veronica was still absent too, but he was tired and very confused. He had a shot at Dusk? How could that be? And did Veronica really try to kill her? Deep down, was she still the creature that nested on the bones of her victims? Could she ever really change?

And yet the hurt in her voice had seemed real.

His thoughts become lost in shadow, as he finally drifted into sleep.

S he struggled, trying to free her wings. He held her firmly until she pecked at his face, and then he did let go. With a shriek she beat at the air, but then his nimble hands had her again. And he said a word.

It was just a sound, the first time, but the next it seemed as if it meant something, and though her heart shivered beneath the black down of her breast, she listened a third time, and a fourth.

Aster.

A spark kindled in her head. It sputtered for an instant and then suddenly exploded, and for the second time, so did she. She stretched high and far and returned, slapping back together, and this time she had arms instead of wings, and feet instead of claws, although the legs they were mounted on failed to hold her up, and she collapsed onto the red rock.

"Wow," she said. "That was—wow."

"Are you well?" Billy asked.

"I think so," she said. "Shaky. And—" She suddenly realized the unforeseen consequences of her transformation.

"And naked," she finished. She felt a blush go down her whole body, but she had barely gotten the words out when Billy's shirt settled over her head.

"Thanks," she said, pulling it on. It smelled like him, like juniper and smoke.

She glanced at him, blazing with embarrassment, and saw he was turned away from her, working at the buttons on his pants.

"That's okay," she said, quickly. "This shirt is like a dress on me. See?"

He turned, saw, and nodded.

"I, ah—sorry about that," she said.

"About what?" he asked.

"You know, the whole naked thing."

He smiled slightly. "Didn't intend to look," he said. "But you're pretty."

Something tightened in her, but no guile was on his face. Billy wasn't Jake, trying to peek at her in an outhouse. He had seen her, that was all, and hadn't taken advantage—he handed her his shirt as soon as possible.

But that he had seen her left her feeling vulnerable and confused just the same.

Or maybe she was discombobulated from having been a bird.

"Anyway," she said, brushing her hair out of her face. "Thanks for staying. Thanks for bringing me back. I was almost gone. A raven evermore."

He didn't get the joke, which made her feel even more awkward.

"Did you find what you were looking for?" He asked.

"I did!" she remembered. "We'd better get back to the others."

E rrol rose a little after dawn. Veronica was still nowhere to be seen. Neither, for that matter, were Aster or Billy in evidence. After their victory in Jezebel's village he had felt like they were a team, friends. Now it all seemed to be falling apart, and he realized with surprise and some dismay that he didn't want it to.

He saw Dusk coming down from the tower and a moment later saw why as Aster and Billy came into camp. Aster wasn't wearing anything but Billy's shirt.

"About Goddamn time ya'll showed up," he snapped. "This is a damn stupid time to disappear for the night. For all we knew, anything could have happened to you."

Billy didn't really react, but Aster's eyes widened in surprise, and he realized that his tone must have been harsher than he thought it was.

"Did something happen?" Aster asked.

"Damn straight it did," he said. "Not that you two would care."

"Now listen," Aster said. She was blushing. "I told you I had something to do."

"Well, I guess you did, at that," Errol said.

"This isn't what it looks like," Aster said.

"Really? Cause what it looks like is that you're missing every stitch of your clothes."

He knew he was pushing his luck. Part of him was surprised she hadn't already flown into her usual icy fury.

But what she did was laugh. He had only heard her laugh like that a few times, and it had been a long time ago. And that's how he knew it was real.

"Yeah," she said, when she could talk again. "About that. I'll give you all the details, I promise. But first tell me what's going on here. Where's Veronica?"

Errol felt the anger leaking out of him.

"Okay," he said. "Here's what happened."

Veronica stopped when she saw dawn creeping up the firmament. She found a flat rock to sit on and watched color invade the night, soft coral and dull, thick orange and finally the bloody rim of the sun itself, washing away the last of the sky shadows in a slow flood of turquoise.

She placed her hand on her belly, and felt the bullet hole. It hadn't healed, or even begun to. Why would it? She wasn't really alive.

"Hello, Sky," she said, quietly. "You've got some nice sunrises and sunsets up here. Like none I've seen before. I mean, I don't remember a lot from when I was alive, but I'm pretty sure I've never seen anything like this.

"I wonder if I was this stupid when I was alive," she went on.

"Stupid enough to think I could belong, could be part of something and do no harm to it."

She scratched a line in the stone with her fingernail.

"I don't remember having a boyfriend. Maybe I never did. But Errol — he was really sweet to me, Sky. He was nice to me. It kind of felt like he was my boyfriend."

She looked back up at the azure dome.

"But he turned on me pretty quickly, didn't he? Because he thought I tried to kill Dusk. He didn't even ask if I did it, he just went straight to it. And you know why, Sky? Because it's her he's in love with."

She kicked her legs a few times.

"The thing is," she said, "I *might* have done it. I don't *remember* doing it. Not on purpose. But when I close my eyes, the things I see are just — well, awful and beautiful things. I won't bore you with details. But some of them are desires, I guess, that I push down when light is coming into my skull. Part of me would kind of enjoy seeing Dusk's face puff up and turn black, and hear her shiver out her last breaths. I'm getting stronger. Maybe my dreams are granting my wishes when I'm asleep.

"But — here's the thing, Sky old girl. I'm all about the water. Down in the lowlands — in the creeks and rivers and swamps — I could hear and feel and smell and taste every slithering thing — every lizard, fish, snake and frog. I could listen in on their slight conversations and feel their blood, room-temperature like mine.

"Up here I don't feel anything like that. I didn't even know the snake was there."

She sighed.

"I thought Errol would follow me. I thought I could have this conversation with him rather than you. Not that you aren't a good listener, Sky."

She watched the clouds drift for a few more minutes and then stood up. "Okay," she said. "That's enough of that. Maybe I'll just go back downhill and find a nice river to settle in."

"Naw, don't quit now," somebody said. "You talk about as pretty as you look."

She spun and jumped away from the sound — right into one of Jobe's boys, who had been creeping around the other side of the rock. He slammed her down on the stone and a second later she felt a rough cord bite into her wrists. Then he was pushing her dress up. She kicked back and hit him in the thigh, rather than where she meant to.

"Leave off her," the other boy said. "The Sheriff said not to mess with any of them, just to bring 'em back alive."

"How's the Sheriff going to know? It's just you and me."

"Are you really that big an idiot?" Veronica asked. "I'll tell him, stupid."

"Huh," the boy said.

"Let's just get out of here before her friends show up."

"I wouldn't worry about that," Veronica said. "I don't have any friends."

EIGHT

THE KISS

When Sam and Charlie brought the girl into camp, David at first assumed she was from a nearby village. She was dressed in buckskins, like most of those in the last. But as soon as he was close enough to see her face, he realized he knew her; he just wasn't sure from where.

The boys hooted and jeered, but her face remained calm, almost serene. Her gaze went through the boys as if they were invisible.

But when she looked at him, her brow creased.

"Peek-a-boo," she said, in a low, slow voice. "I see you."

The hairs on his neck stood on end, and he felt a whirling pressure in his body, as if his skin contained a tornado.

"Who do you see?" he asked. "What do you see?"

"I remember you," she said.

"From Aster's house," he realized.

"Sure," she said. "Her father put you in a bottle."

"I'm trying to find Aster," he explained. "I'm trying to help her."

"I know *exactly* how you want to help her," the girl said.

It was as if her words flipped the switch on a movie projector in his head, and he suddenly saw himself with Aster, doing the things that wanted doing, had to be done for everything to be right. The girl blinked and her dark eyes went round.

"Wow," she said. "Usually I have to touch one of you to feel it like that," she said. "You're a bad, bad boy."

"Nothing is either good or bad but thinking makes it so," he said. Then her words sank a little deeper.

"What do you mean, 'one of you'?"

"I don't know if I have a word for you," she said. "But I know what you are, and what you've done and want to do. And you know what you are."

"I wish I did," David said. Part of him wanted to back away, get away from this girl who could see inside of him. But he knew that was the weak part of him, the part that didn't understand.

"I see how things are," he told her. "I see how things should be. I make them that way."

"How should things be, Mr. Watkins?" she asked softly.

The name jarred him. It was his, but somehow it didn't feel right any more.

"Light," he murmured. "Always the light. Aster's light."

He felt his breath shorten. There was something about this girl, something so familiar, so deep. He had never heard her laugh, and yet he could imagine it with absolute clarity. He could imagine other things too.

He stepped closer.

"Hoo-hoo," Jobe said. "The preacher done got religion."

"Shut up, Jobe," he snapped. He saw the surprise in the boy's face, followed quickly by anger.

"Now look here, preacher —"

"I said shut up."

Jobe reached for his pistol.

"You do that, you little ass," David snapped. "See how the Sheriff likes you when he finds out what you did to his pathfinder."

"Hell," Jobe said. "We know where they are. They're stuck hard up against nothing at all, with nowhere to go."

"Take the chance then," David said.

Jobe's eyes looked less human than ever, but David didn't care, he kept his gaze on the boy until he blinked and looked away. His hand eased off the gun.

"What the hell ever, preacher," he said.

"Yeah," David replied. He wondered why he had ever been scared of Jobe. Of anything.

He walked over to the girl, staring at her, until their faces were inches apart.

"What's your name?" he asked.

"Veronica Hale," she told him.

The name sounded familiar, but the shine inside of him wasn't all that concerned with it. He was more interested in her face. There was so much girl left in it. Except for her eyes; in the deeps of them something old lurked.

He traced his finger along her chin.

"This won't hurt," he said. He bent and kissed her, gently.

He felt a shudder run through her, but wasn't sure what it was; only that it was strong. But she didn't close her eyes, didn't even blink, but kept her gaze steady on his until he found himself looking away the way Jobe had from him. When he looked back, her face had changed. She was Aster.

Of course.

He took her by the shoulders, and started to push her down.

"Enough of that," the Sheriff's voice commanded from behind him.

"She's mine," David said.

"She's an abomination," the Sheriff replied, "And she is not yours. She falls under my jurisdiction."

"Now listen—" David began. But the Sheriff wasn't talking to him anymore. He dismounted and strode over to Veronica.

"Anything you want to tell me, girl?" he asked.

"Plenty," she said. "But I don't think you would want to hear it."

She was trying to sound brave, but her lip was quivering. David wondered what would happen if he killed the Sheriff. Would the boys turn on him or follow him? Of course, from what he had seen, it might not be possible to kill him. But at some point he might have to try. To save Aster.

"They've reached the Hollow Sea by now," the Sheriff said. "Have they a way to cross it?"

"They're just sitting around," one of the boys said.

"I'm not speaking to you," the Sheriff said. "I'm speaking to the dead."

As he said it, his tone changed and he laid his hands on her. Veronica made a choking sound, and then her eyes rolled back.

"Please," she said.

"Have they a way across the sea?"

Veronica trembled so violently it looked as though she was having a seizure.

When she spoke, her voiced sounded clipped and almost metallic.

"I don't think so," she said. "Aster was trying to think of something. She was upset."

"As I thought," the Sheriff muttered, and removed his hands. Veronica shut her eyes and gradually ceased her tremors.

"I've no use for you, then," the Sheriff told her.

"Well, then," Veronica said, shakily, "I suppose I'll just be going."

"No," the Sheriff said. "You'll not be going anywhere."

"We can use her," David said. "You saw what she did back at the river. And I heard about what she did in the battle at the village."

"He's got a point," Jobe said. "She ain't with them anymore. Hell, the things she can do—"

"Indeed," the Sheriff cut him off. "If she had been near water when you found her, you never could have captured her, much less brought her back. Up here in the high desert, she has little power. But if we come to water, that will change. And her sort is not trustworthy."

"What are you going to do with her, then?" David asked.

"She's dead," the Sheriff said. "So we'll bury her."

B illy pointed to marks in the red sand.

"Two boys caught her here," he said. "Took her off that way on horseback."

"The Sheriff?" Aster asked.

"Outriders," Billy said.

"But he's still coming," Aster said. "We still have to get to the ship."

"The ship you saw when you were a bird," Errol said. He didn't sound convinced. It was annoying to her that even after all that he had been through, Errol still had the nerve to be skeptical about these things.

"Yes," she said. "The ship. The same ship my father and I crossed the sea on years ago."

"The sea that doesn't have any water in it," he said. "And the boat is still where you left it, waiting for you. No one has bothered to take it in all of these years."

"It won't sail for just anyone," she said. "You have to be able to command the spirit that inhabits it. You have to know its name."

"And you know its name?"

"Yes." She felt a slight guilt. In fact, she didn't remember the name, but she felt certain she would recall it when the time came.

"What of Veronica?" Dusk asked.

Aster had been dreading that question, but here it was.

"She walked away from us," Aster said. "She took her chances."

"Because I basically accused her of trying to kill Dusk," Errol said.

"You may well have been right," Aster said. "Aren't you the one who used to tell me she isn't to be trusted? Because she tried to kill you?"

"That's different," Errol said. "She was something else, then."

"She tried to kill Errol?" Dusk said.

"It's a long story," Errol said. "And it doesn't matter. We can't let the Sheriff have her."

"There's nothing we can do about it," Aster said. "If we go after her, we all get caught. Our quest fails, and no one gets what they want."

"*Your* quest fails," Errol said.

"What?"

"Your quest, Aster. What you're saying is, we don't need Veronica anymore, so the hell with her."

"I'm saying we can't do anything for her."

"If you thought you needed her, I guarantee you would find a way," he said. He looked off southeast. "Well, I reckon you don't need me anymore, either," he said. "So go on. Good luck."

"Errol—"

"I'm serious," he said. "You're right. But I have to try, okay? So get going."

He started walking, and Aster felt her heart sink.

"Errol," she said, "please. You're right, I don't need you anymore. I never did. There were others I could have used. But I wanted to give you a chance. I still do."

He turned, slowly. "You did give me a chance," he said. "Thanks."

She felt her fingers trembling.

"Errol?" She said.

"What?"

"Svapdi."

His legs buckled, and he dropped like a puppet with severed strings.

"We'll have to carry him," she sighed.

But then, impossibly, Errol stirred and then slowly pushed himself to his feet.

"I wondered if you would do that," he said. "Now I know."

He was angry, but then he looked around, and his tone changed.

"We're in the same place," he said. "How long has it been?"

"A few seconds," Aster said.

"You changed your mind," he said. He sounded as surprised as she was.

She wrinkled her brow. "I . . ."

"Thank you," he said. "For giving me the choice."

Then he turned again and walked quickly away, following the horse tracks.

He doesn't know he came back by himself, she thought. How had he done it?

"The ship is west, on the rim," she called after him. "We'll wait as long as we can."

"That's great," his voice floated back to her.

She felt a lump form in her throat.

"Well," she said. "Anyone else want to defect?"

"Errol is a warrior," Dusk said. "He must follow his own heart. My heart tells me to stay with you."

"I'll stay," said Billy.

E rrol heard Jobe's boys before he saw them; they weren't taking much care to be quiet. He found a copse of ever-green bushes and crawled into them, wondering if the Sheriff's dogs would smell him—and if they did, whether they would identify him as something strange.

They came into sight a little later, looking freakier than ever. Would they eventually turn completely into animals?

If the dogs noticed him, they didn't let on. He saw Mr. Watkins, walking up front alongside the Sheriff. He didn't look like a captive.

He did not see Veronica, and that worried the hell out of him.

The second they were out of sight he hopped up and raced back along their trail.

It was hard to know how long he ran—an hour, two, three, more—but for the first time since becoming an automaton he was starting to feel almost—well, *winded*. The lungs he didn't have had begun to ache, and the ghost of his heart seemed almost to be thumping in his wooden chest.

He no longer had any doubt his body was becoming more alive. It had been happening slowly before, but now it seemed to be accelerating.

I'm coming, Veronica.

He thought that again and again, and tried not to think of anything else.

Finally he came to the remains of a camp fire, still smolder-ing slightly. After searching a fair area of scuffed up dirt and horse droppings, he found the trail they had come into camp on.

And no sign of Veronica.

He paced around the camp, feeling helpless. Had she escaped, somehow? Summoned a bunch of snakes or lizards or whatever? Or was she further back? What would they have done to her? Had they *eaten* her, for God's sake? Because they surely weren't completely human anymore.

"Damn it!" he muttered out loud. "Veronica!"

He called a few more times, but his only answer was silence.

He finally decided she must be further south, and was just starting that way when something whirred through the air and settled on his nose. He slapped at it reflexively, but it flew off and he ended up hitting his own face.

It came back, circling him. A dragonfly.

Which was weird. A dragonfly in the desert? That had to mean water was nearby, but he sure didn't see any sign of it.

The dragonfly flew a couple of yards and lit on a bush. Then it flew back to him, circled once, and flitted back to the same bush.

Errol walked toward it. The insect flew once more, another few yards, and lit again. Experimentally, he followed it. Each time, it flew in the same direction.

"Okay," Errol said. "I get it."

He trotted after it, and it stopped landing. It led him up a sandy ridge, and on the top a found a pile of stones and dirt that looked very much like a grave. The dragonfly lit on the mound — and on a smaller mound of dead dragonflies.

"Oh, shit," Errol said. He dropped to his knees and started digging. His big hands made decent progress; digging wasn't the problem; it was what he was afraid he might find.

He got the hole down four feet, and still nothing, except that he realized they had used a natural crack in the sandstone and filled it up; as he dug, it got narrower, and it was already too narrow to lay a body out flat in. What if they chopped her up first?

At five feet he was having trouble getting into the hole to excavate. The crack was only about two feet wide now, and maybe five feet long.

Almost at the limits of what he could reach, his palm grazed over something that wasn't dirt or stone; after a moment he realized it was buckskin. He dug on, more gently, and soon realized he was looking at the bottoms of her moccasin-clad feet.

"Oh, God," he said. In seconds he had both feet sticking out of the soil. He pulled at them; they didn't move. He continued digging as far as he could, which wasn't much farther, not quite to her knees.

So they hadn't cut her up. They had dropped her head-down into a stone straightjacket.

His shoulders wouldn't fit any farther down the hole, so he did the only thing he could; he took hold of her ankles, braced his knees, and pulled.

She came up a little. He changed his position and tugged again, and then he was able to get his feet under him and give it all he had, hoping that he wouldn't hurt her and that there was still something left to hurt.

As soon as her head cleared the dirt she started screaming, a terrifying sound like nothing he had ever heard from her — or anyone — ever before. Her eyes were open, and full of madness. There was little there he recognized, and she showed no signs of knowing who he was. He gathered her in his arms, but she fought, scratching and biting like a sack of wildcats. It hurt, but the damage was only superficial, and so he hung on, until after a time she quieted, and her shrieks became sobs.

"L — let me go," she finally stammered, and he opened his arms. She stumbled back a few feet, staring at him.

"Errol," she said.

"It's me," he said.

"Errol — they buried me, Errol."

"I know," he said.

She looked wildly around and when she saw the hole, pointed to it.

"Buried me," she said.

"I'm sorry," he said.

"Where are they?" she asked. "Are they here?"

"They're about half a day further north," he said. "I passed them on the way."

She brushed at the dirt clinging in her hair.

"You came after me," she said.

"I wish I had come sooner," he said. "I should have followed you right away."

"Yeah," she said. "That would have been nice. But you came after me. Do you still think I tried to kill Dusk?"

"I'm not sure," he said. "But it doesn't matter."

"Doesn't it?"

He took a step closer.

"You know," he said, "at first I didn't believe any of this was happening. And when I did, I just wanted to get through it, be done with it, get back to my normal life. But then I started thinking. It was my normal life that landed me in this mess. What do I go back to? Did you see anybody in that hospital room? Flowers? A get-well-soon card? Even my mom hardly comes by. I don't like my friends, but I want them to like me. Aster's right, I'm like a puppy. I pretend drinking myself sick is fun and I pretend talking about how freaking drunk and sick we got the other day is interesting conversation. I can act happy, but I never am. Mostly I'm angry. My normal life is what killed me, or almost did. If I get it back, it'll kill me again. But with you guys—with *you*—and in this creepy Pinocchio body—I feel more myself. I feel more like the me I thought I was going to be when I was a kid. The Errol who believed he would become an astronomer and find a new galaxy, or maybe a paleontologist digging up pelycosaurs."

"That's nice, Errol," she said. "Good for you."

"Veronica, I couldn't have said any of that to anybody back in Sowashee. Back there, I wanted to belong and never did. Here—I belong. And by here, I mean with you. With all of you, as dumb as that may seem. And I don't want it to fall apart. And it feels like it is. Without you, it falls apart. I—uh—I fall apart."

She stared at him for a long time, and finally smiled a little.

"I didn't try to kill Dusk, Errol," she said. "I'm jealous of her, sure. She's strong and smart and beautiful and—alive. But I didn't have anything to do with the snake. I can't do much up here, where it's so dry. Dragonflies were the best I could manage."

"You knew I would come after you," he said.

"It was the only hope I had, Errol. But you did. You did."

He reached for her, but she leaned away.

"I've just been buried, Errol," she said. "Face-first in a hole. You said a lot of nice stuff, but I have things on my mind. If you know what I mean. And I'm filthy. So don't go grabbing at me."

"Okay."

She sighed and brushed a little more at her matted hair.

"I need a bath," she said. "So what now?"

"Aster turned into a bird and found some sort of boat we can use to cross the sea."

"Wow. A lot can happen while you're buried."

"She said she would wait as long as she could. I'd like to try to catch up. But at this point—whatever you want."

"Well, there is one bright spot, anyway," she said.

"What's that?"

"I remember who killed me."

NINE

LIKE A GIRL WITH NO HEARTBEAT

Aster didn't want company but Billy — who usually never pushed himself where he wasn't wanted — seemed determined to ride beside her, even when she reined back or trotted ahead. Dusk, on the other hand, seemed to get the message and was way up front.

Partly, she was bothered by what Billy might be thinking, after she had kissed him and after the whole nude scene. She was afraid he was going to say something and she wasn't sure what it was going to be or how she would respond. So she was surprised and relieved when he finally did speak, because neither topic seemed to be involved.

"You keep reining back," he said.

"I just don't feel like talking, Billy. Not today."

"I know," he said. "But you keep slowing us down."

"Did I miss something?" she said. "The part where I put you in charge? Because I don't remember that."

"You act like someone who is going the wrong direction," he said.

That hit her in the belly, and for a minute or two she couldn't say anything at all.

"If we had gone with him, he might have had a chance," she finally said.

"Or we might have all died," Billy said. "I understand. Your quest."

"Yeah," she said. "My quest." She looked over at Billy.

She remembered her father, laughing, stroking her hair as they lunged through high seas on a silver ship. She remembered him holding her so tight, and crying, and not knowing why, but knowing he loved her. And she remembered losing him, a little at a time, until he hadn't been able to recognize her face.

She sobbed and kicked her horse into motion.

They had only been traveling half an hour or so when Errol spotted the riders. They were off to the east, and though he couldn't make out much about them, he knew who they were.

"They found my trail," he said.

"They haven't seen us," she said. "They're still going south."

"Yeah," he said. "Aster said the ship was west, so we're maybe half a mile from my old trail. But when they get to camp—"

"They'll see I'm not buried and come after us," she said. "I get it."

"We'll still have a head start, but they have horses. Can you run?"

"Like a girl with no heartbeat," she said.

So they ran as the sun drifted west and quietly set the horizon ablaze. They ran as the familiar stars appeared, more quickly than Errol was used to in the high, thin air.

On a talus slope, he slipped down to one knee, and it took a moment for him to get back up.

"You're getting tired, Errol," Veronica said. "How can that be?"

He started forward again, trying to find a good pace.

"I don't know," he said. "My body is changing, somehow."

"Yes, I've noticed that," she said. "You're getting softer. Some of your wires look more like veins now. Sometimes I think I hear you breathe. Maybe you're going through some sort of puppet puberty."

They jogged on a few more paces.

"Do you think it was that spell the Snatchwitch put on you?" Veronica asked. "Or something Hattie did when she took it off?"

"Maybe," he said. "I did feel a little different after that. But the really noticeable stuff started when . . ." he trailed off, embarrassed.

But she got it. "Oh," she said. "Really? You think my kiss broke the spell?"

"Not so much the kiss," he said. "Remember how you asked me to imagine I had my body back? I think it might be tied up with that."

"Yes, maybe that," she said. "Or maybe true love's kiss." She laughed.

"I wonder," she said, a few moments later. "If your puppet body comes alive—what happens to the other one, the one in a coma?"

"I have no idea," he said. "Maybe Aster knows."

But the thought worried him.

N ear morning, the howling began. Errol was staggering by then, hardly able to keep his feet under him.

"How much further?" Veronica asked.

"I don't know," Errol said, "but I'm tired of running. I think there are only four of them."

"Four dog-boys with guns," she said. "We don't have any weapons."

"Look," he said. "That last bluff we came up. Most of it is too steep to climb, especially with horses—there's just that one slope, at least as far as I could see. I can hold them off."

"With what?"

"Rocks."

She blinked. "Oh. Rocks against guns. This should be fun."

"I'll be the one having the fun," he said. "You'll be off trying to find Aster and the rest."

"The Devil I will, Errol Greyson," she said. "I can throw a rock as well as you."

"You can still run," he pointed out. "I can't. You're our best hope."

"You're only even guessing about where Aster went," she said. "She told you a day west, whatever that means. We're probably ten miles off. If they're even still waiting, if they haven't sailed that ship off into the sunset."

"Veronica . . ."

"Oh, hush," she said. She brushed his forehead and then kissed him lightly on the lips.

"It was a good try, Errol," she said. "A really decent rescue attempt."

"We're not done yet," he said.

He and Veronica made piles of stones, separating them by size. He tossed a few, to get his range, and was pleasantly surprised by how far he could throw. Maybe they had a shot of this after all.

He also found a withered, dead tree with a nice heavy root mass, and lay that by as well.

Then there wasn't much to do but watch them come.

When they were close enough, he hefted a rock and hurled it at the lead rider.

It missed him, but nearly hit the next guy. He took aim and let fly with another. That one went true, slamming the creature that had once been a boy with a sickening, fatal-sounding thud. He dropped from his saddle.

The other three took that as their cue to dismount. One took a shot at him, but the bullet glanced from the stone he and Veronica were using for cover. Errol kept throwing, feeling an odd calm settle over him. More shots rang out, but he ignored them. One of the dog-boys dodged violently to avoid a rock thrown by Veronica, moving directly into Errol's next throw. He went down with a yelp.

The other two dropped to all fours and came bounding up the slope. Errol threw frantically, and hit one of them on the head, but he kept coming, moving much, much faster than Errol had anticipated. He didn't throw his last rock, but used it to belt the creature in the chin.

That worked okay; he pitched back down the slope, but the other was leaping toward him, and he was still off-balance from the punch. He tried to get back around in time, but the dog-boy seized him with unreal strength and yanked him down the bluff. They tumbled, the both of them, head over heels.

He started up with the muzzle of a pistol in his face and for a moment felt paralyzed, his mind unable to register what was about to happen.

Then something flew down from above and sort of wrapped itself around the boy's head — Veronica, who had hurled herself from the rock, a fall of over twenty feet. The pistol went off, but Errol didn't feel anything.

He scrambled up. Veronica was clawing at the boy's face. His pistol lay on the ground. Errol reached for it, but a loud report and shattering pain in his gut stopped him. Gasping on the promise of a scream, he saw the other three boys coming for them.

The boy on the ground threw Veronica clear. She came right back at him, but two more shots rang out and she fell over, darting Errol an agonized gaze. He heaved himself back to his feet, but a thunderbolt seemed to strike him in the knee. White light burned away his sight, and when it came back he saw Veronica was coming unsteadily back upright.

"Bitch doesn't know when to stop," one of the boys said.

"I'll shoot out her Goddamn eyes. Maybe that'll slow her up." He lifted his gun.

Errol realized his hand was on one of the stones he'd thrown earlier. He closed his fingers on it and hurled it with everything he had in him. It hit the boy in the side of the jaw. Errol saw shards of teeth fly from his mouth.

Then he heard a gunshot. He winced involuntarily, but didn't feel any new pain. Only two of the boys were standing now, and the others weren't looking at him, but past him, where Billy was calmly taking another shot as Dusk charged down the slope wielding her gleaming sword. One of the boys set a bead on her, but a wind suddenly started; dust swept up around the feet of the dog boys and in the next instant a small tornado formed, lifting them bodily from the ground and hurling them like the hand of a giant, one to each direction of the compass.

The last of Errol's strength left him. His face dropped into the dirt. He could still hear the sounds of the battle. It seemed to him it didn't last much longer.

In the end, two of Jobe's boys wouldn't get up again, thanks to the edge of Dusk's sword. The other two made it to their horses and rode off.

Errol and Veronica were a mess. Veronica had been shot several times. It wasn't clear to Aster exactly what that meant, except for the damage to her leg, which prevented her from walking. Other than that, though, she seemed okay, if that was even a word that could be applied to her.

Errol's injuries were worse and stranger. He'd taken a shotgun blast to the gut and a bullet to his knee. The damage to his torso shouldn't have mattered—it was mostly a box to hang the limbs and head on. Or had been. But now that the breastplate was compromised Aster could see something inside she hadn't put in him; a mass of gelatinous fiber. In places it had congealed, or tied itself in knots, almost as if it was trying to form organs. Where the bullets had torn it, a viscous yellow fluid oozed.

Other changes Aster knew she should have noticed earlier. Some of the wires that moved his limbs had actually somehow been enveloped by the outer layer of his "skin", becoming more like actual tendons.

"Does it hurt?" she asked him.

"Jesus, yes," he muttered.

"Try some of Shecky's ointment," Veronica suggested.

"I don't know what's happening here," Aster said. "It might do more harm than good."

"Just try a little," Veronica insisted.

Reluctantly, Aster applied the salve. It hissed and fizzed a bit. Errol made an odd sound.

"Does that hurt more?" she asked.

"No," he said. "It feels better."

She treated all of the wounds.

"You're turn, Veronica," she said.

"It won't work on me," the girl said. "I don't like the smell of it."

She was probably right, Aster reflected.

"Can you ride?" she asked.

"Yes," Veronica said. She seemed uncharacteristically subdued, which Aster supposed was entirely reasonable.

"Then we'd better go, before the most of them show up."

"I'm still invited?" Veronica asked.

"I came back for you didn't I?" Aster said.

"You came back, anyway," Veronica said.

They rode hard, and without much conversation, although Aster had plenty of questions. They entered a forest of pale, slim trees. Coppery sunlight slanted their shadows long, while small birds flitted in the branches and rustled the slender leaves. When the wind blew, Aster thought she heard faint musical notes.

By nightfall they reached the rim of the Hollow Sea and wound their way through the night forest. The restless landscape turned once again as hills rose south of them so that soon they had a low range of mountains on one side of them and the emptiness of the sea on the other. It felt precarious and exhilarating at the same time.

A soft rushing ahead announced the presence of a small waterfall, running down from the hills and filling a small pool. The pool in turn overflowed into the Hollow Sea. It was a pretty spot, green with horsetails and fern. They rode uphill, to where the stream was fordable, and crossed it.

Veronica hung back, gazing at the water.

"I think I need a bath," she said.

"Now?" Aster said.

"It's the first water we've seen for a while," Veronica said.

Aster paused. Veronica was in bad shape. Being what she was, the water might help her out. And they were all tired; she had fallen asleep in her saddle twice already, once nearly falling out of it.

"Okay," she said. "We'll ride up a bit and give you some privacy. We'll rest until sunrise."

"Thank you, Aster," Veronica said.

They set up camp without a fire, and Billy took the first watch.

J ake slowed his horse; he could still hear them talking, but he couldn't pick out the horses' hoof-beats anymore. Likely they had stopped for a rest.

He dismounted and checked to be sure his rifle was loaded. Jamie had gone back to find the Sheriff, to let him know what had happened, but Jake reckoned to shadow them, so he could give report in case they did anything strange.

Riding alone had brought other things to mind, though. Like how Aster had humiliated him back at the house, stung him in the eyeballs and all. And just when they had the dead girl and the wood man ready to take apart, she'd shown up again with her Hell-witch ways and brought the sky against him. Then the other girl killed poor Eldridge and Peas.

So now he thought maybe he might sneak close to the camp and put a bullet through her head while she was asleep. He could run faster than any of her friends. Hell, maybe he could pick them all off, one by one.

So he eased through the forest, quieter than a spider's breath, until he came to a little waterfall, and a pool.

He saw the horses had worked around it uphill, and was starting that way himself, when he noticed something in the water — somebody was in there, sunken down so only their eyes and the top of their head was visible. Those eyes glimmered the green of rusted copper.

He brought his rifle down to bear, just as she rose up out of the pool.

At first he just saw the girl-shape, and he felt the lust. Then he saw it was her, the girl they had buried.

"You just keep quiet," he murmured.

"I can be quiet," she said.

"Yeah," he said, trying to get his mind straight. Only he couldn't.

"You just come on out," he said.

"I'd rather you came in," she replied.

"Holy Moses," he said. "You *want* it?"

"I want you. To come here," she said.

"Well, that's okay then," he said, dropping his rifle and wading out toward her.

The water was cold, but when she wrapped her arms around him and pressed close he forgot about that, even though she was cold too.

"You're the prettiest thing I ever saw," he said.

"So pretty you were going to leave me buried forever," she teased.

"Well, that was then," he tried to say. Except he sort of choked on the last couple of words on account of the water in his mouth. But she was still hugging him—harder than ever, in fact. He kissed her and pushed her down, deeper, toward the bottom.

Billy had just rousted Aster for her watch when Veronica came strolling into camp. Her limp was not only gone, but she had a bounce in her step.

"You look like you feel better," Aster said.

"Well, water works wonders," Veronica replied, walking her way. "At least it does for me."

She was close enough Aster could make out her face in the moonlight. Her eyes gleamed faintly verdigris, and something in her expression made Aster take a step back.

"If you're tired," Veronica said. "I'll take the watch."

The moment passed as quickly as it had come.

"Sure," Aster said. "I'm glad you're feeling better."

"Thanks," Veronica replied.

They set back off just after dawn, just rested enough not to tumble from their saddles. An hour into it, the baying began, and it didn't sound that far away. Aster cursed that they had stopped at all.

But then she saw the gleam ahead. She took her mount to canter, her heart thumping strangely.

"It has to be," she murmured to the breeze.

And as she came around a copse of trees, there it was.

Her throat closed and tears welled in her eyes. She wasn't crazy. There was a ship. Her ship. It hadn't been a fantasy, her metamorphosis into a raven some sort of hallucination. It was all real, everything she remembered. She had been telling herself that for so many years. Had believed it almost as much as she wanted it.

And yet madness ran in her family. Her father had said so more than once.

"Wow," Errol said.

"Yeah," she replied.

She was a sailing ship, with two great square sails and one triangular lateen. The sails were put away, of course, but the rest of the craft—every bit of it—gleamed in the young sunshine.

"Funny," Errol said. "It looks like it's built of metal."

"Silver," Aster replied. "Billy, how far back are they?"

"Won't be long," he said.

But she knew that. The hounds sounded close.

She nudged her mount forward. It was just as she had last seen it; no leaves had settled on the deck, no vines entangled it.

Well, there was one difference.

"That's disturbing," Errol said.

The gangplank, still extended, was covered with human bones. It looked like ten or more individuals.

"No one can board her unless they know her name," Aster said.

"Which you do," Errol said.

Aster closed her eyes, remembering another place, a quay in a great city, her father whispering a name she could only just make out.

"You do know it, right?" Errol said.

"Just give me a minute," she said.

"You said you knew it."

"I may have been exaggerating a little," she confessed. "But if you don't give me some peace, I'll never remember."

She took a step toward the ship, and another. A breeze came, and the faint music of the trees whirled up. The name, the name, she hadn't really heard it, she had been too far from him, but the shape of his lips, the slight hiss at the start.

She had one step to go before joining the bones. The hounds were closing fast. It was forward or nothing.

She set her foot on the gangplank.

"*Streya*," she whispered. "Your name is Streya."

She did not die. She took another step, and again she did not die. She walked to the top of the gangplank and stepped down upon the silver deck.

"It's okay now," she said. "You can board."

She turned, so they would not see her wipe the cold sweat from her forehead.

Down along the way they had come, she saw the Sheriff and his beasts racing through the trees.

"The horses," Dusk said.

"There's a place for them below," Aster said. "Quickly."

The nearest dog—the black one—came snapping as the last of the horses came on board. Billy shot it and it rolled away and came back up without an obvious wound. Errol jerked up the gangplank as it leapt again and its white brother joined it.

A bullet struck a silvery note on the ship.

Aster pointed north. This part she remembered clearly.

"*Airdi*," she said, and with a hiss and flap of wind the sails dropped down.

Another shot rang out.

"*Vetas*," she commanded, and a wind came up, billowing the sails taut.

"*Plaikdi*," she said.

The ship lurched forward as if pushed by an invisible force, into the gulf. Her belly went light as they fell, and she heard one of the others yelp. But then the keel slapped hard against something, and spray came over the bow, soaking them all as around them the sea came into being.

And she laughed.

Behind, on the shore, a few more shots rang out, but soon enough they were well out of range, and not much later far from the sight of land.

They found Jake's horse near a pool that drained into the abyss the Sheriff called the Hollow Sea. They found Jake, too. He didn't have a mark on him, but the light in him—small as it had been—was gone.

"Drowned," Jobe said. "Damn fool."

It was just then that David began to tremble. It was curious, at first. He wasn't cold, or afraid, and when he held his hands up they seemed steady. The shivering was deeper, inside of him.

"She's close," he realized out loud. "Very close."

"Yes," the Sheriff said. "It's time to run, boys."

And so they ran. The boys had changed further over the course of the last day. Their fur had thickened, their faces begun to protrude. They had sharp ears, and their mouths seemed wider.

And they were fast. In a sprint they could easily outdistance a horse; but they couldn't keep up such a pace for very long.

But they didn't need too. David could feel a slight warmth on his face when he looked in Aster's direction.

And as the boys went howling through the woods, David recognized the trembling in him as hope, hope such as he had not felt in a very long time, longer than his body had been alive. And that hope built as the warmth became heat and finally a glorious burning.

At first he thought she was a star brought to earth, so brightly did she shine in the grey morning. He jumped from his horse and broke into a run. He could see now that although Aster shone the brightest, another star blazed nearby, along with another, fainter light and also a shadow of some sort, a darkness a bright light might cast.

But this constellation was receding from him.

"Aster!" he yelled, running all the harder.

Then something gripped him tight around the knees, and he toppled forward. He screamed, kicking, fighting to get up, but more of the boys piled on him.

"Let me up!" he screeched.

"Look," Jobe said. "Just look, you idiot."

His breathing was coming in short chops, and black spots filled most of his vision, but they kept him pinned until he saw the endless drop below.

"Too late," Jobe said.

David pulled his vision back up and saw the ship, sails billowing, scudding away from him on a pool of rippling yellow light.

"That's her," he said.

"Yeah," Jobe said. "Too bad."

"Let me up," he commanded.

"I'd just as soon let you jump in," Jobe said. "But the Sheriff—"

"Let me up."

They did, and David stood as if rooted, felt the shivering in him all but gone and despair oozing in.

But he remembered more of himself now. He remembered despair that would make gods weep. He wasn't sure how, or why, but it was there, along with the determination that allowed him to survive it.

And the need. He had an empty place in him where that star fit, and he would never be whole until he possessed it.

He walked over to where the Sheriff sat, watching the boat go.

"What now?" he asked.

The Sheriff scratched his chin. "You didn't know what she was?"

"I don't know what you're talking about."

"The girl. Aster. Does she have a mark on her forehead? A star? A moon? Anything?"

"No," David said.

"These things can be hidden. Her father. The man who sent you? What was his name?"

"I never met him before the other day," David said. "I never had to deal with him. But Aster's last name is Kostyena."

For the first time, David saw two things he had never seen in the Sheriff's expression before—genuine surprise and fear.

"Kostyena," he said, slowly. "Is it possible?" He rubbed his head, and seemed to be in pain.

"Describe this man."

"Ah—red hair, lots of tattoos. An alcoholic, I would say."

"I knew this," the Sheriff hissed. "Once I knew it." His gaze stabbed at David.

"Why didn't you tell me any of this before?"

"Are you kidding?" David exploded. "You didn't ask! And when I do try to talk, you usually dismiss me out of hand! Why didn't I tell you? I can't even believe you're asking. And that name might mean something to you, but it doesn't to me."

"It's not his name," the Sheriff said. "His name is Kostye Dvesene. 'Kostyena' means 'daughter of Kostye.'"

"Well, who is he?"

"A nightmare," the Sheriff said. "We hunted him. We failed. I was exiled to your—" His face twisted. "No," he said. It ground out of him. "I went after him. I exiled myself to find him. And then I forgot—the curse made me forget. I thought we were chasing the whelp of some Marchland imp. If she hadn't annoyed me I would have turned my attention elsewhere a long time ago."

"And now?"

"Kostye Dvesene." He said it like an obscenity.

The Sheriff stared after the ship for a little while longer.

"Pick one of the boys," he finally said. "I don't care which one. Bring him to me here at sundown."

PART FOUR

BEYOND AND BEYOND

ONE

TWO STARS

W ell, that's really weird," Errol said.

"Yes," Aster replied, watching the sea fill ahead of them and fade in their wake. Out to maybe a hundred feet it shimmered on all sides. Veronica cried out in glee as three dolphins leapt, one after the other, then laughed in astonished amusement as one arced beyond the water and became a skeleton in midair. Flying fish skipped by, doing the same trick, crumbling into little clouds of dust.

But beneath them she could feel the swells, the absolute reality of the water they sailed upon.

"Well, sure, all of this weirdness," Errol said. "But I actually meant that." He pointed at her face.

"What?" she asked.

"You've got a star on your forehead," he said. "Like Dusk."

"What?" She felt for it, but her fingers only encountered skin.

Dusk, who had also been marveling at the now partly-filled sea, turned quickly at Errol's pronouncement. Her mouth dropped open, and she hurried over.

"By the Vast," she murmured. "I should have known. How—why did you hide this?"

"I don't know what you're talking about," Aster said.

The lie came out before she even considered telling the truth, and it felt natural. After all, until a few days ago, she really *hadn't* known about it.

Dusk seemed to buy it.

"You really didn't know, did you?" she said.

"A star. Like yours?" Aster asked, hoping she didn't sound obviously disingenuous.

"Near," Dusk said, and reached to trace it with her finger. Aster flinched, but allowed the little intrusion.

"We're family, then," she said. "There can be no doubt. Who are your parents?"

"I never knew my mother," she said.

"But your father?"

She felt her heart pounding. She wanted to lie about that, too, but Errol knew her father's name, and Veronica probably did.

"My father's name is Kostye Dvesene," she said.

Dusk tilted her head. "That name is unknown to me," she said. "What more do you know of your family?"

"Nothing," she said. "He tells me nothing."

"How curious," Dusk said. "But now I understand why I was drawn to help you. We are cousins, distant or near. Our fates are bound together."

Aster was torn. On the one hand, she desperately wanted to know more about her family—Dusk's family. On the other, she wanted this conversation to be over. Her father had hidden her away from everyone, family included. Maybe especially from family. She desperately wished she could talk to him before things went any further. Or that he had told her a little more, dammit.

"Well," Aster said. "This is all very confusing. To have a cousin, all of a sudden. You'll forgive me if this comes as a shock."

"Of course," Dusk said. "We'll talk when you're ready."

So she doesn't really want to get into this either, Aster realized, and wondered what that could mean.

"Why don't we have a look at the ship?" Veronica interposed. "For all we know an ogre is hiding below decks, waiting to make a meal of us."

Instead of an ogre they found cabins with beds made up in silk sheets and down comforters, a dining room (Errol called it a mess) complete with a table set with china and crystal. The hold had a steep ramp that allowed the horses to enter it from the middle deck, and that was empty as well.

They found no stores or cupboards, but when Aster returned to the mess at noon she found the serving plates plenished with lamb chops in a green sauce, a whole fish, croquettes of some sort, peas, and a clear soup with tiny star-shaped dumplings. The horses were likewise supplied with grain and sweet grass.

She, Dusk, and Billy ate while Errol and Veronica watched.

"Errol, you almost seem to have an expression on your face," Dusk remarked. "I wonder if that's possible."

Aster shrugged. "Something is certainly going on with him I can't explain."

"You've no idea?" Errol asked.

"Well," she said, patting her napkin to her lips, "the soul is a strange thing. I put yours in a body of wood, wire, bone, and ivory, and with a little magic, I made it believe it was in a real body, that the wires were tendons connected to muscles, that those spheres are eyes, and so on. And because your soul believed that, you can see, and move, and feel. I thought that was about as good as I could do. But maybe here, where magic isn't a faint memory but a part of everything, maybe here what your soul believes can do more. Maybe it is actually making your body human."

"Maybe," Errol said.

"Maybe," Aster agreed. "I do not want to give you false hope. But the further we travel in the Kingdoms, the stronger magic feels to me, and the more I remember of what I've studied."

"What do you mean?"

"It's like I can't remember a spell until enough magic is present to use it," she said. "Or I can, but not perfectly enough to pronounce it."

"That is the nature of things," Dusk said. She leaned back in her chair. "So many revelations in so few days."

"Yes," Veronica said. "And I have another one."

"Geez, I almost forgot," Errol said. "What with all the running and getting shot."

"Makes you forgetful," Veronica said, patting his arm. "So easily distracted."

"What is it?" Aster asked.

"Your teacher," Veronica said. "Mr. Watkins. He's the man who killed me."

For a very long moment, the table was absolutely quiet. Then Aster found her voice.

"Veronica," she said, "that's impossible. You died before he was even born."

"Sure," she said. "I know that. But it's also still a fact. I wasn't absolutely sure until he kissed me, but now there's no question. He doesn't look the same. Back then he was older, and taller, and his face was sort of longer. His name was Mr. Robertson and he lived about a half a mile from us. I always thought he was nice."

She looked away, out the porthole at the sky.

"I don't want to go into details, okay? But it was him."

"You mean to say he's reincarnated or something?" Aster asked.

Veronica met her gaze. "I believe," she said, "that in his case it's 'or something'."

D avid found Jobe half-asleep and nudged him awake with his foot. He snarled and bounced up, his strange, wiry frame taut and his eyes flashing with anger.

"What do you want?" he snapped.

David met his gaze levelly, looking past his eyes and into the light that burned in him. These people here had so much of the quick—not as much as Aster, but more than most in the dim world where he'd languished for so long.

"Listen," David said, quietly, "things were different when we met. I've learned some important truths about myself since then. It seems laughable to me that I was ever afraid of you, but you need to understand that time is over."

"Whatever you say, preacher," Jobe said.

"And stop calling me that," David said. "Now come along, the Sheriff wants you."

"The sheriff," Jobe muttered. "I reckon we're about quit of him. There's no following them where they've gone."

"You're giving up?"

"Just doesn't seem like there's anything in it for us any-more," he said.

"It's not like you can go home," David pointed out.

"Why not?" Jobe said. "Sure, the folks will be sore. But even if they don't take us back in, I reckon we could manage on our own, me and the boys."

"Well, but you've changed," David.

"Some, I reckon," Jobe admitted. "I reckon I've done some things I might not have done before. You know, if the folks were around like they're supposed to be."

"No," David said. "Literally. Your bodies have changed."

Jobe looked down at his pelt. "What do you mean?" he asked.

"Look at me," David said. "Can't you see the difference?"

"You're older," Jobe said. "Your hair is lighter."

"Okay," David said. "What about the others? Do they look the same as when I first met you?"

Jobe looked around. "They look tired and half-starved, that's all."

David wondered if none of them knew what had happened to them or if it was just Jobe, retreating into fantasy.

He realized he didn't care.

"Come on," he said. "The Sheriff." He started to walk.

"Yeah," Jobe said, following.

The Sheriff was waiting for them by the Hollow Sea. The shadows were long now.

"Sunset," David said. "As requested."

"Come here, Jobe," the sheriff said.

"Yes, sir," the boy replied.

"Jobe," the Sheriff said. "I need you to remember something."

"What's that," Jobe asked.

"Melzheyas," he said. "It's a name."

"A funny name," Jobe said.

"Say it back to me," the Sheriff said.

"Meljeys," Jobe attempted.

"Melzheyas," the Sheriff said again.

"Melzheyas," Jobe said, this time getting it right.

"Good, Jobe," the Sheriff said. "Good."

David didn't see the Sheriff draw the knife; maybe it had been in his hand all along. He was almost as surprised as Jobe, who suddenly had it buried in his heart.

Jobe tried to pull away, but the sheriff hung on to him. He said something. David thought it was "Mama." His light shone through the break, dimming in the air like frosty breath on a winter's morning.

Then the Sheriff wrenched the knife out and sent Jobe spinning over the cliff. David had one last look at the boy's confused face before he was gone.

The Sheriff wiped his knife clean on a cloth.

"Why did you do that?" David asked.

"Should have known you would pick him," the Sheriff said. "Just as well. If he'd decided to go back, they might have gone with him. As it is, they'll stay with me."

That didn't answer his question, but David didn't think he should repeat it. He would find out in time.

He did, and it didn't take long.

The stink came first, an unbelievable hot billow of putrefaction. Then, in the last light of the sun, Melzheyas rose up from the Hollow Sea.

His huge wings reached over the rim and beat once, twice, before his head — or more appropriately, skull — came into view, followed by seemingly endless coils of serpentine corpus. His wings were tattered, with a few feathers clinging here and there; the head was the size of a car, and the body was bones and clinging rot.

Clearly, Melzheyas had seen better days.

David knew it was impossible that such a thing could fly, even if it were alive and its wings intact. But he was long past worrying about such matters.

"Hello, Melzheyas," the Sheriff said.

The monster settled on the cliff in a coil, like a rattlesnake.

"Hello, Banished," the dragon said. Its voice was like wind rattling through leafless limbs, but it was comprehensible.

"Whatever have you called me for? Conversation?"

The Sheriff snorted. "Kostye Dvesene. The man who killed you."

The serpent was silent for a moment.

"You have my attention," it said.

"His daughter is passing over the Hollow Sea as we speak."

"She was passing over it when he killed me," Melzheyas said.

"She has returned."

The monster's wings twitched and rustled in agitation. Sulfurous light gleamed in his empty sockets.

"Is her father with her?"

"He is not," the Sheriff said. "He is where you cannot touch him."

"Then we shall kill his whelp, is that it?"

David started to object, but the sheriff did it for him.

"Her we need alive," he said, "to get to Kostye. Her companions you may kill as you please."

"How shall I capture her?" Melzheyas asked. "With my teeth?"

"No," the sheriff replied. "You'll take us with you."

They sailed through days and nights that were much the same. The skies were clear and at night the moon seemed twice the size it should be. Aster had the odd feeling that the sea was somehow curving up very gradually. It seemed so especially at night.

Given how things had been since they had entered the Kingdoms, she had expected anything and everything from the Hollow Sea — sea serpents, storms, pirates — but when Errol shouted that land lay ahead, nothing of the sort had imperiled them.

The land Errol had spied was the uppermost peak of a jagged mountain range. It took another day to sight the shoreline, a rocky shingle brooded over by a deep, evergreen forest.

"Well," Errol observed, "I don't see an orchard. Or any giants."

"No," Aster said. "I don't guess it's going to be that easy."

"Maybe you should change into a bird again and have a look," Veronica said. "I missed that before; I wouldn't mind seeing it now."

The suggestion was both tempting and terrifying. She had nearly lost herself the first time. What was disturbing was that part of her had enjoyed it, reveled in the simplification of thought and memory, the loss of control. She feared the next time she transformed she would be even more inclined to remain an animal.

"If I have to," she said. "But let's have a look first. Dusk, do you have a suggestion for which way to sail? East or west?"

"Things generally get stranger when one travels west," she replied.

"West it is, then," she said.

About noon the next day, Errol spotted something on a high hill that looked built rather than natural. The closer they got the more it became clear it was a tower or castle of some sort. Aster brought the ship up to the stony shore, but from there the structure was obscured by the trees.

"I don't think we should all go," Aster said. "Someone should stay with the ship."

"That means you, then," Veronica said. "You're the only one who can make it go." She smiled. "Maybe Billy can stay here with you."

Aster frowned her little frown and shook her head.

"Billy is probably best in the woods," she said.

"Agreed," Dusk chimed in. "I can accompany him."

"You're probably second best," Errol said. "You should stay here in case we need finding."

Dusk conceded that with a nod.

"So it's just me and the boys," Veronica said.

"I'd rather you stayed, too," Errol said. "It's just up the hill and we won't be gone long."

Veronica gave him the stink-eye and then took him by the arm.

"Errol," she said, "may I have a word with you in private?"

Errol actually felt his face warm a bit, and wondered if his 'face' was actually reddening.

"Sure," he said.

He followed her below.

"What?" he said.

She lifted her arms and clasped her hands behind his neck.

"You wouldn't be trying to coddle me, would you?" she asked.

"I just—you, know, just the other day I pulled you out of a hole in the ground," he said.

"Is that a yes?" she said.

"I guess so," he said. "I don't want to see you get hurt again."

"I'm dead, Errol."

"Yeah," he said. "Still."

She sighed, conceding the argument. "This time I'm going to interpret this as you being sweet. Next time I'm going to tell you to jump off a cliff. Okay?"

"Okay," he said.

"You had better kiss me now."

So he did.

"It's not far," he said. "We'll be back soon."

I t didn't *look* that far," Errol complained, as he followed Billy up yet another steep slope.

"Not far for birds," Billy said.

"Yeah."

He looked back. He could see reflected bits of sunlight through the leaves and maybe part of the ship. He wasn't sure how high they were, but they had been climbing for hours, and it was starting to get dark. A few birds and a chipmunk accounted for all of the wildlife they had seen thus far, but this felt to Errol like the sort of place where nasty things might be met at night.

By the time they reached the building, he was sure they were going to find out. The sun was no longer visible, and the sky was the color of slate.

What they found was a ruin. The structure he had seen from the sea was a pair of towers connected by a wall. Now he could tell there had at one time been eight towers, but the other six and their walls had fallen—oddly, all in the same direction. As if they had been pushed down.

"Looks like no one is home," Errol said.

Billy just nodded. Sometimes he wished Billy had a little more to say. It made him nervous to do all of the talking.

Probably his taciturn nature was what Aster liked about him.

They searched through the ruins anyway, but there wasn't really anyplace for someone to hide. The towers were empty columns; only a few wooden struts remained to suggest the stairways that had once led to their summits.

Now stars were appearing, as the moon, nearly full, brightened in the sky.

"Can you lead us back down?" he asked Billy.

Billy seemed to consider that for a long time.

"That's not such a good idea," he said. "I don't know these woods. I don't know what lives here, and the path is steep. Better we camp here and go back down tomorrow."

It was obviously the right answer, but Errol was still uneasy. He felt better when Billy had a cheerful little fire going.

The moon seemed huge here, as it had above the Hollow Sea. As if they were closer to it. The dark blotches seemed somehow more foreboding, and he shivered involuntarily.

"They tell a story about Him," Billy said.

"Him?" Errol asked.

"The Moon."

"I thought the Moon was a 'her'."

"No," Billy said. "At least not in this story."

"How does it go?"

Billy settled back onto one elbow.

"There was a woman," he began. "Some say she was the Sun, or maybe a daughter of the Sun. And this man came into her house every night and fornicated with her. But it was so dark she didn't know who it was. So one night she put her fingers in the ashes of the fire and when he came to her she touched his face. The next day, she looked around the village for the man with ashes all over his face."

Errol thought he would go on, but the silence stretched out.

"I get it," he finally said. "The guy was the Moon. That's why he's all smudged up."

"The guy was her brother," Billy said. "He was so ashamed when everyone knew what he'd been up to he went up into the sky and stayed there."

"Oh. Wow. That's kind of creepy."

Billy didn't say anything, and an owl or something made a weird sound in the distance. Looking at the moon, Errol had another little shiver. In that moment he remembered Aster's workshop, the clockwork sun, moon, and star. The moon had been clear and unmarred at first, but then it had flipped around to look as it really did, bruised and battered.

"The moon, actually, is a satellite," he said. "They think it used to be part of the Earth. The dark marks are craters and seas of dust."

"Yeah?" Billy said.

"Men have walked on it."

"Have they?" he said.

"Yes," Errol replied.

"Huh."

Errol thought maybe Billy would defend his story, but he didn't.

"You sleep," Errol finally said. "I'll take first watch."

"Have you ever done that?" Billy asked, quietly.

"Done what?" Errol asked. "Sleep with my sister?"

Billy looked uncomfortable. He sat back up, crossed his legs, and looked into the fire.

"With anybody," he said.

The question froze Errol for a moment, both because it was unexpected and because he didn't know what to say.

"Yeah," he finally admitted.

"How was it?"

He looked at Billy. If Phil or Tommy had asked him that, it would have been with a leer — or even a sneer. But Billy's eyes were as without guile as a child's.

"It was — weird," he said. "I was nervous. I was happy, too, you know, because . . ." he stopped. "Now I wish it had never happened."

"Why?"

"Because it just makes it worse," Errol said. "That she dumped me."

He knew he would be crying now, if he could. Like a girl. But somehow he knew Billy wasn't judging him.

"Is this about Aster?" Errol asked. "Did you —"

"No," Billy said. "No, we haven't."

He studied Billy for a moment. He felt sort of knotted up inside, and wasn't really sure why.

"Look," he said. "I'm not sure what's going on with you two. But I've known Aster for a while. And maybe I haven't been the friend to her I should have for most of that time, but I don't want to see her hurt. So you'd better not be planning on just—you know—and then moving on, right?"

"No," Billy said. "I like her. I just want to make her happy. I know fornication makes people happy sometimes."

"Yeah," Errol said. "Sometimes. Why don't you just start with giving her flowers, or something?"

"Okay," Billy said.

"Now go to sleep."

Billy nodded and rolled over.

"Billy?" Errol said.

"Yeah?"

"Don't tell anyone anything I said just now," he said. "Especially don't tell Aster."

"Why?"

"Lisa didn't want me to tell anyone we did it. So I didn't. Nobody knows, okay?"

"Except me," Billy replied.

"Well, you don't exactly go to my school," Errol said.

Billy didn't reply to that. He just sort of slumped forward, like he had fallen asleep sitting up. The fire flickered and took on a bluish tint.

"This talk sounds very naughty," a soft, high voice murmured. For a moment, Errol wasn't even sure he heard it. But then he saw her, just a few feet away, crouched in the vines between two fallen blocks of stone. A hot wave of shock pulsed through him. Where had she come from? She was right in front of him. How could he have not seen her arrive?

Her eyes were what he mostly saw; blue like the fire — which now was deep turquoise. Her hair glowed the same color, but the rest of her was dark, and he realized it was mostly her outline he saw, limned in a faint glow.

It was very cold. The girl stood up and stepped toward him.

"Billy?" Errol said. "Are you okay?"

She took another step.

"Don't come any closer," Errol snapped.

"You aren't like him," she said, ignoring his warning. He scrambled up, unsure what to do, but knowing he had to do something.

He could see her features in the azure glow of the fire now. She was smiling, and when he raised his fist she puckered her lips and blew. The fire suddenly swirled up and surrounded him. He felt his legs go heavy and sat down, hard. His arms were difficult to move, but he tried, reaching toward her as she knelt down at his feet.

"Here we go," she murmured. "Don't fret." And she touched his ankles, very gently. It felt as if his feet had been dunked in cold soda water, and the effervescent sting worked quickly up his legs, to his torso. When it reached his head he had a moment of giddy confusion before oblivion.

TWO
THEY WENT INTO THINGS

"G irl's night is always such fun," Veronica commented, as the sun settled on the horizon. Something warbled in the distance, and something closer answered it.

"Yeah," Aster replied, staring up at the dark, forested hills. "Really fun." She sighed. "They're not going to make it back before nightfall, are they?"

Dusk shook her head. "Someone just built a fire up there," she said. "See the smoke? Climbing down in the dark wouldn't be sensible."

Aster stared hard to where she was pointing, but didn't make out much.

"Learn that in girl scouts?" Veronica asked.

"I don't know what that is," Dusk replied. She sounded irritated. The camaraderie that had developed between Dusk and Veronica seemed to have dissipated. Aster wasn't sure why — although it probably had to do with Errol — but it was something of a relief to Aster. If they were sniping at each other, they weren't ganging up against her.

"Errol and Billy," Veronica said. "All alone in the woods. Whatever shall they talk about? Girls, perhaps?"

"Billy doesn't talk much," Aster said.

"Yeah. I figure that's what you like about him. He's quiet. Does what he's told. Quietly."

"Not a quality Errol values apparently," Dusk said.

"Oh," Veronica said. "There is no accounting for who Errol is going to like."

You can say that again, Aster thought. Dusk, however, did not let it go by.

"Errol is a kind person," Dusk said. "He finds an injured bird and he tries to fix its wing, even if it pecks at his eyes. But his kindheartedness blinds him to a simple fact—that some things are broken beyond fixing, and to continue the effort hurts everyone."

Aster was slightly shocked; it was the meanest thing she had ever heard Dusk say.

"Wow," Veronica said. "That was a good one. When the boys are gone, I guess you figure you can drop your act."

"I've no idea what you're talking about," Dusk said.

"Why are you with us, Dusk?" Veronica sked. "You've never explained that. And yet odd things keep turning up. Everybody we meet acts funny around you, like you're something special. Now suddenly Aster is a relative of yours. What are the odds? And that snake—I didn't call it up. I doubt very much it crawled up on you on its own. So how did it get there? I was the obvious one to blame."

Dusk pursed her lips. "I'm not accustomed to being spoken to in that manner," she said, softly. "I give you my aid—risk my own life—and this is my payment?"

"I'm on to you," Veronica said.

"If you have something to say, *nov*, say it."

Aster felt a little shock at the word from her father's language.

"Ouch. Name-calling too," Veronica said. "Shall we move on to hair-pulling?"

"You guys—" Aster said. But it turned out she didn't have to interrupt them. The whirlwind settling on the deck of the ship did that.

Dusk swore and yanked out her sword, while Aster spoke an adjuration to Calm Winds. She felt the power of it as it came through her throat into the world. She felt her mind envelope the rough moving surface of the air.

Then everything flashed blue-white, and spasms wracked her body, sending her down to the deck. For long moments she knew only agony, but then the pain slacked, and her muscles returned to her control. She pushed herself up.

The whirlwind was gone. In its place stood a boy with a blaze of red hair and beetling eyebrows to match. He wore a long shift of felt with swirled patterns of umber, red, and black and dark yellow pants tucked into high boots that turned up a bit at the toe.

"Don't let's try that again, eh?" he said. "It's not as if I'm an ordinary wind."

"Haydevil is actually more ordinary than he imagines," a softer, feminine voice said. This came from the slight young woman settling on the deck near the boy. She was dressed much like he was, but her colors tended toward late autumn gold and brown and her hair fell in long, black braids. They were both beautiful in a delicate way.

The girl also held what looked remarkably like Dusk's sword, and a glance at the warrior-woman's empty hands confirmed it. Aster wondered how that had happened.

"Oh, sew it in your lips, Mistral," the boy said. "She knows my power to her bones."

"Aster was defending us," Dusk said, helping Aster to her feet. "Your arrival was abrupt and strange."

"That's a fine description of him, abrupt and strange," the girl—Mistral—said. "Let's all be easy. No harm was intended. But this is our country, and you are strangers in it."

She stopped, and waited expectantly.

"This is Dusk, and she's Veronica," Aster said. "As Dusk said, my name is Aster."

"What are you doing here?" Haydevil demanded.

"Give them time, brother, they will tell us, I'm certain," Mistral said.

Aster regarded the two and then cast a little glance at Dusk.

"We've nothing to hide," Dusk said to Aster, in the language of her father. For an instant, Aster considered pretending not to understand, but Dusk shook her head.

"You bear the mark of my kin," Dusk said. *"And I've heard you spell in the old tongue. There's no use in pretending, with me or them. The danger here is in deceiving them and being discovered. Speak plainly."*

"Yes, please do," Mistral said, in the same tongue. When she saw their surprise at knowing the language, she smiled. "I am well-traveled."

"Then maybe you can help us," Aster said. "We've come in search of a certain orchard. One with—ah—well, a giant."

Mistral blinked. Haydevil pursed his lips, but remained silent.

"I know that place," Mistral finally said. "May I ask your intentions?"

"I'm not really clear on that," Aster replied. "I'm supposed to find an orchard, and a giant, and he's supposed to help me somehow."

"Help you?" Haydevil scoffed. "A giant? Help you to the grave, maybe. Plant you straight in the ground."

"There is danger, that is true," Mistral said. "But if you seek him, I can help you."

"Thank you," Aster replied.

"Well," Mistral said. "That's settled then. Are you ready?"

Aster blinked. It all seemed a bit too easy.

"Errol," Veronica said. "Billy."

"Right," Aster said. "Two of our companions went ashore last night. We're waiting on them." She pointed up the hillside.

"Waiting on them?" Haydevil said. "Well that's useless."

"What do you mean?" Aster said.

"Well, the Brume has them," he said. "We thought you knew."

"What do you mean?"

"Well you sent them up there," Mistral said. "That's begging the Brume to make off with them."

"You must not have liked them much," Haydevil put in.

"No, we like them well indeed," Dusk snapped. "What is this Brume?"

"She's awful," Mistral said. "Really awful."

"Some sort of monster?"

"All sorts of monster, I would say," Haydevil said.

"Has she — are they dead?" Aster asked.

"No, not yet. Dragged off to her lair, by the looks of things."

"And where is that?" Dusk demanded.

Mistral looked thoughtful. "That's two favors you're asking of us now, and the second one is a great bother."

"I would be very grateful," Aster said.

"I am *so* certain of that," Mistral said. "But I'm minded that there are traditions about this sort of thing. You know that, I think."

"I have some things," Aster said. "Magical things."

"Indeed you do," Mistral replied. "And one very nice one."

"What do you —" she closed her eyes as it sank in.

"You mean the boat, don't you?"

"Eh—yes," Mistral said. "After all, it did once belong to our father."

"No it didn't," Aster replied. "It belonged to mine."

"Both things are possible," Mistral said. "I was just a little girl, but I remember Father giving it over. Made a deal with a traveling wizard. Red-headed fellow, had a little girl . . ." she stopped and smiled. "Why that was you, wasn't it?"

"I don't . . ." Aster began. But she did remember a man, talking to her father in a huge hall of stone. Was there a little girl with dark hair? Maybe.

"Well, you see, that brings us all back around," Mistral said.

"But I need the ship to go back home," Aster said.

"Well, then," Mistral said. "You will have it. And the Brume shall keep your friends. It may well be too late anyway."

Veronica walked over to Mistral until they stood eye-to-eye.

"Where is Errol?" she asked. Her voice was quite low. "I'd like to know."

"Take it up with your friend Aster, then," Mistral said. Her eyes began to flash and glint, and Aster felt the sudden welling up of power. Veronica didn't budge. Mistral reached and touched her shoulder, and Veronica's hair stood straight out; sparks played along her arms and legs, crackled between her fingers. She crumpled without a sound.

Aster stared, aghast.

"What have you done to her?" she gasped.

"She is no more alive and no deader than she was before," Mistral said. "She was summoning the beasts of the deeps, and so I did no more than defend myself. I have no wish to harm anyone."

"Why do you want my ship?"

"It was my father's, and all things of his are dear to me."

Oddly, her voice had a certain gravity that it hadn't up until now. It felt to Aster as if she was telling the truth.

"Fine," she said. "If you take us to Errol and Billy and if you show us the way to the orchard and the giant, then I'll give you the ship. I'll find another way home."

"Done," Mistral said. "Sail west along this coast. My brother and I shall guide you."

I told you things grow stranger in the west," Dusk said.

"I see that," Aster replied. She hadn't noticed the oddness about the trees at first, the slant was so imperceptible, but as they went along the trees bent more and more towards them. They looked as if they had grown that way. But as her gaze wandered up the hillside, it was apparent that the trees weren't all leaning in one direction—instead they bent away from some common single spot, as if a great explosion had pushed them all down.

The only exceptions were the youngest trees, the saplings. They stood straight.

On the deck, Veronica began to stir, and after a little while she stood and joined them. When Aster asked if she was okay, the other girl nodded slightly, but didn't say anything.

Not much later they reached the epicenter of whatever had happened, the place everything slanted away from.

It was not empty, as Aster had half expected. They sailed into a little bay. Beyond that a small mountain rose up in three tiers, almost like a wedding cake. The cliffs and slopes were of white stone, but Aster could see green upon the flat surfaces. The upper part of the mountain had been carved into strange, flowing shapes with odd, irregular openings which she remembered were windows and doors.

"I've been here before," she whispered.

"Have you?" Veronica murmured, to Aster's chagrin. She hadn't meant to say it so loudly.

"Is this where the Brume is?" Dusk asked.

"Yes," said Mistral. "From here we must go on foot. Bring lamps, unless you can see in the dark."

Aster landed the boat at the quay, the same quay she and her father had boarded it from. But a lot was missing. She remembered a city, and colorful pennants, other ships, the smell of bread baking. All that was gone, perhaps swept away by whatever bent the trees.

"The people who lived here," she asked Mistral. "Where are they?"

"They were changed," Mistral replied.

"Into monsters? Like the Brume?" Aster replied. "Your parents?"

"This is not your business," Haydevil snapped. "It's this way."

Mistral seemed content to let Haydevil lead. When they reached the cliff, he suddenly reached out his hand toward Aster.

"What?" she asked.

"Take it," he said. "You too, hold my other hand." The last was directed at Dusk.

She did as she was told, feeling the hot prickle of magic against her palm.

"Now you two join hands."

She took Dusk's hand and felt how hard it was, how calloused, and realized it was her sword hand.

"Now, run widdershins," he exclaimed, tugging.

They followed him, faster and faster until she thought they would fall, and then her feet did go out from under her, but not in the usual way. They were airborne, whirling round and round. Haydevil was laughing, the anger in him temporarily absent and replaced by joy, and Aster herself felt a burst of exhilaration.

Mistral had taken Veronica's hands and they were dancing rather than spinning, long gliding steps taking them higher and higher.

Soon they all settled on the grassy surface of the lower tier.

"Here we go," Mistral said.

"I hope we're not too late," Haydevil said.

They followed the siblings through a door carved in the rock. It was vaulted but slightly irregular, as if the stonemason had been trying to suggest it had been fashioned by nature rather than a chisel.

There were no steps inside, but the corridor sloped alarmingly downward. The stone was very smooth, and she wondered if she would be able to climb back up it.

It grew colder as they descended, and the passage became slick with condensation. Eventually it opened into a large chamber.

Like the door and passage, it was a little unclear whether they were in a cavern carved to look like a room or a room constructed to resemble a cavern. Pillars rose high into the darkness, but they seemed so thin and fragile it was hard to believe they were holding anything up. The cold, wet air stank of decay.

Beyond the light of their lamps, Aster made out another source of illumination, greenish blue in color.

"Yes, that's the way," Mistral confirmed.

Haydevil went ahead, striding quietly. Aster heard a voice or voices. Almost they seemed to be singing.

Haydevil stopped, suddenly.

"Eh," he said. "Too late for sure."

"Too late?" Aster repeated. She pushed past him, her heart thrumming, terrified of what she would see.

"We told you she was awful," Mistral sighed.

The light came from a shaft of sunlight falling down through a hole in a roof choked with moss and ferns. In the dim circle of light stood a table and chairs. The table was set with silver and ivory tea service. Billy and Errol were seated, dressed outlandishly in lacey feminine garb.

With them was a girl who appeared to be around ten or eleven years old. She had long, tangled blackish-green hair and was appareled in what might have once been a pink ball gown. It appeared as if she had been wearing it for weeks, if not longer.

She looked at them as they came in.

"These boys have been naughty," she said, in a chirpy little voice. "But I have given them tea, and they are thinking better of their ways."

"We're thinking better of our ways," Billy agreed. His voice sounded strange.

Errol waved.

"Let's have a song, boys," the girl said.

Horribly the two boys began to sing an odd, childish little melody.

Drip and drop
Plip and Plop
Put the spiders in the pot
Boil them up, then we'll sup
Spider tea from our dainty cups

"That's the Brume?" Veronica asked.

"Yes," Haydevil said. "Horrible isn't she? Look how she's dressed them."

"But they're alive," Aster breathed.

"Well, sure," Haydevil said. "But high heavens, the embarrassment."

"Have you come to join us?" the Brume asked.

"I'm afraid not," Mistral replied. "The boys' friends have come to fetch them."

The girl frowned. "But it's been such a short time."

"I know. But we've made promises."

"Not for me, you didn't," the Brume said, petulantly. "I make my own promises."

"They've given us something very nice to get their friends back. You can see it if you want. Now, let them go, little sister."

"Sister?" Aster snapped. "You tricked us."

"How so?" Mistral asked. "Could you have found them without us?"

"You probably sent her after them!"

"As it happens, we did not," Mistral said. "We all went to see you and your ship, but the Brume does what she does. It's nothing to do with us." She frowned. "You're not considering going back on our deal?"

Aster held herself defiantly for another moment. "No," she finally said. She knew that if she did, odds were that none of them would leave this place. "Just—make them right. Make them well."

"I hate you all," the Brume said. Then she brightened. "What did they give us?"

"Let them go, and you shall see," Mistral said.

"Fine," the Brume said. She pursed her lips and inhaled sharply, making a little whistling sound. Errol and Billy instantly stopped singing. Errol looked at the Brume, then over at them, then down at himself.

"What the hell?" he blurted.

E rrol sat staring into the biggest fire and fireplace he had ever seen. He still felt chilled to the core.

"You know," Veronica said, "if Aster hadn't given away our only way home, this all might seem kind of funny."

"Yeah?" Errol said. "I'll take your word for it."

"I'm just talking, honey." She touched his arm. "It's warm," she said.

"From the fire," Errol replied.

"No," she said. "It's not. It almost feels like skin. And your face." She traced her finger along his cheek. "Look, it moves a little."

"That tickles," he murmured.

"You're changing," she said. "But I'm just staying the same."

"That's okay," he said. He hesitated, and then put his arm around her, even though he knew Dusk and Aster would see.

A ster saw Errol put his arm around Veronica. She had been about to join them at the fire, but now thought better of it.

"What about the orchard?" she asked Mistral instead, who sat a few feet away sipping wine from a tear-shaped glass.

They were in the great hall of her memory. Like everything else it seemed less than it had been. Not less large—it was huge—but before it had bustled with servants and children. A few new faces had appeared in the evening—about twelve all told—but she gathered they were all siblings or cousins of Mistral, Haydevil, and the Brume.

"The orchard," Mistral said. "Come."

She followed the older girl from the hall onto a balcony. Mountains rose under the moon, fantastic and breathtaking and seemingly as distant as the moon, but Mistral gestured below, to where a stone wall enclosed about a hundred small trees in neat little rows. Over half of the enclosure was empty ground.

"Mother's orchard," she said. "The giant will not come tonight, but he will tomorrow night."

"What happened to your parents?" she asked. She expected the question to be dismissed as it had been before, but Mistral shrugged.

"They changed," she said. "They went into things."

"You said that before. What do you mean?"

"A curse came over the mountains," she said. "I do not know how. Much less why. My father went into the water, into the Hollow Sea, and sleeps there, perhaps forever. He fought the curse—you can see that in the trees, can you not, in the smiting of the land? But he did not win."

"And your mother?"

"In the orchard," she said. "In the trees."

To Aster's vast surprise, she saw that Mistral had a tear on her cheeks.

"What is it?" she asked.

"The giant comes once a week and uproots a tree," Mistral said. "When he has pulled them all, my mother will be no more. Even if the curse is lifted."

"Why don't you stop him?"

"He is a giant. Our natures are of no use against him. Perhaps yours will be."

"I . . . I did not come here to slay a giant," Aster told her.

"Then you shall be slain by one," Mistral said. "And my mother will die."

She turned and went back into the hall, leaving Aster to stare at the half-ruined orchard, trying to remember, to think about what tomorrow night held.

And to hope.

But it seemed a stupid hope, for a lot of reasons. Actually, all of her hopes seemed stupid now.

She was about to go back in when a hand fell lightly on her shoulder.

"Hey, Billy," she said. Her voice felt shaky in her throat. "What's up?"

"Do you want to be alone?" he asked.

"No," she said.

"Okay," he said. And then he didn't say anything.

"That's the orchard," she said, waving a hand toward it. "The giant comes tomorrow night."

"That's good, then."

"I don't know," she said. "It sounds like another thing we have to fight. And Mistral and her family can't beat it, so what chance do we have?"

"I guess we'll find out," he said.

"Yeah," she sighed. "I mean it's what we came for. But I don't know anymore."

"You gave the ship away," Billy pointed out.

"Yes," she replied.

"To save Errol and me."

She nodded, not looking at him.

"I think I'm going back in," she said. "It's cold."

"Okay," he said.

"Unless you—"

It seemed to happen in slow motion, just like in one of those stupid movies. Billy's face was near, and then it was closer, and she wasn't *sure* what it meant. If she leaned forward, and she was wrong, it would be too embarrassing to deal with.

She leaned forward half an inch.

She wasn't wrong.

She had been kissed before, by Brett Perkins. It hadn't been horrible, but it had been awkward and felt kind of silly. She had certainly not seen what the big deal was.

This was a big deal. When Billy's lips touched hers, she knew in the same instant that he wasn't thinking about anything but her. Everything seemed *more*—the sounds of the night, the distant chatter inside, the cool wind on her arms. All of her self-consciousness melted away, and she kissed him back, trying to show him how she felt, what she never had the courage to say with words. His arms closed around her.

After a moment he stopped kissing her and stroked her hair.

"I couldn't find any flowers," he said.

"What?"

"So I hope that was okay."

"That," Aster said, "was *very* okay."

THREE

A GIANT MISTAKE

H ow big is this giant?" Errol asked.

"Eh, bigger than you," Haydevil said, biting his nails and then looking them over.

"Well, that's helpful," Errol said.

By day it was easy to see the gaping holes in the ground where the giant had pulled up the apple trees, roots and all. He was trying to imagine something big enough to do that, and not liking the image it was conjuring.

"I don't suppose you guys have a cannon or a catapult or something?" he asked.

Haydevil just blinked at him and whirled up into the air.

"I've shown you," he said. "That's all I promised Mistral I would do."

"Anything can be killed," Dusk asserted, crossing her arms as she examined the area.

"Maybe it has a weak spot, like the Snatchwitch," Veronica suggested.

"Hopefully, we won't have to fight it at all," Aster said. "I really don't understand this. It flies against what the oracle told me."

"Oracles are not entirely to be trusted," Dusk said. "They may give you the right advice, but twist it up a bit. You came here to find an orchard and a giant. Here we have both."

"But maybe it's the *wrong* orchard, the *wrong* giant," Aster said.

"Starting to second-guess ourselves a little, are we?" Veronica said.

Aster frowned, but she did not reply immediately.

"None of you need come here tonight," she eventually told them. "I will try the giant alone. If he attacks me, I'll run, that's all."

"You needed me to find Veronica," Errol reminded her. "You may need us both to—I don't know, make friends with the giant?"

She shrugged. "Maybe."

"So I'm in," Errol said.

"Whither Errol goes," Veronica sighed. "Let's just get this over with. I'm not that keen on hanging out here, and we can't go back. Forward seems like the only way."

"Thanks," Aster said.

Errol was wandering along the rim of the Hollow Sea when he noticed Dusk riding toward him. She was running Drake full out, decked out in battle gear except for the helmet. Her long hair streamed behind her like copper smoke.

She drew near and dismounted. Her eyes were bright.

"This should be a challenging fight," she said.

"Yeah," he replied. "I was just wondering if we could trick him over here, push him off the cliff."

"Psshaw," Dusk said. "We'll beat him by force of arms. We'll hamstring him and make short work of it. Don't forget our battle with the Sheriff."

"The one where you nearly got killed?"

"The one where you saved me," she said. "I never repaid you for that."

And before he could move she was kissing him.

What surprised him was how warm her lips were, how supple. Dusk was full of passion, but he had never thought he would feel it like this.

But still.

She broke it off.

"Did you not want that?" she asked. "Could I be so wrong?"

"No," he said. "No, I really wanted that. It's just . . ." he held up his arms.

"Look at me."

She laughed. "Is it your seeming that worries you? The world is full of curses and charms and false appearance. If you do not look beneath such things, you will never know happiness, and perhaps be eaten by something you mistook for a flower. I see *you* Errol, not with my eyes but with my heart."

"I . . . Wow, I don't know what to say."

"And yet," she said, now sounding a little vexed, "you don't seem worried about your appearance when you're near Veronica."

"Well, that's because—" he stopped, aghast at what he had been about to say.

"Because you think you are both monsters," she said.

"That's not what I was going to say."

"Because you think only a creature like her could love a creature like you. But it's not true. I could love you, Errol. You think on that."

And with that she kissed him again, very lightly, though it sent shocks all through his strange body.

Then she mounted up, and—before he could find his voice—rode away.

Aster was at the orchard a bit before sundown and waited as the others arrived, one at a time.

"Mistral says the giant comes from the north," Errol said. "What if we tied a rope or something, something he might trip over?"

"I will hide behind the wall," Dusk said. "If he doesn't trip I'll slash his ankles as he steps over."

"I don't want to fight him," Aster said. "I certainly don't want to attack first."

"We should be prepared, though," Dusk said.

"If he sees we're waiting to ambush him, he might fight, even if he wasn't going to," Aster said.

"So we're just going to wait?" Dusk said.

"Yes," Aster confirmed.

Dusk sighed. "Well, we shall see, then."

The night grew darker, and the wind picked up. Aster strained for the any sound of the giant's approach, but all she heard was the spectral cry of a nightbird.

"Have you fought a giant before, Dusk?" Veronica asked.

"Yes," she replied.

"And did you win?"

"My brother and I killed it," she said.

"And how tall was it?"

"Thrice the height of a tall man," she replied. "Perhaps a bit more."

"How did you kill it?"

"We brought it down in a charge with our lances. After that it was sword work."

"Thrice," Errol murmured. "Like eighteen or twenty feet?"

Dusk shrugged. They sat in silence for a few moments.

Veronica noticed it first.

"The birds have stopped," she said. "Everything has stopped."

She was right. Other than her words and the sound of their breathing, the night had gone as quiet as it was dark.

Aster had imagined they would hear loud footsteps approaching, feel the earth rattle. Neither happened.

North she could see the dark line of the mountains against the slightly lighter sky.

And then she saw something else—a shadow showing above the mountains, moving. It was small at first, but it grew, a dome shape, and then a head, and massive shoulders. And still it came on.

"Holy crap," Errol said.

"Yeah, I think this a little more than thrice," Veronica said.

Aster kept thinking it was on them, but it just kept getting bigger. When it reached the wall—which was ten feet high—it didn't even come up to the giant's calf.

The giant stopped at the edge of the orchard. Even this close, the light was too dim to make out a lot, except that he seemed to be naked.

Aster had planned to say something but her mind just wouldn't work. Sure, a giant was supposed to be big, but this . . .

The giant stepped over the wall and covered the distance to the trees in two strides. It bent down, reaching for the nearest tree.

"Wait!" Aster called.

At first it didn't seem to hear her at all. It just grabbed the tree. But then it turned toward her.

And growled, a low rumble that shuddered the air.

"Wait," she said again. "My name is Aster . . ."

She didn't get any more out. The giant screamed like a jet engine and dashed his fist at her. She saw it coming down, but couldn't force her feet to work.

It was Errol who saved her, tackling her from the path of the monstrous hand. She saw Dusk's blade gleam and flash.

She shook herself and stood, terrified but also angry.

"*Laikas!*" she shouted, and light shattered the darkness as every mote in the air around them became a tiny sun.

Aster almost vomited. The giant was indeed naked, and hairless, and as far as she could tell, sexless. Its face was only faintly human, like a clay figure sculpted by a child — simple, and weirdly proportioned.

The light made it shriek again and straighten, shielding its face. Dusk and Errol were running at it.

It's not supposed to be this way, Aster thought.

But it was, and her friends were about to get smashed like bugs.

So she exclaimed the most terrible Recondite Utterance she knew, the one she had been going over all day, just in case - the Utterance of the Heart of Lightning.

She felt all of the hair on her body stand out.

The giant flashed like the inside of a thunderhead, red in the center so they could see the shadows of his ribs and the gigantic sacs that were his lungs. White lightning played all along his body and shot from his eyes.

Errol and Dusk stumbled back.

"Wow," Veronica said. "Remind me not to get you riled again."

The lightning flickered out, and the red glow in the giant faded.

And he laughed, a low, horrible grating sound.

"Impossible," Aster murmured. Her father had killed half an army with that utterance. And a leviathan, if he was to be believed. The giant had not turned her magic back, as when she attacked Haydevil. It had simply shrugged it off.

Dusk cut at the giant's leg, but her blade had no effect. Nor did the giant acknowledge her presence. Instead he stooped and reached for Aster.

She yelped and broke into a run, but the monster was fast, and hard, cold fingers closed around her, lifting her up toward that awful, unformed face.

She looked down and saw Billy. He hadn't moved from his place by the trees, hadn't taken a single step or raised his gun.

But as the giant lifted her, she heard Billy say something, although it was only a whisper.

"Oh," he said. "I remember now."

Then he was bigger. And as she watched and the giant lifted her, Billy grew past the height of the trees, and more swiftly, so they were knee-high to him. By the time the giant had brought her up to his unshaped face, Billy was there, too, gripping her captor's wrist in his now titanic hand.

And still he grew, his head rising past the giant's. He twisted the monster's wrist so it loosened, and gently plucked her from it. Now he towered over the first giant. It looked up at him, its mouth forming a huge "O."

Billy picked him up by the neck and began to walk, each footstep leaving Aster breathless and dizzy. The giant flailed at him, but it was no use. In less than ten strides Billy reached the Hollow Sea and pitched the giant into it. Its scream went on for a long time.

Then Billy lifted her in his palm, until she was even with his face. It was still Billy's face, although it seemed simpler somehow. He didn't have any hair. His eyes were dark, and she couldn't see any emotion in them.

She remembered, then, what Hattie had said.

"Well, when you have part of something, you reckon the rest will be along directly. Needs tend to find one another."

"Of course," Aster said to Billy.

"You were my giant all along."

E rrol watched Billy — or the thing that had been Billy — toss the first giant into the Hollow Sea and then turn back toward the orchard. It was like watching a movie or something, like he didn't have anything to do with it. How could that be Billy?

He realized Veronica was right next to him, and he put his arm around her. She felt cold.

The gigantic figure bent and his hand came down, and there was Aster.

"All aboard," she said.

"You're sure about this?" Errol asked.

"I'm not sure about anything," she said. "But here is the orchard, and here is the giant."

"Billy?" Errol shouted. "Is that really you?"

The huge brow furrowed slightly, and then the massive head nodded.

Still, Errol hesitated.

Veronica did not. She strode up onto the giant palm and sat next to Aster.

"Will you convey Drake as well?" Dusk asked. "He is my companion as much as my mount. I would not care to leave him."

Again, Billy nodded.

Drake snorted and skittered, but he went up as well, as Dusk soothed and gentled him.

When Errol joined them, Billy stood. He did it mindfully, but it was still like they were on a fast elevator with no walls or ceiling.

For a moment they were still, high above everything.

Then Billy began to walk.

The wind was gentle at first, but as he picked up speed it rushed hard against them, stinging Errol's face. Aster said something he didn't understand, and the wind suddenly abated, although it still hissed and hushed all about, as if it had been bent around them. Errol wondered how fast they were going. It was hard to tell in the dark.

Dawn came, and—if anything—Billy seemed even taller than he had been. The mountains were long gone, and now they rushed over a strange, broken landscape of moss and stone. They came to another sea, this one full, and with no hesitation Billy waded in. It was deeper than his waist, so he had to lift his hand higher, but they could see the flying fish skipping across the water below, and dolphins, and once even a sailing ship that nearly capsized in the waves created by their passage.

Night came again, and another day. Billy set them down occasionally so that Aster, Dusk, and Drake could see to the needs fully live creatures had. But then they would go on.

"How far have we come?" Veronica wondered.

"How far do we have to go?" Errol replied. "This is a big place."

"Bigger than big," Dusk said. "The kingdoms have borders, but some say no end."

"That doesn't actually make sense," Veronica pointed out.

"Neither does riding in the palm of a giant," Aster said.

Seven days Billy walked. It wasn't all wilderness; they came near several villages and one city with high walls and towers. Aster urged Billy to take care not to step on anyone, but whether that had any effect, it was impossible to say.

And as they traveled, Errol changed more, and faster. His heart beat; odd, coarse hair began to sprout on his head. He began to feel a little hungry, and on the sixth day his lips actually parted. Parts of him that Aster hadn't included began to grow, and he was glad he was wearing clothes.

On the seventh day, Billy stepped from miles of uninhabited forest onto a broad grassy hill that sloped down into a marsh with hundreds of gleaming creeks that wound about one another like a nest of silvery serpents. Beyond that, another sea stretched to meet the horizon.

But that wasn't what Errol noticed first. It wasn't what got his attention. The floating mountain held that.

It looked as if someone had cut it from the earth and placed it in the sky, but they had done it carefully, because the four sides and the bottom formed an imperfect cube—imperfect because the top wasn't flat, but was instead an irregular cone. On the spiky peak a castle stood, tiny with distance, but glittering red-gold in the noonday sun. He could make out a sort of trail of buildings winding down from the castle and around the mountain, corkscrew fashion, until they were hidden by a high stone wall and a gate. There the buildings ended but the road they verged continued down, around another, larger wall and then out into the air, becoming a delicate little bridge supported by long, absurdly thin columns with their footings in the marsh. The bridge crossed to a high, natural pillar of eroded stone, and then to another, slightly lower one—seven upthrust rocks in all, each a little shorter than the last.

Billy walked them to where the bridge met the earth and set them down.

And he began to shrink. In a few moments he looked like Billy again, no taller than he usually was, but bare-butt naked. The girls had all turned away from him.

"Good thing we brought your pack," Errol told him, digging out some clothes.

At first the clothes seemed to puzzle Billy, but then he nodded and clumsily put them on.

When he was dressed, he started walking up the bridge. He hardly seemed to know they were present.

The bridge was bigger than it looked from a distance, wide enough for maybe forty people to walk side-by-side.

"Billy?" Aster said. "Where are we?"

He didn't turn to look at her. "The place," he said.

"Are you okay?" Veronica asked.

"I'm small," Billy replied, continuing on.

After seven days in the palm of a giant, Errol was used to heights, but the bridge still made him queasy as they ascended. It seemed somehow precarious. When they reached one of the eroded rock pilings he felt a little better, but the bridge went through tunnels in them, and they were quickly passed.

The tunnels had huge gates, but they were all open.

It took them nearly the rest of the day to reach the mountain. The walls they had seen from below were huge, but they didn't go all of the way around the peak; they were more like retainers for the road. They wound around the lower wall, across a long field of beveled stone, and through a gate in the upper.

When they came to the first building, he understood he'd been wrong about the scale. It had been built by something bigger than humans. Not as big as Billy at his tallest, but definitely bigger than normal people.

"Is this where you're from, Billy?" he asked.

"No," Billy said. His voice sounded a little more natural. "I was here, though. Long time ago."

"Do giants live here?"

"Not like me," he said. "And not anymore."

"What happened to them?" Aster asked.

Billy shook his head and shrugged.

They passed through a vast, empty hall, then across a paved courtyard where weeds and vines had obviously had their run of things for a while. Towers and spires jutted up around them, but only along the narrow strip that coiled up the mountain, a strip no more than a hundred feet wide at any given point. Given how regular it was, it had obviously been carved. "This is all connected," he realized. "This isn't a road anymore—it's a castle."

"Indeed," Dusk said, as if this was all so very normal.

Night came, but Aster wanted to push on, so she made light for them. They walked through arches carved in strange figures that might have been language, past sculptures of weird beasts and trees. Errol never saw any depiction of anything he would guess could have built this place.

Finally they reached the top.

"It's made of gold," Veronica said, as they stepped into the first hall. "Or something that looks an awful lot like gold."

"Red gold," Dusk said.

Drake's hooves on the floor had a metallic ring to them.

Billy wound his way through a labyrinth of rooms, large and small, until they came into an enormous courtyard. Unlike the others they had seen, this one appeared tended. The grass was regular and short. Trimmed hedges formed a maze in the center, and it was into that maze Billy took them.

It ended in what amounted to a smaller courtyard, and a small, clear pool of water overlooked by weeping willows.

Aster stopped and stood rigid, her hands in fists.

"The water of health," she finally murmured.

"We've done it. We're here."

FOUR

THE WATER OF HEALTH

I t was a still, perfect, beautiful moment for Aster. The garden in the golden castle, the sky, the pool.

Of course Errol ruined it.

"This seems too easy," he said.

"Easy?" Aster said. "Easy? Are you kidding me?"

"No," Errol said. "Here, now. Shouldn't there be guards or something? Or a riddle we have to solve?"

"I think the journey was quite enough," Dusk said. "We have fought long and hard, and here is our prize."

Aster took off her backpack and reached in deep, withdrawing a little case about a foot and a half long and four inches high. She opened it; inside its velvet lined interior, each in its own little space, were seven crystal vials. She took them over to the pool, but now she was starting to worry; Errol sort of had a point.

"How do we *know* this is the water of health?" she asked. "What if it's just plain water—or worse, water of horrible dying?"

"Or perpetual flatulence," Veronica chimed in.

"That's a fair question," Dusk said.

"Veronica," Errol said, after a moment. "If it gives Veronica a heartbeat it's the right stuff."

"Hah," Veronica said. "Sure. Give it to corpse girl. She'll try anything."

"I just—" Errol began.

"I'm not sure I like the idea of being experimented on," Veronica said. She suddenly seemed a bit subdued.

"But if we don't do something like that, we'll never know if we have the real thing," Aster pointed out.

"It's the real thing," Billy said. "I know it."

"How do you know?"

"I've seen it used."

"Okay," Aster said. "Okay."

She took the vials to the pool. Without much surprise, she saw the handle of a little golden dipper sticking out of it. She filled one vial, then another. After she filled the fifth and reached for the ladle again, she saw with a start that the water was gone.

"What happened?" She gasped.

"One for each of us," Dusk said. "I have heard this. It makes sense."

"You mean it's gone forever?" she asked.

"No," Billy said. "Only for us."

"Oh," Aster said, uncertainly. "Okay. That's that, then." She placed the vials back in the box, and the box in the backpack.

"I'll keep them safe," she said. "But I have one for each of you."

"Wow," Errol said. "I guess we did it. But I still say that was way too easy."

"It isn't easy at all," Veronica said.

"What do you mean?" Errol asked.

"Has anyone stopped to wonder how we're supposed to get home?"

A long silence followed her remark. What Aster noticed most about that next minute or so was Billy, who seemed to be studying the ground.

"You know what?" Aster finally said. "We've done one impossible thing today, and I'm tired. Let's save the next impossible thing for tomorrow, shall we?"

B illy had found them some rooms overlooking the ocean, huge suites with outsized furniture. Aster chose hers, but before turning in she took Veronica aside, leading her through the castle until she was sure they were out of earshot of the others. There, in a hall of crystal columns, she handed Veronica one of the vials.

"You're the only one who can benefit from this immediately. I'll keep it if you want. The choice is yours."

Veronica stared at the water for a moment, then reached for it.

"Thanks," she said, uncertainly.

Aster returned to her room and unrolled her sleeping bag on the floor; the bed seemed like it was still okay, but it was dark, and she didn't care to risk what might be living under the covers after all this time.

She lay quietly, trying to summon back the sense of accomplishment she'd had at the pool, but it was elusive. Formless doubts worried at her.

But that wasn't the only reason she couldn't sleep, and eventually she had to admit it. Quietly she rose and went to Billy's room.

He wasn't asleep, either, but stood on a golden balcony in his room, staring out over the sea. The moon was up, and the breakers churned silver in its soft radiance.

"Hey, Billy," she said.

"Aster," he said.

"Can't sleep?"

"No," he replied.

"Me either."

She was standing by him by then. His hair had returned when he shrank back down; he looked just like he had the night he had kissed her. Except his eyes, which seemed dreamier, more distant.

"So," she said. "You're a giant."

"Yeah," he said.

"You could have told a girl," she said.

"I didn't know," he said. "I forgot. That happens when we stay little too long."

"What happened, to make you forget?" she wondered. "I mean, do you know?"

He looked at her, and bent, and kissed her, and for a long time she didn't ask any more questions. But eventually he drew back, and led her to a small bench, and put his arm around her.

"We are lonely," he told her, "we giants. We never meet one another. We walk by ourselves. We stay mostly in the distant places, where people like you do not live. When I am a giant, my thoughts are big and very slow and mostly about the world around me—the stars and the sea, the clouds and the sun—mountains. And I don't feel the little things you call pleasures and pains. But sometimes I remember those things and wish to feel them; to have skin that can appreciate a hot bath, to eat bacon and sugar, smell a wood fire." He smiled. "To kiss, I know now. To do those things, I have to become little. Usually only for a day or two, because it's dangerous—like when you became the raven. We forget."

"Yes," she said, remembering. "I get it."

"But it's true the other way, too," he said. "I almost forgot to become little again, when we got here. I almost put you down and kept walking."

"But you didn't."

"Because I want to be with you," he said. "A lot."

"Oh." *But that's great*, she thought. She just couldn't quite say it.

He hung his head. "I can help you return home. There are ways around the Hollow Sea that I remember now. I can carry you home in ten days. But then I really will forget. I will take you home and then walk away. It might be a hundred years before I become little again."

She absorbed that for a moment, feeling a sort of black ball form in her chest.

"Are you sure?" she asked. "Sure you would walk away?"

"Yeah. It's too long."

She took his hand and laced her fingers into his. She thought of her father, and everything she had gone through.

"I must think of Errol," she said. "And Veronica. I promised them things."

"I know," he said.

She took a few deep breaths, wondering how they could hurt so much.

"I want to be with you, too, Billy," she managed. "I'll find some other way."

When she started the sentence she didn't believe it. But by the end of it she did.

"The water of health," she said, excited. "It's also known as the water of restoration. It might return your memories, restore you to human form."

His eyebrows lifted a little. "It might," he said. "But my true form is giant."

"I think it will work," she said. "I'm sure it will."

And she was sure, Billy saw it and grinned, and kissed her again. She closed her eyes and just felt, trying to stay in the moment and not let her mind race ahead. It was going pretty well, but it ended abruptly when something sharp pricked her in the back.

"*Gelde*," someone said. Aster felt a chill go through her, dragging a hard frost behind. Then everything stopped.

Errol saw Veronica slip past his room; she paused for a moment at his threshold, maybe thinking him asleep. Then she continued on. After a moment, he got up and followed her. He found her in the garden, gazing at the pool. She had one of the vials in her hand. Overhead the stars blazed, bigger and brighter than he had ever seen them before.

"I wondered if you were awake," she said. She lifted the vial.

"How did you get that?" he asked. "I thought Aster was safeguarding it for the time being."

"She gave me one," Veronica said. "I think she's hoping I'll try it out." She slipped it back into her pocket.

"Yeah. Look, I'm sorry I volunteered you. It wasn't my place. I just—"

"Want me to be alive again," she said. "I know, Errol. And so do I. Sort of."

"What do you mean, 'sort of'?"

"I can do a lot of things like this, Errol. I'm more powerful here dead than I could ever be alive, back home. And anyway, back home? Nothing seems right about it. Everything looks weird. Everybody I knew who isn't dead is old. I'm just not sure that going back there is for me. If I stay here, who knows what I might become, how powerful I could be?"

He remembered her riding the monster amphiuma, the battle at Chula's village. What she might become—was a little terrifying.

"You'll have me," he said. "Things aren't as different as you think."

She gazed at him for a long moment, and he looked at her, really looked at her. He saw the sadness and pain, but he also realized just how beautiful she had become to him, how much he wanted to make all of her pain go away. He reached and touched her cheek. She closed her eyes and nuzzled into his hand.

"You made me that long speech about how you don't belong there either," she said. "You seem to be turning into a real boy just fine on your own. If your body back home dies, I'll bet you won't know the difference. It might be dead already. Why don't we just stay here?"

"You really want to be like this forever?" he asked. But she had a point. What was there for him back home?

"Errol," Veronica said, "I've been killed once already. Like this, I can't be killed. I'm safe."

"I wouldn't go so far," a familiar voice murmured.

Dusk stood at the entrance to the willow garden. Drake whickered behind her.

"Anything can be slain," Dusk went on. "But now you see, Errol? However she may seem, whatever she may say, she is a *nov*, a seductress, an eater of life. And she likes what she is."

"This is a private conversation," Veronica snapped. "You aren't wanted here."

"Of course, you're right to be suspicious of the water of health. Its effects on a thing like you are—at best—unpredictable."

"You can leave anytime," Veronica said.

"I intend to," Dusk said, walking forward. Errol watched her come, wondering what she was up too, and he was still wondering that when she whipped out her sword and jabbed it at him. He just watched it happen, unbelieving.

But Veronica believed. She slammed into him, sending him off balance and out of the path of the sword.

Then Veronica screamed, the same hideous inhuman shriek she'd let loose when he dug her out of her hole. With horror, he saw the sharp tip of the blade sticking out of her back.

The weapon flashed a cold, white color, and then Dusk yanked it out and in a single economical motion cut through Veronica's neck and sent her head rolling across the grass. Her body wobbled on its feet for a few seconds, and then toppled over.

"Oh, my God, no!" Errol screamed, and lurched toward Dusk.

She sidestepped and he went stumbling by.

"I offered you my love, Errol," she said. "My companionship. I still offer it. You can come with me."

"I don't understand," he said. "Why?"

"My reasons are my own. I need the water of health."

"Aster said we could each have one."

"I don't trust her," she said. "And even if I did, I need more than one vial. I'm sorry; it's just the way it is."

"Leave Aster alone," he said.

Dusk smiled, a beautiful and terrible smile. "It's too late for that," she informed him.

"What have you done?" he asked, stepping a little, trying to judge the distance.

Her face set in grim lines.

"It's too late, isn't it?" she said. "I can never trust you. You loved that *thing*."

"Arrh!" Errol shouted, slapping at her blade and diving forward.

The blade suddenly wasn't there; she avoided his hand with a simple flick of her wrist. He stumbled and turned.

Just in time to see the blow that took his right leg off at the knee. He thudded clumsily to the ground. The pain was so immediate and impossible that he couldn't even scream, at first. But he got around to it.

"I like you, Errol," Dusk said. "So I'm not going to kill you unless you make me."

She turned and briskly walked over to Drake. Errol tried to push himself up.

"Really," she said. "Stay down."

She patted Drake on the muzzle. "Time now, my beauty," she said.

The horse seemed to shiver, as if seen through a hot haze. When it was done, Drake still looked something like a horse, albeit with burning red eyes and black-feathered wings. And he was bigger, much bigger.

Dusk swung up onto his back.

"Farewell, Errol," she said, and gave Drake her knee. He reared up on his hind legs, flapped his dark wings, and leapt into the air. They vanished over the top of the hedge and reappeared a moment later, a strange shape against the sky, dwindling.

Errol meant to call something after her, but all that came out was a scream of rage. Then he collapsed.

It was all over. Aster and Billy were probably dead. Veronica was decapitated. He'd screwed up again.

The world seemed to flicker in and out, dark and light. He saw himself in the hospital bed. He saw the woman in white and her face, turning toward him.

He saw Veronica, headless on the grass.

"No!" he snarled.

One vial of water remained. Dusk didn't know Aster had given Veronica one of the vials. But if she stopped to count them, she might come back. He still had a chance, a chance to make all of this as right as he could.

He pushed himself up on one knee and crawled toward Veronica's head.

"Veronica?" he gasped. "Can you hear me?"

She didn't answer.

He found her with her eyes open, but they were glassy and still. Starting to sob, he dragged the head back over to her body and tried to stick it back on, but it wouldn't stay.

"Oh, yeah," he muttered. He reached into her pocket and pulled out the little vial. He opened it with trembling fingers.

Was she supposed to drink it? He remembered Aster had just flicked the water of life onto her, back in her in-between.

He sprinkled some along both sides of her severed neck.

"Please," he said. "Come on, please."

He pushed the body and head together.

Nothing happened.

"Veronica," he said. "Come on." He sprinkled a little more of the water on her face and abdomen.

Then Veronica opened her mouth and finished the scream Dusk had so abruptly cut off. Her eyes darted about wildly.

He looked at the bottle. It was half empty. He stoppered it and put it in his pocket.

Veronica sat up and her gaze focused on him.

"Again," she gasped, feeling her neck. But he didn't even see a scar. The wound in her belly was gone, as well.

"You used it, didn't you?" she murmured. "The water of health." She seemed dazed, which more than made sense.

"Yeah," he said. "Sorry, but you were—I couldn't leave you like that."

"It's okay," she said, wrapping her arms around him.

Then she eased back.

"Still no heartbeat," she said. "Still no breath. Dusk was right."

"It's okay," Errol said. "I don't care about that. I don't."

She smiled and touched her forehead against his.

"Why did Dusk do it?" she asked. "I knew she was up to something, but—"

"Aster," Errol gasped. He struggled to rise and then remembered he couldn't.

"What's wrong with you?" Veronica asked.

"Dusk cut off my leg," he said. "It hurts."

"Cut off your leg?" She pushed him back and saw.

"Well, that's not right," she said. She got shakily up, found his leg and brought it back.

"Was there any water left?" she asked.

"No," he lied. "I had to use it all."

"We'll get some of Aster's then."

"Dusk already has the rest," he said. "We've got to find Aster and Billy."

"You can't walk!" she said.

"Find me something to use as a crutch," he said, "and I'll for damn sure walk."

She looked around, but he could see as well as she that there weren't any fallen branches at all, much less one in a convenient shape. Finally she bent and put her shoulder under his arm.

"I'll be your crutch until we come across something better," she said.

Aster first became aware of hands stroking down her arms and legs, and warmth following them. Her abdomen and face came next, flushing full of blood and heat. When her eyelids finally unstuck she found Billy beside her, features full of concern.

"Good," he murmured.

"What happened?"

"Dusk froze us," he said. "You more than me. I was giant a few hours ago, so I'm still a little in-between."

"Dusk *froze* me?"

"Like the river," he said.

"Yes, I remember," she said. "I meant *Dusk* froze me? Why?"

"Uh, huh," Veronica said. She was sitting on Billy's bed. Errol lay next to her. "I hate to say this, but I told you so."

Then she frowned a little. "Actually, no, it felt pretty good to say that. All in all."

"She took the water of health," Errol said. "She said she needed more than one vial."

It was then that Aster noticed Errol's—injury.

"What the hell happened to your leg?"

"Dusk cut it off," Errol said.

"Right after she cut off my head," Veronica put in.

Aster stared at her, wondering if she had heard her right.

"She cut off your head?" she said, at last.

Aster slumped back against the banister, feeling sick. How could everything go so completely and suddenly wrong?

"After all of this," she said. "For nothing."

Then she remembered. "Wait. The vial I gave Veronica."

"You notice her head is back on," Errol said. "I used it."

"Oh. Of course." She looked back at the stump of Errol's limb.

"I'm so sorry," she said. "All of you. I thought I knew what I was doing. The arrogance, to think I—" she suddenly couldn't talk because she was bawling. She knew she should be embarrassed, but all of the dams she had built to keep her tears in were swept away in an instant.

"What have I done?" she sobbed.

"You gave us a chance," Errol said.

"Look at you!" she said, waving at his stump. "And all of us, so far from home."

She put her face in her hands so she didn't have to see them. Nobody said anything while she cried herself out, until great heaves finally gave way to hiccupy sobs.

"Everyone," Errol said, then. "Could you leave Aster and me alone for a minute?"

Billy looked at her, and she nodded. She watched the two of them file out, wiping at the tears still running down her cheeks.

"You remember," Errol said, when they were alone, "when we used to do those comic books together?"

"Yes," she said.

"Why did we stop doing that?"

"Because you stopped liking me, Errol."

"I didn't," he said. "I don't know what happened. I mean I do, but it wasn't something I did on purpose. And I wish I never had. I wish we had kept doing that stuff together, because if we had maybe my life wouldn't have gotten so screwed up."

For a moment she could only stare at him in astonishment.

"Or maybe just screwed up in a different way," she said at last. "I mean, look at me."

"Anyway, I'm sorry."

"You were my only friend, Errol," she whispered. "My only friend in strange place. And you abandoned me."

Then she covered her face again. "Oh, God, I didn't mean to say that."

"But it's true," he said. "That's how it turned out. But we're friends now, right? Again?"

"Are we?"

"I think so. Look—you saved me, Aster."

"I wanted to save you, Errol," she said. "But without the water of health—"

"I don't mean like that," he said. "You know what I mean."

She studied his nearly-human face, and felt something like a little flower bloom in her, something good amidst everything awful.

"I wanted that too," she admitted. "I hoped if I brought you here, and we had a little adventure together . . ." She didn't finish.

"Yeah," he said. "I know."

He took a deep breath and reached into his pocket.

He pulled out a half-empty vial.

"It only took half to put her back together," he said. "I didn't tell her because she would have wanted to use it on my leg, and I'm not sure I could have stopped her."

Her heart seemed to stop in her chest as she gazed at what he held.

"Errol," she breathed.

"Is it enough to help your father?"

"I think so," she said. "It should be. But . . ."

But your leg, she thought. *And Billy.*

"I'll get along without my leg," he said. It felt like he was reading her mind. "Heck, maybe you can reattach it. I'm still not a real boy. If I was, I would have bled to death. So I'm a work in progress."

She slowly reached and took the vial from him.

"Thank you Errol," she said. She put the water in her pocket.

"Thank you," he returned.

Then she gave him a hug. It felt awkward at first, but when he squeezed her back, it was nice.

There came a little knock at the door. She pulled away from Errol a little guiltily.

It was Billy.

"Sorry to interrupt," he said. "But trouble is coming."

FIVE

THE TROUBLE THAT CAME

F or David, the days, nights, forests, deserts, seas, and grasslands all streamed by in his peripheral vision, as if he were flying through a tunnel with his gaze always fixed on the light at the end of it. The shining star now had his complete attention. The smell of rot, the chatter of the boys, and the tug of the lashings that kept him on Melzheyas became meaningless sensations. He had become his purpose.

They reached the floating mountain during the night, but David could see the light shining from the little castle at its summit. The dead dragon circled and then landed in the courtyard, the place nearest Aster that would accommodate his size. Then Melzheyas flew again, coiling himself around the uppermost tower to keep watch.

"Force them up," the Sheriff told the boys. "Find the ways down and guard them."

And so they entered the castle. David noted without much interest that it was made of gold.

Z hedye," Aster swore. "How did they get here?"

"I don't know," Billy said. "I didn't hear them until they were already in the castle."

"That means they probably have the lower floor pretty much locked up," Errol said. "If we go down, we go into an ambush."

"Why don't we go up?" Veronica suggested.

"Because we can't fly?" Errol rejoined.

"But there might be a place up there where Billy can do his giant thing again, and we can just walk out of here. Obviously as long as he has a roof over him he can't."

"Maybe," Billy said. "I know of a tower lookout that might be big enough. The footing would be tricky, and coming down the causeway dangerous—that's why I didn't carry you up it. But I think I can do it."

"Billy, wait," Aster began and stopped. She frowned her dangerous little frown.

"Let's—let's just make a stand," she muttered.

Holy socks, Errol thought. *Has she lost it?*

"I'm missing a leg," he pointed out. "And we don't have Dusk anymore. I know you've got some pretty strong juju, but still . . ."

"Sure," Aster muttered. She was still thinking. He could practically see the wheels spinning in her head, but toward what he couldn't tell.

"They're coming," Billy said. "We have to go."

"You wouldn't have to be a giant long," Aster said. "Just long enough to get us away from here. Then we think of something else."

"Yeah," Billy said. "Come on. I know where the closest stair is."

He got under Errol's arm, and together they made for the stair. Errol wondered at Aster's odd comment. What was the problem with Billy taking them all the way to the Hollow Sea, at least? Because the sheriff had obviously found a fast lane, too. He was missing something.

Somewhere, the hounds were baying.

They came out of the stair into a huge, darkened room. The sky showed through four large archways, one of which was quite near. In the center of the room a water fountain cheerfully rose and cascaded into a marble basin. For a moment, Errol wondered how they drew the water up, but then realized he was being ridiculous — they were, after all, on a floating mountain.

Through one of the archways was another tower, another spiraling stair. Billy went first, practically carrying him. Veronica and Aster brought up the rear.

High above, Errol could see a slice of night sky.

It seemed a long time before they reached the top of the tower, but finally they stumbled from the uppermost landing. Crenellated walls enclosed a courtyard roof the size of a basketball court.

Which was already occupied by a very large pile of something that stank to high heaven.

"A corpse," Aster gasped.

"Of what?" Errol demanded.

"Dragon," Billy clarified.

Veronica didn't say anything, because she wasn't with them anymore. Errol stared back down the stairs, but she was nowhere in sight.

"Veronica!" he shouted.

She didn't answer.

"Oh man," Errol said. "What the hell does she think she's doing?"

But he was pretty sure he knew the answer to that.

"We'll go back," Aster said. "We'll go back and fight."

She was willing to. He saw it in her eyes.

"No," Errol said. "Not 'we'. Billy — would you please give me your gun?"

"Errol," Aster said. "No."

That's when the dragon corpse raised a head the size of a Buick.

"Aster Kostyena," it hissed. "You are now mine."

"*Zhedye*!" Aster squeaked. They ducked back into the cover of the stairs.

"Okay," Errol said, after a moment. "Now we know how they got here."

"This is a problem," Aster said. "Big problem."

"And not one I can do much about," Errol said. "You deal with this. I'll go get Veronica."

She sighed, and their gazes locked for a long moment.

"Yes," she said, softly. "Okay. But hurry back."

"Yeah," Errol said. "I will. Billy?"

Billy handed him the rifle and the pouch he kept his shells in.

"Thanks Billy," Errol said. "You're a good guy."

"You too."

"So long," Errol said, and began hopping down the stairs, supporting himself against the wall.

David led the Sheriff and his posse through the golden castle, trying not to let on how sick he was. The man he had been when this journey started would never have managed it, but he had found his ancient, obstinate core. He couldn't keep it up forever, but he knew that soon an opportunity would present itself.

He was right. They passed into a gallery filled with crystalline sculptures of fabulous beasts, and at the end of it a doorway that actually had a door in it. Like the castle itself, it appeared to be made of gold. It stood slightly open, and a golden key protruded from a lock beneath the handle.

"She's through there," David said. "Not far."

The Sheriff didn't say anything, but David knew the drill. He dropped to the back; the Sheriff didn't want his compass getting tagged by a stray bullet.

One of the boys—they were difficult to tell apart now—eased the door open. To David's relief, a corridor ran on from it, with another door at the end.

"There," he said. "Down there."

He waited until the last of them was in the corridor and then threw himself at the portal. It was substantial, but not heavy enough to be solid gold. He guessed it was just plated. Still, it was bulky enough that he almost didn't get it closed in time; one of the boys yelped as he slammed into it.

David turned the key and felt the tumbler click. Then he pulled it out and ran toward where Aster really was.

"Mine," he muttered under his breath. "Not yours, Sheriff. Mine."

He knew he couldn't beat Aster and her friends in a fight. He didn't have to. All he had to do was convince them he wanted to help. The Sheriff wouldn't stay locked up long, but it might give them time to escape. He would deal with Aster's friends at his leisure.

He raced up a series of passages and stairs. It seemed Aster was making for the highest point of the castle. Did she have a means of escape? Did the silver ship fly as well as sail on invisible seas?

Did she know about Melzheyas?

He broke into a huge room with four tall Ogee arches open to the sky and a fountain in the center. Like the rest of the castle, it reminded him a little of medieval Spanish architecture.

Aster wasn't far, now. He could see her shining above.

"Wow. This is more than I hoped for," a soft voice said.

He froze and turned, and saw her, a shadow with glowing green eyes, half-submerged in the fountain.

"Who is it?" he said.

"Think you're going to come to her rescue, do you? And then what, I wonder?"

He saw now she had a light in her, too, encased in shadow but present, nonetheless. And familiar, so familiar, like an old friend.

"I was expecting a crowd," she went on. "I thought I might be lucky enough to get my hands on you when you went past. As long as the Sheriff has you, Aster can't ever really escape, can she?"

David was torn. He wanted to follow Aster, but here was something that also belonged to him. He remembered now.

"Veronica?" he murmured.

"Hello, Mr. Robertson."

He felt a little dizzy.

"You had new tennis shoes," he remembered. "You were really proud of them. You were running around everywhere."

"Yes," she said. "I was. But you put a stop to that, didn't you, Mr. Robertson? Why don't you come here?"

He took a step forward. It was too dark to see well, but he remembered her golden hair.

"I watched you grow up," he told her. "Such a little thing at first. The light got so bright in you. I was afraid."

"Afraid of what?"

"Girls like you," he said. "They begin to fade, at a certain age. They diminish and become common. I couldn't let that happen to you. I wanted to keep you always like you were that day you wore your tennis shoes. Keep you safe in here, like the others." He tapped his temple.

"How many others, Mr. Robertson?"

"It doesn't matter," he said. "You were special."

"Well, of course," Veronica said.

He was close to her now, almost touching. He remembered kissing her, back in the desert. The Sheriff stopped him then, but now they were alone.

"I missed you," he said.

"I know you did," she said. "I didn't die quickly enough. The Creek Man got me instead. You must have been so disappointed."

He touched her cheek.

Aster, he thought. I can't . . .

But then she wrapped her arms around him.

"Come on, Mr. Robertson," she said. "It's time to go."

C ome out," the dead dragon said. "You have nothing to fear from me, at least not at the moment. It isn't you I want."

Aster peeked out and saw him reared against the sky, grey with approaching dawn. His shape seemed so familiar . . .

"I know you!" she said. "You chased us across the Hollow Sea. My father and I. You tried to kill us."

"Kill you? No. Apprehend you, yes. Your father committed a terrible crime. We were charged with setting things right. We are still."

"Who is 'we'?"

"Seven of us began the hunt, but in the end only two remained—the man you call the Sheriff and me. Your father killed me, but the Sheriff continued. The curse caught him, and his mind was damaged, I think. He's forgotten a lot."

"You want me in order to get to my father?"

"Obviously none of us was a match for him," the beast said. "Doubtless it is still the case. But with you to bargain with, things might go differently. I make you this condition. I will not harm you. Your friends may go free."

Aster thought of Errol, hobbling down the stairs. Of Veronica and Billy.

"I am my father's daughter," she said. "I have power of my own. I bet I can take you."

"Possibly. Possibly not. I am—after all—already dead. But if you attack me and I win, your friends will die. Even if you succeed, they will likely perish in the battle. And there is still the Sheriff to consider."

Aster gritted her teeth. She knew she didn't have much time. The sheriff must be close, now. If Errol went against him, Errol wasn't coming back. That didn't mean he would die, just that he would be in a coma again. But she remembered how much that scared him. If she could save him . . .

"Okay," she said. "I agree. But my friends must live."

"No," Billy said.

She pulled him close. "If I'm alive and you're alive, we have a chance," she whispered. "Maybe I can escape or you can rescue me or my father will destroy them anyway. If we fight here, my gut tells me it won't turn out okay."

Billy kissed her, and nodded. She thought he was agreeing with her.

Then he stepped out onto the roof and began to grow.

"Billy!" she screamed, as the dragon's head darted at him.

When Errol got to the bottom of the stairs, he heard the sheriff and his dogs, close. He didn't see any sign of Veronica, and after calling her name a couple of times, he took a seat on the lowest step and examined Billy's gun. His fingers had thinned out, become much more human, although they remained alternating black and white. Little nails had even begun growing on them.

The rifle was lever action, like the ones in the old westerns. It held seven bullets at a time.

He sat on the stair, listening to them come, remembering his father's Scotch and pain pills and he finally faced it down.

"I did want to die," he murmured aloud. "I wanted to die, and I mucked it up. Now I want to live, and I've mucked that up, too."

He sighed and aimed the rifle at the head of the stairwell, and realized something else.

Something was happening up top. A loud crackle and heavy thudding like a giant's feet on stone.

Exactly like that, maybe, he hoped.

The first of the boys appeared, sticking his head from out of the landing. Errol fired the gun and heard the bullet spang against gold. He scooted back up a few steps, until he couldn't see the room anymore, except for the bottom step and a bit of floor.

"Next one I see gets it in the head," he shouted.

He was lying. The thing he had realized was this — as much as he didn't want to die, he didn't want to kill anybody, either.

He could hear them clustered below, baying. Crazy things were happening upstairs. He couldn't save Veronica now, even if she needed saving.

One of the boys bolted toward the bottom stair. Errol fired again, aiming in front of him. The boy yowled and backed off. Errol thought he'd just hit him on the foot.

Suddenly they all quieted.

"Stand down and live," a hard voice said.

"Sheriff?" Errol said. He scooted back another couple of steps.

"Yes. My word. I've lost interest in you. You can go."

"What about Aster?"

"She's mine," the Sheriff said, "but I won't hurt her."

"No? Then why are you trying so hard to catch her?"

"My reasons don't concern you. Surrender. You go free; I'll take her unharmed if I can."

"Yeah, it's that 'if I can' that worries me," he said. He kept working up the stairs a little at a time, but he still had a long way to go. If he could keep stalling . . .

"If that's how you want it," the Sheriff said. "Boys."

So much for stalling. Here they came.

None of them were in view yet, but he fired anyway. He went up another stair and shot again, and twice more. Then they were there, coming shoulder to shoulder. He put one of their heads in his sights. It was an easy shot, and at least one of them would be sorry.

"Screw this," he said. He threw the gun at them, jerked himself up on his one leg and dove down the stairs, arms swinging.

T he monster clamped its jaws on Billy's shoulder, and blood spurted. Aster said the Utterance of the Heart of Lighting, and both the dragon and Billy lit up like roman candles. It bothered Billy no more than it had the last giant, but the dragon twisted away and thrashed on the ground.

Aster brought a whirlwind and sent it spinning out into the air. Billy grew.

The dragon fought off her wind and dove at Billy. It hit him, hard, pushing him off-balance and back. He stepped to compensate, but there was nothing to step *on*, and he toppled over the edge, carrying the dragon with him.

Aster watched it all happen as if it were in slow motion. Then they were gone.

"Billy!" she whispered.

She heard gunfire, and the boys-turned dogs coming up the stairs. She looked to where Billy had vanished, then back at the stairs.

"Okay," she said. "Okay, here we go."

She backed up across the roof until she had her spine against the wall and watched them come pouring into the yard.

When she thought most of them were out, she spoke a Profound Recondite Utterance.

Not the whirlwind she had brought against Shecky or the boys back near the Hollow Sea or even the dragon just now, but something more ancient and far more dangerous.

The boys looked up as the cyclone descended and its grey-black walls sucked them in. She stood in an eye that was no more than a yard wide and felt the tremendous force an all sides threatening to crush her. She held it as long as she could, but after a few moments she felt her control slipping, and then the wild wind began to turn on her, lifting her from the ground. Almost too late she commanded it away; it made a try for her before it went and failed, though it sent her spinning across the stone.

As she tried dizzily to get up, she saw him, the Sheriff. His two hounds were by him. She didn't see any of the boys.

"You are your father's daughter," he said.

Aster began a Recondite Utterance, but the Sheriff pointed at her.

"*Keidi*," he snapped.

Something in her throat closed, and she gagged.

"You defeated Melzheyas," he said. "Impressive. But it only makes it more difficult for us to get back home. I will find a way."

Aster managed to climb to her feet. She clutched at her throat, trying to somehow loosen it up so she could say something, but it was if her vocal cords were tied in knots. She gripped at the spell with her will, and met the Sheriff's resolve. She pushed back, hard, and managed to gasp a little. He frowned, and her throat went even tighter.

The white and black dogs prowled closer.

Veronica left the body at the bottom of the pool and rose up, feeling sick. When she broke from the water her belly heaved as if trying to throw up, although she had nothing in her stomach.

Something came out, anyway, a black, oily gas with little orange lights flickering inside. She reached after it, but it thinned away before her eyes.

And as it vanished, she felt better.

"I should have known he wouldn't agree with me," she murmured to herself.

Only then did she take in her surroundings.

The room was empty, but she could hear some sort of commotion up the stairs. She started up them.

She didn't get very far before she found Errol. Or the parts of what had been Errol.

"Oh, Errol, what did they do to you?" she sighed. She found his head, shattered, and for a moment felt a little hope. But the little bone doll was broken, too. Weeping a little, she gathered up the tiny pieces and put them in her pocket.

Billy's rifle lay abandoned on the stair. She picked it up and kept walking, tears streaming down her face.

When she got to the top, she didn't see anyone but the Sheriff and his two dogs — and Aster. Aster was backing toward the edge of the roof top.

Veronica pointed the gun, took a deep breath, and pulled the trigger.

The rifle kicked her in the shoulder way harder than she thought it would. She stumbled back and saw the Sheriff jerk and stagger too. Then he spun and stalked toward her, pulling a saber from a sheath at his side. He was bleeding, but he didn't act like he was hurt.

"Enough of you, *nov*," he said. "I'll chop you up into so many pieces no one will ever put you together again."

Veronica pulled the trigger again.

The hammer clicked on an empty chamber.

Behind the Sheriff, the first slice of the sun appeared on the horizon, and Veronica's lungs suddenly billowed inside of her, filled like balloons. The breath went in and sighed out. It was the most beautiful feeling imaginable, and she remembered it all, the smell of peaches and honeysuckle and catfish frying. Her heart thumped in her chest. She dropped the gun, hardly noticing the Sheriff anymore as he raised his vicious-looking weapon.

But then the wind came, and sent him whirling over the edge of the tower. Aster was a few feet away, staring at her.

"Veronica?" she asked.

She looked into Aster's eyes. "I'm alive," she said. "Actually alive."

Aster at first didn't understand, but then her mouth made a little "o."

"Wow," she said. "That's . . . huge."

"Yeah, it is," Veronica said. "Thanks, by the way."

"Sure," Aster said. "Did you see Errol?"

Her joy faded away, and for a long moment she said nothing, as tears formed in her eyes.

"They got him," she said. "They smashed up his little body."

For a moment, Aster just stood watching her, but then she took a step, and another, and took Veronica in her arms. Veronica accepted the embrace.

"There is hope," Aster said. "If we can get back, I can build another automaton—"

"Where's Billy?" Veronica interrupted.

"Billy!" Aster cried. She ran to the side of the tower. Veronica followed.

Billy was standing in the sea, looking up at them. Down around his feet a mess of some kind was slowly sinking.

"Well, there has to be a story there," Veronica guessed.

Aster didn't say anything at first, but the look of relief on her face was a statement in itself.

"At least we have a ride home," Veronica said. "At least as far as the Hollow Sea. Then I say we steal your ship back—"

"No," Aster said. "Billy can take us all the way back."

"Well, that's good, right?"

Aster nodded, but she was crying.

"Nothing's left for us here," Veronica said. "We can go back, you can build Errol a new body. We can try again."

"Right," Aster said. She sounded tired, and sad, which she had every right too. Then she touched Veronica on the arm.

"We'd better go. While he still remembers."

"What do you mean?"

"Just—we had better go. Thanks for saving me, Veronica. If you hadn't distracted the Sheriff, I wouldn't have got my voice back."

"He was going to chop me in half," Veronica said. "I think I probably still owe you one."

She looked at the rising sun, and thought it was the most beautiful thing she had ever seen. She felt the pulse in her wrist.

Alive.

Aster picked up her backpack at the head of the stairs and started down. Veronica followed. She tried not to look at what had once been Errol.

When the sun set and they were very far away from the golden castle, riding in the palm of a giant, Veronica's heart stopped beating again.

"Well," she sighed. "It's like that, is it?"

He remembered dying and being born, many times, and he remembered the frustration of always having to start again in an infant's body, the years spent helpless, knowing what he needed but with no way to obtain it.

But that was in the Land of the Departed, the grey, lightless place he had been consigned for more millennia than he cared to remember. Here, where light shone in everything, he saw other possibilities.

He found the Sheriff in the marshes below the floating mountain. He was broken, but not dead. His body would heal, given time. But part of him had leaked out through the wound in his head. That too, might return in time; the Sheriff was a patchwork of ancient enchantments.

But that was not what David wanted. He burrowed into the man like the larva he was, and began to incubate. Plenty remained of the sheriff that he could use; memories, Utterances and Whimsies, all the things denied him in the frail bodies he had traveled in since before he could remember.

He lay in the marsh, and healed, and became himself — but as always, something new as well.

And this time better. Much, much better.

SIX

THE REIGN OF THE DEPARTED

D elia wasn't sure who she was expecting when she answered the door. The police, hopefully, or maybe a mailman with a package.

What she didn't expect was a young woman dressed in knight's armor. A horse stood attentively at her shoulder.

"Ah, yes?" she asked. She noticed the girl had a star on her forehead.

"I'm here to see Kostye Dvesene," she said, in accented but understandable English. She sounded, in fact, very much like Aster.

"Oh, I'm afraid he's unavailable."

The woman cocked her head, and a sort of dangerous expression went across it, but then she seemed to notice something.

"Interesting necklace," she said.

"I suppose," Delia said. "If you like that sort of thing."

"Which—I take it—you don't."

"Well, not so much," Delia agreed, but found she could not follow that with anything stronger or more specific.

"May I see it?" the young woman asked.

Delia was certain she would have said no, but before she could say anything, the girl had taken it and lifted it over her head.

"Oh thank God," Delia gushed. "Thank you. You have no idea—"

But then the girl dropped the necklace right back on.

"What's your name?" the girl asked.

"Delia Fincher," she said, her hopes evaporating like morning dew.

"Mine is Dusk," she said. "And from now on, you do what I say."

"Yes," Delia said miserably. "I suppose I must."

"The first thing I want is for you to tell me everything you know about Kostye Dvesene and his daughter. You are not in any way to endanger me or raise any sort of alarm. Do you understand?"

"Yes," Delia said. "This could take a while. Why don't you come in?"

So they went in. Delia talked for a while. Occasionally Dusk asked a question. Finally, she couldn't think of anything else to say.

Dusk sat pensively for a few moments.

"Here is what we're going to do," she finally said. "Next time he's asleep, you're going to go in and take all of the pictures off of the wall. You can leave up the other things, the writing. And from here on, you will refer to me as Aster or Aster Kostyena, do you understand?"

"Yes," said Delia, "I do. But I don't think this is a good idea, young lady. He is a rather—unstable man. You should reconsider."

"Thanks for the advice," "Aster" replied. "Now, don't bring it up again."

T he darkness around Errol eased from black to grey. He was sitting up, but he wasn't sure where. He remembered going at the boys with his fists and after that a good bit of pain followed by a whole lot of nothing. Now night birds and crickets sang and he smelled honeysuckle.

The wind blew and something creaked, and he realized he was sitting on a swing—not just any swing, but one of the two on the set his dad built for him in the backyard. But the last time he had seen it the seats had been broken, and he hadn't cared much about swinging, anyway.

He could see the house, and the road going by.

The wind blew again, and the swing next to him moved, squeaking again.

He looked along the road again and saw her coming. Her head was down, so her hair covered her eyes. He felt the fear rise up from his belly.

He had hoped he could meet her better than this, unafraid. Proud. Knowing that this time he had died *doing* something.

But, oh God was he scared.

It took everything in him to stay in the seat, to not run like he had before, because he knew it was useless.

He wished he knew if he'd helped, if Aster and Veronica and Billy made it. He reckoned it had to be good enough that he had tried.

She was closer now. He started to shake.

The swing next to him creaked, and creaked again.

Errol looked over at it.

His dad sat in it, looking like he had before he got sick. He reached over and cupped Errol's head.

"Dad?"

His father nodded yes, but he didn't speak. He just turned Errol's head away from the woman and pulled him close. Errol studied the wide, familiar face—the thick broad nose and quick, dark eyes. Errol could tell he wanted to say something, but he couldn't.

"I miss you Dad," he said. "I miss you so much."

His father pulled him to his shoulder and wrapped his arms around him, and for the first time in a long time he felt safe, even though he knew he wasn't.

The woman was close, now. He could feel her like a chilly wind.

"I'm not scared anymore, Dad," he said. "Well, just a little maybe. I love you."

The light was coming from behind his dad now. His father held him closer, trying to shield him, but it was no use. He began to fade. He looked sad, and distressed.

"I'm okay, Dad," Errol said. "It's not your fault."

Then his father was gone, and the woman in white was only a yard away.

Her head rose slowly. Errol straightened his back defiantly. He lifted his head.

"Come on, then," he said.

He saw her chin. He saw her nose.

He saw Aster and Veronica staring down at him. Above, long fluorescent tubes cast a pallid light.

"It's a miracle," Aster said. "Hallelujah."

"You lied to me, Errol," Veronica said, patting his cheek. "You told me you used all of the water of health on me. I'm very cross."

"What?" he croaked. He turned his head.

His head. He was in a hospital bed, in his own body. His throat hurt like fire, and he had an awful taste in his mouth.

"You used it on me?" he croaked. "What about your dad?"

"You needed it more," Aster said. "I—" She turned her head quickly, as if to hide something. Was she crying?

"Excuse me, okay?" she said. "I'm going to tell the nurses about your miraculous recovery."

He waited until she was out of the room before asking the obvious.

"What about Billy?"

"He brought us home," Veronica said. "Or at least to the edge, where we came in. The Marches. And then he just turned around and walked away. Didn't even say goodbye."

"Poor Aster."

"Yes," Veronica said. "To be honest, she said some things that made me think he might not have left if she'd used the water of health on him. So you should be doubly grateful to her."

"I didn't ask her to do this," he protested.

"Would you rather be dead? You were about to be when we got here. They said it might be just a few hours."

He digested that for a minute.

"I do want to live," he said. "I'm glad to be alive." He reached for her hand. "I tried to find you," he said.

"I know," she answered, knitting her fingers into his. "Of course you did." She smiled. "Notice anything different?"

She *was* different, he realized. Her skin was pinker than he had ever seen it. She almost seemed to be shining. And her hand was warm.

"You're alive?" he gasped.

"Well," she said. "About half the time. When the sun is up. But that's not half bad, is it? Or maybe it's exactly half bad."

He studied her with wonder. But then he remembered.

"You said you didn't want to come back here," he said.

"Well," she said. "I'm not so wild about the idea, but I've kind of developed a thing for you, Errol Greyson."

"Have you?" he said. "Really? The kind of thing where you want to strangle me at the bottom of a swimming pool?"

"I *wasn't* thinking about strangling you," she said. "But I am now."

"Well, back up a little," he said. "What *were* you thinking about?"

"Something more like this," she said, and she bent over and parted her lips. The kiss was warm and sweet and altogether amazing.

"And that is exactly how I should like to kiss you," she said. "Now that I am alive."

"I'd like another please," he said.

But then the doctors and nurses arrived, and things were kind of a mess for a while.

A ster managed to convince Veronica to leave the hospital with her. It wasn't easy, but at some point someone was going to want to know who the strange girl was, and that could lead to a whole lot of trouble.

From the outside her house looked like it had when she left it. Not so her father's room.

Aster was sitting against the wall, quietly sobbing, when Veronica came in. She was munching on a peanut butter sandwich.

"Oh, this is soooooo good," she said. "I had completely forgotten how wonderful *tasting* is."

She saw Aster was crying, stopped, and looked around.

"What's wrong? What happened?"

"He's gone," Aster told her. "My father is gone."

"I thought he was trapped in here."

"That was the theory," Aster said. "But clearly . . ." she gestured at the room.

"All of it," she said. "For nothing."

"Nothing?" Veronica objected. "Errol is well again. And I'm alive, more-or-less. And we beat some bad guys. I'm sorry about your dad, but this isn't over. We'll help you find him, if that's what you want."

"You don't owe me anything," Aster said. "You've done your part."

"Me, you, Errol—we make a good team," Veronica said. "If you want to boot me out, that's one thing. But if you're going back in, I can still help. I'm sure Errol feels the same way. I can't believe you would just give up now."

"It's not a matter of giving up," Aster said. "It's that I don't even know where to start."

"Well, I'll tell you one thing," Veronica said. "This all stinks of Dusk. I can practically smell her. Did you notice the horse poop in your yard?" She knelt down and tapped the star on Aster's forehead.

"I suggest you start with that. With her."

Of course, Aster thought. She was stupid not to have seen it sooner.

"She must have come here and pretended to be me," she said. "It wouldn't be that hard, at least not at first. She took the pictures down—ah, *zhedye!*" She jumped up and raced to her bedroom. It was in shambles. She looked under the mattress where she kept her diary.

It was not, of course, there.

"That bitch!" she shouted.

"Now you're talking," Veronica said. "That's the Aster I like to see."

"Yes," Aster said, feeling her anger rise. "I am Aster Kostyena. And she will regret this."

"That's right!" Veronica said. "We'll find her, get your dad back—"

"And chop her bloody head of with her own sword," Aster finished.

"That too," Veronica said.

Aster looked up at Veronica, who was offering her a hand. She took it and stood.

"Put the sandwich down," she said. "How long has it been since you had a hamburger?"

Veronica's eyes went round as quarters. "Hamburgers? I completely forgot about those."

"Come on, then," Aster said. "I'm buying."

ACKNOWLEDGEMENTS

T hanks to Cory Allyn for overseeing this manuscript becoming a book; to Jeremy Lassen for editing and Joseph Foster for the nitty-gritty of copy editing. The wonderful cover art is by Micah Epstein, the cover design by Claudia Noble, and production by Joshua Barnaby. Thanks also to my first readers, Lanelle Webb Keyes and Tim Keyes.

GREG KEYES

was born April 11, 1963 in Meridian, Mississippi. When his father took a job on the Navajo Reservation in Arizona, Greg was exposed at an early age to the cultures and stories of the Native Southwest, which would continue to inform him for years to come. He earned a bachelor's degree in anthropology at Mississippi State University and a Master's degree at the University of Georgia. While pursuing his PhD at UGA, he wrote several novels, one of which — *The Waterborn* — was published, along with its sequel *The Blackgod*. He followed this with The Age of Unreason books, the epic fantasy series Kingdoms of Thorn and Bone, and novels from several franchises, including Star Wars, Babylon Five, The Elder Scrolls, and Planet of the Apes. He now lives and works in Savannah, Georgia with his wife Nell, son John Edward Arch, and daughter Dorothy Nellah Joyce.